SNOW

Landon Beach

Landon Beach
Visit my website at landonbeachbooks.com

Printed in the United States of America

First Printing: October 2025
Landon Beach Books

ISBN-13 978-1-959783-06-0

"*Snow* is thrilling fiction, gripping and sexy, with twists and turns charged with the effects of human fallibility and the consequences of paths not taken. It is as page-turning as Beach's most suspense-filled action chillers—from the first sentence, I was all in."

—Pamela Dillman, actor and audiobook narrator

"*Snow* is a heartwarming holiday novel about the family we're born into, the friendships that sustain us, and the detours in life that can change everything. Reading it had me thinking of the joy found in family traditions and community connections. It is incredibly touching and engaging, with charming characters and a reminder that love can find you when you least expect it."

—Ali Gifford, audiobook narrator and voiceover artist

"Landon Beach's *Snow* is a richly detailed, evocative love story to Christmas. The changing points of view from character to character keep the plot fresh and perceptions satisfyingly entwined. No spoilers, but the ending both surprises and delights. *Snow* is deliciously entertaining and vivid. A perfect book for the holiday season."

—Becky London, actor, audiobook narrator, and coach

"Landon Beach, known for his compelling thrillers, flexes his 'Hallmark Christmas Special' writing muscle and spins a moving story of a fractured family, emotionally distant parents, and a young woman with an unrealized dream of a music career. Jean Mercer throws herself into the high-stakes, high-glitz, and fast-paced world of New York City's marketing industry, where she can forget who she is and cloak herself in wealth. Then, on a trip to rural Michigan at Christmastime to oversee the sale of her deceased grandmother's house, a historic snowstorm strands her with strangers, and Jean begins to see herself with wide-eyed clarity. A master of plot twists, Beach serves up some surprises in *Snow*, a gentle, feel-good holiday tale."

—Anne Marie Lewis, actor, singer, and audiobook narrator

"*Snow* is indeed a warm, feel-good, and thoughtful holiday page-turner, but it is so much more! It is a story of triumph over loss, the struggle between the trappings of success and the insight to consider the long-term consequences of our decisions. Beach has a way with inner dialogue, a powerfully intimate POV that kept me engaged, and his knowledge of the Montana, New York, Michigan, and Santa Barbara regions had the meticulous detail of a local. If *Snow* were a movie, it would feel like it was shot in real time, capturing the nuance of the human condition and the dance of dropping one's long-curated guard to allow love and vulnerability in once again. An a-ha, *Sliding Doors* type twist at the end is not to be missed. Every book from this prolific author has held a refreshing surprise, so immersive that it has left me wanting more!"

—Claudia Dunn, actor, audiobook narrator, and voice actor

"Landon Beach has entertained us as a master of suspense with many previous novels. In *Snow*, he creates suspense of a different kind, one involving family secrets, hoping to find and fall in love with the right people, and the keys to self-discovery. What better time and place to 'find' oneself than when snowed in during a Michigan blizzard? The central character, Jean, is a strong but pained hard-charging executive whom you will definitely root for to make the right choices as Beach offers up a fascinating cast of supporting characters, some loving and helpful, others downright dangerous. Reading this novel as Jean negotiates her emotional journey is both suspenseful and entertaining!"

—Jordan Rich, WBZ Radio Boston, iHeart Media

"Landon Beach, the master of thrillers, is now also the king of human emotions, of the human condition. *Snow* is outstanding from start to finish. Don't miss this experience—have tissues available."

—Wendi Flint Rank, top NetGalley reviewer

For all the broken families and lonely hearts out there, and for future generations, who will have to carry on long after we are gone.

SNOW

PROLOGUE

Billings West High School, Billings, Montana – Saturday, December 10, 2011

It was standing room only in the Billings West High School auditorium, which was decorated to resemble a winter wonderland. Wreaths with red bows were hung along the walls; cardboard snowflakes marked the ends of each row; and garland with strands of white and red lights wound around it was strung across the stage's apron. Wearing her black choir dress and singing in her final Holiday Traditions concert, seventeen-year-old senior Jean Noel Mercer stood on the stage's top riser and looked out into the audience, waiting for the pianist, Ms. Janie, to start the last song of the night. Jean's choir director—mentor, second mother, friend, and shining light in her life—Ms. Norman had told the choir before they took the stage that the principal had just informed her that the auditorium's 967-person capacity had already been reached. Jean's spirits had lifted at the news. *My parents have to be here,* she thought.

For the past hour, during the short breaks between songs, her eyes had searched the rows and rows of people wearing formal dresses, snazzy suits, pretty blouses, heavy sport coats, and festive sweaters for her mother and father. When she hadn't found them, her eyes had moved down the outer aisles and across the back wall where people were standing shoulder-to-shoulder, even in front of the main doors, as if they had decided to make a human chain around the entire seating area. The rule follower in her said, *We're now beyond capacity, which is a hazard if anything happens and the auditorium needs to be evacuated.* The romantic in her said, *It's so good to see the community here celebrating the season together.* She saw some of the other choir members' parents who had shown up late and were standing—Caylee's, then Mark's, then Ashley's . . .

Her parents were nowhere to be seen.

Where are they? They must be here somewhere. They said they'd come.

The first notes of "Snow" sounded from the piano, and Jean's eyes locked in on Ms. Norman, who was turned toward Ms. Janie and moving her right arm up and down to the beat.

Suddenly, Ms. Norman snapped back, front and center, facing the choir and smiling as she raised both arms, and with a quick downward jab, the choir began singing.

Jean focused on the music, singing as if there was no tomorrow.

In a way, it was true.

She had been a member of the choir for all four years, and this would be the last time she would sing a Christmas song with Ms. Norman directing her. This was her last Christmas at home—she would be graduating at the end of May and leaving for college. She had spoken with Ms. Norman about majoring in music, and Ms. Norman had encouraged her to pursue her passion. However, Jean's parents, who were paying for her education, had not been supportive of this path. In her entire high school career in choir, they had not attended a single one of her performances. The excuse was always the same:

work. She was the only child and had grown up in comfort, not realizing how much money her family had until she started to spend the night at friends' homes and witnessed that not everyone had a pool, game room, or their own private bathroom. She had wanted for nothing.

Except for her parents to show some interest in one of *her* interests.

The bitter irony was that they liked music, especially holiday music. However, that fact had given her ammunition in her logical argument for why, if there was one choir event of hers to attend, the Holiday Traditions concert— her *senior-year* concert—was the one. She had also snuck into their home office and checked their calendars that morning. They had nothing planned for the evening, which had strengthened her argument, and she had enjoyed watching her mother and father exchange nervous glances after Jean had presented her reasons why they should attend. After an exhale, her father had shrugged; then, her mother had said, *"Okay, we'll come. What time does it start?"*

The choir was nearing the end of "Snow," which was one of Jean's favorite songs, and she found herself fighting off the feeling of loss, which was not the feeling that Ms. Norman wanted everyone in the auditorium to leave with.

"It is almost impossible to hear that song, my dear darlings, and not be filled with joy," she had said. *"Energized and hopeful about the days to come—that's the spirit we want to promote. Pure jubilant liveliness."*

As Jean sang the final word, "Snow," and held it, her eyes left Ms. Norman and focused on the audience. She might have missed her parents during her earlier searches, or perhaps they were delayed and squeezed in while she was looking at another area of the auditorium.

She looked for them again. Up the far-left aisle, across the back, down the far-right aisle, row A, row B, row—the song concluded, and the seated audience members leaped to their feet, joining those already standing around the perimeter, and started an ovation that lasted for over a minute. Ms. Janie stood behind the piano and bowed. Then, Ms. Norman bowed and blew the audience a kiss. She turned around and faced the choir, tears streaming down her face, and mouthed, "I love you."

Jean's eyes started to water, but, mercifully, Ms. Norman dismissed the choir, and Jean was soon surrounded by parents hugging their sons and daughters, presenting them with flowers and words of affirmation.

"You were spectacular."

"Wonderful!"

"I'm so proud of you."

"I can't believe this is your last one. I just love you, kiddo."

Jean tried to make her way off the stage, still looking into the dispersing audience for her mom and dad. As she weaved through the hugs and pats on the back, her emotion gave way to the practical matter of: *If they didn't come, how am I going to get home?*

She had gotten a ride to the event with her friend Marissa, and she had done it on purpose. *When my parents come to the performance, I'll be able to ride home with them. Maybe we can go out for hot chocolate, and they will tell me how much they enjoyed the concert—maybe they'll let me know I did a good job. Maybe they'll see me.*

By the time she made it to the downstage-right stairs, the crowd had thinned. *I'll take a look around before heading to the choir room to get my things. Maybe Mom and Dad already exited and are waiting around in the area just outside the main doors. They know I didn't drive my car here.*

As her right foot touched the first stair, she heard, "Jean!"

She stopped and looked back over her shoulder. Marissa stood on the first riser and waved her over.

Jean backtracked and made her way across the stage. She saw Marissa step down from the riser. Her friend's parents, along with her younger brother and sister, were nearby, and Marissa held a beautiful bouquet of roses in her hand.

"Hey!" Marissa said, while hugging Jean. "I can't believe that was the last one."

"I know."

"My mom wants to speak with you."

The hug ended, and Jean said, "Oh. Okay."

Marissa moved around her and soon returned with her mom.

"Hi, Jean. Beautiful singing tonight," Marissa's mom said.

Jean managed a smile. "Thank you."

"Your mom texted me and wondered if we could bring you home."

"Were they here?" Jean asked. *Please, tell me they were here and had to leave early.*

Marissa's mom frowned. "She said something came up at work and they weren't able to make it tonight. She sent the text right after the concert started, and I saw it after the first song ended. I'm sorry."

Jean started to sway as if disgust, sadness, fear, and anger were people who had ropes around her and were engaged in a 4-way tug of war, each trying to dominate the other emotions. Would she yell? Would she cry? Would she collapse? Would she find something and break it? She looked like she was losing her balance.

"Oh, sweetie—oh, are you okay?"

Get it together. You're fine. She steadied up. *I will not break down here. I will not break down anywhere.* Her mouth was dry, but she got out, "Thank you. I'll get my things from the choir room and be right back."

She turned and started speed-walking away. Behind her, she heard Marissa say, "Hey, Jean, wait up."

But Jean did not slow down.

She would never wait for anyone again.

She would never depend on anyone again.

Out of the corner of her eye, she saw Mark's parents presenting a vase holding a red poinsettia to Ms. Janie, and Ms. Janie placing a hand over her heart. *She can't help me.* Then, she saw Ms. Norman hugging a choir member.

My hero can't even help me. I'm all alone. Jean's heart ached and her hands shook as she stormed away. She closed her fingers and thumbs, making fists.

And . . . I will never sing *for anyone again.*

PART I

Flurries

13 Years Later . . .

1

Pier Sixty, New York City – Friday, December 20, 2024

Jean stood tall in her square-neck, gold sequin Versace dress and looked out at the snow falling onto the dark Hudson River through the floor-to-ceiling windows of Pier Sixty's six-thousand-square-foot Majestic Room. Her black, silky hair was styled in a tight bun, and, given the occasion, she wore contacts, which highlighted her blue irises. She had already lost count tonight of the people who had said, *"My God, your eyes,"* or something similar. Laser surgery was on the horizon, but her glasses had become a fixture of her identity since she put on her first pair in second grade. On nights like these, she was reminded of the freedom that came with having one less thing to worry about. However, she planned to put in a full day tomorrow, which was Saturday, and would return to her work persona, her default persona, which required her to wear glasses. She would work half a day on Sunday, again wearing her intellectual armor. Perhaps her frames had always given her a layer of security with which to disguise herself—they distorted who she was and put up a Teflon front to outsiders, protecting and preserving who she was, or at least who she thought she was. And so, because her spectacles deflected inquiries into her inner sanctum, she kept putting off the surgery. She was logical, and this decision made no logical sense.

She held a flute full of Moët champagne, which a waiter wearing black pants, white shirt, green cummerbund, and red bowtie, in the spirit of the season, had just poured for her at the elegant bar stationed in the center of the venue's Olympic Room. "I've Got My Love to Keep Me Warm" by Dean Martin echoed through the space, mixed with the murmuring and laughter of the nearly five hundred people—mostly guests and retired employees—who had gathered for her company's annual holiday party. And right now, that cheerful symphony of voices and joy had yet to drown out Dino's smooth voice, which meant that the night was still tame. In another hour, Jean knew that she would have to be near a speaker to hear the music. She had joined the Fortune 500 company Renault Impact, an elite advertising agency located on the fabled Avenue of the Americas, right after graduating college, and every gathering for the past eight years had progressed in this fashion—cheerful and polite cocktail hour followed by glorious dinner and focused program, and then . . . a race to empty the bar of its expensive alcohol. Her rule of thumb after enduring the first party—getting well-oiled and waking up with a head-hammering hangover—had been: nurse a club soda and cranberry juice cocktail before dinner, enjoy a glass of red or white wine with dinner, and when the room goes dark except for the lights on the enormous Christmas tree in the corner *after* dinner, it is time for one glass of champagne and then a cab ride home.

But tonight, she might have to stay and weather a stretch of the debauchery.

Grasping the stem between her thumb and her long, delicate index and middle fingers, she raised the glass of sparkling wine and then hesitated before taking a sip, her attention held by the bubbles rising inside the flute, contrasted with the snow falling outside in the freezing temperature. *An apt mosaic for this past year at work,* she thought. Ups and downs. Gains and losses. Triumphs and failures. Opposing forces in different sectors, somehow affecting each other in an all-encompassing melee.

And yet. Chantel just promoted me.

That would be reason number one she should stay longer tonight: gratitude. The sudden jolt of surprise when the announcement had been made less than thirty minutes ago had still not subsided—her arms still tingled, and her smartwatch kept asking her if she would like to record the workout it thought she was performing. *Deep breaths,* she told herself, *deep breaths.*

Some of her fellow employees, especially the thirty-to-forty crowd in her department, which she had just passed over, would see her lingering presence as a victory lap masked as gratefulness. There had already been narrowed eyes, gritted teeth, patronizing smiles, limp handshakes of congratulations, and other vise-tightening handshakes delivered while locking eyes with her for an extra second. Well, they would not be wrong about the victory lap. It came with the territory, and every single one of them would be taking it if he or she had received the giant promotion she had just been given. They would have also gloated; she would not. Like any other major corporation, her agency operated according to a pyramidal system. Employees at or near the bottom had little to no power; employees in the middle reached for more power and either ascended or fell down the ladder of hierarchy; employees at the top possessed immense power. Because of her promotion, she would finally have tremendous power. Still, her ambition to reach this level had centered on gaining greater control to make the company more successful. In contrast, many in the cohort of competitive colleagues who had jostled for the position and lost had sought the exclusive and lofty reaches of the pyramid's top echelon to only, at long last, wield power over those beneath them—a singular vision of reward and retribution doled out based on loyalty that, in her opinion, had little or nothing to do with the health of the business.

Her elbow bent, and the curved lip of the flute met her lips, which were glossed in scarlet lipstick, and the cool liquid slid into her mouth and then down her throat as she swallowed.

She thought about the past week. *I should be staying at The Westin hotel at the Detroit Metropolitan Airport right now.* She shrugged. *Things have a way of working out.*

The holiday party was initially scheduled for Friday, December 13th, but on Wednesday, the 11th, her boss changed it to Friday, the 20th. Jean had gone to her immediate supervisor, a mover and a shaker in the industry, the handsome forty-year-old Urian Phineas Nikolaidhts, hailing from Palaio Psychico, perhaps the wealthiest suburb in Athens, Greece, and told him that she would not be able to attend the rescheduled party on the 20th. What struck her was his reaction. For a man who was so in control of his emotions, his face betrayed a mixture of being let down and the sudden paranoia of *"Uh oh, this will ruin our plan."*

Ten minutes later, she followed Urian into the company's largest C-Suite corner office to see Chantel Nadine Renault, the CEO of Renault Impact.

"I hear you won't be able to make the holiday party this year," Chantel said.

"Yes, that's true. As you know, my grandmother passed away in October, and we're having trouble selling her house. I'm flying to Michigan to meet with the realtor and see what we can do." She was also meeting with her late grandmother's best friend for dinner, but decided not to mention it. Unless it was company or industry gossip, Chantel wanted the bare minimum.

"That's sweet," Chantel said, and then peered over at Urian. *"Don't you think that's sweet?"*

The man, whose nationality highlighted the cosmopolitan metropolis that New York City had become, nodded and said, *"Very sweet."*

Chantel took off her designer glasses and leaned back in her leather chair. *"And even so, we need you at the party on the twentieth."*

"You do?" Jean said.

She watched as Urian and Chantel exchanged a playful glance.

"Yes," the reclining fifty-five-year-old CEO, wearing her staple charcoal suit, said. *"We're going to be honoring you, and you must be there."*

As if it were choreographed beforehand, Urian jumped in. *"We'll reschedule your flight for you and pay for the change. Flying first class, right?"*

She shook her head 'no.'

"Really? Well, we'll upgrade you to first class and also take care of getting you a top-of-the-line rental car to use." He looked to Chantel, who gave him a grin of approval, and then swiveled his eyes back to Jean. *"Since the party is moving to Friday the 20th, most people will be leaving for vacation that weekend. Now, I know you're a workaholic, but what if we moved the flight to Michigan to Monday the 23rd—morning, I assume? Out of JFK?"*

What are they honoring me with? she thought.

After a few seconds, she nodded and told them the change would be fine but that she could handle the finances. And she wasn't lying. At thirty years old, she was already a millionaire, living in a 2-2, 1250-square-foot, $2.7-million condo on West Broadway in SoHo, about a mile and a half southwest of the Renault Impact office on the Avenue of the Americas. The condo was home, but it was not Urian's $7.5-million mansion in Tribeca, nor was it Chantel's $38-million condo in 53 West 53. *Was she being promoted? If so, to what position?* The buzz around the company was that Urian was the heir apparent whenever Chantel decided to step down, but that might not be for years. Still, Jean wouldn't mind sliding into Urian's post when that happened. Right now, there were approximately three rungs on the ladder between her current position and Urian's. There were also rumors that his deputy was planning to retire. *Perhaps I'll be taking that soon-to-be-open post?*

Chantel smiled and waved her hand. *"Nonsense. We'll pay for everything. It's the least we can do. And we'll pay for your flight from Detroit to . . . well, where are you going for the holidays?"*

"I planned on working through the thirtieth, and then I was going to just stay here through the new year."

"Christmas?" Urian asked. *"Family plans?"*

"I haven't been home for the holidays since I left for college. I usually put in at least a half day on Christmas. It's so quiet."

He shook his head. *"You should take some time off."*

Jean gave a sportive shrug. She didn't know what to say.

Chantel tapped her fingers on her chair's armrests. *"We'll get you a flight out of Detroit that evening back to New York City. Drop by my secretary's desk when you leave here in a minute and work out the details. Tell her to file the trip under 'research.'"*

"Research?"

"C'mon, Jean, you're trying to persuade your real estate agent to sell the house faster. Sounds like an advertising consultation to me."

Urian slid the tip of his tongue across his upper lip and added, *"Me too."*

"So, you won't have to take any personal days." Chantel sat up straight. *"But, you should be taking personal days over the break. We'll discuss that later. I'll probably have to pressure you at the party to stop working. But until then, off you go."*

Jean said, *"Thank you,"* and Urian motioned her toward the door. In the hallway, leading to Chantel's secretary's desk, Jean thought, *Where would I even go on a vacation?*

Now, a week and a half later, she still didn't have any holiday plans for after her short trip to Michigan. She lowered the flute of champagne and allowed herself a quick grin as she watched the snow continue to fall. Chantel's power of perception was as sharp as ever. *She knew I wouldn't have any plans yet.*

"Happy you let me change your flight?" a voice from behind her said.

Speak of the devil.

The snowflakes disappeared as Jean's eyes focused on the window, using it as a mirror to see Chantel approaching her. *You just promoted me to the executive team,* she thought. *I'm now fourth in line behind you.* She turned and said, "Yes, I am," to her boss.

Chantel, by no means short at five feet seven inches, stopped next to the five-foot-ten-inch Jean and gave her a warm side-hug before parting and shifting a few feet to the right to talk.

"You're staying for more than just that one, right?" Chantel said, pointing at Jean's flute with her index finger, the emerald polish on her nail matching her radiant, draped gown, which was cut low and exposed her stunning cleavage. Jean considered her own frame athletic but would never risk wearing a cut that deep, especially to a work party.

"I plan on it," Jean said and then took a sip.

Chantel raised her glass of scotch, and Jean watched as the powerhouse of a human being took a long pull and then smacked her lips. "That's what I wanted to hear."

Chantel's pixie cut of brunette hair was on the longer side but still trimmed to perfection, and everything about her appearance was pristine, calculating, and magnetic. "When you break it down, the catering company is charging us fifty bucks per glass of this single malt." Chantel paused, studying the amber liquid in her Collins glass. "And I'd pay a hundred for it."

They laughed.

If it were like previous parties, Jean knew that her boss already had two hundred dollars' worth of the amber liquid in her.

For as prim and professional as Chantel was during the workweek, she became a different animal after hours. Other senior employees had remarked to Jean that perhaps the startling transformation was merely the daughter mimicking how her father, company founder Marsilius Alain Renault, had operated: being a statue of class and stoicism while "on guard" and then morphing into a charismatic charmer when the proverbial five-o'clock whistle blew. Create intrigue. Let there be devilish rumors. Above all, stay *mysterious* to your employees and clientele.

In terms of beauty, she came from prime stock—Marsilius, a ripe apple from the Cary Grant lookalike tree, and her mother, Fae Leena, a mythological model for Dolce & Gabbana, Giorgio Armani, and Dior. However, Chantel kept her sensuous curves hidden.

Which is why when new employees first saw her abandon her constitutional, rotating array of conservative charcoal, black, and indigo suits for form-fitting dresses or tight turtleneck sweaters and skinny jeans, the shock was so severe, it invariably led to instant whispering, and, in the case of a nineteen-year-old boy who worked in the company mailroom, an inappropriate outburst to a twenty-two-year-old Jean by the bar at her first holiday party. *"Holy Christ, Chantel has boobs."* Immediately seeing the astonished look on Jean's face, and apparently coupled with his own surprise at the verbal expression of what was supposed to stay safely housed in his mind, he had added, *"I mean, Chantel has news for all of us tonight. I hear we are getting bonuses."* Jean had given a polite nod and watched as the young man, after receiving his drink from the bartender, almost dropped it as he scurried away into the crowd.

Until a year ago, Chantel's chameleon-like maneuvering with new and prospective clients had remained a rumor to Jean. Then, Jean had accompanied her on business trips to Houston, Los Angeles, Sydney, Tokyo, Zurich, London, and Nassau and witnessed that Chantel was indeed following her father's social playbook.

Looking back, Jean should have seen the promotion coming. Other than Urian and another member of the executive team, Jean had been the only person to travel alone with Chantel to meetings outside of the New York City hub.

Beyond her boss's supreme intelligence, divine business instincts, gift of gab, and quick wit was her stunning figure, which eased forward as a lethal weapon during informal talks that had taken place in 5-star hotel bars, where Jean observed Chantel coerce bottom-line-obsessed, overly-aggressive clients who, at the end of formal proceedings, had requested to meet with her in a more relaxed and low-key environment, which were the business world's code words for: *unfiltered* and *unrecorded* environment.

Expecting some of these informal talks to lead to one-night stands, Jean was surprised and impressed—she also felt guilty for her stereotypical assumptions—that, adhering to a true advertising ethos, Chantel would put her beauty on exhibition, but never allow the yearning, sometimes near-panting, wide-eyed clients to experience anything further than the aesthetic pleasure of enjoying her flirtatious company. *"By all means, let the drinks go down; delight with the devious grin, and let the talk wander to the margins. But the dress stays on, Jean. Remember that. After the deal is made, always promise future casual chats."*

Jean had just nodded, and later found out from Urian that Chantel adored her husband of twenty years, Alec Rio Mar. *Inseparable—I've never seen two people more in love or more devoted to each other,* Urian had said. *She joked with me once, saying that they had made monogamy sexy again.* It was none of Jean's business, but it made Chantel's advice to her make more sense and carry more weight.

"People want what they cannot have," Chantel had gone on to say, *"but they can always be seduced into buying what they don't need, which is why we'll always be in business. And, in business dealings, our clients can have the services of my* company; *they just can't have* me. *Now, whether or not I give each suitor of Renault Impact the* impression *that he or she might also have an opportunity to court or bed me is . . . not my concern."*

Later, at 35,000 feet, flying home in the company jet, Chantel had asked Jean, *"So, did you think I was leading them on?"*

In a decision fueled by liquid courage—they were on their second bottle of champagne—Jean had said, *"Yes,"* even though she believed what Urian had told her.

After a beat, Chantel had leaned back, crossed her legs, squinted, and then smiled. *"You're god damn right I was. My father always said that sex sells, and maybe in his time it did. But I have found that the possibility of sex sells more . . . and keeps clients coming back. Advertising is flirting, and so flirting is never unethical. It's funny, they all know Alec is the only one for me, but every single one of them thinks he or she has what it takes to be the first to lure me away. Not a chance."*

"I've Got My Love to Keep Me Warm" faded away and was replaced by "The Christmas Waltz." The vocals started, and Chantel asked Jean, "Is that Natalie Cole?"

"I don't know."

Chantel took another sip of scotch and then said, "I believe it is." She broke off, listening, then motioned with her glass toward a ceiling speaker. "My favorite holiday song. I didn't know she sang this one." She cocked her head to one side. "What's yours?"

Jean reluctantly searched her memory, scrolling through dozens of holiday tunes that she mostly couldn't stand because her parents overplayed them while she was growing up, and, there was also another reason. "Don't know if I have a favorite."

Chantel's eyes moved beyond and to the left of Jean. "Think *he's* got a favorite?"

Jean looked in that direction, and seated by himself half a dozen tables away was Kenneth Lars, the executive she was replacing, who had been given a standing ovation when Chantel had announced his retirement and brought him up on stage for a hug and a toast five minutes before declaring that Jean had been promoted and would be taking his position on the lead team. *He looks tired.* "Maybe his is 'Sleigh Ride,' as in 'I'm outta here.'"

Chantel let out a loud laugh. "God, your random humor hits." She squeezed her arm. "Perfect. I *was* right about you."

Jean lowered her head. "Not the only thing you were right about."

Her boss put her index finger underneath Jean's chin and raised it until Jean made eye contact with her. "You still don't have vacation plans. I checked with HR before leaving the office today to get ready for tonight, and Chuck said you hadn't submitted for any time off." She removed her hand from Jean's chin and grasped Jean's bare shoulder with a firm grip. "You *are* taking time off, understand me. What is it? Worried about not holding your own with the other executives? Sweetheart, I would have never dragged you around the world with me or promoted you if I thought you weren't up to the task. Now, will you learn a lot in the next few months? Yup. But you're hungry and smart, and you have me and Urian in your corner, and there's no better duo to have than us." She stopped, raising her free hand toward her face. As her index finger and thumb rubbed her nose, she added, "The two of you may be running my company one day." She lowered her hand.

Jean recognized the move. In a crowd like this, there were always a few lipreaders, thirsting for gossip. Whenever Chantel wanted to share a private thought, she always spoke into her hand while rubbing her nose. Jean was thrilled with what her boss had just said. Not only was she excited about the possibility of being promoted further, but she was relieved to hear that Urian had faith in her. He was smooth, which made it difficult to know where you stood with him; the never-rattled demeanor was intimidating. But, like her, he was also a workaholic, which had drawn them closer since she started traveling with Chantel.

Wait a minute, she thought. *Why is he getting off easy? Surely, he's working over the holidays to get ahead, too?*

She decided to start with Chantel's plans and then pivot to Urian's.

Jean took a sip of champagne and then said, "Looks like I need some mentorship in the vacation department. Where are you heading in the next few weeks?"

Chantel turned and made eye contact with a man and a woman wearing black suits who were standing approximately twenty yards away. Immediately, the duet approached and took station five feet apart from each other and ten feet away from Chantel and Jean, forming a loose perimeter. The two were familiar to Jean: Marcus and Ariel, Chantel's bodyguards. Was there a specific threat to Chantel here tonight? No. There wasn't much of a threat anywhere she traveled. Both were fully trained and capable threat eliminators—no doubt there were weapons within arm's reach underneath their suit coats, but, on social occasions, Chantel had them accompany her for a more practical reason: they limited access to her, especially during exclusive moments like the one she was having now with her protégé—Chantel's word, not Jean's.

In her travels, Jean had seen them grant access to certain people and turn others away. Whenever they were around, people took notice, which was why, as she took a quick look around the room, people were giving them a wide berth. Now that Marcus and Ariel had taken their official positions, her chat with Chantel would go undisturbed.

Her boss raised her glass and drank . . . when she lowered it, the glass was empty. "That's an aspect of you that I appreciate. Your willingness to be guided." She held Jean's gaze for a beat. "You haven't heard over the years where I go?"

The answer was "no," but the addendum to the truth was that she had never been interested in where people went for vacation. She was too busy working and had never asked. "No," she answered. "Although I assumed it was someplace sunny and warm because your skin was always the color that it is now at the holiday party, and when we gathered a few weeks into January for the annual new year kick-off luncheon, your face had a sun tan."

Chantel's mouth slid into a sly grin, exposing her unstained, straight, and perfect teeth. "Yet another trait that has found favor with me—your powers of observation. You're curious, but you don't cross the line."

Movement to the right caught Jean's attention, and she saw a male waiter being intercepted by Marcus. After a brief exchange of words, the bodyguard allowed the waiter to approach Renault Impact's CEO.

Without breaking eye contact with Jean, Chantel held out her empty glass, and the waiter took it, placing a recharged glass in her hand. Not waiting to be thanked, he backed away and disappeared into the crowd.

After a sip, Chantel said, "In two days, I'm heading to my family's winter sanctuary, St. Barths. We've vacationed at Eden Rock for Christmas and New Year's since the mid-1970s—started by staying at the hotel and, over the years, have worked our way up to a villa. Even after traveling the world, it is still the only place I'd rather be than New York City. Dad, Mom, and my brothers, along with their families, will all be there. Since we're all going this year, we've rented two side-by-side villas. When growing up, we were always told that Santa knew we'd be away from the city and to bring our presents to the island. And, Alec loves the place," she said, motioning to her husband, who was at the bar talking to . . . *My God, it's the hottest director in Hollywood right now.* Chantel, no doubt noticing Jean's excitement at who Alec was speaking with, gave Jean a high-spirited tap on the arm and said, "*He* might visit us while we're there. Ah, Christmas is . . . well, there's nothing like it, right?"

For as amiable as her boss could be when networking or securing a deal, Chantel's statements oozed of who-you-know hierarchy and where-you-stay conceit, but Jean sensed that they were also of genuine affection and not just laced with nostalgic charm. *Unfortunately, these are areas where we have nothing in common,* Jean thought. *Am I a bit jealous?* She did not like the answers her conscience was giving her. Jean neither lived a lavish life nor mingled with celebrities. She was not intimidated by people of fame, but she did not seek them out for conversation or company. Yet.

Jean's family was not close—she barely knew of her late grandmother, with whom she had been charged with selling her house; holidays, especially Christmas, while she was growing up, were a time of great stress and anxiety. It was why she had never gone back for any holidays after she had left for college. And perhaps that was why she worked so hard each year during these three weeks: so that she would not dwell on the fact that her parents had never talked to her about it. This was why she had been hesitant to take a vacation, fearing that too much free time would lead to thinking, and thinking might lead to a sad, hollow feeling that she had experienced once and vowed to avoid ever since. She would tell Chantel none of this.

However, she was open to taking a vacation. It would just need to be structured, and even various pleasures would have to be scheduled as items to be checked off once accomplished. She needed to feel like she was making progress each day, even if the reason for being productive was to relax within the parameters of an event to be on time for and execute the evolution effectively. Massage at 2 p.m. Show up to the boutique at 1:45, undress, receive your massage, shower, dress, and leave the boutique. Next event!

"Nothing like this time of year," she lied, raising her flute in a toast.

Chantel touched glasses with her. "Which is why you need to get out of here at some point. Don't get me wrong, other than St. Barths, New York City is the place to be for Christmas. The soul of this city awakens. But you've got to get away after that. And I don't mean Michigan. I think it's wonderful what you're doing for your late grandmother, and, yes, the temperatures there around this time of year are comparable with the temps here, but, c'mon, it's bore, snore-city in the Midwest."

"Any suggestions?"

Chantel angled her body a point away from Jean so that her eyes could survey the room. While giving her a sly grin, she said, "Oh, I don't know . . ." Then, her eyes settled on someone, and Jean followed with her own eyes until they rested on the handsome and tall figure of Urian—black curly hair, thick five-o'clock shadow—holding court with half a dozen employees and their significant others.

Jean smiled at Chantel. "What?"

"You might ask him where *he* goes."

Their eyes returned to Urian, and, after a few seconds, he met their stares, toasting them with his flute of champagne.

"Well, I have a few more palms to press and rounds to make with prospective suitors for our business's expertise. It never ends—well, it will for a bit when I touch down in paradise. Now, off you go to make plans for your vacation." She leaned in and gave her a politician's hug, accompanied by an awkward kiss to the side of the head. Whispering in her ear, Chantel said, "Safe travels to *Michigan*. But finish your business there and get somewhere fun. I want to see a refreshed and excited *you* at the kick-off luncheon. We're going to make a killing this year."

Jean was not a hugger by nature, more at home giving handshakes and forming an intellectual connection with someone, versus an emotional one. However, in the past year, she had learned the art of the social hug and air kiss to the side. It had nothing to do with feeling; it had everything to do with optics: the impression of respect and camaraderie—So good to see you . . . We're in this together . . . We *know* each other . . . We work together . . . I'm with him . . . I'm with her . . . I *trust* you—at least for now . . . etc.

"Merry Christmas, happy 2025, and safe travels," whispered Jean. "I'll be ready."

They parted.

Chantel said, "I know you will," and then walked away with Marcus and Ariel in tow.

Jean watched as her boss spied the first target: a pharmaceutical baron who was thinking of hiring Renault Impact to tell his company's revised brand story. She heard Chantel say, "Roger," right before performing her hug and cheek kiss. Roger said, "Hey!" and performed his half of the ridiculous public ritual.

She took a long sip of champagne, thinking about how nice another full flute would be, when she heard, "Staying a little longer than usual."

Turning, she saw the welcoming face of Urian Nikolaidhts look down at hers from a few paces away.

2

Most men in the company were at Jean's eye level or below, but Urian was six feet four and one of the few whom she still had to tilt her chin upward to take in the handsomeness of his chiseled facial features. On many occasions when he would pause at work—refilling his coffee, stepping aside in the hallway, pondering a question in a conference room meeting—she thought he would make a magnificent statue, placed somewhere in Athens, signifying beauty, strength, and wisdom.

He stopped and clinked glasses with her.

"Couldn't dash out too fast after that surprise promotion," she replied.

"It couldn't have been *that* much of a surprise."

She gave a half-serious grin. "It was."

He went to say something but waited, studying her. Not in an unflattering or creepy way. *Just one human being appreciating the presence of another . . .*

Wait a minute, am I talking about him or me? She tried to hide a smirk as she thought, *It's me. He's being a statue again, a beautiful, stoic, stimulating statue.*

After a drink from his flute, he said, "Well, I hope you know how much Chantel and I . . . well, how much *everyone* on the lead team thinks of you now."

Jean wished she had her glasses on. *I still struggle with accepting compliments.*

As the COVID pandemic had spread across the globe, Jean felt, like many others, the uncertainty of what effect the disease would have on her if she were infected. Her bubble of safety, certainty, and comfort was shattered early. So, reasoning that tomorrow was not promised, she decided to finally risk being vulnerable in an attempt to unpack her past, perhaps, before it was too late. *I want to know* myself *at least before I die.* She found a psychologist, Samuel something or other, who would meet with her online, and they had commenced their sessions in August of 2020. Behind the good doctor's massive salt-and-pepper beard, long black hair, black turtleneck, and tortoiseshell glasses lay a discerning intellect. They met for half a dozen Zoom sessions, and after two, Jean discovered that, to some extent, she had repressed her emotions for the majority of her life, building a sizable wall around her core. Samuel had told her that the reason she was not yet equipped to handle praise was that, for her entire childhood, she had been made to feel unworthy of it, no matter how much she accomplished.

There were tears; there were more questions; there was the beginning of healing.

Then, the vaccines were rolled out, and she felt reassured of her chances of survival. There was no need to probe any deeper—certainly not about singing—now that she could return to her usual routines and efficient modes of operation. Samuel had also mistakenly stood up during their last session, revealing that below the black turtleneck he was only wearing tighty whities— *"Oh, my God. I am so sorry. These goddamned computers."*—and she canceled the next session.

Then, she canceled Samuel, deleting his emails that started with an apology for his unprofessionalism, then moved to queries of wanting to continue their work if she was still willing to be vulnerable, to a video of him playing basketball with a group of elementary school kids—everyone masked up—and him accidentally tripping and plowing a boy to the ground, to ending with a final message containing the solitary sentence:

I wish you peace.

Peace? What did that mean? What did that concept ever *mean in terms of the human condition? And what is the framework for me to apply such ubiquitous words of encouragement?* She had no time to consider these questions. There were essential tasks to be completed, mountains of stimulating work to tackle, and she happily lost herself once again in the cutting-edge ecosphere of Renault Impact, which shaped economic consumer behavior and ultimately influenced the world.

"I'm just eager to get started," she said to Urian. *There. That's safe.*

She observed him as he gave a slight tilt of his head and squinted his eyes. After a quick pursing of his lips, Urian said, "I never thought I'd find someone who loved work as much as I do."

She raised her eyebrows.

"But, I think I've met my match."

"Maybe you have."

With the fingers and thumb of his left hand, he rubbed his facial hair as if she had asked him what he thought about a scandalous celebrity memoir. *Does he read or listen to books?* On the company jet, he was always on his phone with his AirPods in, but that was all she knew. If he was consuming literature, he didn't talk about it.

"Okay. Time to put it to a test," he said, continuing to massage his immaculately trimmed five-o'clock shadow, his manicured fingers like a wire comb pulled through a thick carpet.

Her breathing was picking up, and not because she was nervous about the test. *Slow down,* she told herself, but her body did not listen. "What's the test?" she asked, trying to get him to at least speak again and give her something to concentrate on other than being drawn further into his looks and easy manner.

He moved closer, and she got a whiff of his marvelous cologne. *Armani? I'm sure of it.* She finished her flute of champagne. Feeling warmer, she thought, *Ready for the next one!*

"It's simple," he said. "Are you taking any vacation time over the next three weeks?"

"Were you lip-reading?"

"What?"

A waiter arrived with a fresh glass of champagne, and Jean took it, inclining her head to say thanks.

"Chantel and I were just talking about holiday plans."

Urian's eyes moved over the room. "Standard fare around here, I suppose." When his eyes had worked their way back to Jean, he added, "So, what is your answer?"

"How is this a test?"

"I'm not following you."

"Well, we discussed this last week in Chantel's office. You already know the answer."

"Ah, but there's the test. I want to know if you changed your mind. Or," he said, pointing with his glass at Chantel, who was giving another woman around her age a hug and air kiss, "if *she* changed your mind."

"Okay, I have two answers."

"Fair enough."

"One. I usually don't take any days off this time of year." She registered the defeated look on his face.

"I think you love work more than I do. I bow to your highness," he said while leaning over and then straightening back up.

She played along and gave him a nod of acknowledgment. "Two. My talk with Chantel has me rethinking that approach."

His eyes opened up. "I couldn't agree with her more. The last thing we need you to do is get burned out."

She rolled the flute's stem between her thumb and fingers, as if she were attempting to use the friction to start a fire. "The question now becomes, I suppose, *where* should I go, *if* I were to go someplace?"

"Are you looking for suggestions?"

She stopped rolling the flute's stem. "You know I like data when making a decision."

"Of course," Urian said. "But first, what climate?"

"Anything warmer than New York City."

"So, sitting on a beach in a swimsuit, having a drink with a tiny umbrella in it is in play, but we're not limited to that slice of paradise, right?"

"Correct." *Say Greece, say Greece.*

He grinned. "Ever been to Greece?"

And now her heart was POUNDING. *Am I blushing? Who cares? I can always blame it on the champagne. Get a hold of yourself. You can't make this easy.*

"No, I haven't," she said, attempting to sound uninterested.

"Well, Athens is a wonderful city, and I am proud to call it home, but my family spends its vacations at our seafront villa on the island of Mykonos. Like you, I have been around the world with Chantel and seen beautiful places, but no place compares to Mykonos." He pointed at their boss with his drink. "She thinks that St. Barths is tops, but that's just her childhood reminiscences of the place clouding her logic. The beaches, the nightlife, the vibe of Mykonos is, well, *potent*." He made a dismissive wave with his hand. "Has it become known for tourism? Yes. And has that spoiled it for native Greeks? A bit. Still, there is nothing like sitting on our patio with a drink in your hand, high above the turquoise Aegean, and feeling a stiff wind blow against your face, carrying the scent of fresh flowers. Mykonos's nickname is actually 'The Island of the Winds.'"

"And you're going there for the holidays?"

"I always go there this time of year. Gives me perspective." He peered down at his watch in a symbolic gesture. "I'm flying out tomorrow."

There was silence between them for a few beats. *Trust yourself. You're reading the signs correctly.* She said, "If I didn't know any better, I'd say you were inviting me."

His face froze.

Oh, no, I've misread him.

Then, he exhaled. "Am I that obvious?"

She relaxed, gulping champagne to calm her nerves. "Not at all. I took a guess."

"You're too generous. I slipped into my pitch mode. Can't help it. Everyone should experience Mykonos."

She took another sip. "Temperature right now?"

"Okay, stay with me on this."

She nodded as if to say, *Proceed.*

"It's not the mid-eighties like it is in summer, but it's not the thirties and forties of New York City either." He paused. "The days are usually mid to high fifties, breaking sixty every once in a while. Lows, mid-40s. Perfect for sweatshirts, bundled-up walks on the beach, and fires at night to cut the cold."

I would be fine with that, she thought. *I hate to sweat, and I hate to freeze.* "If I were interested, would you have any recommendations for where I could stay?"

He did not hesitate. "With me, of course."

She thought she would drop the champagne flute, but somehow held on. Her facial features must have registered surprise because he quickly added, "I mean, at my family's villa. We have a guest suite on the far side of our pool and cabana. You'd have your own living room, kitchen, study, bedroom, and bathroom. We always keep the pool heated, so you'd only have to take a few paces across the patio to take a dip."

"No one else is using it for the vacation?"

"Correct. My brother and his family have their own place in Chora, and my sister and her wife are staying in Athens until the middle of January, so it will just be me and my parents living in the main house along with the house staff."

"The house staff?"

"Yes, my parents have a full-time cook, gardener, butler, nanny, maid, and they each have a personal secretary. They've all been with us for years and are like family. Our nanny, Theora, helped raise my brother, sister, and me, and now she looks after their children when they come to visit my parents. She'll adore you for sure."

"I couldn't impose." *Yes, I could.*

"Oh, you wouldn't be. It would be *our pleasure* to host you." He waited. "However, if it would make you more comfortable, I can recommend some places to stay. It's just that my family knows how much I love my work, and they would be happy to host a colleague of mine, especially a rising star. Besides, they've done it before. Chantel, her husband, their two children, and their nanny stayed at the guest house last summer. Ha! Another reason she knows deep down that Mykonos edges St. Barths—nothing like experience, but she still won't face the truth.

"They had started their vacation in Australia and were going to stay a few weeks in London before heading back, so I invited them to stay with us for a few days in between. My mother and father enjoyed the visit, and they *love* Chantel and her family, especially her husband, Alec." He laughed. "I think my parents love Alec more than they love *me.*"

And now I can proceed. "It does sound like it would be a beautiful getaway, but are you sure? Would the other members of the lead team be comfortable with the arrangement?"

"Absolutely! They've all been there, too! A few winters ago, we had a mini-summit at the villa on our way back from Istanbul." He laughed.

"Looking back, I think that is where I sold Chantel on stopping over for a less formal visit."

"I have to travel to—"

"Michigan, right?" he said, interrupting.

"Yes. On Monday."

"There's no timetable on my end. You can come whenever you want and stay as little or as long as you desire."

You have no idea what I desire, she thought. *Or, maybe you do.* "I'll only be in Michigan for a day, so I could see about getting a flight out of New York City after I return?"

"Perfect. There's a seven-hour time difference between here and Athens, so you can sleep plenty when you first arrive to acclimate. We would have the guest house all ready for you." He let out another short laugh. "Or, if I let my mother know tomorrow, our maid, Iris, will have it ready before *I* even get there."

She shared the laugh with him and said, "Looks like efficiency runs in the family."

"She's the one who taught me!" he said, laughing again.

So, I'm going to Greece . . . to relax—something I'm not good at—and to spend some time with Urian. What if something happens?

Stop it. He is just a co-worker making a generous gesture. Just because we're both single—his relationship with that Broadway star ended, what, two months ago?—doesn't mean anything. Chantel and he just want me to be rested before the pressure-filled winter push. With our new partnerships, this spring is going to be busy. I cannot fail at my new position.

"Okay," she said, "it seems like destiny has taken a hand."

"Casablanca!" he cheered. "We'll watch it at the villa in our theater room. We'll make a night of it with dinner beforehand, followed by dessert and a bottle of twenty-year-old Vinsanto from Santorini. It's the sweetest white wine you'll ever taste. My parents are good friends with the owners of Estate Argyros on the island." He stopped speaking, as if he had been muted by someone pushing a button. He gave her a self-deprecating grin. "There I go again, getting ahead of myself, and, ugh, dropping names. Sorry, it's a habit I have when I let my guard down and show someone that I'm excited."

He's excited? He knows Casablanca well enough to recognize a line. Impressed, she filed the information away. *But, I'll have to confess that I'm not a movie buff—I just love* that *particular movie. And he wants to watch it and serve me fine Greek wine.* "I like the excited version of Urian," Jean said. "I'll start looking for tickets tomorrow."

"Excellent."

They toasted.

Motion off to her right caused her eyes to wander back over to Kenneth Lars, the executive she was replacing on the lead team. Urian's eyes moved with hers.

An older gentleman, whom she did not recognize, gave Lars a pat on the back and then walked away, leaving the retiree alone at his table again. "You'd think Kenneth would have a little bounce in his step tonight," she said.

Urian took a drink and then frowned in measured disappointment as if a board member had just said something embarrassing in a meeting.

"Who was the guy that just gave him a pat?"

Urian brought his free hand up and tapped his fingers on the side of his glass. "Gary Woods. He was Chantel's father's number two for years. Normally, I would be surprised to see him here; he's not an emeritus has-been who shows up to company functions to drain our alcohol and talk about the good old days when he was in charge. Usually keeps to himself."

Their eyes followed Woods until the old lion stopped at a table filled with people, all around Woods's age, whom Jean did not recognize.

As if he had anticipated her question, Urian said, "Those are all people who worked for the company around the same time as Woods did. Chantel told me that tonight was an informal reunion for most of them since they, like Woods, don't usually attend company functions even though the ones who still live in the city are invited."

"Oh," she said. "They all look miserable. They aren't even speaking to each other." Jean hesitated, looking back at Kenneth Lars, who was staring into his drink. "And why isn't Kenneth over at their table. Surely he worked with some of them."

Urian shrugged. "I thought Kenneth was a solid guy, but I didn't know him outside of work. Even when he stayed at my family's place, he kept to himself." He finished his drink. "I agree with you, though. I thought he'd be in good spirits tonight. I could be wrong. He's sixty-one, and this past year has been one hell of a roller coaster.   Maybe instead of emptiness and sadness, it's relief we're seeing in his eyes."

If Kenneth Lars's posture is the definition of relief, then I never want to feel it, Jean thought.

Urian shook his head. "I've been meaning to visit that other table all night. I was new to Renault Impact when most of them were in their final years, but I did work with a few." He pursed his lips while studying the table. "I don't know. It's just not the same when you fall out of touch. When you work together, you always have something to talk about, and most of the time, you unite to solve a problem. But when that central tether frays, it can be a little awkward." He straightened up and exhaled as if gathering his courage. "But, it doesn't matter. I need to go pay my respects." He gave her shoulder a polite rub. "Which will be infinitely easier knowing that I now have your company to look forward to over the holidays—I might even break down and talk some business with you." She gave him a mischievous shrug. *What am I doing?* "Let's touch base after you've got your tickets."

"Done," she said.

"Again, congratulations on your promotion, Jean." He gave her a warm smile, then turned and headed for the table of former employees.

Jean saw that two of the women were now chatting, but their expressions remained unchanged as each statement and reply was made. Urian was the only person approaching the table, a wolf homing in on a circle of wounded prey.

A discomforting question entered her mind: *Kenneth Lars aside, why aren't any of the older, current employees going over to chat with any of them?*

The impersonal nature of the whole thing was unsettling. These people had worked together for years. Now, even after a year of record profits, something every company member, past and present, should be rejoicing about, it was as if the former personnel of Renault Impact had been discarded or at least forgotten.

She watched as Urian arrived at the table and stood behind one of the seated men, then began massaging his shoulders while making a statement to the entire group. As his words hit their mark, there were a few smiles, and the man receiving the classic "Urian Treatment" gave a polite smile back over his shoulder at him. Then, the charming current executive motioned toward the bar. A waiter was soon on his way with a tray full of flutes of champagne, and just as the waiter started to hand out the glasses, Chantel arrived and delivered, in assembly-line fashion, hugs and air kisses to each seated person.

Feeling a touch better, Jean turned away and peered back out the window. The snow continued to fall, and through the speakers, just above the murmur of voices and pockets of growing laughter, she heard Andy Williams begin to sing "Winter Wonderland."

At least it wasn't "There's No Place Like Home for the Holidays." She hated that song.

3

M-20, Michigan – Monday, December 23, 2024

Jean drove her rental car, a Mercedes-Benz A-Class, down the highway and away from Midland, Michigan, toward her turn off onto White Pine Road a few miles ahead. Snow had started falling soon after she had picked up the car at MBS International Airport in Freeland and continued to fall at a steady pace. The sky had become a sheet of gray, which made structures off to her right and left stand out more than they usually would, like the enormous red barn on the edge of a clearing and the lit Christmas tree in the front yard of a home.

She lifted the large Dr. Pepper she had ordered from the McDonald's in Freeland and sipped from the paper straw, which had become a bit soggy. *Not going to lie, I miss plastic straws,* she said to herself. Setting the drink down, she rolled her eyes at the huge *plastic* top to her cup. The drive, without any stops, to her grandmother's was supposed to take thirty minutes. However, as soon as she had started down West Freeland Road toward M-47, the hunger pains began, and she realized that she had not eaten since her breakfast of coffee and a blueberry scone at JFK. So, instead of taking a right onto M-47, she had taken a left and pulled into her childhood favorite restaurant. Her order was the same as it had always been after she graduated from ordering Happy Meals: two cheeseburgers plain, large fries, and a large Dr. Pepper. Now, the smell inside her Mercedes was a mix of Mickey D's and "new car smell," as the vehicle had only 62 miles on it when Jean drove it away from the rental car lot around 12:45 p.m.

It was now 1:25, and she slowed, seeing the brake lights on the sedan in front of her. Instinctively, her right hand reached out toward the volume knob on the radio, and she turned Taylor Swift down a few decibels. She had resisted listening to any music for the first few minutes of her drive, but the overwhelming need to establish a comfortable atmosphere for herself in a place she did not know had overridden her usual preference for silence. Even though she avoided Christmas music and anything that might remind her of her years in choir, she was still able to enjoy pop music, especially tunes from her college days.

Living in New York City, she didn't own a car, but she missed driving, especially her old Ford Fusion, which had seen her through the last two years of high school and her college years. Saying goodbye to her "blue baby" when she moved from Montana to the Big Apple had been one of the few times she had experienced the uncomfortable feeling of emptiness that accompanied loss. It was only a car, but it had been *her* car, her responsibility. As her hand regripped the leather wheel, she realized that she could have turned the SiriusXM volume down with a touch of a button on the wheel console, which, ironically, she had used to turn the volume up fifteen minutes ago, but years and years of conditioning coupled with the distraction of driving in bad weather had overridden convenience and logic. It was a small detail, but it bothered her. She was in an unfamiliar place, and the pace, compared to New York City, seemed to have been slowed to a crawl. Ever since she had driven away from the fast-food haven with delicious food that she hadn't tasted in years, everything had slowed down and gone uncomfortably quiet. That is, with the exception of the thoughts running through her mind. Even with her singing companion on the radio to distract them, they had sped up and come from regions she had not drawn from in forever.

My first kiss. My first plane ride. My first sip of alcohol . . . What is this all about?

It was starting to snow harder, and she turned on her headlights. *Why didn't I do that earlier?*

As the red lights ahead extinguished, she peered down at her speedometer.

49 miles per hour.

The speed limit was 55, and, according to her mother, Lori—who preferred to provide bits of trivia and small talk centered on the weather instead of discussing anything of substance—the locals, including Jean's late grandmother, Shirley Ruth White, had argued for years to have the limit upped to 65. Typically, Jean would have tuned out the inconsequential facts and figures her mother seemed to vomit up every time they spoke, but that particular nugget had been different. Not because of the speed limit, but because it was one of the rare times that Jean's mother had spoken about her own mother.

Jean had no memory of Shirley Ruth, despite having visited her as a toddler. Not even flashes of images or jolts of feelings.

And yet, I'm having visions of my younger years scroll through my mind right now.

. . . There was another one—Jean, standing next to her locker at school, looking down at her phone. The text from her boyfriend reading:

I'm sorry, J. I like . . . need some space right now.

She had not been able to attend her grandmother's funeral in October while overseas with Chantel and Urian; she had also not been able to attend the funeral of her grandfather, Martin, Shirley Ruth's husband of nearly sixty years, in 2021. However, that absence had been a result of the short conversation she had with her parents when they called to notify her of his death.

"Your father and I are flying to Michigan for the funeral."

"I don't know him," Jean said.

"It's fine. You aren't expected to come."

A similar exchange had taken place in October when Shirley Ruth had passed away, but her parents, high-profile lawyers in Billings, Montana, were currently tied up in a huge case and needed her to handle the meeting with the realtor. The phone conversation last week had ended with her mom saying, *"Do whatever you need to sell the bitch—fast."* Her father, Patrick Mercer, had added, *"You're not coming for the holidays, are you? I'm afraid we won't be good company if you are . . . basically living at our firm right now."* She had said that she wasn't planning on it, and he had replied, *"Probably better that way. We may be able to visit you later this spring. Your mother still wants to see* Wicked.*"*

Other than a rehearsal of what to discuss with the realtor and the tremendous amount of snow that Michigan had been hit with in the past week, the speed limit on M-20 had been the only thing Jean had discussed with her mother last night. She hadn't told her that she was flying to Greece on the 27th and staying until January 4th.

A digital readout on the Mercedes's center console told her that the temperature outside was twenty-three degrees, and there had to be at least three feet of powdery snow lining the highway with even larger piles at the ends of driveways that had been cleared with snowblowers or back-breaking shoveling. Greece, sweatshirt weather, wine, rest, and Urian sounded better every minute.

After another two miles, her smartwatch started to vibrate, and her phone directed her to turn right onto White Pine Road, which her mother had told her was named after Michigan's state tree. A voice inside her said to turn the radio off, and so she did.

I'll catch up with you later, Tay.

After pulling the wheel over and then steadying up on the narrow side road, she took a quick sip of her Dr. Pepper and watched as the pine trees, shagged with ice and snow, traveled down both sides of her car. Jean could hear the bitter wind outside, and it carried snow across the road as if a person were standing on the shoulder with a powerful broom, sweeping the powder off the bank and onto the pavement. She slowed to thirty-five miles an hour.

Another few miles down the quiet stretch, her watch vibrated again, and her phone announced that she had reached her destination. She looked for the house, but there was nothing but a wall of trees off to her right. Seeing that no vehicles were heading toward her, and after a quick check in her rearview mirror to confirm that no cars were approaching from behind, she slowed the Mercedes to a crawl. She concentrated on the dark, rectangular mailbox coming up. Moments later, she could make out the name "WHITE" in gold letters on the side, and then she saw a strip of black asphalt, situated between two high banks of snow, a few yards beyond the mailbox. She turned in.

Jean was relieved to see that the driveway had been cleared, as there was only a thin film of snow covering it as she passed between the high banks, lined with towering pines. The storm, which had threatened to delay her trip, had ended two days ago. *Who cleared the driveway?* she thought. *A neighbor? The real estate company?* She glanced up at the sky. *If this keeps up, they'll have to clear it again. The last thing we want is for the house to be unable to be shown because prospective buyers can't access it.*

The drive bent to the right, and soon the trees opened up to a spacious yard, covered by snow, with her grandmother's two-story house centered on the plot and a detached garage off to the left. The snow on the roof reminded her of a gingerbread house in a snow globe she had received as a party favor a few years ago at a small holiday gathering at Chantel's condo that overlooked a snow-covered Central Park. Urian had been there as well as other members of the executive team—only Jean and another non-lead-team member had been invited. Looking back, perhaps that was the moment that had led to the promotion on Friday night. She had been awed by Chantel's residence on the seventy-first floor of 53 West 53rd's eighty-two-story building. At nearly 6,000 square feet, the $38 million condo had exposure in all four cardinal directions. It provided her boss with exclusive access to a fifteen-thousand-square-foot wellness center, which included a sixty-five-foot lap pool, golf simulator, regulation squash court, sauna, steam rooms, private high-energy and low-energy studios, and a full suite of strength and cardio training equipment. There was a housekeeping service, dry cleaning and laundry service, floral delivery and care, pet walking and grooming, and a twenty-four-hour concierge, porter service, and doormen. All the creature comforts that Jean did not have.

The evening had started with wine tasting in the octagonal double-height wine tasting room—vintages she had never heard of before but so memorable that she had been tempted to order an assortment of bottles . . . until she had seen the prices the following afternoon, awaking in a haze. Could she afford the wine? Yes. Would she pay that much per bottle? No. Drinks and heavy hors d'oeuvres were next in the building's premier restaurant, 53, followed by dinner in its private formal dining room. Chantel's husband, Alec, seemed to be everywhere—giving hugs, patting shoulders, sneaking in kisses with Chantel, laughing loudly as an obscene joke hit its mark, making jokes of his own and then pointing at his listeners as they joined him in amusement, and shaking hands as if each time he had closed the biggest deal of his life. This was all during the cocktail hour—at dinner, he gave toasts; he gave compliments; and he gave investment advice to those seated near him. Jean had marveled at how magnetic a couple he and Chantel were. They couldn't keep their eyes off each other.

Then, the party had traveled up to the forty-sixth floor's double-height lounge with Central Park views for more drinks. Again, Alec ruled the room.

And then upward they all went again, stopping at Chantel's home on the seventy-first floor, where Jean and the others had received a "gift bag" at the door from Chantel's butler that was actually a "Scuba Navy" colored luxury rolling carry-on suitcase named the "Aviator" made by Paravel. Chantel had hinted at the surprise while they were at dinner, stating that a friend from the Academy of Motion Picture Arts and Sciences had given her an idea for a gift bag of sorts from the "Everyone Wins" bag given to the hosts of the Oscars, along with the nominees for the major acting and directing categories. Alec had feigned obliviousness to his wife's words, mouthing "Wow" after Chantel's teaser. As each cart was rolled out for the party guests, Chantel pointed a finger and said, *"Don't open it until you get home, and don't thank me until you have used at least one of the invitations."*

As Jean lay in bed the next day, scrolling through wine bottles and their exorbitant prices on her phone, she spied the rolling cart next to her dresser. She remembered searching "Oscars gift bag" on her phone's internet browser at some point last night—perhaps, on the cab ride home? She wasn't sure, and she didn't remember the contents of the bag, but she did recall the rumored total value of the contents.

$150,000.

Surely, Chantel would not go to that extreme for a holiday party, she thought.

She had not opened the stylish piece of luggage when she returned home at . . . well, she couldn't remember when she got home.

She rolled the cart to the kitchen and then made her go-to hangover cure cocktail: the Virgin Mary—three ounces of tomato juice, half ounce of lemon juice, one dash Worcestershire sauce, one teaspoon celery salt, freshly ground black pepper, two dashes of Tabasco hot sauce, a pickle spear, and one stalk of celery. After a few revitalizing sips, she set her drink down on the breakfast nook table and zipped open the case.

Her eyes popped at the price tag of the first three invitations:

A $40,000 invitation for a 3-day stay at a ski chalet in the Swiss Alps.

A $20,000 invitation for a 7-day stay at a spa in Southern California.

A $15,000 invitation to attend a private performance from one of the world's top jazz singers—location and singer a surprise.

Chantel had not been exaggerating about the "Everyone Wins" nature of the gifts.

There was a check for $20,000 to be used for home repairs.

Then, the gifts took on a local flavor—a $2,000 gift certificate for two Broadway premium tickets to any show, two courtside seats at a Knicks game, two tickets for seats in the Field MVP Outdoor Suites rows behind home plate in Yankee Stadium, and a $2,000 gift certificate for a return trip to 53 for dinner—the only catch being that she would have to invite Chantel and Alec.

There was $10,000 worth of "rejuvenation procedures" from a plastic surgeon, a $1,000 life-coaching session with a wellness expert, and over $1,000 worth of skin-care products. Her head still pounded as she took another pull on her Virgin Mary. She could not believe what she was pulling out of the case.

After removing an assortment of snacks, she finally reached the last item: a square cardboard box. Opening it, she found the snow globe, whose gingerbread house resembled the home she had now stopped her rental car in front of.

After putting the car in park, the memories of glamour and expensive pampering dissipated as her eyes studied the forest-green-sided house with white trim and pillars painted white on the front porch. She removed her glasses, wiped them with the soft cloth from her case, and then put them back on.

From her study of the listing on Zillow and the realtor's website, she knew that the house was just over thirty-five hundred square feet, and yet, seeing the empty house set against the snow-covered tree line in the distance with darkening skies and snow pouring from it, the place seemed smaller than the pictures in the carousel the realtor had featured online.

Perhaps it was because the photographer had taken the pictures during the two weeks in October when the changing leaves were at their peak color, and the reds, yellows, and oranges, along with the green carpet of freshly mowed grass, gave the home a warm, welcoming, and expansive feel. She remembered thinking that the black shingles of the roof against the blue sky above had been a stark contrast, highlighting the structure's top with a clean-cut outline. It was like a picture frame within a picture frame, which gave a hint of class and stability, as if the home had been there for a long time yet remained unchanged in its rugged beauty.

Perhaps the home seemed smaller now because the snow covering the roof seemed to blend in with the snow falling, making the roof almost disappear as if it had been erased. There were no signs of life. Smoke did not rise from either of the two chimneys. No lights were on in the house. The brick walkway, leading from the driveway to the porch steps, was covered in snow, as were the steps, making the entire porch look as if it were floating in the air. There were also drifts of snow on the porch's rectangular surface, making it seem like the structure was a boat with white waves frozen at their crests across the deck. The porch appeared unkempt and smaller, which was not an appealing look when trying to sell a house. Whoever had plowed the driveway had not cleared anything else. Jean typed a note into her phone, reminding herself to mention this to the realtor. As she thumbed the letters, she noticed the time.

1:36 p.m.

She was to meet her family's real estate agent, Sarah Todd, at 2:00 p.m.

Perfect, she thought, typing the last of the note and then putting the phone down on the center console. She had wanted to be able to take a walk around the property before Sarah arrived, mostly for business reasons, but now, staring at the home of a relative she had never known, she admitted to herself that there was also a reason to do so based on curiosity . . . sentimentality? . . . At this point, she could not distinguish between the two. Everything outside of the car existed in a purely physical world, and the atmospheric cues—smells, sounds, and sights that would normally trigger memories—would not prompt her to recall things that had taken place here because she had no memories to retrieve.

However, that did not mean that her senses would fail to provoke feelings of some sort, hence the confusion between curiosity and sentimentality. She was already recalling events in her life that she had not thought about for a long time. Once she left the bubble of the Mercedes, her senses might come to work on her, encouraging her brain to conjure up scenes and events, as well as imaginary renderings of what *might have happened* here if she had visited and gotten to know Shirley Ruth and Martin White. Or, going back to her hours on Zoom with the pant-less, coffee-drinking, self-aware and yet, apparently, self-conscious, Samuel-the-psychologist, her senses might unlock the creative part of her brain, usually reserved for creating dynamic ad slogans and superior branding campaigns, which could author memories she *wished* she had of this place, the people who had lived here, and the desired interactions she would picture a granddaughter having with her grandparents over the course of a childhood.

Or, would her advertising persona ease forward in the realms of her subconscious and work on her in the opposite manner, using her supposed judgment-free and unbiased observations to seduce her into further believing that the absence of memories that took place here, real or imagined, was the desired state of mind? A narrative would be built around logic, pragmatism, and the reality that no emotional anchors were welding any of her feelings to this house and plot of land; nothing had happened to her here, so there was nothing to discover; there was only a piece of real estate to sell.

Jean put on her winter hat and scarf, zipped up her purple Marmot down hoodie jacket, and then turned the car off. She put her phone in her purse, took out the key to the front door that her mother had given her, placed it in her jacket's right pocket, and zipped it up. She had dropped a key in deep snow before, and it had been no fun trying to locate it. Lastly, she put on her navy-colored Burberry cashmere gloves, which were fashionable but would prove to be impractical if she had to survive outside for any length of time. A memory from a few days ago flashed across her mind: Jean standing at the open hallway closet in her SoHo condo holding the pair of Burberry gloves in one hand and a pair of L.L.Bean GORE-TEX PrimaLoft Ski Gloves in her other . . . pursed lips followed by a shrug . . . placing the ski gloves back in the closet and shutting the door.

She frowned.

Wrong choice.

With the vehicle keys in one hand, she grabbed her purse and black leather Renault Impact padfolio with her other hand and opened the door, stepping out into the Michigan cold.

Even though the temperature was the same as when she had first stepped outside the MBS Airport terminal, it felt colder due to the biting wind. Snowflakes tickled her cheeks as she shut the door and placed the keys inside her purse. She flexed her free hand a few times and then looped the purse over her right shoulder before starting to walk toward the sidewalk that led to the front porch.

After a few steps, she heard a tapping sound and looked in the direction it was coming from.

A small section of siding had come loose near the corner of the house where the porch bent around and continued down the left side of the house. She made a mental note as she carefully stepped onto the brick path that was covered with knee-high snow. Jean watched as each boot disappeared into the powder as she made her way toward the front steps. Other than the sound of the wind and her exhalations, there was the crunch her boots made as they compacted the snow and then lifted off.

More and more snowflakes landed on the lenses of her glasses.

She reached the steps, and, gripping one of the two round entrance pillars, ascended and stepped across the decking until she was at the crimson-colored door with a brass handle. Looking down, she could see the top of a brass kickplate just above the uneven line of heavy snow that had drifted up against the door.

Tucking the padfolio under her right armpit, she unzipped her jacket pocket and carefully withdrew the key. After a few seconds of massaging it into the lock, the key turned, and she cracked open the door. Jean had studied the floor plan online and was surprised by the functionality of the room layout, especially on the first floor, which would be important when trying to sell the house. Whereas many cookie-cutter midwestern homes from fifteen years ago seemed to give a claustrophobic vibe with low ceilings and closed-off spaces, which created a lack of flow, her grandmother's house's rooms were open and spacious.

As she opened the door, hearing its loud creak like she imagined old knee joints sounded when an elder's leg was straightened for the first time in the morning, she glanced down at the berm of snow that had been up against the brass kickplate.

For the moment, it stayed upright, not caving into the home's interior.

Jean opened the door farther and took a measured step onto the wooden floor, immediately feeling the room's warmth. Then, she lifted her other leg and slid her entire body inside. Satisfied that her entrance had brought in little to no snow, she closed the door, and the sound of the wind dropped off to a dull hum, like a box fan placed on low speed.

For a few moments, she just listened, hoping to hear nothing more than the subdued wind. She didn't think that anyone would break into the house—there was nothing to steal other than the appliances—but it never hurt to be on guard. When temperatures dropped, people without shelter could become desperate, although they would have to travel miles into the countryside to reach the house.

Hearing just the wind, she locked the door, zipped the key back in her pocket, and removed her gloves. She wiped the lenses of her glasses again and then took in the view.

The house's interior was dark, but there was enough light to see the foyer and the stairway in front of her that led up to the second floor. She removed her hat and scarf and unzipped her jacket. She laughed at herself, thinking that seventy-two degrees inside compared to the twenties outside felt like a sauna. Her mother had left the heat on not only for showings but also to help prevent the pipes from freezing. *"Each faucet should have a slow drip,"* she had said. Jean wondered if she would have thought of the second reason. Thankfully, none of this was her responsibility. She was simply applying her business skills to help her parents. At least that was what she kept telling herself.

Besides feeling the warmth and protection from being inside, her nose picked up a light scent of cinnamon as if a Yankee Candle had burned for a decade and a half straight before being extinguished in October. It surprised her because Jean's favorite scent was cinnamon. Plugged into the outlet in her own foyer was a Pura diffuser loaded with a Cinnamon Woods cartridge. *"As a guest walks into your home for the first time, you want the smell to be a welcoming first impression,"* her lawyer had told her when she had closed on the condo in SoHo. Then, she gave Jean a plastic bag with a box inside. *"I've used a Pura for years, so I'm giving you one as your housewarming gift. Plug it in next to the front door, and your blood pressure will lower instantly when you return after a day at work. Your guests will feel like they've entered a relaxing oasis. Trust me."*

Wait a minute, she said to herself, as her eyes scanned the room. Had the real estate agent installed a diffuser? She searched the foyer, peeking around a half-wall and then surveying the side of the staircase.

Nothing was plugged in.

She walked down the narrow hallway that separated the foyer from the kitchen, noting the blank walls that still had tiny holes where nails had been hammered in to hang picture frames or paintings. Jean's mother had decided to adopt the "completely empty" philosophy for the showings, reasoning that the rooms would appear larger and give a more "move-in" ready appearance. The other option had been to adopt a minimalist approach, staging certain arrangements of furniture and hanging pieces of art throughout the house to give the buyer a glimpse of what the home might look and feel like, while still positioning everything to make each space appear as roomy as possible. As she entered the kitchen, she saw the value in having nothing in the house as the breakfast nook looked spacious, and the huge island stood out, as did the granite countertops. She bit her lower lip and scanned the kitchen cabinets, which she had been told were hand-crafted by a noted local builder. They were beautiful and understated. Her eyes moved to the imposing family room. *I would have staged a few pieces of furniture, but I don't think that's why the place isn't selling.*

She stopped at the island and set down her hat, gloves, scarf, padfolio, and purse. Then, she slid out of her jacket and laid it next to her other things. She wore a cranberry-colored turtleneck, and after straightening the top so that the fold was perfect, she picked up the padfolio and opened it. Removing the blue pen, she made a note on the canary-colored legal pad to share with Sarah Todd when she arrived about plugging in a diffuser to the half-wall outlet in the foyer. She enjoyed the natural cinnamon scent she had noticed upon entering, but thought that a more pronounced scent might help. Anything to make a future showing go better. From what she had read on the flight from New York City to Detroit, selling a house had become as much about enhancing a prospective buyer's experience during the showing as it was about the actual floor plan. People respond to pleasant smells; otherwise, there wouldn't be a lucrative market for candles and diffusers. Association was also a powerful tool of persuasion, as she had learned in advertising—seeing the beautiful hardwood floors in the open foyer while smelling hints of apple cinnamon would not only reinforce a feeling of home and warmth but also remind the prospective buyer of the holiday season. If the showings extended into the spring, she would have the scent changed.

She set the padfolio and pen down and moved into the dining room, where her intuition, confirmed by her study of the floor plan at her condo, was confirmed. Not only did the house have a relaxed feel, but it was perfect for entertaining. The dining room bled into the formal living room, which bled into the foyer, giving the spaces a seamless flow. The rooms were open, expansive, and functional. As she walked into the living room, she automatically framed the room, placing imaginary furniture where she thought the pieces fit best—a couch here, a love seat there, a coffee table right here. Jean stopped by the imaginary couch, thinking about the conversations that could have taken place where she stood. Is this where her grandmother would meet her best friend, Annie, for tea? Is this where she would talk with Jean's grandfather about life, out of reach of the television or other distractions?

The furniture disappeared, and she stared at the blank space.

Is this where the falling out had taken place?

Jean stood and looked out the window in one of the two upstairs guest bedrooms. Like the inside of the house, the backyard and patio were clear of any furniture. The blanket of snow covering them was growing thicker as snow fell from the sky. Her eyes moved across the patio, and her brain played the role of decorator again. *A grill could go there; a large table with six chairs could go there; I'd put a bench and two loungers over there . . .*

In the far back right corner of the yard, she could see the tops of the concrete blocks that made a square fire pit. *If it keeps snowing, you won't be able to see it soon,* she thought. As she envisioned four lawn chairs spread around a roaring fire on a cool autumn evening, she started to wonder who had sat in those chairs and what the conversations over the years had been. Immediately, this took her back to her final thought in the downstairs living room: *Is this where the falling out had taken place?*

She shook her head and exhaled, wanting to push the thought away. *Find something else to concentrate on,* she told herself. Her eyes moved to the firewood port that had been built behind the garage. It was empty.

Like I feel right now.

Then, an unstoppable wave of nervousness overtook her. She no longer felt in control of the situation or of her mind. *It's too quiet. I'm too alone. I'm in a house where . . .*

She turned and walked out of the room. After a glance in the other bedroom, the hallway closet, and the bathroom, she stopped in the brown-carpeted passage, seeing the open doorway to the master suite at the far end.

She couldn't get down the stairs fast enough.

Reentering the kitchen, she headed for the island and picked up her phone.

1:55 p.m.

She texted her real estate agent, Sarah Todd:

Hi, Sarah. We still on for 2:00 p.m.? I'm inside the house—everything looks great.

She hit send.

Okay, I don't know what is going on with me, but I need to distract myself.

Taking a seat on the floor with her back against the island, she opened her favorite game on her phone called "Free Fall" and started to play. At 2:05 p.m., she finally heard back from Sarah. The text read:

Sorry! Last showing ran over. Weather a factor. Should be to you by 2:15.

Jean sighed but decided not to get upset. Sarah was sweet and a good agent, and delays happened. She tried to immerse herself once again in "Free Fall," but a nagging thought made it difficult. *I could have gone to see her and been back by the time Sarah gets here.*

Jean had promised her mother that she would make a quick visit to Shirley Ruth's best friend, Annie Brady, before she drove back to the airport for her two-leg return flight to New York City. Annie lived five miles away, and Jean planned on dropping by after she met with Sarah. She was not looking forward to it—especially now, given the unexpected emotions she was feeling—but a promise was a promise. And Jean did not break promises. Annie meant something to Lori. What it was, Jean did not know, but her mother was adamant that Jean visit Annie, almost to the point where selling the house was secondary.

She checked her smartwatch. 2:06. *Damn. If I had known that Sarah wouldn't be here until 2:15, I would have skipped stopping here first and gone straight to Annie's and squeezed in the visit.*

Let it go, she told herself. But she couldn't. She hated being inefficient; she hated it even more when other people's inefficiency prevented her from being efficient. This spirit had served her well at Renault Impact, but in the good old blue-collar state of Michigan, it seemed it would only bring her disappointment. Time is money, but the rules of "Midwestern nice" say: time is money . . . but you can wait a bit when there's bad weather. *What am I even supposed to say to Annie when I see her? "Hi, I'm Jean, Shirley Ruth's granddaughter. I'm thirty and haven't seen her since I was a toddler. Sorry for the loss of your friend. My mom wants me to give you a hug, which I am not comfortable with. Hope the house sells soon, um, Merry Christmas, and, well, that's it. Goodbye."*

Jean sat, staring at the kitchen desk that was an extension of the counter underneath a long row of cabinets. *Concentrate on your work here. Your job is to help sell this house.*

She completed four cycles of box breathing and then focused on the floor plan. She had visited every space upstairs except for the master suite. Downstairs, she had walked through the foyer, formal living room, dining room, kitchen, family room, bathroom, and den. There was a downstairs master suite next to the den, which Jean had thought was ahead of its time for a floor plan like this and a major selling point for the home. From her study of the pictures online, she knew that the master suite upstairs had large windows with beautiful views of the woods. It was where her grandparents would have stayed until they got older and moved downstairs to the first-floor master suite. Climbing stairs became a pain, both figuratively and literally, as homeowners aged, which is why many retirees opted for one-story homes or apartments or condos where they could reach their floor by elevator.

Jean turned her head away from the desk and in the direction of the hallway, which wound to the right and led to the den and eventually the master suite. She wondered how old her grandparents had been when they moved downstairs and what the conversation had been like. Was it a difficult one? A bending of the knee to Father Time? A graceful surrender? A bitter acknowledgement?

Stop thinking about it.

She twisted her wrist, and the time on her smartwatch now read 2:08. *The visit with Annie can wait. Sarah will be here in seven minutes.* Jean went back to playing her video game.

Sarah opened the front door at 2:31 p.m.

5

"I think we've got a great plan," Jean said to Sarah as they exited the front door and stepped onto the porch.

"I agree," replied Sarah. "Yeah, definitely need to get the porch, steps, and sidewalk cleared before the next showing. I'll see if he can also do the back patio, deck, and fire pit. Whoa, look at it come down." She turned back toward Jean. "Does it snow like this in New York City?"

"It's been a while since I've seen this much." It was 2:57 p.m., and the snow continued to fall as they left the porch's protective roof and made their way to their vehicles. The Mercedes's windshield, roof, and back window were already covered, and Sarah's F-150 already had a thin layer over the portion of the windshield where her wipers could reach.

"I'd give yourself some extra time to get to the airport. This doesn't look like it is letting up anytime soon." The realtor gave a sarcastic laugh. "Forecasters wrong. Again."

Jean reached her car and stopped, tilting her head back. Cold flakes blew onto her face as she squinted up. She brought her chin down in time to see Sarah kick her boots against the truck's front tire and then open the driver's side door.

"Be safe. We'll get it sold."

Jean said thanks and watched as Sarah started the truck, turned on her wipers, and then drove off. *Well, I guess it was worth the trip,* she thought, and then got inside her car. Annie Brady's address was already in her phone, so all she had to do was push the green "Go" button on her phone when she was ready.

It didn't take long for the vehicle to heat up, and she removed her hat and gloves, setting them on the front passenger's seat next to her purse and padfolio. She cleaned her glasses again and then checked her email on her phone, only to see that she had no new messages. *Stop worrying,* she told herself. *Your flights will be fine. They're not getting cancelled—especially* that *one.* Jean was referring to her flight to Greece, which departed JFK on December 27th; she had built in a day of rest before Christmas and a day after to pack and prepare for her vacation to see Urian. Even if there were a delay in getting back to New York City, it would not be a *four-day* delay.

She brought up Annie's address and went to press the "Go" button, but stopped. Part of her wanted distractions as she left, and part of her wanted silence so that she could reflect.

So that she could feel?

She chose silence and put the phone down in one of the center console's cup holders. Soon, the windshield and back window were clear of snow, and she completed a three-point turn and drove down the driveway. As she approached the bend, which would put the house out of view, she stopped the car.

Looking through the rearview mirror, she studied the grand house one last time, memories of what could have been flooding her mind. When her eyes started to water and her chin started to shake, she swallowed, then picked up her phone and started her route to Annie's. After Siri's introductory directions, Jean set her phone back down, looked ahead, and drove off.

The house disappeared behind the trees.

We'll get it sold.

Sarah's final words echoed through her mind as she turned onto the road and headed away from a house that should have meant more to her—maybe it was starting to, but she needed to take care of the quick visit and then get to the airport.

Greece awaits, so stop being emotional. Focus on the details of the new plan.

As if she were reviewing a meeting agenda—only this time, the meeting had already taken place—Jean went back over the ground that she and Sarah had covered.

While facing each other, sitting on the bench in front of the living room's enormous bay window, they had discussed the past two months of trying to sell the house. Shirley Ruth had died at the end of September, and Jean's parents had come and cleaned out the house in a week. Then, they had it professionally cleaned by a local service and hired Sarah as their realtor. The house officially went on the market during the second week of October, and Jean's parents had promised Sarah a ten-thousand-dollar bonus if she could sell the house by December 1st. There had been a handful of showings, but the first of December had come and gone with no further interest.

The house was built in 2008, so the HVAC, water heater, and roof were all sixteen years old. Jean could not believe that the water heater had lasted that long—typically, they lasted eight to twelve years—but sweet, mild-mannered, and spunky Sarah Todd had grinned and shrugged, saying that sometimes they just did. The trim was painted in 2020, and in another four years, the house would be due for a new paint job.

Selling the house was like walking on a tightrope between skyscrapers with one of those long poles to keep your balance, Sarah explained. The fact that it was a seller's market and that they had a great house with gorgeous property should have made the walk easy. Except, a nasty little force called inflation was pulling down on one end of the pole, threatening to plunge the sale into the chasm below. Adding additional weight to that side of the pole was the age of the HVAC, water heater, and roof, which meant the asking price was probably even more inflated, despite all three being in good working order.

So, what they had decided to do was perform what Sarah called "a little real estate magic." She said that the HVAC and water heater could be replaced in one day if the two crews started early in the morning. The roof still had ten years left on it, so they wouldn't touch it. She would take the house off the market, deleting the former asking price and home details. Then, after the HVAC and water heater had been replaced, she would relist the house at a slightly lower price, highlighting the upgrades.

New HVAC!

New Water Heater!

It's like buying a new house!

They would all still clear plenty of money at the new price, but the most crucial goal was to sell the house as soon as possible, and doing "the magic" would ensure that goal was achieved. After agreeing on the new price, Jean sweetened the deal by saying that her parents would now offer Sarah a *fifteen*-thousand-dollar bonus to sell the house by mid-January. If she sold it by January 1, she would receive a *twenty*-thousand-dollar bonus. For that to happen, though, Sarah explained that the HVAC and water heater would have to be replaced in the next week. Jean had raised her eyebrows at that point and said—*maybe* in a slightly mocking tone—*"Then the magic needs to . . . POOF! . . . happen soon."*

Jean's phone rang.

It was Sarah.

She answered.

"Hey, I just got off the phone with my HVAC guy and my water heater girl," Sarah said. "They told me they both had the units that we discussed in stock, and that, because it's *me*, they could replace them both tomorrow."

"Great," Jean said.

"Well, sorta. They said that this storm is a monster, and they didn't know if they'd be able to get out tomorrow due to the roads. Worst case scenario, they can get to it on the 26th or 27th because the storm should be cleared out by then." There was a pause. "Well, hell, what do I know? I'm not a weather forecaster. It could be the 28th or 29th before they get to it. Still, though, it will be done. That *magic* be okay with you?"

Is she mocking herself and *me now?* Jean peered out the windshield at what she had to admit had become a blizzard. "Storm will be that bad, huh?"

"Pretty sure. Those two teams go out in all kinds of weather to stay on schedule, so you know it's going to be nasty if they say they might have to wait a few days."

Jean watched her wipers go back and forth across the windshield. "Okay. Hopefully, it won't be as bad as they're saying, and they can get to it tomorrow. It would certainly increase your chances of getting the bonus. You never know who might be visiting the area over the holidays."

"You got it, boss lady," Sarah said, her chipper voice never changing. "I'll keep you updated. Now, watch those roads. It's gettin' dicey out."

The call ended, and Jean increased the speed of her wipers. The weather was working in her favor. She could make her visit with Annie shorter, claiming that the weather was getting worse and she wanted to make sure that she made it to the airport on time for her flight. Glancing at her phone, she saw that she had 3.2 miles left to go. She thought about her flight, but then relaxed.

It's Michigan, which is just like New York at this time of year. Even a snowstorm doesn't halt life around here. They've got the infrastructure to deal with weather like this because they live with it most of the time.

My flight will be fine.

If only Jean could have known how wrong she was.

62

My flight will be fine.

If only Jean could have known how wrong she was.

6

The respectable and trustworthy voice of Siri told Jean that she had arrived at her destination, and she turned into the long driveway that disappeared into the woods ahead. *What is the deal with all the long driveways?* she thought, stopping the route on her phone. Slowing the car, she tried to read the name on the mailbox, but it was covered in snow, the entire structure looking like a white-globed sucker had been stuck into the ground. However, the driveway had been recently plowed—*like in the last half hour,* Jean guessed—as there was less snow on it than on her grandmother's drive. The rising banks on either side looked like white, chunky vomit. Someone had taken a snowblower to it—*Annie, perhaps?* She was eighty-three, but Jean's mother had said that Annie still mowed her own yard, that it was a point of pride.

She focused on the drive ahead, but her concentration could not keep out the thought that was moving forward to the front of her mind, like a school bully, a head taller than his classmates, skipping his way to the start of a long lunch line:

I know next to nothing about this woman.

When asked, Jean's mother had only provided a few tidbits—Annie and Shirley Ruth had been high school teachers together at Midland's H.H. Dow

High School; their families vacationed together every summer in two side-by-side cabins on Big Manistique Lake in Curtis, Michigan, which was in the Upper Peninsula; and Annie still rode her John Deere around her property, cutting the grass, once a week from late March until early November.

That was it.

Why does my mom want me to meet with her? Why did I even have to meet with the real estate agent? I could have had a phone call, a FaceTime call, or a Zoom call with Sarah.

The driveway angled to the left, enough so that she could no longer see the road in her rearview mirror, then the path straightened out, and she saw only trees in front of her. Some of the snow that had been launched from the snowblower had piled around and stuck to the bases of the towering pines that lined the driveway, making it look like they had on white hula skirts. Admiring the accuracy of her description while she studied the trees as they passed down the sides of the car, she almost drove straight into one of the snowbanks as the drive made a sharp turn to the right. She corrected her steering in time, and, similar to the approach to her grandmother's home, the trees disappeared on her right and left, and the driveway cut an enormous front yard in two.

The great log cabin had two peaks and two stories with huge glass windows and an expansive front porch. The driveway split ahead, with one path leading up to the large concrete pad in front of the attached three-car garage and the other path leading to a sizable pad in front of a giant log pole barn, which had a firewood port that ran down half its length. The port was filled with stacked firewood, ready to provide hundreds of blazing fires to a hearth within the cabin. Jean thought of her grandmother's empty port, snow piling up on its roof, threatening to crush it, and drifts overtaking the space below. Heat. Cold. Robert Frost.

Fire and ice.

Which is more powerful?

She watched as the wind blew over the top of a drift, spraying the white powder across the yard of snow.

Mad as the sea and wind, when both contend which is the mightier.

Hamlet.

The two remnants of her undergraduate education held the spotlight on the stage of her mind for a few more seconds . . . and then receded into the darkened wings, doubtful that they would ever make an appearance again.

Although the brief visitation to the realm of past scholarship had opened another line of questioning, perhaps this was the lasting value her professors had preached about, that, at the time, she had not understood. Had her grandmother studied some of the same eternal works? When, if ever? Her grandmother had been a high school teacher, so she had also attended college. But where? And what had she majored in? Had she ever found profit in recalling bits and pieces of literature at certain moments, long after graduation when the books containing those poems, plays, and stories collected dust in a cardboard box in the attic or, slightly less depressing, on a bookshelf next to a chest of toys her young children played with on the living room carpet? A bookshelf that had become more of an untouched piece of furniture, a museum artifact with an unmistakable description on the pedestal in front of it:

Here lies the information that made me who I am today—the collective wisdom I once possessed or was supposed to possess, now frozen in time: the words, phrases, equations, and so on, receding, symbolizing the version of human being our society was attempting to produce during the years . . .

Her frustrating refrain returned.

I know next to nothing about this woman.

She looked away from the firewood port.

There were no vehicles in the driveway, but the front porch light was on, as were the three lights on the garage, one on each side of the two doors.

However, what caught her attention the most was the lit Christmas tree on the far end of the porch next to the beautiful log swing. Surprisingly, snow was not accumulating on the porch like it had at her grandmother's. However, the wind was making the Christmas tree sway back and forth.

She drove the car onto the concrete pad, completed a three-point turn, and then backed up until the Mercedes's proximity alarm sounded as the rear bumper neared the single garage door. After putting the vehicle in park, she tapped her phone's screen and swiped up.

She had one new email message.

Uh oh.

As soon as she tapped on the sky-blue app with the white envelope in the middle, her heart sank. The email was from her airline, and the subject line read:

FLIGHT CANCELLED

"Damn," she said, tapping the message.

Ten minutes ago, her flight from MBS to Detroit Metro had been cancelled, and there was no current information as to when it would be rescheduled.

Jean looked at her watch. Even if the weather was perfect and she left for Detroit now, she would not make her connecting flight from Detroit to JFK.

A new email appeared—the subject line read:

FLIGHT CANCELLED

She tapped the message and read.

Great, now my flight from Detroit to JFK is cancelled.

She turned her head and peered out the window. "C'mon, the weather isn't *that* bad!" she yelled. "Ugh!"

Seconds later, she received two text messages that said her flights were cancelled.

Wait, wasn't there a 10:30 p.m. flight leaving Detroit for LaGuardia? She had researched flights and come up with backup plans before leaving New York, in case of delays or cancelled flights. She opened her "Notes" App on her phone and confirmed the alternate flight.

Then, she checked.

Cancelled.

Jean leaned her head back against the headrest. *What to do . . . What to do . . .*

Flint! If I can get a flight out of there to . . . well, anywhere east, west, or south of Michigan, then I can get a connecting flight to JFK or LaGuardia.

She opened her web browser and started typing.

A minute later, she let out a sigh.

All flights out of Flint had been cancelled.

Chicago!

All flights out of Chicago had been cancelled.

"Shit!" she yelled, tossing her phone on the passenger's seat.

She was now stuck—stuck in Michigan, stuck in Midland, stuck in this driveway. After a few more forceful exhalations and a swat of the steering wheel, which stung her fingers, she closed her eyes and did box breathing for four cycles.

As she calmed down, she chastised herself for losing control, which was something that rarely happened to her.

You're okay. The weather will clear tomorrow, and you'll still be back in plenty of time to catch your flight to Greece.

Then, all at once, she became overwhelmed by her emotions—things were not working out the way they were supposed to, the plan was changing without her approval, and her insides were stirring up without any warning.

What if the storm is bad? How long might I be stuck here? Greece!

She opened her eyes.

Relax. It's just a snowstorm. You're not leaving Michigan tonight, but tomorrow, they'll have everything plowed, the weather will clear, and you can catch a flight. Hell, if the roads are good enough, you can drive the Mercedes all the way back to New York City and be there in eleven hours. This is not *an emergency.*

"And this is why we never travel without our aviator," she said, thinking of her Paravel rolling carry-on suitcase that she had received from Chantel, which was in the trunk of the Mercedes. Inside the aviator was everything she would need for an overnight emergency stay: toiletries, pajamas, workout attire, running shoes, and a change of clothes. She always figured that if she had to stay somewhere longer than that, she would have access to a washer and dryer and, therefore, could extend her stay by recycling her outfits.

"Okay," she said, picking up her phone, "let's find a place to stay." After a series of taps and swipes, she found a Holiday Inn. *That will work,* she said to herself, zooming in on the map displayed on her screen. *Good. There's a mall, a cinema, and plenty of places to eat . . . yes! They've got a BW3's—I haven't eaten there in ages.* She tapped on the hotel, called the number, and made a reservation for one night.

She was going to send her mom a comprehensive text from the airport while she waited for her flight, but she decided to send a quick message now and then send a detailed one later from the hotel. She typed:

Bad weather. Flights cancelled. Staying at a Holiday Inn. Mtg w/ Sarah productive—details later. Seeing Annie and then heading to hotel. Will try to get flight tmrw.

. . . and hit send.

Immediately, she saw bubbles underneath her message, and a few seconds later, she received a reply:

Sorry to hear. Looking forward to recap of mtg. Stay with Annie a bit longer?

Jean hesitated, her right index finger hovering over the screen's keyboard. *Stay longer?* She squinted, biting her lower lip. "Wouldn't hurt you to say, 'stay safe,' Mom," Jean said. She considered writing something back, but then decided to give the message a safe "thumbs up" emoji and closed the chat.

All right, I'll do my duty of saying hi to this person I don't know, hopefully, that won't be too uncomfortable, and then it's off to the hotel, and then Bee-Dubs.

She went to turn her car off, but stopped as movement out the passenger's side window caught her attention.

Standing on the porch, in front of the open door, was a tall, lithe, silver-haired woman wearing jeans and a red crewneck sweater.

7

J ean turned her car off, thought about putting on her hat, gloves, and scarf, but decided not to as it was just a short walk to the front porch. *I'll be back here in ten minutes.* She checked her makeup in the rearview mirror and gathered herself by taking in a breath and then exhaling. *Be pleasant.* She put on her best smile, grabbed the keys, and opened the door.

Immediately, the frigid wind blew her hair across her face, tickling her cheeks. As she felt the outside of the driver's side door with her right hand, it felt like she was touching a block of ice and that her warm palm would freeze to it. She shut the door and looked at the porch as she started to make her way around the car.

The woman waved and said, "Jean?"

"Hi," she replied, trying to brush her hair away from her face.

"I'm Annie. Can I help with anything, dear?"

In a few hurried steps, Jean reached the walkway leading up to the porch. "No, I've got it," she said. A half a dozen steps more, and she reached the steps. Climbing them, she felt the shelter of the roof as the snow blowing down and across her field of vision let up as if someone with a remote control that regulated snowfall had pushed "pause." She stepped onto the porch and was out of the wind enough now to pull her hair away from her face so that she could get a clear view of Annie.

The stately woman was nearly as tall as Jean, maybe an inch shorter, and she smiled while shaking her head. "Dear girl, you're the spitting image of your grandmother when she was your age, glasses and all; your mother was right. I—I cannot believe the resemblance. Look at those long legs; five feet ten, right? My God, just like Shirley Ruth—she was six feet tall."

Jean had no idea how tall her grandmother was. It had never been discussed, and she hadn't thought to ask her mother about it. Yet, her mother had told Annie what Jean looked like and how tall she was. *Why didn't Mom tell me that?*

Lori was five feet eight, so Jean assumed that her grandmother was tall. However, now that she knew her grandmother had been six feet tall and had long legs like she did, it somehow made her more real. She tried to hide the surprise by maintaining the polite smile she had practiced in the car and stopped a few feet short of Annie, extending her hand. "It's a pleasure to meet you."

Annie had magnificent green eyes . . . *Were they tearing up?* She couldn't tell as she blinked due to a rivulet of water reaching her right eye from snowflakes that had melted near her temple. Her host took Jean's hand between both of hers, and she felt the slender, bony, yet smooth hands clamp down, rub, squeeze, and then release. "Come in, come in," Annie said.

As Jean followed her inside, she hoped that her outer veneer had not betrayed the shock she had just experienced. *I look just like my grandmother when she was my age?* She felt a mix of anger and frustration at the statement because she didn't know what to do with it, which was why she had ignored it, maintaining her Jean-meeting-someone-for-the-first-time smile and shifting her attention to the formal greeting. *I have no idea what my grandmother looked like at any age, let alone at thirty.* The only picture she had ever seen was the one accompanying Shirley Ruth's obituary in the *Midland Daily News*. It appeared to be a recent photo, as her hair was all white and fell across her forehead, the bangs nearly touching the large glasses with black plastic frames. Perhaps, there was some similarity between their faces. Still, Jean thought the picture had poor lighting, and the domineering glasses and wrinkles made it difficult to imagine Shirley Ruth at an earlier age. *Apparently, she wore glasses when she was thirty, too.*

She felt anger bubble up even more as they entered the expansive foyer, and Annie moved back around her and closed the door. Her mother must have seen the similarity. Why hadn't she shared this, especially before Jean met Annie?   Or, she wondered, was this just another way of her mother manipulating her, knowing that Annie would find her the spitting image of her grandmother?   Her mother was not above doing it, but Jean could not understand *why* she would want to.

Why is it so vital for me to meet Annie?

The warmth of the room matched her rising anger, but Annie's light touch on her arm, followed by, "Could I take your coat for you?" calmed her.

With a mix of grace and purposefulness, Annie helped Jean out of her coat, and then Jean watched as she opened a closet door and hung up the jacket on a bare rod, except for a blue windbreaker and a puffy, hooded red jacket she assumed were Annie's.

For some reason, she had feared Annie would have an old lady scent—she had learned about it on Reddit—but was surprised to get a whiff of a fruity-scented perfume as she walked by after closing the closet door. *The aroma was familiar . . . my gosh, is that Eternity Moment by Calvin Klein? I used to wear that!*

The wind wailed, and Jean looked out a window at the Christmas tree, still upright on the porch.

"Oh, it'll be fine," Annie said. "How did the house look?"

"It's nice," Jean said. "I think Sarah, our realtor, will be able to sell it soon."

Annie nodded. "It's a beautiful home. How is your mother?"

"She's good."

"And how about your Uncle Brett?"

Jean knew next to nothing about him other than that he lived in Alaska and her mother spoke to him occasionally on the phone. He was a trucker, divorced, and had one son, Brandon, with his ex-wife. Her cousin was four years younger than she was, and she had never met him. Seen pictures of him? Yes, but that was it. One thing Jean *did* know about her uncle, though, was that, like her mother, he had little to no contact with his parents. Jean hadn't seen him since he had passed through Billings in his truck when she was . . . five? . . . six? "Fine, as far as I know. I haven't seen him in a long time."

Annie's face was stone. "Hmm," she said.

The utterance was followed by a few seconds of silence, and Jean wondered what her host was thinking.

"This way," Annie said, waving her down the hallway. "I prepared a snack for us to have by the fire while we chat." She glanced back over her shoulder as she walked. "Still cannot believe you're here." She flashed a welcoming smile and turned forward again before Jean could react. "Hope you can stay for a while, but I understand if you have to be back on your way to the airport on account of the weather. Heavier snowfall than I was expecting today."

"I—"

Annie cut her off. "With the amount that came down this past week, I didn't think there was any left in the sky."

They rounded a corner, and the hallway opened up into a large kitchen on the left with a dining room on the right. The floorplan was open so Jean could see an enormous family room, bathed in only the orange flames from the fire in the massive brick hearth, and the red, blue, and white lights on the towering Christmas tree in the corner—half-a-dozen presents were spread out underneath the bottom branches as if the tree had given birth to a litter of packages wrapped in brown paper with white string, which made a perfect cross in the center of each gift. For a moment, her mind wandered, wondering who the gifts were for, but then a heavenly aroma focused her attention on trying to determine what was producing the delightful combination of scents. After a quick survey of the spaces, she had it. The smell of the fire, along with a cinnamon candle burning on the granite countertop of the kitchen bar, filled the air, and Jean thought the mixture would give her Pura diffuser a run for its money.

Cinnamon.

The room smelled similar to the inside of her grandmother's home, and Jean wondered if her grandmother had given this candle to Annie as a gift.

As the calming scents grew stronger, she said to herself, *What am I talking about? This natural scent is far superior to a diffuser. I could never have a real fireplace in my condo.*

She glanced over at the towering Christmas tree.

But what about the trees? Her friends would say.

Looking around the house *made of trees* and the cut-up trees burning in the hearth, she thought, *Maybe it's okay if the trees lose sometimes.*

As she moved to the kitchen bar, she discovered yet another smell. *What is it?*

She watched as Annie stopped by a small crockpot on the opposite counter, lifted the top, took a whiff, and then set it back down.

Before her host could say the words, the overpowering and delicious scent reached Jean, and she knew what was cooking.

"Just a little chili for dinner tonight," Annie said. "I'm baking some homemade bread to go with it." She moved to the tea kettle on the stove and picked it up, pouring hot water into two heavy brown mugs that already had tea bags inside. "Tea and gingersnaps for our snack. Do you bake?" she asked.

Gingersnaps were her favorite cookies. *How did Annie know this? Mom? Maybe.* Her mind drifted back to the conversation. She had been asked a question. *What was it? Oh, right, do I bake?* "No," Jean said. An uncomfortable silence grew as Annie set the tea kettle back on the stove and moved toward a plate covered in aluminum foil. Feeling that she should fill the silence, Jean added, "Never had the time." *Damn, that sounds ridiculous, pretentious, and, jeez, it's just not true. Fix it.* "I mean, I always wanted to once I got established in my career."

Annie peeled the aluminum foil off the plate, revealing a dozen or so ginger snap cookies, and said, "And are you established in your career?"

I made over a million dollars last year. "Um, well, I'm getting there."

Annie gave her a polite grin. "I'm surprised your mother didn't pass on the family gift. Your grandmother was the best baker I've ever—" She broke off, staring up at the ceiling as if to receive guidance in how measured her words should be. After a few blinks, her eyes lowered to Jean's level. "She was special in here," Annie said, motioning her hand across the kitchen. "Special everywhere. Your mother was very good, too." They held each other's stare for a moment, and then Annie pointed at the plate of cookies. "I've got the mugs of tea if you can grab the cookies."

Jean nodded, and soon they were walking across the beautiful wooden floor of the family room.

In addition to the magnificent tree, the entire room was decorated for Christmas with a classic and balanced touch; nothing was overwhelming, gaudy, or out of place. Lights were woven through a garland that hung down from a bookshelf, ran behind a Smart TV, and then on top of a bookshelf on the other side, continuing onto and across the entire fireplace mantle, where one sizable red stocking, bulging from the gifts inside, was hung from a candy cane hook. Thick, green felt letters spelling "Scott" were sewn across the top quarter of the stocking, and, for a flash, Jean surveyed the entrances and exits of the room, anticipating "Scott"—Annie's companion?—to appear at any moment. She envisioned a wiry man with thin, freshly cut white hair, a clean shave, wearing tortoiseshell glasses, a plaid shirt with a white t-shirt underneath, perhaps a cardigan over it, corduroy pants with diabetic socks, and a pair of slip-on leather shoes.

"Grandpa Scott" of the L.L. Bean family.

Retired "Professor Scott," outfitted by Orvis.

"Senior Scott" wearing an eternal "Scott for U.S. Senate" smile, sucking on a Werther's Original, previous occupations unknown.

Or even "Scottie"—eighty but acting eight, bouncing on his tiptoes, raising his eyebrows up and down while waiting to open his stocking and tear into the presents under the tree.

With the character options for her commercial to sell an article of clothing in the company's "Christmas with Old Saint Scott"—or, the more general "Holidaying with Scott"—campaign solidified, her eyes scanned the room with precision, noting every camera angle and lighting choice that could be leveraged to highlight whatever the team decided to sell: Scott's shirt, his shoes, his watch, a bottle of his favorite whiskey, which he would find by unwrapping one of the presents. The camera would close on his face, and "Grateful Scott" would give a nod as rich as the fifteen-year-old liquid in the bottle his weathered hands held.

And, suddenly, she was no longer in the cabin but, instead, in the Renault Impact conference room, seated across from her client, and saying, *"And that's just the base package. The premium package, which Urian, Chantel, and I believe is a perfect fit for the holiday season, would allow us to get—"* She delivers a perfectly placed knowing grin. *"—a certain character actor to play Scott in the commercial."*

No one entered the room, and the advertising realm of her brain simmered down as Annie walked by the hearth. *I can't help it,* she thought, *this room is perfect for a holiday ad.*

There were two leather couches facing each other, with a heavy wooden coffee table in between, resting on a rectangular, thick, navy-colored rug. The far edge of one of the rug's two shorter sides was perhaps six feet away from the hearth's brick bench, which could seat four or five people when there was no fire. *Great for family pictures,* she said to herself. On the end tables, which matched the coffee table, were simple lamps and cork coasters. A hardcover book was on one of the tables, and next to it was a wooden Christmas tree, perhaps a foot tall, painted green with silver bells hanging from each branch.

The bookshelves underneath the garland were bursting with books, DVDs, CDs, and even a row of records, but in front of them, on each shelf, was a decoration for the season—an elf sitting in chair working on a toy, Santa in his sleigh, reading a scrolling list, a snow globe with Yukon Cornellius, Rudolph, and Hermey riding Yukon's sleigh being pulled by the prospector's dogs (she almost laughed out loud), a manger, the Grinch on his ramshackle sleigh being pulled by poor Max, a diorama of Charlie Brown and Linus standing on either side of the Christmas tree they had found, and, finally, the word "Peace" unevenly carved in a block of wood . . . a present that one of her children or grandchildren had made her?

Centered behind one of the couches was a component stereo system in a wooden case with a glass door. Brown cords ran along the floor in both directions, ending in tall speakers at the corners of the end tables. Behind the other couch was the most impressive object in the room: a Steinway & Sons Grand Piano, made of wood that was a deeper and brighter shade of red than traditional mahogany—it gave off a unique reflection, a throb as if it were alive, and had a perpetual shine.

"Do you play?" Annie asked.

Was I staring too long? Probably. "No, I don't, but I know the brand." A few years ago, Renault Impact assisted Steinway & Sons with an advertising package targeting churches, conservatories, and university drama schools that specialize in musical theater.

It was also the brand that Ms. Janie played at all of Jean's high school choir concerts.

A vision of Ms. Norman, Jean's beloved choir director—the woman whose heart Jean had broken—entered her mind, and she watched as her childhood idol, the woman she had trusted more than anyone, stood in front of the risers full of choir students and then turned, giving a bow to Ms. Janie, who was behind the piano. Ms. Janie bowed back and then started to play . . .

The vision vanished.

"Other than books, winter fires in the hearth, walks outside in the fall, and good films, playing the piano is my sanctuary." Annie gave a nod to the Steinway. "That's a Model B Classic Grand Piano made of African Pommele— I fell in love with the texture and the natural glow."

"It's beautiful." *Please don't play it.*

"It's seen a lot of songs."

As Jean walked toward the couch in front of the piano, she passed by an ornate rocking chair next to the hearth with a gorgeous Pendleton blanket folded and hung on the backrest. She recognized it immediately: it was the Crater Lake National Park version—navy blue with a band of stripes—white, light blue, light green, dark green, orange, orange-red, and red—on each end. The reason she recognized it was because she had a Pendleton blanket that hung on the back of her living room's couch. The choice had come down to either the Crater Lake National Park version or the Grand Canyon National Park version.

The Grand Canyon version had won.

Did it look as good on her couch as the Crater Lake blanket looked on Annie's rocking chair? No.

Annie placed her mug of tea near the edge of the coffee table in front of the couch with the stereo behind it, and Jean's mug near the opposite edge.

Jean set the plate of cookies down in the middle, and Annie grabbed a handful before sinking into the couch.

Jean took two cookies, picked up her mug, and sat down, feeling the brown leather mold around her rear. She could feel the Steinway behind her as if it were pulsating, waiting to fill the room with melody. The last time she had heard live piano music was at Chantel's home. At first, it was soothing and beautiful, but after a while, she started to remember her days in choir and how it had all ended, and she excused herself to use the restroom, where she had a panic attack. Here, in the living room of a log cabin decorated for the holidays—the very definition of festive—with a blazing fire, Jean thought the sound of a piano would be sublime, but she knew it would take her back, and that was not good.

Her eyes stole a peek out the window next to the glowing tree; there was so much snow falling that it was as if someone was on the roof pouring buckets of it down in front of the window. *It's getting even worse out there. Will I even be able to make it to my hotel?* She took a sip of tea and met Annie's eyes. Her host blew on her own tea and then took a careful sip, and Jean wondered if she should bring up her change in plans. Annie had cut her off as she was about to say something earlier, or maybe she hadn't heard the start of Jean's reply. *When you speak, you're not shaky at all. You're confident,* Chantel had said, *and I like that. It's just that your voice is so soft. You have to remember to raise your volume when we're in meetings with clients.*

As she lowered and then cradled her mug, she convinced herself that Annie had not heard her. After all, Jean had been speaking to Annie's backside while following her. Jean's eyes glanced out the window again—it was a sheet of white flurries. *Should I mention that my flights have been cancelled and that I'll be staying in Midland for the night?* It would be weird for Annie to find this out later, most likely from Jean's mother, who could not keep anything a secret . . . except her family's past.

Deciding that there was only one way to proceed, Jean said, "Both of my flights got cancelled because of the weather. I just got a notification on my phone." *It doesn't matter when I found out,* she thought.

Annie's eyes opened in surprise, and then Jean saw something in them that she had not seen in someone's eyes in a long time: hope. "Oh, my," her host said and then gave a perfunctory look out the same window by the tree.

"So, I'll be staying—"

"Here, of course!" Annie broke in with.

"Well—"

Annie continued to ignore her, or not hear her, as if her mind had been given a shot of adrenaline, awakening, energizing, and then initiating bed-and-breakfast and emergency-manager instincts that had been dormant for decades. Perhaps, there was a loudspeaker now going off in her head, saying: *Clear the way, I'm coming through. Nothing will prevent me from having company stay the night in this house!* "Oh, you'll stay, won't you? We'll have a full house!"

"A full house?" Jean asked.

"Yes," she said, looking at her watch. "My grandson—"

The doorbell rang, and Annie Brady gave Jean a wink before lifting off the couch and walking toward the front door with gusto. The sheer power of her movement momentarily took Jean out of processing what she had just heard as she thought, *There is no way she is eighty-three.*

The front door opened, and she heard Annie yell, "Scottie!"

Then, she heard a deep voice reply, "Hi, Gram."

She couldn't place the exact age of the voice, but the depth told her that Scott was not a teenager. *How old is he?*

The door jingled as it shut, and she heard Scott say, "Is she still here?"

8

Jean rose from the couch and had taken two steps when Annie entered the room, followed by Scott. The last words she had heard Annie say were, *"Yes. Follow me and meet her."*

He was tall—at least six feet one, compared to Annie, who was around five feet nine—and wore brown leather hiking boots with classic red laces, jeans, and a tucked-in black mock turtleneck, which showcased his fit waist and massive shoulders. He looked like a bodyguard following Annie into the family room, but his smile put Jean at ease. As he got closer, she took note of his trimmed black hair and dark five-o'clock shadow—no gray anywhere. He wore a bulky watch with a black band and a yellow bezel—sporty yet classy. Everyone, including her, seemed to own a smartwatch these days. Still, she always enjoyed seeing someone wear something different—just a watch—that prompted only an occasional glance at the wrist, rather than an obsessive check every minute with awkward screen tapping, dial pushing, dial turning, and *speaking* into the device. It was not lost on her that the gesture of simultaneously lowering her chin and bending her neck gave the impression that she and an ever-growing percentage of the earth's human population were bowing to their devices.

Urian wore a Rolex, and, like her boss's fingers, there were no rings on any of Scott's.

They rounded the couch, and she completed her pre-greeting assessment. He was anywhere from the late twenties to the mid-thirties, and if she were to categorize his looks, attractive was an understatement. Thinking back to her visit to Shirley Ruth's house, Jean thought that since Annie was her grandmother's best friend and their houses were close to each other, there was a strong possibility that Jean would have met Scott much earlier if her parents had taken her to visit Shirley Ruth when she was growing up. However, her grandmother's house wasn't built until 2008, so the meeting would have taken place at a different home in Midland. Still, she could see the two of them, in elementary school and on summer break, playing in her grandmother's backyard like some OshKosh B'gosh commercial.

"Jean, this is my grandson, Scott."

He stepped to within a few feet of her and stopped, and the vision of them playing freeze tag in overalls, t-shirts, and Keds disappeared. The scent of him reached her. It did not smell like cologne but rather body wash, which gave off a crisp and clean odor. He reached out a large hand to her and said, "Hi, Jean. Didn't know if you'd still be here when I arrived. Pleasure to meet you."

His handshake was firm and his greeting warm, but she could also hear in his voice and see in the way that he carried himself that he was someone who could take charge when the situation called for it. There was a reserved confidence about him, no trace of cockiness, secure in who he was and where he was at this moment in life. She had seen it in only a few of the executives of her company's more impressive clients. It was rare. Annie couldn't stop beaming as she watched his every move.

"Nice to meet you," Jean said.

Their hands parted, but he held her in his stare for a few moments more, almost as if he recognized her. *What is that about?* she thought.

Annie commanded, "Sit, young ones," as she maneuvered around the table to check the level of Jean's tea. Scott broke his gaze and took a seat on the far end of the couch, but Jean still felt the effect of his weight as the cushions underneath her shifted as he settled in and then crossed his legs.

Annie headed for the kitchen and returned with a green Stanley thermos and a mug, which she set down on the coffee table near Scott. After unscrewing the top, she poured steaming coffee into her grandson's mug. "Made it an hour ago when you called."

"You know me too well, Gram." Scott picked up the mug and took a sip.

"Well, I've had thirty-one years to study you," she replied, tapping the tight mound of his left shoulder.

Jean hid a satisfied grin behind her mug as she took a drink of hot tea. *Thirty-one—my reputation as an accurate age estimator is safe.*

Annie took her seat across from them.

Now, let's see if my instincts about character are still sharp.

"You know, you might have the best first-impression read of any young executive I've ever worked with," Chantel had told her after Jean's assessment of a potential client had ended up being right. She had told her boss that after fifteen minutes with him, she believed there to be at least an anxious, if not insecure, man behind his charm and fixation on his own company's internal numbers, which he had provided, a bit prematurely, in her opinion. *"We should wait to close the deal,"* Jean had said. After some hesitation, Chantel had phoned the company's CEO and said, *"Because your needs are so specific, and we want to make sure we can deliver what you are asking, we'll need a few weeks to draw up the contract and run our models."* The CEO had seemed confused by the call but agreed to the extended timeline. A week later, they learned that the man they had met with had been let go, and Chantel was relieved and grateful that the partnership had not been finalized. Later, they learned that after Chantel's phone call with the CEO, the CEO had grilled the executive who had met with Chantel and Jean and discovered that the

executive had been cooking the books to conceal the fact that the company was headed off a financial cliff. The meeting with Renault Impact had been a desperate effort to get the advertising giant to rescue it through direct marketing, branding, and a robust mobile and social media campaign. Two weeks after the executive had been let go, the company filed for Chapter 11 bankruptcy. When the CEO reached back out to Chantel with an apology and asked to meet, Chantel declined the invite.

From that point forward, Chantel built in a twenty-minute debrief between only her and Jean—it was in Chantel's corner suite if the meeting was at the company's office in Manhattan or in Chantel's hotel suite if the meeting was away from New York City.

"I'll get right to the point," said Scott.

"Spoken like a true park ranger," Annie quipped and then focused her attention on Jean. "He's a federal park ranger who runs the national park in Munising." She sat back, tapping her cup of tea with her bony fingers. "Michigan has seven national parks that fall under the National Park Service, and he's the youngest park ranger of them all."

"Gram, stop. You're embarrassing me."

"No, no," Jean said. "That's impressive."

"You're so humble, child," Annie said to Scott, beaming with pride. "I get to brag about you. I'm your grandmother."

He went to reply, but stopped.

Annie set her cup of tea down. "Now, what was it you had to tell us?"

"My flights for tomorrow have been canceled."

Annie's eyes shot over to Jean and then back to Scott. "Oh?"

"Yeah. I just found out when I pulled in the driveway and checked my email. Then, I got text messages."

Annie pointed at Jean. "Her flights for today were cancelled."

"Sorry," Scott said. He motioned toward the window next to the Christmas tree. The wind howled, and a feather of snowflakes hit the glass and then swirled away. "I don't think anyone is going anywhere for at least the next few days."

"Including you?" Annie asked.

"If the forecasters are a little off, then things could be up and running later tomorrow. If they're off the other way, then it might be until late on Christmas Day when some stores and airports reopen. Maybe as late as the 26th. We'll know more in the next few hours. I think if they had to do it all over again, they would have issued the winter storm warning earlier. Usually, they give those twelve to twenty-four hours in advance, but the storm that dumped all that snow out there at the end of last week must have thrown their models a curveball—you usually don't get back-to-back storms like these. When the other one ended, they backed all the way down to a winter weather advisory instead of a winter storm watch." He shook his head. "This is going to be bad." He looked straight at Annie. "Blizzard of '78?"

Annie pursed her lips. "Could be. That a boy, remembering your history."

"You told me the story how many times while I was growing up?"

She gave him a guilty grin. "A few."

Jean resisted the urge to pull out her phone and look up the blizzard that had occurred in 1978. The last thing she wanted to do right now was be rude, and looking at her phone in the middle of a conversation—especially with people she didn't know—would be bad-mannered. She would look it up later, but she still wanted immediate information about the storm, so she asked, "How bad was it?"

As if pulling the internet page up in her mind, Annie said, "In Midland, we saw thirty-four inches of snow and winds of fifty to seventy miles per hour. Across the affected states, fifty thousand miles of roadway were blocked, over one hundred thousand vehicles were abandoned, fifteen thousand people found themselves in shelters, and almost four hundred thousand homes were without power."

"And you both think this storm could rival that one?"

"Wouldn't surprise me," Annie said.

Scott added, "Two days after the storm, ninety percent of Michigan's roads were still impassible, and the entire state went under a Presidential Emergency Declaration." His attention returned to Annie. "Studying that storm was part of my official ranger training."

"I know. Will you be needed up north?"

"No. My deputy, Jessica, is working Christmas this year, and I'll be working New Year's. I'm not due back until the twenty-ninth; she leaves for her vacation on the thirtieth." He glanced at Jean and said, "We flip-flop every year," and then focused on Annie once again. "I checked in with her ten minutes before I arrived here. They aren't getting hit that hard, but even if they did need me, with what we're getting in the lower peninsula, I'd only make it an hour or so north before I'd have to get off the highway. Looks like everything south of the Mackinac Bridge, all the way into northern Ohio, is going to get the worst of it. It's as if Lake Michigan is a trough of snow that is about to be propelled over the Lower Peninsula by an enormous snowblower." He stretched his arms. "The park is in capable hands; Jessica is already going through her checklists. They'll be ready." He sat back and rubbed his whiskers. "Yoopers are the very definition of being prepared for weather like this. They shovel roofs up there. We'll have to see how the situation progresses. There were a lot of vehicles on the road on my way down here," he said, looking at Jean, "visitors who are traveling to see family for the holidays. Everyone needs to find a place to hunker down by dinner time."

"I didn't think it would be this bad," Annie said.

Scott leaned forward. "You know the old saying in Michigan, 'Everything is treated as normal until there are three new inches of snow on the ground.'

Well, we're almost at three now. If they are already cancelling flights for tomorrow, then we're in for something enormous today and tonight—even more than last week, because at least with last week, you didn't have the wind, and the temperatures hovered around thirty degrees. Now, you've got the additional snowfall, plus the wind blowing the massive amount that got dumped last week. We'll have seven . . . eight-foot drifts. Maybe bigger." He looked at the Christmas tree lights. "And I think we're looking at widespread power outages, too. Mind if I extend my stay?"

"Of course not! I've already extended the invitation to Jean."

"And I'm grateful for that," Jean said, "but I feel like I would be imposing. I've already made a reservation at the Holiday Inn Express."

Her statement paused the conversation, and the only sounds were the screams of the biting wind outside and the disintegrating log falling in the fireplace, which sent embers sparking up into the chimney.

Annie joined her hands and said, "Well, you wouldn't be imposing at all, and I'm not sure that there will be any stores or restaurants open after tonight. I'd hate for you to be stuck there. Since it's on the other side of Midland, we might not be able to get to you for a while, depending on the storm."

She hadn't thought of this angle. What if she got to the hotel and everything around it was closed? What if she stopped at a grocery store on the way to the hotel to get supplies and became stranded there? What if she went straight to the hotel but became trapped there for two days or more? She shuddered at the thought of eating a continental breakfast morning, noon, and night. And that was if they had enough food to feed everyone there for that long. Knowing that Scott's flights for tomorrow were cancelled had eliminated her hope of only losing a day and getting back to her condo. Now, it seemed that the day after tomorrow, Christmas, might also not work out, depending on the storm. *Do I remain stubborn, unwilling to accept help, and head to the hotel anyway?*

Or, do I do something entirely out of my introverted comfort zone and stay in an enclosed space with two people I don't know for at least a day and a half?

In her life, she had mastered whittling down options to two good ones, where, no matter what she chose, the result would be pleasant and in her favor. Call it overpreparing, call it the need for control, or even call it robotic living, she had always been able to engineer plans, make decisions, and steer scenarios to stay on schedule and remain in her bubble of guaranteed outcomes and inescapable, unalterable—and, hence, *unsurprising*—destinies. Now, she was faced with two unfavorable options, and, due to the lack of data and time, would be forced to make a decision based on the most unreliable foundation of all: her feelings. She felt her phone vibrate in her front pocket. Yes, she could excuse herself and pretend to use the restroom while she scoured the internet, studying meteorological models and predictions, but how accurate would they be? This morning, the weather had looked manageable, and her flights were a go. No, she would not learn anything new in the five minutes spent hiding in the bathroom.

She looked at the Christmas tree lights. But what about the power? The hotel would have generators, so at least she would have heat. Her eyes moved to the hearth. Annie had enough wood next to the pole barn to heat the cabin until next year, but that would mean all three of them would need to hang out in the living room, and, at night, probably *sleep* in the living room. She winced inside, thinking about sleeping in the same space as strangers. *Ugh. What. To. Do?*

"Thank God, I've got a generator that runs on natural gas and powers the entire house," said Annie. "We'll be comfortable here."

And that piece of information tipped the scales for Jean. Would she be staying with strangers? Yes. Would she be safe, comfortable, and not wondering where her next meal was coming from? Yes. Plus, she had to admit that she found Annie warm and generous, even if she was a bit pushy. And

Scott . . . she found him intriguing—a person her age who was living a very different lifestyle than hers in the city.

She was about to talk when Annie added, "Jean, your grandmother would not want you getting stranded in a hotel with nowhere to stay for Christmas. If she were still alive, she would never forgive me if I let you walk out my front door right now." She made a wicked smile. "Yes, I'm trying to blackmail you emotionally."

Knowing that this was true, which could have tipped the scales in the other direction, she chose to believe that what Annie was saying was from the heart. Still, her answer would now be a result of logic that overrode any emotion she might be feeling. "From what I just learned from you and Scott, this is the place to be right now." She gave Scott a grin of thanks and then faced Annie and said, "If it wouldn't be too much of a hassle—"

"No hassle at all," Annie interrupted, clapping her hands together once. "Let's get to work." She was up and moving toward the hallway. "Now, the two of you go get your belongings from your vehicles. Scott, your usual room is ready. Jean, I'll have yours put together in a few minutes." She looked back over her shoulder. "Then, we'll meet in the kitchen and talk logistics."

And with that, Annie disappeared down the hallway.

Scott was first to his feet. "There's no stopping her," he said. "Do you need help bringing anything inside?"

"I don't have much, so I think I've got it," she said. "Thanks, though."

They moved into the hallway, heading for the foyer. "No problem. I'm glad you're staying. This storm is going to be dangerous."

"Dangerous?"

Scott opened the door to the foyer closet and grabbed her coat first, handing it to her before removing two items for himself. One was a down sweater jacket, which he donned, and the other was a black Patagonia Stormshadow Parka, which he put on next and zipped up. From the left sleeve of the parka, he removed black Gore-Tex gloves and a black watch cap and put them on. He was dressed for the outside before Jean had gotten her second arm through her coat.

"For the next few hours, everything will seem pretty normal. Traffic will slow, but people will still be able to get to their destinations. Yes, the airports are closing, but that call was made to give everyone enough time before the weather gets bad enough that travel will start to get challenging." He looked into her eyes as she zipped up her coat. "If the snow and wind keep up, people are going to get stranded, and then the sun is going to go down, and the temperature is going to drop. The last I heard before I got here was that it might hit minus ten tonight." He started to move toward the door. "That's when the real problems are going to start because at that temperature, people will freeze to death if they can't find shelter, and the only thing that will keep them warm is if they can keep their car running. But their vehicles are going to run out of gas sooner than they think." He opened the door. "At that point, they will have to make a decision: stay in their vehicles and hope that help is on the way, or take a tremendous risk and leave their vehicles to find shelter in subfreezing temperatures. And, with the widespread loss of power we could experience, there is no guarantee that the place they make it to will have electricity, a wood-burning stove, or a fireplace. I know what we said about the blizzard of 1978 and what could happen." He hesitated, tapping his gloved hand on the door frame. "I just hope—" His voice trailed off, and he looked at her head and hands. "Do you need a hat and gloves?"

Startled by his assessment of the worsening situation, it took her a few seconds to respond. "Uh . . . no—no, I left them in the car."

He gave her a nod. "Okay, here we go."

They stepped onto the porch.

One look at the monstrous blizzard in front of her, the top of her car already looking like it was wearing a hat of snow, and Jean knew she had made the right decision.

9

Scott knocked on the sliding door to Annie's den, and moments later she opened it and ushered him inside, closing the door behind them.

As he looked around the room, he felt transported from one winter wonderland to another. This was his grandmother's "Christmas Room," which stayed decorated year-round. *"Any time I need to take a rest from the world, I come in here and get lost in happiness,"* she had once said when he asked her why she devoted an entire room in her cabin to Christmas. *"Sometimes, I lose track of time, smiling and staring, and I'm in here for an hour before I go back out and rejoin the cruel game."* The decorations were more elaborate, including a Lemax village with over twenty lit buildings and structures on a massive table covered with a white tablecloth that reached the floor on all sides, giving it the feel of a tiny town perched on a plateau at the top of a snowy mountain. There was a Christmas tree exclusively adorned with red bulbs and white snowflakes, and it had two-inch green ribbon wound around it from the base to the top, where a white angel sat. Running parallel to the ribbon was a string of white lights that highlighted the bulbs and snowflakes. Underneath the tree were an assortment of decorative presents—silver boxes with large red bows. He had opened one once when he was a child and found it empty; his grandmother had explained to him that they were just for show, to make the room look like Santa had visited. He had been confused and avoided the room for years.

Next to the tree was a gas fireplace made of fake stone with a wooden mantle painted white. Two small red stockings hung from ceramic statues of Santa and Mrs. Claus, the loops of the stockings secured to the Clauses' hands, giving the observer the impression that the couple was holding the reins of a sleigh that was out of sight below.

The entire floor was covered in lush, navy carpeting, and a long white couch ran along a wall with a red throw blanket dotted with white snowflakes draped over the backrest. Nat King Cole's version of "The Christmas Song" finished, and "Underneath the Tree" by Kelly Clarkson started up as he joined his grandmother on the couch.

"You look surprised," Annie said.

"I didn't expect to hear Kelly Clarkson in this room." He smiled. "She's of my generation. I thought you only played the old classics in here."

"I'm open-minded," she said, and then told her Echo to pause—the music stopped. "Jean upstairs?"

Indeed, Scott thought.

They had brought in their belongings from their respective vehicles, and, after shaking off the snow and stowing their coats, Scott had shown Jean to one of the guest suites on the second floor. Jean said, *"This is beautiful,"* when she entered the room. He peeked in and saw that Annie had already made the Queen bed and placed fresh towels on the purple bedspread. The door to the bathroom was open, and he could see a candle flickering on the counter next to the sink. *She still doesn't miss a thing,* he thought as he told Jean that he would be downstairs and to holler if she needed anything. Hearing her soft voice reply, *"Okay,"* and watching her delicate right hand pull her rolling suitcase behind her as she entered the suite had made his heart skip a few beats.

As he walked down the hallway to the door of his suite, he had said to himself, *I don't even know her, but*— He shook off the thought and entered the room where he always stayed when he came to visit Gram, hefting his large duffel bag onto the black-and-red checkered bedspread of the King bed. Although this time, he regarded the bag with contempt: Almost everything in it had been packed with warm and sunny California in mind, not bone-chilling Michigan.

"Yeah, she's getting settled in," Scott replied.

"Good." Annie reached into her pocket. "Here, take this."

Into his palm, she placed a folded piece of paper. Surprised by its thickness, he unfolded it. Inside was a small stack of bills, with a fifty-dollar bill on top. He glanced at her and then peeled back the fifty. There was another . . . and another . . . and another . . .

"There's enough money there for the run."

Before he could question her, Annie continued, "On that piece of paper is a small list of gifts I want you to buy for Jean. The remaining money will be used for groceries and supplies. I checked, and the mall is closing in two hours, but Meijer will stay open for another two hours after that, so we have time. The plows are already running."

"Gifts?"

"I already have something for her, but since she is staying for at least another day, I want her to have some things to open when we do our usual exchange." She waited to speak, having to swallow as if her emotions were starting to take over. "We don't know what the weather will do, but I haven't had anyone in my home on Christmas in so long . . . well, I don't want to miss the chance if it does happen. The only person I always saw on Christmas day besides your grandfather was—" Her voice drifted off.

Scott put a hand on her knee and gave it a loving pat. "Shirley Ruth," he said. "I knew this holiday would be difficult for you." He met eyes with his grandmother. "I'm glad my flights got cancelled."

He did not make the statement only to comfort her. Being here and around Gram and Jean, he was relieved not to be traveling to Santa Barbara. Not because of the weather, which was beautiful, or the city, which was vibrant, or the beaches, whose warm sand and cool Pacific breezes revitalized him. In particular, he enjoyed Butterfly Beach with a post-beach-day stop at the Honor Bar in Montecito, where his father made the same embarrassing toast every visit: *"Here's to honor—gettin' on her and stayin' on her."* No, his skepticism, his aversion to visits out west, was centered around what the sun-dappled vista in California represented in his mind: a fractured wing of his family. His parents, J.J. and Kayla Brady, had divorced in 2016 during his senior year in college.

It had devastated him.

Now, eight years later, each holiday trip reminded him that his family would never be whole again, a yearly dagger that depressed his spirits and pierced his conscience. Ever since the split, he had alternated holidays with his parents. Last year, it was Thanksgiving in Santa Barbara with his father and his father's new wife, Megan, both humanities professors at UC Santa Barbara. Christmas was spent with his mother and her husband of six years, Stephen, in Tampa, Florida, along with Scott's sister, Heather, who was three years younger than him and a chemistry professor at the University of Central Florida. As difficult as the divorce had been on Scott, it had been even worse on his sister. She had seen things unravel in real time, from their mother's discovery of their father's affair to the final papers being signed. Scott had been away at college and spared the late-night screaming matches, slamming doors, broken furniture, and shattered dishes. What he had not been spared were the phone calls and texts, at all hours of the day and night, in the aftermath of each fight. And there had always been three perspectives: his father's, his mother's, and Heather's.

Reflecting years later, he had concluded that it was having to listen to or read about a recap of each explosion three separate times that had physically and mentally worn him out and emotionally crippled him.

He was still in contact with Heather, perhaps making a phone call every time a season changed, in addition to the once-a-year visit. However, something about her being present during the worst of their parents' imploding marriage had forever changed their relationship. Was it her possible jealousy that he had been away at college, many miles from the worst of it? He'd never asked her. Or, was it the emotional damage she had sustained, witnessing the destruction from their father's infidelity, that had made a part of her forever inaccessible—unreachable, he questioned, because he had not experienced the terror firsthand? The subject had not come up. Or, was it that she had felt alone, perhaps abandoned, and had wanted him there for support? He wished he could have been. Their father's affair with a colleague had fizzled after a year, and they had neither seen nor heard of the woman again. Some wounds had healed. Still, every time Scott was in his father's presence, along with Heather, a tension simmered just below the routine pleasantries that they all displayed during the holiday duty calls.

The visit to his mother over Thanksgiving a month ago had been okay, unremarkable except for the celebration of Heather's first published article as an Assistant Professor. Stephen had asked him the same, and usually *only*, question he asked Scott during every visit, *"How are things up north?"* and then seemed to tune out when Scott gave his answer; Scott's mother had given her typical smile, accompanied by the bouncy shaking of her head as if to say, *"Why didn't you put your university education to better use than being a park ranger?"*

But Thanksgivings were always manageable, whether they were celebrated in Florida or California. He still pitied his mother for what she had endured, and Scott was relieved that Kayla had found love and happiness again with Stephen.

His father's new bride, Megan, he could do without.

There had been a soap opera titled *Santa Barbara* that had run from the mid-1980s to the early 1990s, which Megan had adored. Somehow, every year she forgot that she had told Scott all about her teenage years watching and, in her words, "learning from" *Santa Barbara's* glamor couple, Cruz and Eden, and how *she* had discovered Robin Wright as a talented actress before the world knew who she was. *"Everybody always talks about how they've known her since she starred in* Forrest Gump. *Well, I've known her since 1984 when she played Kelly Capwell on* Santa Barbara." He would always politely nod, affirming her knowledge, and then start the whole exchange all over again the following year, when she would casually ask, *"Did you know there used to be a soap opera named after this city?"*

Anyway, the holidays of his father begging forgiveness from him—and Heather, if she was there—were in the past. The position at UC Santa Barbara and his revitalized life with Megan had tilted his father's emotional openness with his children in the opposite direction. He had become remote and matter-of-fact with Scott and Heather as if he had surrendered to the fact that he could no longer influence their decisions, and, because he no longer needed to emotionally manipulate them into boosting his wounded soul, he chose to focus his attention on Megan's young son from her prior marriage, reinventing himself as a caring and emotionally available father, a role he had abandoned eight years ago at the moment of discovery of his secret relationship with a fellow professor . . . which had been just after Christmas vacation when Scott had returned to school.

And so it was the annual Christmas visit, no matter if it was to his mother's or his father's, that was always the more difficult of the two holidays to endure. The first reason was obvious: Each parent always tried to recreate the experience they all had shared before the divorce. They failed every time. The second reason was simple: Christmas had always been the Brady Family's rallying point, the day when they huddled at Gram's to connect and find peace, strength, and calmness away from the outside world. He had not known it at the time—no one had known, except perhaps his father—that the Christmas of 2015 would be the last family gathering at Gram's. The divorce would not only shock and devastate Scott, but it would also overwhelm Annie. She had found it difficult to forgive J.J., but she had done it and never understood why he would not come home for Christmas ever since then, choosing to stay in Santa Barbara even in the years when he was single. Yes, J.J. had invited his mother—and his father, when he was still alive—to spend Christmas out west every year since, but Annie always declined.

After Scott's grandfather, John, had passed away five years ago, Annie had become even more stubborn, refusing to leave her cabin for Christmas in the hopes that one day everyone would return. But after her first holiday season alone, except for the company of Shirley Ruth, Scott knew that his grandmother had accepted the fact that no one was ever coming home for Christmas again. Not even her daughter, Michelle, Scott's aunt, who with her husband, Rick, ran a restaurant (their yearly excuse), came home after the split. But, in a moment of surprising honesty that, for once, did nothing to serve himself, J.J. had told Scott that Annie and Michelle had never been close, and that also went for Michelle's daughter Victoria, who at twenty-two was Scott's youngest cousin. And Scott knew that this estrangement had wounded Annie more than the one with her daughter, for Victoria was a senior at Middlebury College in Vermont, studying creative writing and literature—the subjects that Annie had once taught for forty years. *"It's the tangential carnage that one doesn't always see,"* Gram had confessed to Scott one fall after receiving her unopened letter, marked returned to sender, that she had mailed to Victoria. *"Michelle always thought I preferred J.J. to her, and, maybe I did, but when he and your mother got divorced, I think Michelle thought she would get more attention now that the "golden child"—her phrase, not mine—had a chink in his armor, but, as you know, I went the other way and poured all of my energy into helping J.J. get through it, although I detested what he did. We don't do forgiveness very well in this family, Scottie."*

In any event, the good times, the memories, and the drawing near had abruptly ended, without warning, when Kayla came home early one January 2016 night to find J.J. and his mistress together.

Now, the annual Christmas visit to either Tampa or Santa Barbara—"Santa" was even in the *name!*—had become a chore. He had once heard that most members of the military spent their leave time visiting family instead of taking time for themselves, and, now, as he sat in his grandmother's Christmas room, he realized through that long-forgotten nugget of insight that he had been doing precisely that for the past eight years, which was why he welcomed the change to stay with Gram for a few extra days. He was the only member of his family, other than Annie, who still lived in Michigan. She was his special grandma, and he drove down at least once a month to check on her. Perhaps the fact that both of his parents required him to visit them over Christmas, when it was their turn to host him, was their way of trying to hold on to what once was. And that yearly attempt to repackage the experience in a new place with different people was what made it cruel and painful.

The Christmas gatherings at Gram's were gone forever.

Then, as he rubbed his grandmother's delicate forearm, he arrived at another moment of clarity, perhaps brought about because he finally had an unimpeachable reason why he could not travel: His routine of staying one night at Gram's, exchanging gifts, and then leaving right before Christmas had been good of him but, also, it must have torn the heart out of Annie each time he pulled out of the driveway to catch a plane to Florida or California. He felt a deep and heavy sadness weigh him down. He felt ashamed.

"Everyone eventually leaves Michigan," Gram had once told him. *Well, not me,* Scott said to himself.

Annie's eyes were glassy, and she gave them a quick wipe. "I'm so happy you're staying," she said, regaining her composure. After clearing her throat, she immediately switched gears, *like only she can,* Scott thought. "Okay, let's check our supplies and make the grocery list."

They exited the room, and Annie slid the door shut, making the room seem as if it were a present to be opened.

"You going to show Jean that room?" he asked as they walked down the hallway that led back to the foyer.

"I thought we might all have a hot chocolate in there later."

"Of course," he replied. "Didn't know if you were going to let her join our tradition or not."

"Might as well," she said over her shoulder.

Scott heard footsteps coming down the stairs, and soon he saw Jean take the last few steps, joining them in the foyer.

"Good timing, my dear," Annie said. "Is your room okay?"

"It's wonderful," Jean replied without hesitation. "Thank you again for letting me stay."

Scott studied her. She had pulled her hair back into a ponytail, which exposed her long and narrow face, the smooth skin glowing in the light from the chandelier overhead. She had also slipped out of her boots, and he liked seeing her black-stockinged feet on the polished wood floor as if she lived here.

"Easy peasy," Annie replied, waving for them to follow her down the far hallway. "Let's get down to it."

With the matriarch in the lead, marching with a purpose, Scott eyed Jean and grinned, and, after a beat, Jean gave him a grin back as they walked behind Annie until reaching the kitchen.

Annie motioned for Scott and Jean to take seats at the bar, and as they did, Scott watched as his grandmother opened a cabinet above the kitchen desk and pulled down a 3-ring binder.

"Okay, first things first. Let's make sure we have everything."

"Gram, you know you do."

"You never know, young man." She opened a drawer and removed a pen and a pad of paper, then shifted her gaze to Jean. "And this young lady might find it interesting to learn a little bit about survival in Michigan."

Jean nodded.

"All right," he said, "I'm not stopping you."

Annie lifted her chin a few inches into the air, while keeping her eyes glued to Scott, a Queen taking a measure of her subject. "No, you're not."

She flipped open the front cover, glanced at the first page, and then turned to the second.

"What was on the first page?" Scott asked.

"My emergency checklist for Crickett."

"Oh, sorry, Gram."

"It's okay . . . a part of life."

Crickett was his grandmother's beloved golden retriever, who had died the previous spring at the age of twelve. He had yet to get used to not seeing the old girl lying in the foyer, awaiting his arrival, which he would have mentioned today had it not been for the storm and the surprise of meeting Jean. Annie had told him about her visitor, but he thought Jean would be long gone by the time he arrived. Naturally, Annie had not told him the *exact time* she thought she would see Jean. In contrast to his friends' grandparents, who were obsessed with time, punctuality, and repeating the daily schedule multiple times when asked, his grandmother had become a little loose with things like meeting times. Hence, his statement to Jean earlier of, *"Didn't know if you'd still be here when I arrived."* And yet, if Annie was *in charge of the schedule*, then she behaved exactly like his friends' grandparents, and other things—like the emergency binder she was now going through—remained as cornerstones to her routine, which she swore by. *"They keep me safe and keep me dancing, dear child,"* she had said.

Annie pointed to a picture of Crickett she had on the countertop next to the fridge—she had always joked that she kept it there because the dog liked food so much—and said to Jean, "Crickett was my last baby. I lost her in March."

"Sorry," Jean replied. "That must have been difficult."

Annie put her palm on Jean's forearm and squeezed it. "Thank you, dear."

There was something about Jean that stirred feelings in Scott he had not experienced in a long time. Her beauty was striking, yes, but how many pretty women had he seen come through the gate to the national park who ended up being pretentious, annoying campers?

"They're making too much noise."

"Ma'am, they have a baby."

"Not my problem. Move them to another site."

"No."

"Fuck you! We're leaving!"

There were too many to count.

No, what attracted Scott to Jean was her display of genuine empathy and honesty. There was one unmistakable skill his grandmother possessed, and it was her ability—by simply being her normal, spunky, caring, and gossipy self— to reveal another person's character. It was akin to a nugget of wisdom he had once received from his high school football coach: *Football doesn't* define *your character, but it* exposes *it.* Could his initial observations still be classified under the umbrella of first impressions, which were not to be completely trusted? Yes. But if she was putting on a front, he knew that being around Annie would eventually break down that front. For now, he enjoyed being in Jean's company, but the situation couldn't help but be a bit awkward. He asked himself, *When was the last time you stayed in a house with a stranger?* His mind traveled back. College—those halcyon, foolish days of yore? About to abandon that line of thinking, an image popped into his mind. Twenty-two-year-old Scott Joseph Brady waking up on an apartment floor in his get-buzzed-and-make-out attire of Vans, ripped jeans, and a Quicksilver hooded sweatshirt . . . with a Maine Coon cat on his chest. Then, as if someone pushed play on the still photograph, he watched as young Scott slid the monster furball onto the foul-smelling carpeted floor, struggled to stand up due to his pulsating headache and queasy stomach. Then, realizing that he did not know where he was or the identities of the partiers who were asleep on the floor around him and on the dark room's ratty couches, he tiptoed, teetering from side to side, toward the door and exited.

"Okay," Annie said, taking her hand off Jean's forearm and pointing at the top of the next page in her binder. "Here we go."

For the next minute, Scott and Jean listened to his grandmother go over her personalized home emergency cold-weather checklist. She kept all of her supplies in the kitchen's large walk-in pantry.

Water—three gallons per person, purchase at Meijer

Food—a three-day supply of non-perishable food per person, purchase at Meijer

Prescribed medications (she still had a month's worth of all of her pills)

L.L. Bean battery-powered & hand-crank dynamo emergency weather radio

Rayovac Industrial 2D LED Flashlight and extra "D" batteries

First aid kit

Whistle

Important family documents—in waterproof and fireproof safe, check on them

Moist towelettes, garbage bags, and plastic ties for personal sanitation

Plastic sheeting and duct tape

Wrench and pliers to turn off utilities

Multi Tool

Can opener

Light sticks

Emergency candles

Matches in waterproof container

Paper plates, paper cups, paper towels, plastic utensils

Emergency cash and change

Fire extinguisher

Down sleeping bag

Medicine dropper

<u>Winterize home:</u>

    Insulate walls, attic, and crawlspace—Done

    Insulate pipes that run through walls and attic—Done

    Check on water valves

    Clean gutters—Done

    Clear storm drains along curb—Done

    Back-up heating source: 1) Home generator, 2) Wood-burning fireplace

    Install battery-powered carbon monoxide detectors near every sleeping area and check batteries—Done

After reviewing the list, she sent Scott to check on the water valves and the attic. When he returned with a thumbs up, he found a fresh cup of coffee on the counter in front of him. He took a sip and said, "Pipes next?"

"Yes," Annie said, flipping to the next page. "Once the temperature reaches twenty degrees outside, which it has been for the past week, I do the following: Keep my garage doors closed, open kitchen and bathroom cabinet doors to allow warm air to circulate around the plumbing . . ." She looked up. "None of the bathroom sinks are on an exterior wall, so I usually only open the cabinet doors before I go to bed and then close them in the morning. However," she said, pointing to the kitchen sink, "since that is on an exterior wall, I keep the cabinets cracked six inches all day and open them wide after dinner for the rest of the night.

"As far as faucets are concerned, I turn the handles on each one just enough to start a drip. If you can both ensure the upstairs faucets are set like that tonight, I'll take care of the ones downstairs. I usually do this at night when the temps dip below twenty, but it looks like the temperature is going to stay below twenty for at least the next few days, so we'll leave them dripping until things warm up outside again."

Scott and Jean nodded, and then Scott observed Jean typing a note into her phone.

Annie chuckled as she wrote a note to herself on the pad of paper with her pen. "Everybody's got their own system. If that gadget works for you, my dear, then don't change anything."

Jean finished and set her phone down. "I set an alarm for 9 p.m. just in case I forget."

"Smart," Annie said. She twisted her head in the direction of her grandson. "Scott?"

I may be the only person under forty to think this, but I hate *cell phones.* "Yes?"

Annie and Jean laughed, and then Annie asked, "What's your system for remembering things?"

Without hesitation, he raised his right hand and tapped the side of his head with his index and middle fingers while saying, "Right here."

"Ha! You never change, Scottie."

He pointed at the binder. "Pole barn and vehicles and then the grocery list, right?"

"Keeping us on point. Love it."

And now it was Jean and Scott who shared a laugh. Annie acknowledged the chuckles with a smile and then dug back into the binder.

"Pole barn. I've got the space heaters positioned." She flipped back a few pages. "Got the ones in the garage ready, too." She flipped forward again. "I did my walkthrough this morning. The snowmobile and SnowCoach are ready, still hooked up from two weeks ago."

Scott noticed Jean's confused look and jumped in. "She's got a Ski-doo Grand Touring snowmobile in her pole barn, along with an HD bumper hitch and SnowCoach MPV. Every winter, when we have enough snow on the ground, I come down here, hook everything up, and then take her for a ride. It's one of our favorite traditions." He motioned toward the window next to the Christmas tree. "She has nine miles of trails back through the woods that she shares with two of her neighbors, so she gets in the SnowCoach, and we go on a tour. Sometimes, we even drop in for a visit and have a cup of hot chocolate with them."

Annie snapped her fingers. "That reminds me—I need to call them after you head out. Tammy and Rob have a generator like mine, but Carole and Geoff and their two toddlers, Brittany and Ethan, don't, and they don't have a fireplace."

Scott gave her a nod. "Make sure to tell them to keep their cell phones charged. With this much precipitation, our CB radio range will be significantly decreased, and they don't have a landline phone, do they?"

"Tammy and Rob have cell phones and still have a landline like me, but no, Carole and Geoff only have cell phones."

"Tell them all to turn on their CB radios, and do a radio check with them. I'm guessing, even with the large antennas you've all got mounted on your roofs, the signal won't reach. Great if it does, but tell them to keep their radios on, regardless, because I should be able to reach them from the trails using the CB I installed on the Grand Touring. But, *make sure* they charge their handheld radios—especially Carole and Geoff—because, beyond cell phones, if the power goes out, that's the only way we'll be able to communicate."

Annie had picked up the pen and was writing more notes down on her pad. When she finished, her eyes returned to the pole barn checklist in the binder. "All ten five-gallon Jerry gas cans are filled and lined up against the north wall. Rob helped me out last week."

"Perfect," said Scott. "So, we've got plenty of fuel. Snowmobile suits, helmets, and boots?"

"All in the mud room. What about your suit?"

Even though the contents of his duffel bag upstairs—shorts, t-shirts, sandals, sunglasses, swimsuit, etc.—had been selected for his now-cancelled trip to Santa Barbara, he had brought his snowmobile suit—an orange Polaris TECH54 Backcountry Monosuit. In past winters, he would leave the suit here, but last November, he had purchased his own snowmobile, a Polaris 650 INDY Adventure 137, to ride on the over 3,000 miles of groomed trails in Michigan's Upper Peninsula. Being a park ranger, constantly thinking of worst-case scenarios, had pushed him to acquire the machine for large winter storms. And so, he brought the suit back and forth between Munising and Midland. Additionally, in the winter, he always traveled with his green Patagonia alpine suit stowed on the back bench of his truck's cab—he could layer his clothes underneath it, and it was perfect for working outside in frigid temperatures. Earlier, while unloading vehicles with Jean, he had brought both suits in and hung them in the foyer closet. "In the front closet," he replied to Annie.

"Must have snuck them past me."

"You were in the kitchen when I brought them in."

He watched as she studied Jean for a beat.

"You'll fit in my snowmobile suit without any problem, Jean, if you want to go on a ride. We'll have to see what this weather does."

"I've never been snowmobiling," Jean said. "Though I have been jet skiing, and heard that it is a lot like it."

Scott tilted his head, trying to concentrate on the similarities in the experiences, but the mention of jet skiing had pulled a bait and switch on his mind, and he now wondered what Jean would look like in a bathing suit. "Pretty comparable," he said.

Annie flipped to the next page in her binder. "Okay, car checklist," she said. "When the snow hit last week, I checked my Expedition, so I'm all set. But, unless either of you needs it, my pride and joy is staying put in the garage." She raised her right index finger and used it to make a circle in the air while saying, "I do not drive around in this garbage."

"Is my car blocking the way out?" Jean asked.

"No. Where you parked is fine." Her attention returned to the page. "Ready, Scottie?"

Annie had given him the exact checklist they were about to go over when he had gotten his driver's license at sixteen. Since then, he had kept the copy she had printed out for him in every vehicle he had owned. In his mind, he could see the folded paper, tucked inside the leather sleeve that also held his registration and insurance information, in the Raptor's glovebox right now. The average snowfall in Michigan was around 60 inches per year, but in the Upper Peninsula, the average was between 100 and 200 inches per year; in Munising, nicknamed "The Snowmobiling Capital of the Midwest," where Scott lived and worked, it was 140 inches per year; and to Munising's northwest was the Keweenaw Peninsula, the uppermost part of the state, where snowfall sometimes exceeded 300 inches per year. Cold, inclement weather, especially freezing temperatures, was not something you messed around with during December, January, and February. Small towns sprinkled across the vast Upper Peninsula were known for their preparedness for winter and the efficiency of their snowplows and emergency services when a big blizzard hit, but there were long stretches of road going in every direction where there was nothing, no help if you became stranded. Therefore, Scott's truck was always stocked with enough supplies for his survival, along with anyone he would stop to render aid to. Even when he was away from the national park, he considered himself on duty. It was one of his traits that Gram said she admired most, but, after all, she was the one who had trained him to be that way.

He knew, and so did she, that his vehicle was ready, but he also realized that it gave her comfort to go over her checklist with him. He also had to admit that Jean seemed interested in the preparations needed to get through a major winter storm. He imagined that living in New York City during the winter did not involve any of the things they were reviewing right now. *You are entirely reliant on your building's superintendent to deal with any power issues and on your city officials for anything else,* he thought. Numbers from a training manual, studied long ago, popped into his head. With 1.7 million people living on Manhattan Island—72,000 people per square mile—everything has to work all of the time.

No. Thank. You.

"Ready," he said.

Annie used her pen to tap items as she began to read down the list. "You've got the proper mix of antifreeze and water in your truck's cooling system?"

"Yes."

"You've checked your tires' air pressure, topped off your windshield washing solution, and replaced worn windshield wipers?"

"Yes."

"You've had your radiator system, engine, heating system, defroster, brakes, brake fluid, oil, lights and hazard lights, exhaust system, fuel and air filters, and car battery checked?"

"I had an oil change and tire rotation last week, and the vehicle was completely winterized in early November."

"Gas level?"

"I filled it up right as I got off ten."

"Good," Annie said.

Scott caught Jean's eyes and added, "You want to keep your gas tank at least half full at all times during winter. That way, your fuel lines won't freeze up, and it prevents ice from building up in your tank."

"Makes sense," she replied. "The Mercedes has over half a tank in it right now."

Both Annie and Scott nodded before Annie continued. "Now, to your car kit. Portable solar generator, battery-powered and hand-crank-powered emergency weather radio—I know you've got that because I bought yours for you—flashlight, extra batteries, cell phone charger, windshield scraper, hand broom, work gloves, high-visibility safety vest, high-visibility yellow blanket, duct tape, hooded windbreaker poncho, hand warmers, waterproof matches, jumper cables, shovel, extra blankets, a change of clothes, flares, three days of non-perishable food, three gallons of water, first aid kit, tire repair kit, 'Help' sign, toolkit with extra screwdrivers, wrenches, pliers, and wire cutters." She stopped. "You still have your knife?"

Scott reached inside his right front pocket and, with a bit of shifting his hips around, pulled out a Victorinox Swiss Champ XXL 73 Function Large Red Pocket Knife. "Always have it on me."

"As you should," Annie said, grinning. She continued, "Reflective triangle, manual can opener, extra set of gloves, scarf, winter hat, boots, and jacket, snowmobile suit, balaclava ski mask, sleeping bag, large tarp, parachute cord, tow strap, fire extinguisher, carpet strips, spare tire, jack, portable air compressor, tire gauge, tire chains, full bag of salt, and a full bag of sand."

"A full bag of sand?" Jean asked.

"Sand can help the tires gain traction if your vehicle gets stuck," he said, "I also use salt to melt ice."

Jean ran a hand through her hair and exhaled. Then, with a sheepish grin, she asked Annie, "You wouldn't mind if I took a few pictures with my phone of your checklists, would you?"

"Of course not," the Brady family matriarch replied while closing the binder. "I'll hand it over right after we put together the grocery list. Speaking of that, do you need anything, such as toiletries? Scott said you brought in a travel suitcase."

"I'm all good. I always pack a carry-on in case I get stuck for a day or two. As long as you've got a washer and dryer, I will be fine."

"You were made for each other," Annie said.

Scott and Jean shared an uncomfortable look.

Annie laughed immediately. "Oh, I mean in the way you are both prepared."

Was it a nervous laugh his grandmother had just given, like she had accidentally said something she had been thinking? Or was it a laugh, realizing that her words had come out the wrong way, and that she had intended to make an innocent statement? He did not know, but he did respect the fact that Jean appeared self-sufficient and prepared. But, how real was it? Some in his generation had been raised to overthink and overprepare—almost to the point of paranoia, worrying about what could go wrong at the expense of simply living life—which made them seem equipped to handle sudden changes, but, after the recognition of the deviation in plan, ultimately unable to deal with the fallout. And some members of his mid-twenties-to-mid-thirties cohort had been conditioned to underthink and underprepare, having faith that someone would be there to direct them and take care of them if unforeseen obstacles appeared, which had caused them to live life both a little too freely and a little too safely at times, each path coming with its disappointments, costs, setbacks, and yes, also coming with some seemingly short-term benefits. It was doubtful he would get a full measure of Jean during their time together, so he chose to believe, for the moment, that she thought ahead but wasn't frozen in her ability to live life by doing so. Why he was leaning that way, he didn't know. Maybe it was the fact that she hadn't been on her phone. Maybe it was because of how attentive and respectful she was when Annie reviewed the safety checklists. Jean was more patient about the whole thing than he was.

Annie continued, saying, "The washer and dryer are down the other hallway off the foyer. Detergent and dryer sheets are in the cabinet above the washer. Help yourself."

"If it's okay, I'd like to shower and change after we put together the grocery list, and then I'll start a small load. Might need to wear this outfit again."

"Sweetie, you don't have to ask permission. You are done asking for permission right now. What's ours is yours, right, Scottie?"

Damn, she likes to put me on the spot. "Absolutely," he said, and they settled in to figure out food and drinks.

After ten minutes of discussion, Annie handed Scott the list, and he put it in his pocket with the other list. His stomach started to rumble just thinking about what they had agreed upon, his grandmother steering the decisions toward her favorite meals to make. However, Scott and Jean insisted that they be allowed to help. Annie gave them a mischievous stare and said, "I may be eighty-three, but I am still the host. We'll see."

Tonight's dinner was already set: chili, freshly baked bread, and beer.

Tomorrow was Christmas Eve, and they settled on coffee and blueberry muffins for breakfast, soup and sandwiches for lunch, and then Italian for dinner: lasagna, garlic bread, Caesar salad, and a bottle of Cabernet Sauvignon.

For Christmas, they would go all out. There would be croissants and coffee early in the morning, followed by a heavy breakfast of bacon, eggs, toast, French toast, and fresh fruit, accompanied by butter, apple butter, and maple syrup. Cheese, crackers, and grapes would be paired with Pinot Noir—he'd never had it—for afternoon snacking, and dinner would be served at 6 p.m., featuring a honey-glazed ham, corn casserole, potato casserole, cranberries, and freshly baked bread. The beverage would be, in Annie's terms, "a full-bodied Merlot," and for dessert, she would serve her legendary raspberry pie.

The twenty-sixth would be leftovers, and, with any luck, the weather would clear that day, if not before.

As they had added some odds and ends to the list after the meals had been planned, Annie explained that she already had a few of her staples on hand for this time of year: hot chocolate, whipped cream, candy canes, eggnog, a bowl of salted peanuts and M&Ms, sparkling water, Coca-Cola, scotch, and champagne. Scott had watched as Jean's eyes lit up at the mention of all the goodies. Then, Annie had presented them with her famous final question, which Scott had heard her ask before going grocery shopping his entire life: *"Anything else?"* When he was little, the question overwhelmed him, and his mind would often go blank. Then, in his teenage years, he was ready for it and listed off a dozen items of junk food with pride. Now, he observed Jean wrestle with the open-ended invitation. As she bit her lower lip and shifted her eyes side to side, Scott watched Annie turn her attention to him. He had been ready. *"Reese's Pieces and popcorn—in case we have a movie night."* Annie had immediately given him a knowing glance that said, *Good point* and written the items down. Then, Jean had said, "I can't think of anything."

This had prompted Annie to prod and poke, forcing Jean to add something, until the young woman finally said, *"I would never turn down Sprite with Maraschino cherries."* The old lady had tittered at that, saying, *"Oh, that's easy, dear! You're still young at heart. Love it!"* And she had added them to the list, ending with a resounding tap of the pen on the pad before tearing the sheet of paper off and handing it to Scott.

Now, lists in pocket, he stood and stretched his arms to the ceiling. "I should be able to make it back in two hours."

"I want you focused on the road on the way over, but you check in the moment you pull into the parking lot, sir."

"Yes, Gram," he said.

"While you are out, we'll get Jean settled all the way in, and then I'll try to radio the neighbors."

They were all moving toward the foyer.

"But, before you head out, would you please bring in some wood for tonight and tomorrow?"

"Sure—"

"I could get it," Jean said. "That way, he can leave right away. My shower can wait."

"Oh, wouldn't dream of having you do that," said Annie. "You go ahead and get upstairs and relax."

They reached the foyer and stopped.

"No, I insist," Jean said. "The weather is only going to get worse, and the sooner Scott leaves, the better." And it was now she who gave his grandmother a coltish tap on the shoulder. "A nice little workout would do me some good, too. Then, I will have earned my shower."

Okay, I like her, Scott thought.

Annie, seemingly taken off guard by having someone else leverage spunkiness and wit on her, said, "Well, dear, if you want to . . ."

"I do."

"I'll be right back," Scott said, dashing back toward the living room.

He returned half a minute later with a canvas log carrier that had two leather looped handles. "Here's the beast," he said, handing the carrier to Jean.

She took it without hesitation and asked Annie, "How much do you need?"

Scott grabbed his coat, hat, and gloves from the front closet and started to put them on.

"I think if you brought in twenty-four logs, we'd have more than enough to keep the fire going tonight and tomorrow."

"I can usually get five or six logs in the carrier at a time," Scott said, zipping up his coat. "Did you see where the wood is stacked?"

"The firewood port is on the side of the pole barn closest to the house, right?"

"Yeah."

Annie reached down and picked up her Sorel Caribou Waterproof Pac Boots and then handed them to Jean. "Use these."

"Thanks," said Jean, and Scott watched as she slid her feet into the boots. "Toasty."

"You're heading out into the real winter now," Annie said, "That's deep snow on the yard you'll be walking across to get to the firewood."

Jean walked to the closet and grabbed her coat.

Scott smiled inwardly as he saw her pull her hat, gloves, and scarf out of the coat's left arm; she told him she had seen that he had stowed his hat and gloves in the left arm of his jacket earlier and had remarked that it was a good idea.

After adjusting his hat, he said, "All right, you both be safe. Gram, I'll call you when I arrive."

Annie gave him a hug and then a kiss on the cheek, and he turned to leave.

"Be safe," Jean said, zipping up her coat.

He gave her a nod of thanks, held her stare for a moment, and then headed out into the storm.

Two steps across the porch and he was already starting to think about her.

PART II
Drifts

10

Sitting on her bed, Jean rubbed her stockinged feet, both hands working on one foot at a time. Her feet were not cold, but they were stiff after having been laced in tight to the boots she had worn outside to fetch firewood. She saw her rosy cheeks and nose in the mirror above the dresser as she exhaled in exertion and then concentrated on her right foot, grasping all five toes in one hand and bending them back and forth. She did the same with her left foot until she could wiggle all ten toes freely.

And I was only out there for fifteen minutes, she thought.

Annie had supervised her while Jean made a neat stack of wood next to the hearth and then welcomed Jean inside after her final trip to the firewood port with a mug of hot tea. Even the coldest winter she had experienced in New York City was no match for what she had just faced outside. She cupped her hands and blew warm air into them, and then gently rubbed her nose and cheeks. On the bedside table next to her charging cellphone was the cup of tea, and she slid over on the bed and picked it up, feeling the warmth of the ceramic mug.

After a few rejuvenating sips, she set the mug down and tapped her phone's screen.

She had a text message . . . from Urian.

She checked her charge: 97%

Jean twisted her wrist, and her smartwatch's screen illuminated—it was 47% charged. She unstrapped it and placed it on the watch charger she had plugged in next to her phone's charger. Maintaining close-to-fully-charged accessories gave her great comfort, and since the rest of the night was uncertain—*it is uncertain, isn't it?*—she wanted fewer things to have to worry about if circumstances arose later that demanded her attention. Even though she had convinced herself otherwise, a voice inside her mind whispered that tonight would be the one time that Annie's reliable generator didn't work, and there would be no way to power her devices. Her rental car? The voice told her it wouldn't start . . . no, better yet, she wouldn't even be able to get to it. Same for Annie's vehicle and Scott's truck. The power was going out, and she and Scott would be carrying in firewood morning, noon, and night for the next week . . .

She let out a soft laugh. *Calm down, girl. None of that is going to happen.*

Being prepared and organized was a way of life for the young advertising executive. In an unfamiliar setting with unfamiliar co-habitants, she leaned on her habits and, unfortunately, her vein of paranoia. Although the more time she spent with Annie and Scott, the more she felt her guard lowering, which relaxed her. Thinking of Annie, Jean was supposed to meet her downstairs after a quick shower to help her make homemade bread to go with their chili for dinner tonight.

But now, an important person in her everyday life, Urian, had entered the picture, interrupting her mind's loop of dread, and she was curious to see what he had written to her. She unplugged the phone, moved the protective case's rubber tab back over the outlet, and then opened the message.

Hey! R U okay? Nasty weather in "Middle America." lol
It better clear by 12/26!

At first, there was a swirl of butterflies in her stomach, knowing that he had checked in on her. It was not out of the ordinary for co-workers, who were friends like they were, to reach out over vacations, but this was different because she was going to visit him. *He's thinking about me,* she said to herself. *He knows I fly out on the 27th and that I need to be back home by the 26th to get ready.* She smiled, liking the direction this was headed. Could she do without the "Middle America" comment? Yes, but he wasn't from the United States, and she figured that anyone who had been born into wealth like he had and now lived as an elite in his adopted country was bound to appropriate pejorative statements expressed by fellow elites. She wondered, *If I had not just met Annie and Scott and experienced their warmth and genuine natures, would I be typing the same thing if I were in Urian's shoes?*

She didn't like the answer that came to mind. She inhaled, held her breath for a few seconds, exhaled, and then typed:

Thanks for checking in! Flights for today cancelled but the 27th is still a go—certain that the weather will clear in the next day or so. Everything good with you?

There were immediate bubbles, and she waited until the message came through.

Things here are PERFECT . . . except, there's no YOU. Guest suite already prepared for your arrival—Iris! There's no stopping her.

Jean searched her memory . . . *Iris was . . . right, Urian's family's maid.* In her mind, she could see the guest suite: fresh flowers, superior bath towels made of Turkish cotton—extra absorbent and plush, a new honeysuckle-scented candle burning, a bottle of champagne chilling in an ice bucket, plantation shutters with a view of the sea, varnished wood and stone masonry everywhere . . .

There were footsteps in the hallway, followed by a knock at her door. Annie said, "Jean, I've just placed a bag of Epsom salt outside your door in case you want to take a bath."

How sweet. She looked over at her suitcase. *I need to get cleaned up and help her with dinner.* "Thank you," she answered. Her phone vibrated, and she looked down at the screen.

What hotel R U staying at? Do they even have hotels there? Haha

Jean's eyes surveyed the beautiful room she was staying in. She could tell Annie had decorated it with care. It looked lived-in and inviting. Her eyes stopped at the door, and she envisioned the bag of Epsom salt on the other side. She started typing.

Staying at my late grandmother's best friend's log cabin— BETTER than a hotel.

He answered:

If you say so!

There were bubbles again for a few seconds, followed by:

All right: Stay safe, Merry Christmas. Let me know when U R headed back to NYC . . . and then across the pond. Excited to host U.

Good, he's signing off. Although Jean didn't want the conversation to end, she didn't want to keep Annie waiting. When texting with subordinates at work, she always made a point to be clear that she was signing off, so that the person on the other end did not feel any pressure to keep texting due to the power imbalance. Even though Urian would be hosting her at his home, which would soften some of those junior-senior boundaries, she still felt uncomfortable ending their communications before he did. She typed

Thanks.   You too.   I'll text when I leave Michigan. Looking forward to the vacation.

and hit send.

A few seconds later, he liked the comment—she also had a habit of liking whatever a subordinate said last to solidify the end of their exchange. She plugged her phone back in and walked toward the door. She would take a shower now, but thought that a bath tomorrow morning might be nice. Then, an image of a man appeared in her mind, which surprised her. It was not Urian.

It was Scott.

As she opened the door and picked up the bag, she wondered how he was doing on his trip to the store.

11

It was five-thirty p.m. when Annie saw the headlights of Scott's Ford Raptor appear in the driveway. The sun had set almost half an hour ago, and the blizzard outside was even more intense, the wind howling. She sat back in her recliner and said, "Here he comes."

"Thank. God," Jean replied, entering the formal living room from the kitchen where she had just put their empty mugs of tea in the dishwasher.

She reminds me so much of her, Annie thought. *It's like I've traveled back in time and am spending an afternoon with my old friend—her mannerisms, her tall, slender frame, the way she moves, the way she speaks.* Not for the first time in the past few hours, she lifted her chin until she could see the ceiling and mouthed, *I miss you.*

While they were preparing to make homemade bread earlier, Annie had almost cried in the kitchen when Jean had put on Shirley Ruth's apron in nearly the same way that Annie's best friend had for the sixty years that they had cooked and baked together. Feeling the hot tears release down her cheeks, she had turned away from Jean and started walking toward the hallway, saying over her shoulder, *"A quick restroom visit, and then we'll start."* As soon as she had closed the bathroom door and turned on the fan, she had sobbed.

Annie watched as Jean stopped and stood next to her recliner, peering out the bay window at the approaching vehicle. "It looks like he'll make it all the way in. I'll get dressed," Jean said, and Annie rose and followed her to the foyer.

Just over an hour ago, Scott had called her and said that his trip had been successful. The mall had been mostly empty, with stores starting to let employees go home early while maintaining a skeleton crew to stay on until close. Meijer had been a different story. *"It was packed,"* her grandson had said. *"Every aisle was a battle to get around people and grab what we needed. By the time I reached the checkout line, many of the shelves were almost empty. I've never seen that. The parking lot was becoming a nightmare, but I parked far enough away from the store to avoid the mess. A bunch of vehicles were arriving as I was leaving. I hope they can get in and get out fast—this is one bastard of a storm."*

"Scottie!"

"Oh, sorry, Gram."

She told him that she had successfully made contact with the neighbors and that so far, everyone still had power. *"Their CB radios are on, and they are charging their hand-helds. We tried to do radio checks, but as you suspected, the storm has decreased the effective range."* Forty-five minutes later, he had called her back and told her that he was making progress but that traffic was heavy and a few cars had already been abandoned on the side of the road. *"I got lucky about ten minutes ago and slid into a gas station that only had a few vehicles in line. I topped off and, fingers crossed, I should be back to you in around fifteen minutes."* There had been a pause, and then he had asked, *"How's Jean doing?"* Grinning at the question, Annie had moved out of earshot of Jean and told him that she was fine. *"Brought in a bunch of firewood, had a shower, and helped me make homemade bread for dinner. Nice girl, Scottie, don't you think?"* There had been another pause before he replied, *"Yes. Definitely. I'll see you both soon."*

She had hung up the phone, tapped her palm playfully with it, and thought, *He likes her.*

They entered the foyer, and Annie turned on every outside light imaginable—the porch lights, the pole barn lights, the garage lights, and the Christmas lights, which Scott had hung for her during his last visit. In a minute, Jean had on her coat, scarf, gloves, hat, and Annie's Sorel boots. With a clap of her gloves, the young woman said, "Ready."

"Okay," said Annie, turning her attention to the driveway. Scott's Raptor came to a stop, and she opened the front door. "Be safe, but be quick. The less time out there, the better."

"Will do." Jean exited, and Annie closed the door behind her.

Then, she watched as Jean made her way through the falling snow and gusting wind to the truck, where she greeted Scott as he opened the driver's side door. Less than a minute later, they began to trudge through the knee-deep drifts toward the porch, grocery bags hanging from their gloved hands.

Annie waited in her Christmas room, and soon the door slid open and Scott slipped in, his socks sinking into the lush carpeting; in her grandson's arms were three large bags. She closed the door behind him and followed him to the couch. He was still wearing his coat, gloves, scarf, and hat, and his cheeks and nose were red from the cold.

"Did she see you?" Annie asked.

"No, I waited until she had started unloading the groceries and placing them on the counter. Then, I hurried back to the truck and brought these bags in, which I had hidden on the front passenger seat floor underneath a blanket."

Annie grinned. "Good boy. Now, help her with the groceries. You know where everything goes. I'll take care of all of this in a snap, and then we'll eat dinner."

"Got it," he said, leaning over and then kissing his grandmother's left cheek.

"Oh!" she said, feeling his cold lips touch her skin. "You need to warm up."

"The weather's getting worse. I may need to lend a hand out there tonight." He moved toward the door. "We'll talk about it over dinner."

The door rolled open and then closed. He was gone.

Annie emptied the contents of each bag onto the sofa and arranged the gifts. Scott had done well.

The left-hand cushion held the stocking stuffers for Jean: hand lotion, two packs of gum, a tin of mints, a 3-pack of ChapStick, a family-sized bag of M&Ms, a deck of playing cards, a few travel-sized tubes of scented hand sanitizer, and a candle.

The middle cushion held the items Scott had picked up from Barnes & Noble: a leather journal, a leather bookmark, a fountain pen, and three more important items: a book, a CD, and a DVD.

The tradition that she and Shirley Ruth had established decades ago was to have a Christmas gift exchange as close to Christmas as possible. For many years, it was on Christmas or Christmas Eve, but at other times, when those days were not possible, they would always adjust to make it work. When life was busy with raising children, they would exchange gifts after school before breaking for the holiday, or when they lived far away from each other, they would mail the gifts to each other—the constant always being that they exchanged three gifts and exactly three gifts: a book, an album of music (record, then 8-track, then cassette tape, and then CD), and a film (Betamax, then LaserDisc, then VHS, and then DVD).

Annie did not know what Jean's particular tastes were. She had probed Jean's mom when she had reached out to get Jean's height, weight, and sweater size, but Lori had been unable to provide any help, saying, after a long pause,

"Oh, you know, she's at that age when her tastes are constantly changing. I can't keep up with them anymore." Annie accepted the answer, choosing not to question any further. Still, her impression was that Lori was hiding behind the loose statements, hoping that Annie would not discover that Lori didn't know any of Jean's tastes.

And so, she had abandoned the idea of a nostalgic gift exchange. That is, until she saw Jean in person, and perhaps divine intervention led her to decide to spend the night. At that moment, Annie had decided to take a risk and have Scott purchase the three items. Not knowing what Barnes & Noble would have in stock, she had given him a few options for each item. Looking at the book, CD, and DVD on the couch cushion, he had been able to purchase all three from the list.

The book. *Didion & Babitz* by Lili Anolik. It had just come out and was on her bedside table. Yes, it was about two free and brilliant crusaders—two true artists, two rivals, two feuding titans at the height of their powers—who had given humanity a critical assessment of the world seen through their lenses; Eve Babitz's lens: her experiences, Joan Didion's lens: a cool, semi-removed, prudent, and exacting observer. Babitz had passed away on December 17, 2021, at age 78; Didion had died less than a week later on December 23, 2021, at the age of 87. Even their ages at the time of death suggested a reciprocal relationship—flip the seven with the eight and you get eighty-seven. Annie and Shirley Ruth began reading the works of both literary giants in the sixties and seventies and had devoured every new work since then, but there was something more profound about the pick. One of the women, Babitz, seemed to be well-known, her novels being not-so-veiled tellings of her own life, and Anolik's first biography of her, *Hollywood's Eve*, had given the reader an immersive experience—an eyewitness-like account of the subject's exploits, maneuvers, and reflections.

Didion had remained elusive, an enigma—*who was she?*—until now.

Anolik had been given access to a stack of sealed boxes found in Babitz's apartment after Babitz had died. And in those boxes were diary-like letters that, at long last, gave a peek into the previously impenetrable core of Didion, one of the twentieth and early twenty-first centuries' greatest writers. For once, it was someone close—and of a similar age—to her who wielded the magnifying glass and provided a firsthand impression. Letters, physical pieces of paper—those beautiful capturings of emotional discharges, penned under the condition of immediacy and fueled by feeling. Janet Malcolm had once written in *The Silent Woman*:

Letters are the great fixative of experience. Time erodes feeling. Time creates indifference. Letters prove to us that we once cared. They are the fossils of feeling. This is why biographers prize them so: they are biography's only conduit to unmediated experience.

Annie had, of course, discovered this passage in Anolik's *Hollywood's Eve*, but now it carried even more weight and triggered a melancholy feeling in her. Shirley Ruth, for all her reading life and career as a teacher of reading and writing, had never taken up the pen outside of her profession. There were no physical Shirley Ruth letters. There were only oral letters, listened to during conversations and then filed away by Annie, the keeper of her best friend's memories, experiences, and views. And, until Jean had agreed to stay over, Annie had thought that those spoken letters would die with her. Peering down at the book on the couch cushion, she now confirmed that she had changed course. She wanted Jean to know who her grandmother had been. The question nagging Annie was: *Would Jean be interested?* A part of her, the part that knew Shirley Ruth and saw flashes of her in her granddaughter, believed that Jean would. And so, she had decided that the book, and the approach of the biographer—examining a vault of never-seen-before letters—might spark Jean's interest in the worlds of two of Annie's and Shirley Ruth's favorite writers and might, just might, serve as a subtle hint to Jean, nudging her to ask questions about a wonderful, eccentric woman whom she did not know. Fortunately, *immediacy* and, both fortunately and unfortunately, *time* were on Annie's side: Jean was here, in Annie's house, confined to it by the storm, and both because the storm and Annie would not last forever, and the chances were slim that they would spend any time together in person ever again, Jean might possess the awareness to see the proverbial sand in the hourglass slipping away.

The ironic events surrounding the book's release also influenced her decision to write it down on the paper she gave Scott as her number one choice to purchase. A culminating literary deep-dive event had become the provenance of everlasting loss. Annie and Shirley Ruth had been eagerly anticipating the book's release. Taking the lead as always, Annie had proposed a new book club approach for, perhaps, the final meditation on the two writers who had given texture and depth to the Golden State—particularly Los Angeles—and its people and had shaped a generation's views on a host of issues; the period in which the books were written had also played a role in a particularly formative stretch in Annie's and Shirley Ruth's lives. It only seemed proper, a foregone conclusion, that they should weigh, consider, and wrestle with the concluding reflection together.

Because they both lived alone, Annie had invited Shirley Ruth to stay with her from Tuesday, when the book came out, until Friday. They would read a chapter at a time and then discuss it. Meals, drinks, and snacks had been discussed, agreed to, and planned; Annie had made herself a list to ensure that the guest room was prepared to her friend's specifications—Shirley Ruth was picky, and it was for this reason . . . and the fact that Annie could be overbearing, overprepared, and well, "a bit too much" in her friend's words, that they had decided to not move in together. A five-mile separation was the perfect distance, although they saw each other almost every other day and spoke on the phone at least twice a day. However, under the shared desire to read and unpack *Didion & Babitz* together, they were unified in their belief that they could and *should* co-exist under the same roof for 4 days.

To prepare for the new book, they had been rereading everything written by both authors, as well as everything written about them since the August announcement in *Publishers Weekly*. After having lost their husbands, both within the past five years, they held a healthy respect for the sanctity of time, knowing that tomorrow was not guaranteed. *In all likelihood, this will be our final book club,* Annie had thought. She had felt Shirley Ruth's unspoken agreement in her friend's pauses when the subject came up during the late summer and early fall phone calls.

In late September, the leaves began to change color, and anticipation rose in the hearts of the two lifelong friends.

The book was scheduled for release on November 12th.

Everything was set . . .

Then, at nine o'clock on Tuesday, October 1st, 6 weeks before the release of *Didion & Babitz*, Shirley Ruth did not answer Annie's daily morning phone call—they also spoke every night at seven p.m.—and after repeated calls until nine thirty, Annie drove to her friend's home. When Shirley Ruth failed to answer the door after Annie's incessant knocking and doorbell ringing, Annie used her copy of Shirley Ruth's house key to open the door.

Her fear rose when she did not smell the aroma of morning coffee. Shirley Ruth prepared it the night before so that all she had to do was push the "start" button in the morning. Additionally, Annie did not hear the telltale notes of jazz music playing—Shirley Ruth usually started the day with the likes of Dave Brubeck, Miles Davis, or Diana Krall if it was a slow-moving morning and played exclusively Bossa Nova if she felt a pep to her step or had a busy day ahead and needed an infusion of energy to "get up and go." After calling out her friend's name, she entered the kitchen and opened the top of the coffee maker . . . the glassy surface of the water and the dry filter filled with fresh grounds stared back at her. She closed the top and moved to Shirley Ruth's first-floor bedroom door, which was closed. *Maybe she slept in or slipped on the bathroom floor and needed help.*

She cracked the door open . . .

. . . and found her friend in bed, nestled under the covers and wearing the rose-colored nightgown that Annie had made for her years ago. After one chin-vibrating utterance of her friend's first name and no response, Annie knew. The hearing of no breath, the seeing of no rise in her friend's chest, and the feeling of no pulse on Shirley Ruth's cold neck were formalities, confirmations of what she had already accepted. The arrival of the paramedics and the attempts to revive her lifelong ally, her other half, her rock, and her eternal confidant were a blur to her now.

One thing was not:

Her mind's snapshot of Shirley Ruth's bedside table.

The antique lamp, the thin-framed glasses, the picture of her family taken decades ago when they had gathered for, perhaps the last time before truths blew them apart, the cell phone—plugged in with a full charge, revealing dozens of missed calls from Annie when Annie tapped the screen—the cream-colored Stanley filled with ice water, and . . . two books: *The Year of Magical Thinking* and *Blue Nights*, both by Joan Didion.

Annie's breathing became irregular, and she wiped tears from the corners of each eye. Looking at the cover of *Didion & Babitz* and then at the Christmas room's ceiling, she said, "It's a perfect book. You would have loved it." She shook her head in frustration. The tears slowed, and she dabbed the corners with her fingers until she got her breathing under control. Her eyes moved down to the CD on the cushion.

The Tony Bennett Bill Evans Album.

It was the riskiest and most specific item of music she had listed. Her other two fallbacks were generalizations—"anything by Sinatra" and "anything by Ella

Fitzgerald"—but, ever since Tony Bennett had passed away in the summer of 2023 at the age of ninety-six, there had been the usual re-issue of his life's works, and brick and mortar stores like Barnes & Noble had tried to catch lightning in a bottle by stocking their shelves with all of his albums. The sad news, she realized, was that if Tony had not died, there would have been zero chance that stores would have carried old albums like *The Tony Bennett Bill Evans Album*, no matter how sublime the music. She and Shirley Ruth had listened to that particular album one summer when their families had vacationed together in the Upper Peninsula, and it had become a favorite. And, like the book she had chosen to present to Jean, the album's duo served as a loose metaphor for Annie and her best friend. Bill Evans and Tony Bennett should not have been able to put together the album that they did, but people often forgot that a handful of *supreme* artists were able to put their egos aside and *listen* to one another, accommodating each other by making certain allowances, and that is exactly what the two men had done in the mid-1970s, when disco was in and classic nightclub songs, sung by Bennett, Sinatra, etc. while accompanied by jazz pianists, were under assault. Annie and Shirley Ruth had *listened* to each other and put up with each other since they had met. The rough edges had smoothed over the years into a mature friendship, one of trust where one-time accommodations had become gestures of care and rejuvenation. Friendships became special when doing more for the other person brought greater joy than doing something for oneself. And, for a time, that philosophy had transcended their camaraderie and extended to their families as the two of them dreamed and thought about the future, akin to operating under the ancient Greek proverb that stated: *A society grows great when old men plant trees whose shade they know they shall never sit in.*

Then, one day, it all stopped, and the dreams and hopes had contracted, eventually dwindling to disappointment and survival.

Looking back now, Annie shouldn't have worried about the music. Jazz was more popular than ever; disco—even with John Travolta's fusion-like power plant lighting the '70s music and dance scene—had basically gone the way of the dodo, minus a small cult that thought the '70s had never ended, but even they were overshadowed by the cult that thought the '60s had never ended.

She allowed herself a short laugh, knowing that a part of her would always belong to the sixties and its music and culture. She had been nineteen in 1960 when JFK was elected and felt the historical swerve toward a new and exciting future. Then, three years later, on that fateful late November day, she had felt the enthusiasm and innocence ripped out of her, replaced by a decade of skepticism, strife, and moral uncertainty. Then, in the summer of 1975, a film based on a bestselling novel sent shockwaves through the film industry and the country. So far, the first five years of the decade had been downbeat, full of doubt and cynicism, and represented on the silver screen by a host of anti-heroes, trying to navigate a decaying America. The country needed a summer escape, a piece of popular art to help lower the nation's temperature and provide a communal bonding experience . . .

. . . and the DVD of the film that had accomplished all that rested on an angle on the center cushion's far right, the edge of the rectangular package threatening to submerge into the crack between the center and right-hand cushions.

Jaws.

The first summer blockbuster—a film that had united the viewing public through the universal emotion of fear—fear of the water, fear of the unknown, fear of being torn to shreds by an apex predator in the apex predator's environment. And, there was a secondary terror in the undercurrent of the title: the fear of being ripped apart and destroyed by other human beings.

However, perhaps the two greatest gifts the film had given a pessimistic America were, one) shining a spotlight on the music of then little-known composer John Williams and, through exploiting the usually quiet theatrical period during the summer months, two) providing a viable business model that nudged studios to give young film talent coming out of colleges like USC and UCLA an opportunity to make films that had the potential to reach younger audiences. Yet, the real gift came two years later when these two presents combined to give the world *Star Wars*, which Annie and Shirley Ruth had seen twice in the local theater, and Hollywood had never been the same since.

The trivia, tidal wave of change, and matrix of causes and effects surrounding *Jaws* and the decade during which it was released were enticing reasons for Annie to select it, as was the fact that she still thought it was Spielberg's best film, as was the fact that it had a high probability of being on the shelf at Barnes & Noble due to its classic status, continuing popularity, and the fiftieth anniversary right around the corner.

Additionally, she could have chosen it for nostalgic reasons related to home video equipment. If Annie had one vice it was her determination to create a cinema in her own home, and so, on December 14th of 1978, she had driven all the way to Atlanta, Georgia with Shirley Ruth and purchased Philips's Magnavox VH-8000 consumer laser disc player, which had been released on December 11th, for a whopping $749.

Why had she waited four days to purchase the player?

Because the first-ever LaserDisc (then called DiscoVision) movie, released to coincide with the player's debut, was . . .

Jaws . . .

. . . and it didn't hit the market until December 15th—efficiency was *sometimes* paramount to her. After purchasing the player and film, she and Shirley Ruth drove through the night and arrived back home in Midland early on the 16th.

Before the trip, their husbands had shown some concern about them driving to Atlanta and staying a night, but Annie remembered Shirley Ruth leaning forward at Annie's kitchen table and saying to John and Martin, *"Boys, both of us ladies have PhDs, concealed weapon permits, and have each birthed two children. Nothin' we can't handle on a little jaunt down I-75 and back. But . . . your instincts are right. There is some concern at this table."* She looked at Annie and then back at the men. *"We are a bit worried about you two being able to handle taking care of the kids."* Then, she had given the most wicked smile Annie had ever seen. *"We suggest you all stay under one roof and tag-team the assignment."* Both men had swallowed, made quick eye contact with each other, and then looked away. Grinning back at Shirley Ruth, Annie added, *"I think they've got it in them,"* and gave her husband, John, a half-serious tap on the forearm. The conversation had ended at that point, and the men had survived the three days chasing after the six-, five-, three-, and two-and-a-half-year-olds.

They all stayed the night at Annie's, and, after they had put their children to bed, the adults watched *Jaws* that evening with popcorn and a bottle of red and a bottle of white in honor of Richard Dreyfuss's character Matt Hooper who, when showing up unexpectedly at the Brody's house right after dinner, on the heels of what Annie thought was one of the most brilliant scenes in the history of cinema, says, "I got, uh, red and white—I didn't know what you'd be serving."

Even though Annie would eventually add a VHS player and amass a vast video library over the years, she also remained loyal to her LaserDisc player and rack of LaserDisc films. When the final movie to be released on LaserDisc, *Bringing Out the Dead*, came out on October 3, 2000, she had pouted in the car on the way home from the store. She had never minded flipping a disc over to side two for the second half of a film or inserting disc number two into the machine for a longer film. What she did not like was *change*. The irony of the final film's title, in terms of her hope for a LaserDisc resurgence, a comeback one day, was not lost on her.

Annie had selected *Jaws* as a gift for Jean for none of those reasons.

She had selected it because of the summer of 1975 . . . and what it had started. Yes, *Jaws* had come out on June 20th that summer, and Annie, Shirley Ruth, John, and Martin had all gone to see it together in Midland's Stadium Cinema 1 & 2 in the Stadium Plaza Shopping Center. And as grand an event as it was, it had only set the table for a summer that none of them would ever forget. After celebrating July 4th at home, both families decided to try vacationing together, as there was mutual friendship between the four adults, and their kids had fun playing together. However, living next door in a rustic vacation spot for a month was a different experience altogether. Still, they all agreed to give it a go. The question then became: *Where* would they go? During the school year, Annie and Shirley Ruth had heard from their good friend and fellow teacher, Bob Sympkins, about Curtis, Michigan, a small community in Mackinac County within Portage Township.

Sympkins taught social studies across the hall from Annie and had been part of hers and Shirley Ruth's doctoral cohort at Central Michigan University, located around thirty miles away in Mt. Pleasant, Michigan. The three were from Midland and had started teaching at Midland's H.H. Dow High School after graduating from Central Michigan with their Bachelor's degrees and teaching certificates. However, for the next half a dozen years, the three commuted to Central and took graduate classes until they had all achieved their Master's and PhD degrees. Then, they did something that no one expected: They all stayed at H.H. Dow instead of becoming college professors. The three believed they were making a difference at the high school level and wanted to have families instead of hopping on the seven-year-publish-or-perish tenure treadmill, knowing that tenure would be difficult to attain with babies and toddlers at home. And so the three, with their advanced degrees, helped to bolster Midland's status as the city with the highest concentration of PhDs per capita in the United States, and also became a team within a team on H.H. Dow's faculty.

Sympkins vacationed in a cottage on Houghton Lake during the summer, but had family who lived near Curtis. He told Annie and Shirley Ruth that it was a gem of a retreat in the summer, thanks to the surrounding lakes and remoteness. *"Curtis doesn't even have any legally defined boundaries, but it does have cabins for rent on some of the lakes, and it has a post office. It's the ultimate escape if you like water sports, fishing, hiking, and peace and quiet,"* he had said. *"On the drive north, bring a cooler and stock up on groceries in St. Ignace—it's only an hour drive away from the cabins. Then, when you're up there, Newberry is only twenty miles away from Curtis, and they have everything you need, including a nice IGA."*

So, on Friday, July 11th, Annie and John had loaded up J.J. and Michelle in their brand new 1975 Dodge Coronet Crestwood Station Wagon—a car that would be their family's chariot for another ten years—and Shirley Ruth and Martin had loaded up Lori and Brett in their 1970 GMC Jimmy, and they all headed north for the three-and-a-half-hour drive to the two side-by-side cabins they had rented on Big Manistique Lake in Curtis. It would be the start of a sixteen-year summer tradition, which Annie considered the best years of her life.

Then, everything had changed.

Annie's Echo was silent for a beat, and then "(There's No Place Like) Home for the Holidays" by Perry Como came on. She thought of Scott. Curtis was a little under an hour away from his home in Munising, and this past summer, he had stopped by the old vacation site and reported to her that the cabins were gone. *"Guy up there told me that no one was renting them anymore, and I guess the person who owned the property they were on sold it. A few summers ago, the new owners demolished the cabins. Now there's a beautiful new home where they used to be—nice beach there too. I can see why you liked staying there. Fifty yards out the back porches, and you were at the water's edge."*

Annie closed her eyes, memories appearing and disappearing . . . Como's joyful lyrics filling her ears . . . She fought back tears and then opened her eyes. Spying the extra stocking she had set aside for Jean, along with the wrapping paper, scissors, tape, and string she had laid out on the couch earlier, Annie grabbed the first present and started to wrap it.

12

As Jean savored the last spoonful of chili in her mouth, she saw that there was still enough at the bottom of the bowl for her to mop up with the remainder of her piece of homemade bread, which was still warm in her hand. She swallowed and then scooped out the rest of the serving as if she were behind a pottery wheel, carving her masterpiece.

"Anyone want seconds?" asked Annie.

Scott chewed on his final piece of bread and shook his head no.

Holding the bread, soaked in chili, Jean said, "No, thank you." Seeing Annie frown, she added, "But that doesn't mean I won't want a little later."

Annie gave Scott a look that, to Jean, said, *That's the answer I was looking for,* and replied, "Perfect, my dear. I'll leave the crockpot on low."

Scott took a drink of his Coke and added, "I'll probably have some later, too, Gram." He rose, collected everyone's bowls and spoons, and headed toward the kitchen.

Jean watched as Annie took a sip of her bottle of beer and beamed at Scott as he entered the kitchen. Then, barely audible above the roar of the fire in the hearth, she heard the sound of the dishes being rinsed off in the sink and then put into the dishwasher.

There had been little conversation over dinner as the three of them devoured their meal; Jean had experienced a different kind of hunger after working outside in the freezing temperatures. The heat coming from the fireplace seemed to work in unison with the hot chili and warm bread, thawing each part of her body while replenishing the calories she had burned while bringing in the groceries and transporting the firewood from the port to the living room earlier. Other than the compliments to the chef, squeezed in between bites, the only topic of conversation had been the storm and the power. Would it go out? Or, as Scott had put it, "When *would it go out?*"

She was comfortable with the focus being on the storm. For the time being, it put the usual small talk on the back burner. If she stayed here long enough and there was any amount of downtime, then, if Scott was polite and she had no reason to believe that he wasn't, he would inevitably ask her about her work and perhaps her life. Ever since he had departed for the supply run earlier, she had been wondering how she would answer his question about her career. *What I essentially do is work all day to help clients manipulate various swaths of the population into purchasing the client's goods or services—some of which are necessities and helpful—to increase their profit margins.* Depending on how articulate, tactful, and interested he was, he might probe a bit, posing safe, surface-level questions that suggested challenging, deeper concerns about what she did. *Who are some of your clients?* might translate into *How do you sleep at night, knowing that you help push products and services that are harmful to a person's physical and mental health by making them seem necessary or desirable—a sought-after sign of status? Are you comfortable with creating and enabling addiction?* If the conversation went in this direction, she had tailor-made answers at her disposal, all provided to her through previous corporate training and coaching from Chantel. *Our job is not to judge the perceived pleasant vices and virtues of society. We seek only to provide our customers with humane, robust, cutting-edge, and outstanding service. At the same time, in line with our company's ethos and mission statement, we will always support and defend the free will of customers, potential consumers of our clients' goods and services, to make their own choices.* She could deliver these with ease—they were repeated and reinforced so much that they had become a part of her. Pre-programmed responses were insulation, protection—not a display of being callous, lazy, or robotic; no, they were a result of preparation and insight, which is the realm she liked to operate in. However, considering that she was a guest in Annie's home and that Scott was Annie's grandson, she would probably list a few safe companies that her agency did work for and then try to humbly steer the conversation back to Scott's work as a National Park Ranger, which she was genuinely interested in.

Annie had called her neighbors just before dishing up, and both still had electricity. They promised to call if they lost power, and the spirited elder stateswoman, who had downed not one but two beers during dinner—*"A Sam Adams, a beer with a little attitude, now and then is good for the soul!"*—had said that she would call again later this evening to check in.

Jean took a swig from her beer and watched as Scott returned to the living room and sat down on the other side of the couch from her as before. She wouldn't have minded if he had sat closer. *How many beers have I had?* She looked down at the coffee table. *Right, only one.* She spied Scott's can of Coke. *Why didn't he have any beer with dinner? Does he not drink? Does that matter to me?* As she set her bottle down on the table, she decided that it did not matter at all.

A charred log, worn down by the blazing fire in the large brick hearth, fell and sent sparks outward, like fireworks expanding in the sky, as it succumbed to the heat. She enjoyed the warmth coming from the fireplace and volunteered to add a few fresh logs to the fire. Then, Scott's phone rang, and she studied him as he looked at the screen. "State Police," he said, standing up. "I put in a call to them earlier." He said, "Hello . . . Yes, this is Scott Brady," and then walked out of the room.

Her attention turned to Annie, who had walked over to the window and opened the blinds that she had shut before dinner. "Why would he have called the Michigan State Police?" Jean asked, getting up and then joining Annie in front of the window. It was now completely dark outside, and it was even difficult to see the snow falling. There was no moon above and no outside lights on the backside of the house. The wind, however, continued to gust against the glass and shriek as if someone were trapped outside and screaming for help.

"I don't have a good feeling about tonight," Annie said as she closed the blinds and motioned for Jean to follow her. The women exited the great room and entered a narrow hallway, which led to a sitting room at the back of the house, featuring a sliding glass door that opened onto the back deck. After raising the blinds and flipping the light switch, Annie pointed out the door and said, "My God."

Jean stood shocked as the backyard, from ground level to the sky, seemed like one massive white tornado, making it almost impossible to see the towering White Pine trees that lined Annie's property. "It's getting even worse," Jean said. "I can barely make out the tree line."

"This is why he put in the call. If there aren't people trapped in their cars already, there soon will be."

Using the information she had heard earlier when they had run their checklists, Jean said, "Is he going to try and help, using the snowmobile and snowcoach?"

Annie stared out the glass door for a few more beats and then turned off the lights and lowered the blinds. "I think so," she said. "I need to put on coffee."

They returned to the living room and continued to the kitchen. Pointing to a cupboard above the sink, Annie said, "Could you get me down the large thermos up there, dear?"

"Of course." Jean opened the cupboard door and looked up until she saw a green Stanley thermos on the top shelf—she thought it was the one she had seen earlier, but wasn't sure. Getting up on her tiptoes, she then stretched with her long arms, her hands reaching the thermos, and she pulled it down. After closing the cabinet door, she stood, admiring the container. She had an affinity for retro items—sweatshirts, dishes, appliances, anything old-fashioned—and had many items in her condo that were new but made to resemble those from a prior era. However, the large thermos on the counter in front of her right now was not in that category. This object was an original, with a few dents and scratches. Some of the paint was worn, and the long latch was loose, no longer folding to hug the side of the thermos. "Old school," she said. "I like it."

"Reliable," Annie replied, pouring fresh water into the coffee maker. "It's larger than the one I used earlier." She pointed toward a drying rack nestled into a corner of the far counter. There, Jean saw the smaller green thermos.

She heard footsteps in the hallway, and seconds later, Scott entered the kitchen.

"Talk about irony," he said, putting his cell phone into the right-front pocket of his jeans. "In all of my years working at the park, I've never had to rescue anyone. Tonight, it looks like I might get the chance to finally do one of the things I am trained to do."

Annie put the filter in the coffee maker and began scooping out grounds with a plastic measuring cup from a glass jar. "We just peeked outside." She dumped one last scoop into the maker. "What did they have to say?"

He sat down in the same chair behind the counter that he had occupied when they were reviewing the checklists earlier. "That if I were willing to help tonight, they would welcome it."

"M-20?" Annie asked.

"Yes. I think it's the only place I can make a difference. The twenty-plus miles between Midland and Mt. Pleasant is a lot of road to cover, especially when they are focusing their resources on the major highways. There is State Police Post #63 in Mount Pleasant and the Tri-City State Police Post #31 southeast of Midland, which is the post that called me. While we were talking, I put my phone on speaker and then brought up a map of the area to get a sense of the lay of the land. The Mount Pleasant post will most likely be tied up helping people stranded on US-127, although they might dispatch a few personnel to M-20. The Tri-City post will be working M-47, US-10, and I-75, and was unsure if they could dispatch anyone over to M-20. It will probably be a unit or units from the Mt. Pleasant Police Department and Midland Police Department that will work M-20. I already called both departments and gave them my cell phone number and told them that your snowmobile has a CB radio. Channel nine is the emergency channel, and channel nineteen is the channel used by truckers to report on traffic conditions, so I'll keep it on nine and check in on nineteen. The departments are already reaching out to truckers who are still on the road for situation reports. They've been asked to lend a hand if they see a vehicle on the side of the road. With their large cabs, they can bring people inside and transport them to the nearest city or town. If the truck gets stuck, the truckers can at least keep people warm inside the cab for longer until help arrives. So, I'll be working with the police, truckers, and any other volunteers out there tonight."

Annie pushed the "start" button on the coffee maker. "I'll have a full thermos for you in a few minutes."

"Thanks." He brought out his phone and pulled up the map. Then, he put the phone on the counter, and Jean and Annie hovered over it while he pointed and spoke. "The approximate midpoint of M-20 is South Alamondo Road, and right there is the West Midland Family Center that has a food pantry and the Greendale Activity and Dining Center for Seniors. So, if anyone is stranded near the midpoint, we'll try to get them to the Family Center. If anyone is stranded west or east of the midpoint and closer to either Mt. Pleasant or Midland, we'll try to get them to three primary lodging locations the police have identified and selected. The Mt. Pleasant police will try to get anyone far west of Alamondo Road to the Baymont Hotel, which is just on the other side of the Soaring Eagle Casino. I'll be working the area far east of Alamondo Road with a Midland Police unit, and we'll try to transport anyone stranded to the H Hotel in downtown Midland."

Jean watched as he used his thumb and middle finger to zoom in. She was impressed with how calm he was.

"As a backup, there's the Fairfield Inn and Suites by Dow Diamond. For alternate shelters, I was told that there are a few churches off M-20 that could be open. We'll have to see. The police departments still had a bunch of places to call after I got off the phone with them. Firefighters from Midland and Mount Pleasant were being contacted, and posts are being made on all social media outlets to see if anyone with a snowmobile is willing to lend a hand or at least their machine to our first responders." He turned off his phone and leaned back. "The last thing the state police told me was that the governor was in a meeting discussing whether or not to activate the National Guard."

"Do you think Big Gretch will?" Annie asked, using Governor Gretchen Whitmer's nickname that she explained the governor had embraced after Detroit comedy rapper Gmac Cash had bestowed it upon her in a 2020 song.

Scott shrugged.

Jean said, "Do you think any local snowmobile dealerships would help out?"

Using his thumb and middle finger again, Scott zoomed out and then used his index finger to move the map until he had found the desired location. He zoomed in once more and said, "Yes. Stevens' Sport Center in Midland and Stevens' Cycle Sales Incorporated in Bay City have pledged their support. Mickey's Sleds Motorsports has a sled parts department, and the owner is calling his list of customers to see if they are interested in helping." Scott repeated his hand movements on the screen until a section of Mt. Pleasant was centered on the display. "Central Motorsports in Mt. Pleasant is doing the same, as is Snowmobile Salvage. The reason we need a large number of machines, beyond helping stranded travelers on the roads, is for medical reasons. Many people will need medication. Then, you've got all of the medical emergencies that are going to happen—heart attacks, women who go into labor, prescriptions that run out—" he pointed at Annie, "—not everyone is prepared as you are."

"I know," she proudly said.

He stared back at the screen. "It's a complicated problem. You must be able to respond to those medical emergencies, which will require snowmobiles or 4-wheel drive utility vehicles. But, it's all pointless if there's no medical personnel at the hospital when we get the people there." He zoomed out, moved to a new section of the map in Mt. Pleasant, and then zoomed in. "There's McLaren Central Michigan and MyMichigan Medical Center in Mt. Pleasant, and another MyMichigan Medical Center in Midland. Currently, the personnel still at the hospitals are staying there, but we need to transport the off-duty doctors, nurses, and staff members who are at home to the hospitals, which will require vehicles and time. We have to act now because tomorrow doesn't look good at all."

Annie tapped the phone's screen near McLaren Central Michigan. "EMTs are going to have to ride with snowmobilers, but there's another concern I have."

Jean tried to guess what it was. The EMTs would need to bring lifesaving gear. They could wear a large backpack full of equipment, but for larger gear, they would need something like Annie's SnowCoach that they could load up and pull behind the snowmobile, making it a mini-ambulance. Feeling confident in her assessment of the situation, she offered her guess.

"True," Annie replied, "but it's something more important than that."

What could it be? Jean looked at Scott, who also looked puzzled.

After another few beats, he said, "What is it, Gram?"

Jean watched as Annie sat back and looked at both of them. "The internet and GPS."

Scott looked even more confused.

Now that Jean's brain had a piece of data—the words "internet" and "GPS"—she concentrated, thinking about what the words and all of their associations had to do with the EMTs. When the practical connections and possibilities yielded no answers, the creative part of her brain—the part that had come up with some of the best advertising slogans ever—began to tackle the problem, imagining scenarios that would lead her to the solution . . .

A picture came into focus: A woman giving birth on a snowmobile, which had stopped in the middle of the woods, an EMT saying, *"Push!"* while snow fell on his winter hat and his red, frozen nose . . . the snowmobile driver, a big ole country boy with a Duck Dynasty beard and wearing matching Carhartt bibs and jacket, saying, *"Man, this ain't right,"* while taking a sip from a flask . . . and the woman in labor? She was holding a cell phone sideways, watching an episode of *Yellowstone* while screaming in pain. Meanwhile, a GPS satellite in space orbited the planet, while her mind supplied a steady stream of sonar pinging sounds from the original *Star Trek* television series . . .

Damn it! Jean thought. *Why can't I think of the answer?*

She heard laughter and then Scott's voice say, "It's okay. Neither can I."

What happened? Why is he saying that to me? Looking up into his grinning face, she realized that she had said the words out loud. "Oh, my God. I'm sorry."

Annie was laughing, too. Jean joined in.

They must think I'm crazy. I'll prove I'm not. Her mind continued to scroll through possibilities. *Internet . . . EMT . . . GPS . . . Internet . . . EMT . . . GPS . . . Ugh!*

Annie took her and Scott out of their misery and said, "Directions. If the weather disrupts connectivity and weakens the GPS signal, people won't be able to rely on their phones as much. I know that GPS works independently of the internet via satellites and is designed to function in all weather conditions, but we don't know how well it will perform tonight. And I would guess that very few people nowadays actually know their way around their towns and cities, and that doesn't even cover the maze of country roads outside of these areas. Both City Halls and police stations, and all of the hospitals, had better start printing maps and laminating them for backup."

Before she or Scott could ask, Annie said, "I've got maps for both Midland and Mt. Pleasant. She pointed toward the hallway that led to the foyer and beyond. "In the den, I have my stack of local maps. Got one for all the places that Shirley Ruth and I traveled to. Atlases are nice, but having a town or city map is invaluable when you're traveling to a new place. I still remember enough to get around Traverse City, Grand Rapids, Ann Arbor, Charlevoix, and Sault Ste. Marie." She reached over and pulled open a drawer. After rummaging through it for a few seconds, she removed a notepad and pen and started to write while saying, "I'll get those out for you, Scottie, after we chat, so you can study them and then take them with you tonight. I'll also print out a map of M-20 and the surrounding area between the two cities for you to use. Keep that one and the Midland map with you, but give the Mt. Pleasant map to any police officers you see tonight."

"I will." He held up his phone. "We've become so reliant on these things, I never even stopped to think about what we would do for directions without them. Now, I think their built-in GPS will still work tonight—hell, your Grand Touring snowmobile has built-in GPS that I plan on using—but I agree with you: we need backup maps. Relying solely on technology for navigation tonight is not a good idea. I know my park and the surrounding area inside and out because it's my job, but I've gotten used to using my phone for directions to get everywhere else. I even used it tonight. I knew how to get to the mall and Meijer without it, but I like seeing if the road turns yellow or red because of traffic backups, and also the ETA and alternate routes if needed."

Me too, Jean thought, a bit embarrassed. *I help companies make millions of dollars, and I couldn't even see that people navigating the roads and weather tonight might be crippled by the lack of internet—Google Maps, Google Earth, Google everything—and degraded GPS.* "I'm with you, Scott. I'm so used to traveling by foot, cab, or subway in New York City that I didn't even think about driving directions. I know I needed them to get over to my grandmother's house and to get here from the airport today."

Scott gave her a nod of affirmation, or at least she thought it was a nod of affirmation. She was out of her element and did not like struggling to come up with answers. However, she felt no judgment from either Scott or Annie, which was keeping her from panicking.

"The Midland, Mt. Pleasant, and State Police are in the process of deploying a large portion of their force," said Scott. "They established outposts all over the area and then sent a patrol car there with extra gas, food, water, medical supplies, blankets, and as much cold-weather gear as possible. They're on standby for emergency calls, while another portion of the force is loading up snowmobiles and SnowCoaches to rescue stranded travelers and transport hospital personnel back to the hospitals." He stood up. "Okay, I need to get dressed for outdoors."

Annie was now on her feet, and Jean followed suit. "I'll get those maps for you," Annie said. "What else can we do tonight?"

Scott took a step but then stopped, staring at the mantel above the fireplace.

Jean followed his gaze. *What is he looking at?* Her eyes focused on the stockings and the garland with the string of lights twisted around it on the mantle. Then, her eyes moved up, and she saw the gun resting on two large railroad spikes that had been anchored into the brick hearth.

"I'll think about it while I'm getting dressed," Scott said and then pointed to the gun. "You should get that down and load it."

There was no hesitation as Annie said, "Done."

Jean's stomach became queasy, and bile rose in her throat. *What is going on?* She swallowed the bile and took a deep breath. "I'm sorry, did I miss something here? Why is she loading a gun?"

She watched as Scott and Annie exchanged an amused glance, and then Annie said, "Oh, sorry, dear. We didn't mean to startle you. Everything is fine. It's just an extra precaution. Like other natural disasters, sometimes the worst in humanity comes out. This is just to safeguard us against any possible looters. Though they would skip this house anyway because we'll still have power, and I'll keep the lights on. Don't worry, Midland is about as safe as you can get, but I always like to be prepared." She turned to Scott. "Speaking of which, do you have your sidearm?"

"Always," Scott said. "And I'll be carrying it with me tonight. Might be some people out there who would like to take your snowmobile."

"Just be careful, Scottie. Who knows who might be stranded inside a vehicle on the side of the road? Even good people revert to their basic instincts when survival is at stake."

"Nothing I cannot handle," he said. "Just make sure to keep the doors locked."

Jean could not imagine a stranger knocking on the door of her SoHo condo, looking for shelter. She wouldn't answer the door and would call the police if the person didn't leave. Her mind drifted from New York to Michigan. *What about her grandmother's house? Would someone try to break in tonight?* She had read once about firetrucks that had been abandoned in a winter blizzard and were raided by looters, the criminals stealing radios and the brass nozzles on the vehicle's firehoses. If people were willing to do that, then they would be willing to try to take her grandmother's appliances and maybe even strip the place of its copper pipes. Then, she thought of Annie's log cabin and started to envision worst-case scenarios . . . A large man with rough hands and icicles on his beard pounding on the front door and then breaking it down, his eyes wild with hate . . . A humble woman, claiming to need to make a phone call, being let in by Annie, and then pulling a gun on both of them as the two men they didn't see outside came rushing inside the house . . .

"What *do* we do if someone shows up on Annie's front porch, looking for shelter?" she asked.

Scott rubbed his whiskers for a few seconds. "Good question with no right answers," he said. "I think it's doubtful that anyone would show up in the first place. This house is miles away from M-20, which is the only likely place that strangers would come from, looking for shelter. However, if anyone got stranded on M-20 and decided to abandon his or her car to walk down this road looking for shelter, he or she would reach a half dozen houses before getting to this one."

Jean exhaled, feeling better after hearing his logic.

"Still, it would be good to have a plan." Jean watched as he turned his attention to Annie. "Let's keep the pole barn unlocked and heated. We can stock the fridge in there with water and pop. On the workbench, we can stage some nonperishable food, and I'll place some blankets and pillows on the floor. If someone approaches the house tonight, you'll have to make a judgment call on whether you let them inside or not. If you don't feel comfortable, then suggest the pole barn. Then, try to contact me." He peered up at the ceiling for a few moments and then trained his eyes back on Annie's. "What do you think?"

She started with a slow nod that grew into half a dozen quick nods. "I like it." She looked at Jean. "Does that work for you? Are you okay?"

"Good solution. And, yes, I'm fine . . . just not used to being in situations like this."

"We'd all like to think we'd help our fellow human beings, but inviting a stranger into your home is a big decision. I feel responsible for you, dear, but it's impossible for me not to help out someone who is trapped outside and freezing to death, no matter who they might be. There was a time when this wouldn't even be a discussion. I'd help out anyone, and so would everyone I knew. We never locked our doors at night or when we left the house." She lowered her head and shook it back and forth a few times. "I don't know how we ever got to where we're at now, but Scott's right. We have to go with the safe, middle-ground solution tonight."

"Okay, I'm going to get dressed and then I'll prepare the pole barn before I head out."

"I'll gather the supplies for you after I get the maps," said Annie.

"I can help you, Annie," Jean said, pulling her phone out of her pocket. She tapped the screen and saw that she had a text message from Chantel, and suddenly, she was aware of her bladder as the beer had worked its way down. *I'll head upstairs, use the restroom, check the text quickly, and then head back here to help.* "I'll be right back," she said, looking up from the screen.

Annie and Scott had already left the kitchen.

Jean headed for the stairs.

After using the bathroom, she sat on the edge of her bed and opened the message from Chantel. Above the text was a picture of her boss, wearing a bikini and a straw hat, and sipping from a fruity cocktail. Jean "liked" the image and then read the text.

It's hotter here than where U R at! Urian told me: snowed in . . . and staying in a LOG CABIN with the elderly?! Get out of there and get 2 Greece!

Jean tapped the message to reply, but then stopped, her right index finger hovering above the digital keyboard. The reality that people would be stranded all across Michigan and that first responders would be risking their lives to help them made her cringe at Chantel's picture and tone-deaf message. She regretted "liking" the image, but she couldn't take it back now, as Chantel would already have received a notification, which meant that she would know that Jean had seen her text message.

If I don't respond, she'll think something is wrong, which will invite more communication, and I don't want any more communication with her or Urian right now.

She felt anger and was both surprised and not surprised at the raw emotion. Jean had always believed that people whose lives were not directly impacted by a natural disaster would watch footage of it online, be moved or not, by the death and destruction, but the event would soon leave their minds, replaced by new clickbait. In a minute, the disturbing footage could be five clicks and five stories in the past. On one hand, she couldn't be too mad at Chantel and Urian. How many times had she learned of a natural disaster and forgotten about it minutes later? On the other hand, should her two bosses have shown concern for her safety? Yes.

She thought for a few more seconds and then typed:

Definitely warmer where you are. Yes—snowed in and safe in a beautiful log cabin. Grateful. Huge storm not letting up . . . hoping to get to Greece later this week. Enjoy the sunshine.

There, I said I was safe, which will maybe prompt her to reflect a little bit.

Jean looked back at what she had written, which was an unhealthy habit she had—the grinding of her teeth and the squinting of her eyes as she re-read messages, hoping to find clarity, hoping for relief, and hoping not to see any errors.

She found none, but reading the words "hoping to get to Greece" made her cock her head to one side and purse her lips. *Do I still feel this way?*

Yes?

Maybe?

No?

There were no bubbles from Chantel.

Jean deleted the message, set her phone on the bedside table, and headed downstairs.

As she reached the foyer, she heard hurried footsteps heading her way. Seconds later, Annie came around the corner, looking serious and determined— she did not have any maps in her hand.

"Everything okay, Annie?" Jean asked.

"Carole and Geoff—my neighbors with the two toddlers, no fireplace, and no generator—just lost power."

13

Jean followed Annie to the mud room, and as they stepped through the doorway, Jean saw Scott sitting on a bench. He was bent over and slipping on a pair of black and gray boots that had a large, bright yellow "K" enclosed by a square outline of the same lively color. His legs were in the orange Polaris snowmobile suit, but the portion of the monosuit above his waist was still off, bunched up on the bench behind him with the ends of the sleeves dangling over the bench's edge on either side of him. On the floor, a few feet away from his left leg, were a pair of worn leather hiking boots and a hefty backpack.

"Carole and Geoff lost power a few minutes ago," Annie said. "They're going to call back in five, sooner if power comes back on."

"Tammy and Rob?" asked Scott, looking up from his boots.

Annie said, "I'm going to call them now," and stepped out of the room.

Jean watched as Scott glanced at the room's overhead light and then focused on turning the dial that was centered and at the top of his right boot's tongue. With each turn, the laces tightened. "Smart design," she said.

"Klim Adrenaline Pro S GTX Boa boots." He pointed to a cabinet across the room. "I bought Gram a new pair last year. They're perfect for riding, durable, and keep your feet warm. As long as I'm on the machine or stay close to it when I get off, they'll be perfect for tonight."

"What about those?" she said, motioning to the leather hiking boots.

"My good luck charm." He picked up one of the boots. "L.L. Bean GORE-TEX Cresta hiking boots. Had 'em for five years—best hiking boots I've ever owned. You may have seen my new ones earlier. These are broken-in. I'll keep them in the Grand Touring's rear storage container. If, for some reason, the snowmobile breaks down and I need to walk a good distance to find shelter, I'll switch over to these. The Klims aren't made for hiking."

"Looks like you might be making a few stops before you head to M-20."

"It's a relief. I'd rather get them now and know they're sheltered here before I head miles away. If communications are spotty, you and Gram might not be able to reach me." He switched over to his other Klim boot and started turning the dial to tighten the laces. "I was going to suggest that I pick up at least Geoff, Carole, and their kids, whether the power was out or not. If Gram comes back in here and says their power is back up, I'm still going to get them. Tammy and Rob should be fine unless something has happened to their generator, but we won't know that until they lose power."

"How many can you fit in the snowcoach?"

He finished with the boot and sat up, resting his back against the wall. On the front of his snugly fitted mock turtleneck, she could see the outline of his large pectoral muscles. "I can get Geoff, Carole, and their two kids in there, no problem. There's a heater and interior lights, and it has gas shock suspension and a limited rotational shock-absorbing hitch, so the ride will be smooth and comfortable. Tammy could probably squeeze in, too, and then Rob would ride behind me in the passenger seat, which is heated. There are also heated handholds with air deflectors, so he'd be fine. And, if he had them, Gram's machine even has mobile hookups for heated visors and heated boots. This isn't snowmobiling like when our parents were kids, when luxury meant having a cigarette lighter installed. I'm sorry, going into way too much detail—it's a habit."

Jean grinned. "I've got the same habit. What about comfort for you? Give me the specifics, sir."

"Okay, you asked for it. I'll be spoiled, riding on that thing tonight. Heated seat, heated grips on the handlebars, and for convenience, a 10.25-inch touchscreen with built-in GPS navigation. There's even a USB socket in the glove box, which I could plug my phone into and use the BRP Go! app for navigation, but that probably won't be an option because I'm guessing internet service will be spotty at best." He tugged on the right pant leg of his monosuit. "I'll be warm all night as long as I'm on the snowmobile. How's that for you?"

"I might buy one." They shared a laugh. Then, she asked, "Annie shares nine miles of trails with her neighbors, right?"

"Right. There's a big outer loop and two trails that crisscross on the interior—from the sky, it looks like someone made a fat 'X' inside of an oval. Gram's house is located at the bottom left turn, so I have two options once I leave her backyard. I can hop on the outer loop and head either north or due east, or take the leg of the 'X' that runs northeast across the interior. It's a half-mile straight shot east on the outer loop to Tammy and Rob's, then another mile beyond that to Carole and Geoff's."

"What kind of condition will the trails be in?"

"Perfect. The entire trail is fourteen feet wide, allowing for two-way traffic, and is bordered on both sides by trees. When snowmobiling at night, it's always like traveling down a dark tunnel on a white road. Rob groomed the trail after the big snow last week, so right now, there's less than six inches of new snow out there, which will be fine to ride on. The Grand Touring can handle riding through a couple of feet, but I want to avoid that." He hesitated, shifting his eyes side to side. "I might not have a choice depending on where I go later tonight, but getting to the neighbors' homes will be straightforward."

"How well do you know them?"

Scott reached his right hand up and scratched his nose. "Pretty well. I've been coming down here to visit Gram around once a month for the past few years, more often than that during the winter months." He lowered his hand, resting it on his thigh. "I usually come down on Friday afternoon and head back early Monday morning. On Saturday nights, Gram would host dinner, and then we'd play cards afterward. Tammy and Rob always came, and so did Carole and Geoff. Carole is about as relaxed a person as you'll ever meet. She's an administrative assistant for Gram's dermatologist, and her co-worker has teenage daughters who would babysit Carole and Geoff's kids those nights." He gazed into her eyes for a few moments.

Why is he pausing? she said to herself. *What is he doing?*

"Your . . . grandmother . . . would also come over. She was a spirited card player—vicious."

"I—I didn't know," Jean said.

"Oh, yeah. She and Gram were always partners when we played Euchre— it was after your grandfather passed away. Their old teaching buddy, Bob Sympkins, always came over, which gave us the perfect number of eight adults. To see him with Gram and Shirley Ruth was a show. All three of them trash-talked nonstop, and old Bob had such a good sense of humor, he made us roll over all night . . . Good guy." Scott let out a long exhale. "He was the first to go. Died in June. I'd be checking on him tonight if he were still alive. Lost his wife five years ago, around the same time as I lost my grandfather. For a while, I thought he and Gram would move in together—there was never anything romantic between them, but they were best friends. I thought it was a good idea, but, well, it never happened. I also thought she and your grandmother should move in together, but that didn't happen either." He watched the open doorway, as if to make sure Annie was not in the hallway. He frowned at Jean. "I live alone now, but I'm young."

She jumped in, "Me too."

He nodded. "Sorry, I didn't want to make assumptions about your living situation . . . I'm thirty-one . . ."

"Thirty," Jean said.

"Uh, well, right, so we're both single and we've got . . . time, you know?"

"Yes."

"But, for people like Gram, I can't even imagine what it is like living alone or without family close by." He stopped again. "I think about nights like tonight. Bad weather . . ." His voice trailed off.

After a few seconds of silence, she said, "I wouldn't like it. I'm glad she's got neighbors."

"Yeah," he said. "Tammy and Rob are in their early sixties and are executives at a big insurance company. They're also empty nesters. Their daughter is married and lives in Grand Rapids, and their son is in graduate school at Michigan State." He paused. "Geoff is a professor in the DeVos Graduate School at Northwood University and teaches courses in Organizational Leadership—super nice and smart. He and Carole are about five years older than we are and have the two toddlers, who are both fierce."

She grinned, trying not to laugh.

"I'm serious. Brittany never stops moving, and Ethan is a little tank and wears camouflage all the time. Once, we all had a picnic at the beach down from Bob Sympkins's cottage on Houghton Lake, and Ethan, wearing a camouflage *wetsuit*, put on a mask and fins, and announced to us all, 'Army guy gettin' wet,' before jumping off Bob's dock."

"Sounds like a handful."

"They are. Sometimes, I look at Carole and Geoff and their kids and think they're on another planet." He motioned to her. "We're only a few years away from being their age, but it's like they're fifteen years older than we are. You know?"

"Not quite ready for kids yet," she said with some certainty.

"Right?"

She let there be silence for a longer stretch, wondering if she should innocently ask what his thoughts on marriage were, but then decided to ask more about the card games. Ironically, she enjoyed playing cards too. However, it was online; she'd never played cards with actual human beings as an adult. "Tell me about the card games."

"Do you play? Euchre? Spades? Michigan Rummy? Bridge?"

"Some spades, but mostly poker and solitaire."

"Do you know how to play Euchre?"

"I don't."

"If some of the neighbors end up coming over, we'll have to teach you. It's a lot of fun. Anyway, on Saturday nights, that's what we'd do. Four of us would play at the kitchen table, which was the main table, and I'd set up a card table in the living room, so we'd have two games going on at the same time. Then, winners would play each other in the kitchen, and the losers would face off at the card table. We'd go back and forth for hours." He laughed. "Bob was always my partner, and we spent most of the evening at the card table. Good times . . . Even if your grandmother didn't have a good hand, she would name trump to prevent the other team from calling it. It drove us all nuts, but, secretly, we didn't want it any other way because it made each game even more unpredictable, and her smirk was contagious."

Jean was about to reply when she heard footsteps. Scott's eyes tracked over to the doorway, telling her that he had heard them too.

A few moments later, Annie walked into the room. "Rob and Tammy have power, but Carole and Geoff are still without."

Scott stood. "Okay, let's get the supplies to the pole barn, and then I'll head out to pick up Carole, Geoff, and the kids. I'll have my radio and phone on me, so let me know if Tammy and Rob lose power or if we do."

"I'll get the maps ready while you're picking them up, and Jean and I will get their room ready."

"Thanks. I'm glad you'll have some company while I'm out tonight—I'll head over to M-20 after everyone is settled in."

Jean watched as he put his arms through the sleeves of his monosuit and thought, *If I were stranded in this storm with no heat, there is no one I would rather have come pick me up than Scott.*

14

Jean set down fresh cups of hot chocolate in front of Geoff and Carole Lanning, who sat on the couch facing Annie's enormous hearth, which had a fire blazing inside it. The cups made a *clinking* sound as they touched the glass coasters on the coffee table.

Tiny marshmallows were floating in Geoff's, and whipped cream was on top of Carole's, and the couple said, "Thanks," almost in unison.

"Of course," said Jean.

"Isn't she wonderful?" Annie shouted from the kitchen.

Jean blushed and sat down across from them. Annie had been paying her compliments from the moment Scott had returned with the couple and their two children. She felt uncomfortable, but figured that Annie would continue to say whatever was on her mind, so she took the compliments and remained silent.

"Yes," replied Carole. "I can't get over how much she resembles Shirley Ruth—especially those pictures you showed me from the seventies."

Pictures? Of course. I'll have to ask to see them later.

Annie entered the room, carrying two large, steaming blue mugs of hot chocolate, and sat down next to Jean after placing the mugs on the glass coasters on their side of the coffee table. "That's what I've been telling her," she said.

Geoff took a sip and closed his eyes, seeming to savor the warmth. "Thank you so much for hosting us, Annie."

Both he and Carole gave Jean a positive vibe. Whereas their two children, who were upstairs playing, were rambunctious and talkative, the couple was quiet and easygoing, as if the joining of their DNA had spawned their exact opposite. Even with the loss of power to their home and the stress of having to uproot their family to survive the situation, the two were calm and gracious when they entered the house, immediately asking what they could do to help. This had surprised Jean, and, for a moment, she had wondered if they were handling the situation better than she was.

They were also an attractive couple. His ribbed, cream-colored turtleneck seemed to glow against the brown skin of his hands and clean-shaven face. He had closely cropped black hair and wore wire-framed glasses; his jeans ended in black socks that covered his large feet. He was tall—a few inches north of Scott—and rail thin. His smile was welcoming and a bit mischievous, which immediately captured everyone's attention when he stepped through the front door and said, *"Card time came early."* Carole had smooth, milky-white skin and was short, standing at about 5 feet 1 inch. Her long-sleeved green t-shirt was tucked into her jeans, exposing a trim waist. Her bust and hips accentuated her stocky build, and her blonde pixie cut, combined with her high cheekbones and narrow nose, gave her an assertive demeanor. However, this was softened by her red socks featuring Christmas trees, along with her red ball ornament earrings.

The conversation proceeded, light and easy, and included the usual getting-to-know-you dance, which—outside of her regular business lane—Jean had very little practice with until today. Now, she had introduced herself three times.

Annie interjected a funny statement here and there, but, for the most part, the back and forth was between Jean and the couple. She sensed that the two were still very much in love. The way they sat. The way they looked at each other. The way each listened when the other person was talking. The buzzword for the past decade that described their behavior was "present," and, as overused as it was, Jean thought it was aptly descriptive. They had been together for seven years, having met when Geoff went to the dermatologist to have a mole examined. Carole had checked him in at the front desk and then helped him schedule his follow-up appointment after the examination. Then, after the follow-up, he had asked her out for coffee, and they had hit it off.

When it came to her present situation, Jean stated that she was single, and upon learning this, Carole had casually glanced over at Annie and asked, *"Is Scott seeing anyone?"* Annie had looked into her mug of hot chocolate and replied, *"Not at the moment."* Geoff had let Annie's statement hang in the air for a few beats and then redirected the conversation with a question about what Scott was doing that evening. Jean had welcomed the change in topic, but had also not minded the questions. No one seemed to play matchmaker overtly, and yet, the relationship queries fit in with the previous line of questioning about who everyone was and what they did, ending in a brief glimpse into what lay ahead in their lives. Geoff would be traveling to London this summer for a leadership conference at Oxford; in Carole's annual review this past September, she had put her name in for office manager as the current person in that position would be retiring in May—she was excited to start the interview process in February; Annie was entirely focused on the storm and Christmas—*"I'll think about January when January gets here,"* she had said.

Then, it had come time for Jean to share. She considered telling them about Greece, but decided against it. After all, she might not make it there if the storm continued. There was another possible reason that could be clouding her judgment about the trip, but she was not in a place to deal with it, so she shoved the thought back down and out of sight. She humbly mentioned her promotion and that she would be traveling a lot this year.

The kids had only come downstairs once during the conversation, and that was to drink their mugs of hot chocolate. As soon as they were finished, they had raced back upstairs to play with their toys.

A log in the hearth succumbed to the immense heat and sank into the pile of embers. Instantly, two other pieces of wood that had been leaning on the large log rolled over, sending up a flurry of sparks. Because it had been so quiet due to a lull in the conversation, they all turned their attention to the fire at the sound of the logs shifting.

"We lost the big guy," Annie said.

"Yep, our anchor is gone," Geoff added, cocking his head to one side and studying the fire like a contractor surveying a damaged roof.

Annie rose. "Time to bring in the reinforcements."

"They're needed," Geoff said, nodding his head.

Carole let out a chuckle. "You two and your fires."

Jean watched as Annie walked over to the pile of cut wood next to the hearth, grabbed three logs, and then positioned them in the fireplace. When she was finished, Geoff said, "Nice formation."

Shortly after Scott left to pick up the family, the power went out, and the generator kicked in. Still, they had built up the fire in case it stopped working. When the family had arrived in the living room, Geoff's expression on his face turned into one of boyhood excitement when he saw the fire, and he joined Annie by the hearth and started joking that they would build the best fire known to humankind and keep it going the entire night. Jean had seen Geoff smile and heard him say, *"It's all-out war tonight."* And Annie had put a hand on his shoulder and replied, *"Time to cowboy up."*

And so their little "war" had raged on for the past hour.

Now, Annie directed a satisfied, "Hmmph," toward the fire and turned around and said, "We're back."

"A perfect staging," said Geoff.

Annie rejoined Jean on the couch and then met eyes with Carole. "You all need to get a fireplace put in."

"After what happened tonight, and because he gets infatuated with building the fire and maintaining it every time we're over here in the winter, I'm sold," Carole said.

Geoff rubbed his chin and nodded while studying the fire.

Carole shook her head and laughed. Then, she focused her attention on Jean. "I'm traveling to London with him when he has his conference in June, and my mom and dad are going to watch the kids. It'll be like a second honeymoon because we haven't had a vacation with just the two of us since the kids were born. We'll be there for a week. So, if you happen to be in London during that time, give us a ring and we'll treat you to dinner and show you around Oxford."

"I'd love that," Jean said, but her thoughts were focused on what Carole had said first.

You haven't had a vacation with just the two of you since the kids were born?

It was a world she did not know, one where she could not come and go as she pleased. Jean was comfortable only being responsible for herself. Getting married and having children would be a significant lifestyle change, one that requires energy and selflessness. Even in their short time together, she had observed Geoff and Carole take turns going upstairs to check on the kids. Jean was thirty, ate expensive, healthy food that she ordered from a gourmet food company that many celebrities had signed up for, and worked out every day on her state-of-the-art elliptical and stationary bicycle—all of these were arguments for her ability to handle the physical demands of raising kids. However, how would she handle the lack of sleep, and what about the first time she didn't feel like taking the prepared meals out of the refrigerator? And what about the man with whom she would raise the kids? *Can I tell what kind of co-parent and father he will be ahead of time?*

And then there was the window of time. Five years seemed like nothing; she felt and looked the same at twenty-five and thirty. But, thirty-five . . . well, she'd be old enough to be *President*, and that milestone not only symbolized experience but also served as the signpost welcoming her to the 'middle-aged' trailhead.

What if I get offered another promotion by then? Would I decline, sacrificing more financial security for the sake of parenthood? And not only parenthood, but first-child-I-don't-know-what-the-hell-I'm-doing parenthood.

Annie reached for her hot chocolate, and the motion snapped Jean out of her stream of thoughts.

"I'll call Tammy and Rob again in a few minutes to check on them."

Carole nodded, and Geoff said, looking out the window, "I wonder how Scott is doing?"

15

The Grand Touring's beams found the rear window of the Ford Taurus just after midnight. Scott had almost missed it as the car was no longer running, and, from the looks of the two channels the wheels had cut through the snow on M-20, it appeared that the car had skidded off the road some time ago and landed upright in the deep ditch just off the road's shoulder. The car was painted white, and snow had piled so high that it covered the tires, rear lights, and trunk, making it almost impossible to see. Scott reasoned that if he hadn't been traveling so slowly, making a zig-zag pattern with his machine on M-20, he would have missed the vehicle.

He traveled down the road until his snowmobile was even with the car and made sure to stay away from where the shoulder dropped down into the ditch, which had been difficult to do earlier when there were no snowmobile tracks to guide his way—he had already helped two state troopers get their machines out of ditches. There were no lights on inside the car, and after he turned the Grand Touring off, he heard no noises or voices coming from the vehicle either.

He shouted out, asking if anyone was inside. When he heard no reply, he pulled his Maglite out from the glove box, turned it on, and rose from his warm seat. Standing up, he used the additional height to give himself a better angle as he looked down at the car. Methodically, he swept the beam across the vehicle and then across the snow leading down into the ditch up to where the Taurus rested. There was no apparent damage to the car, and no tracks were visible in the snow. The doors on the driver's side were shut with snow bermed up against them. It appeared that no one had attempted to exit the vehicle on this side. He lifted the light and focused the beam on the far side of the car. Snow was still coming down, and he squinted, trying to make out any disturbances in the drift on the other side . . .

There. Just aft of the rear passenger's side door was a wedge carved out of the drift as if the door had been opened, and, as he moved his light away from it, there were pockets in the snow—footprints?—leading away from the car and up the other side of the ditch.

Scott hopped off.

He moved carefully down the side of the ditch until he reached the car. He wiped some snow off the driver's side windows and aimed his light's beam inside the vehicle. There appeared to be no one inside, but it was dark, and a blanket was spread out on the floor in front of the rear seats.

After knocking on the windows and neither hearing a response nor seeing any movement, he tried both door handles, which did not open. He lowered his light and trudged through the snow around the back of the car until he reached the rear passenger's side door.

As he pointed the Maglite's beam at the ground, he confirmed his suspicion that the door had been swung open at least a few feet, and when he focused the beam into one of the pockets in the snow, he saw what looked like a boot print that was covered with a fresh film of snow. Scott lifted his leg and put his foot down into the pocket, lining up the heel of his boot with the heel of the print— the boot print was a few inches shorter than his own.

He turned around and attempted to open both passenger-side doors, but both were locked. The wind howled, and snow blew against his cheeks. He took one more look inside the vehicle, determined that there was nothing underneath the blanket, and moved behind the back of the car. After a minute or so of digging and scooping out snow, he took a picture of the license plate.

He returned to his snowmobile and, after radioing in the plate and what he had found, changed boots, removed the Digitally Encoded Security System (DESS) key from the Grand Touring, and slid down the ditch, returning to the far side of the car.

Shining his light on the pockets, he began to follow the tracks.

After the second loud *thump*, followed by giggling, Jean decided to head downstairs. She was not angry—the kids were just wound up and excited, and, having had no experience with toddlers, she did not know when they would calm down and go to sleep. *But it's past midnight . . .* There had been no noise from the family's room when she had climbed into bed and snuggled under the covers twenty minutes ago—had one, or both of them, been asleep? Or, had they woken up? Had Geoff or Carole been reading them a story to try and get them back down, and, now that story time was over, were they ready to play again? It didn't matter. Jean was not tired. If Annie had gone to bed, then Jean would enjoy the peace and solitude of sitting alone in the living room by the fire. If Annie were still up, then perhaps Jean would muster the courage to ask her about Shirley Ruth.

Before arriving, this is the last thing I would have considered doing.

She uncovered her legs and swung her bare feet off the bed and onto the cool wooden floor. Her clothes were folded and arranged on top of the long cedar chest that ran along the wall she faced, perhaps three or four paces away, and, for a moment, she considered grabbing a pair of socks and putting them on before heading downstairs. However, for some reason that she hoped would come to her later, Jean preferred going barefoot—her warm feet felt like they had increased grip on the wood's grain as she padded across the room and put on the robe that Annie had provided her with. And even though each anchored step increased her confidence that she would not slip, which was her fear if she was wearing socks, she detected that the sensibility and practicality of going sockless and shoeless was not the primary reason she had decided to do so.

She turned off the bedside lamp and left the room.

Jean found Annie standing with her back to her and staring out the living room window. "Hi," Jean said.

Annie was not startled—*she must have heard my footsteps*—and faced her, saying, "Everything okay, dear? Can't sleep?"

"Everything's fine."

There was a loud thump, as if someone had jumped off the bed and landed on the floor. Annie and Jean looked up at the ceiling and then met eyes.

Annie gave her a wink. "Now I know why you came downstairs."

Jean continued her approach and now stood side by side with Annie. "It's fine. I discovered I'm not that tired yet." She watched the blizzard, which had not lessened since the last time she had stood at the window hours ago. "Must be the adrenaline from the storm. I guess I'm still thinking about Scott. Have you heard from him?"

Annie checked her watch, a small, round-faced timepiece with a gold bezel and thin leather straps. "Maybe an hour ago, right after you all headed upstairs. Doing fine. Busy. He's already transported five people to shelters or hotels." She broke eye contact and stared out the window again. "Scary out there tonight."

Jean put a hand on Annie's shoulder. "I'm glad he's okay. I think it's incredible what he's doing."

Annie gave her a polite grin of thanks. "He's wonderful."

Jean thought it prudent to nod, so she did.

Annie's smile grew wider as if Jean had just answered a vital question correctly.

"Tammy and Rob?" questioned Jean.

"Got off the phone with them ten minutes ago. Doing fine."

"They have any visitors yet?"

"Stragglers looking for shelter? No. All quiet except for the howling wind."

"Think we'll get any more company tonight?"

"There's always the possibility, but Scott said that he had not seen any vehicles on the road or anyone outside on the way to M-20. Everyone is either hunkered down somewhere already or stranded on a major roadway, don't think we'll have anyone coming this way."

They made tea and then sat across from each other on the couches in the family room as they had when Jean had arrived earlier. After talking about Geoff, Carole, and their kids, the conversation hit an expected lull, and Jean decided to ask about Shirley Ruth. "Could we talk some more about my grandmother?"

Annie's hand shook, and she almost dropped her teacup. Carefully, she put it down on the coaster on the coffee table. "Of course." She sat back against the cushions. "What would you like to know?"

Jean took a sip of tea and then placed the cup on her coaster. "Everything."

16

Annie laughed. "Everything?"

"Yes," Jean said. "I know nothing about her."

"Yyyooour mom hasn't told you anything?"

Jean fixed her eyes on the center of the coffee table. She felt a lump in her throat . . . her eyes were filling with tears. *What if they come downstairs right now? What if Scott walks in the front door?*

She took a deep breath and then exhaled. *It is okay*, she told herself. She blinked, and tears ran down both cheeks. *You are okay.* "She's told me next to nothing," said Jean, sitting back and making eye contact with Annie.

"Would you like a tissue, my child?"

More tears came sliding down her cheeks. "Yes."

Annie pulled a plastic container the size of a bar of soap out of her cardigan's right pocket and handed it to her.

Jean had never seen a tissue package this small before and immediately wondered why she had not. *This would be ideal to have in my purse*, she thought. "Thank you," she said, drawing a few tissues out of the container. She removed her glasses, dabbed her eyes, and then put her glasses back on.

"I suppose there's never a right time, just *the* time to talk about matters like this."

Using the same tissues she had wiped her eyes with, Jean blew her nose and then wiped it. "I suppose you're right." She went into the kitchen, threw away the tissues, and returned to the couch.

"Any particular point you want me to start at?"

In the twenty minutes she had lain in bed, listening to the ruckus in the Lannings' room down the hall, she had thought about the jumping-off point in the story of her grandmother's past. As usual, her first instincts were the strongest, and she kept returning to the initial questions her mind had formed as she stared at the log beams over the bed. Finally, like an ad team revising a company's slogan until it captured the essence of the brand and campaign—Just Do It, I'm Lovin' It, America Runs on Dunkin', The Happiest Place on Earth— her brain had cut and then trimmed the questions down to one that, when answered, would open the door to all other answers.

Why did my mother and Uncle Brett stop almost all contact with their parents?

She asked Annie the question, and it hung in the air for a few beats as the fire continued to crackle and pop. Then, as if Annie had come to the same conclusion that Jean had, she said, "That's where Shirley Ruth would have started—right to the point." She took a sip of tea and set her cup back down. "Earlier, when you mentioned that you hadn't seen your uncle Brett in a long time, I thought you might begin with him and your mom."

Jean gave her a nod and then placed the package of tissues on the coffee table. Annie crossed her legs, and Jean noticed she was wearing ruby slippers that looked like replicas of Dorothy's in *The Wizard of Oz*, just without the heels.

"There's no place like home," Annie said.

Jean's eyes broke their stare at the slippers, and she felt embarrassed.

Annie pointed at Jean's bare feet. "And dear, aren't your feet cold?"

The warmth radiating from the large hearth was just enough to keep her toes happy. "No, they feel good," she said. "Sorry for being so informal."

Annie waved her right hand. "Girl, you go barefoot anywhere you like. Just don't be uncomfortable, okay?"

"Thanks. I like the way the wood feels on my bare feet."

"Understand completely. For years, I went around the house with no socks or shoes on." Annie shivered and pulled the lapels of her cardigan closer together. She rose and threw another log on the fire. "Helluva fire we've got goin' here."

"I don't want to see it end," said Jean.

"It won't as long as I'm still awake." Annie lifted the Pendleton blanket from the rocking chair's backrest and returned to her couch, covering her legs with the blanket. "I've got central heating, but I swear there are still nooks and crannies between the logs where the air from outside muscles in."

Jean agreed with her grandmother's longtime best friend—she had felt a few surprising drafts during the night in different locations throughout the house.

The two women studied each other for a moment. Jean would not say there was tension in the air, but there was a sense of occasion, as if secrets that had been buried for decades were about to be revealed. But that is precisely what she had asked for, and she was not worried about what Annie would say. Nothing could change the past. Families become estranged or their members go their separate ways for various reasons. Whatever her family's reasons were had little impact on the life she had lived so far. Her parents were distant, but she had grown up in a stable household. Daycare had led to Pre-K had led to elementary school had led to middle school had led to high school, all without interruption—a smooth journey complete with playdates, youth soccer, and summer camps orchestrated by her mother and father along with tutors, coaches, teachers, and her friend group's parents.

There had also been choir . . .

Jean was sure that her college experience fell securely in the lane of normal—weekly visits to the campus gym, pizza with friends, on-and-off-again study groups, a little partying here and there, football games on Saturday afternoons, and hitting the books in coffee shops, diners, and occasionally the university library. Early breaks were a mix of time spent at home and away with friends; later breaks were filled with internships and traveling. Then, she landed a job at Renault Impact and became a millionaire. No attachments. No family drama. Nothing to hold her back or make her wish that things were different.

So, what is causing my tears?

Her mind searched for reasons, found none that gave her certainty, and surrendered to the probability that they would be realized at a later date. Whenever this had previously happened, she had retreated and become obsessed with achieving a current goal—all A's on her report card in ninth grade, preparing for college every day during the spring semester of her senior year, perfect scores on her final exams in college, crafting the best marketing campaign her company had ever come up with for one of its clients— distracting herself from her unexplained emotions and providing herself with a tremendous sense of self-worth. A two-for-one.

Then, she thought of her cell phone, charging again on the nightstand in her room—*Don't lie to yourself.*

In addition to leveraging her competitive nature and drive to accomplish goals, she also suppressed her emotions by getting lost in her device for as long as it took to push the feelings away. And when they came back, she repeated the procedure. She estimated that she had been doing this since receiving her first phone at fourteen.

She had expected a similar pull now, either to bury herself in her job by working remotely from her phone or disappearing into any one of her dozen apps to distract herself from whatever was bubbling up inside her right now. However, the pull was not there.

Jean felt no need to run from her emotions. The weather, or divine intervention, had created the opportunity for her to discover her family's history. Upstairs, she had also wondered whether it would be better if her mother were here for the unveiling. Whatever Annie was about to lay out, Lori had kept it hidden from Jean for Jean's entire life. Perhaps Lori had discussed the matter with Annie before the trip. Something along the lines of: *I am not close with my daughter, and she has never asked about things, but . . . Annie, it's time she knew. And I'm not in a position to explain things to her. For old times' sake, could you fill in the gaps one last time?*

"I think it would be best if I start with the present and then move into the past," Annie said.

Jean leaned forward. "Whatever you feel is best."

"Your mother and uncle always say that to me."

"How often do you speak with them?"

"About once every few weeks—have for years. Sometimes it's more often with your Uncle Brett since he's on the road most of the time."

Every few weeks? The immediate question that came to mind was: Why had they stayed in so frequent contact?

As if she had sensed her question, Annie said, "I wouldn't say that I have been a go-between for your family members over the years, but you could say that I have been a collector—and sometimes *distributor*—of information. When I sensed the time was right, I would divulge certain pieces of it to the applicable party."

"Between my mother and uncle and my grandparents, you mean?"

"Yes."

"Quite a heavy burden."

"Not really," said Annie. "I put my foot down hard right from the start and told them that I would neither act as a middle person in the situation nor as a referee or counselor. They could choose to talk with me as much as they wanted to, but I would not be a relay station."

"I understand that you and my grandmother were close, but why would her estranged children choose to keep in close contact with you?"

"Everyone needs outlets, Jean, whether they realize it or not. I think your mother and uncle realized it earlier than most."

"But didn't that drive a wedge between you and my grandmother? Wasn't she jealous of you?"

"I doubt it—your grandmother was not a big feeler, more of a thinker. If she was jealous, she never let me know. She certainly never treated me any differently. And, to be clear, I can count on both hands the number of times I passed along information to one side or the other over the thirty-two years that this went on."

"Thirty-two years?"

"The key event took place in 1992."

"Two years before I was born. I had always assumed that the falling out happened after we visited my grandmother and grandfather at their house here when I was a toddler, like in 1996 or 1997." Jean bit her lower lip. "Didn't I meet you then, too?"

"No."

"No?"

"We've never met until now, my dear."

"But I thought—"

"You did go with your mother to visit your grandparents in 1997 after you had just turned three. But it wasn't in Midland."

Jean felt herself losing control. There were many things she didn't know about her family, and she was prepared to face the possible relief and consequences that could accompany learning of that secret past. But, there were things—events—she did know, which gave her comfort. *Knowing* gave her comfort. The visual she had formed in her mind that captured the situation was the progress bar near the bottom of a television screen, which appeared on a streaming platform when a show was paused. In her visual, she had the basic package on the streaming platform, which included ads, and the show had been paused seconds after she had hit play. On the bar, she could see the white markers where the ads would occur; in her current situation, those markers were events in her family's history that she knew of, and the dark sections of the progress bar in between the markers were the vast periods of her family's past that were unknown to her. She had been counting on the markers to keep her centered and anchored when the unknown realms and dimensions were revealed. Now, because of what Annie had just said, at least one of her markers was starting to flicker, threatening to disappear. "That can't be," she said. "My mother told me . . . and I . . . well, they lived in another home in Midland, where my mother grew up. I don't remember it, but I've been there before."

"No. This is the first time you have ever visited Midland."

Jean's breathing became strained. She went to speak, intending to project a tone laced with bravado ignited by the resolve to deliver a crippling inquiry; what came out of her mouth, however, was a voice lowered to an almost inaudible whisper. "What?"

17

Annie rose, put her blanket to the side, and walked over and sat next to Jean. "I am sorry, dear. I got ahead of myself by mentioning how many years the situation has dragged on. I should have known you could do the math in your head that fast. I guess—" She shook her head. "I always know the exact number because as each year turned to another year, I always hoped that *that year* would be the last."

Jean had done the quick math. In 1992, her mother would have been 23 years old. She knew that her Uncle Brett was four years younger than her mother, so he would have been 19 at the time. What about her grandparents? Shirley Ruth was 84 when she died, so she would have been 52. Her grandfather, Martin, was two years older than Shirley Ruth, so he would have been 54.

So, Lori had already been out of the house for five years and would have been in law school, and her uncle would have been a freshman in college. From the practical standpoint of proximity, it didn't make sense. Both kids were out of the house at that point.

Her grandparents were empty nesters.

What happened? And why did my mother lie to me?

She felt a lump in her throat and swallowed, attempting to regain her composure. Looking at Annie, she saw the face of someone concerned, someone who cared about her.

Hear her out on this. It's not her fault. "It's okay. You have nothing to apologize for." She reached over and took a long drink of tea. "My mother hasn't told me much over the years, but I don't know why she would lie to me about the visit in '97."

"I think it was a matter of simplicity. I'm assuming she told you about it recently?"

"Yes. Right after my grandmother passed away."

Annie gave her knee a soft tap. "Knowing your mother, she probably thought the house would sell right away and that you would never travel here. To keep things streamlined, I'm guessing that when she notified you of your grandmother's passing, she said you visited her original house in Midland when you were a toddler—too young to remember—and that your parents were going to sell the newer house. She might have mentioned that it was a bit of a surprise that her mother had made her the executor of her will, but that she would do her duty."

"She did."

"Your mother thought I would be the executor of the will, but I wasn't, and I wasn't surprised at all. Shirley Ruth always wanted someone in her family to take care of her affairs after she had passed, and, regarding me, well, she knew Father Time could come for either of us at any moment, and it would complicate things if I were the executor of her will and died before she did. I mean, she would have just had to name another executor, but even that she would have considered a hassle these days. And so, your mother undoubtedly thought that would be the end of it. But then, the house didn't sell, and she and your father were busy with a big case."

Jean rolled her eyes. "I know. They're still busy with it."

Annie gave a smile of disappointed acknowledgement. "Some things never change. Your mom has always focused on her work and the bottom line."

I am that way, too, Jean thought. *Will I stay that way forever?* She didn't know.

"So, when the house didn't sell, she called me."

"I don't understand why my grandmother would make Mom the executor of her will. They had been estranged for decades."

Annie frowned. "I said I wasn't surprised, and I wasn't. But that doesn't mean that I wasn't surprised when I found out who she willed everything to."

Jean knew the answer before Annie said it.

"She left everything to you and Brandon, dear. I don't think it was an act of cruelty, but I do think making your mom the executor of the will was meant to serve as a summation of the situation. Her son Brett was out of her life. Her daughter, Lori, was out of her life. And both of her grandchildren were out of her life. Her daughter had been the only one to test the waters of reconciliation, which is the visit you accompanied her on in 1997. When that didn't work out, she decided to make your mom the executor and give everything to you and Brandon. The only problem with this was your grandfather, who thought none of you should get anything. She told me that he wanted to name a young attorney in town as the executor and donate the entire value of the estate to charity. And, it looks like he had his way. When your mom checked to see when she had been made executor of the will, it was the day after her father's funeral services in 2021. My old friend rolled the dice and bet that she would outlive her husband. She didn't win many bets throughout the course of her life, but she won that one."

"So, after we sell the house, Brandon and I will split the money from the sale and split the rest of the estate," Jean stated. "My mother never mentioned this to me."

"She was waiting until the house sold. And it will be a good amount of money, but compared to Brett's income and especially your mother's, it won't be much. That's why I don't think it was done in cruelty; Shirley Ruth knew that she did not possess the high card there; any intended message of 'Ha *ha*. Look at what you could have had if you had chosen to stay in my life!' would have been laughed at. I believe that she thought making your mother the executor was a final move to secure the only tether to her family she had left."

"When she called you, did she ask you to tell me about my family's past?"

"The subject came up near the end of the call, and I said I was willing to go there with you but that the conversation would have to be initiated by you." She looked out the living room window. "Without the storm, I'm not sure it would have happened. Am I right?"

"I wanted to make the visit as quick as possible."

"I don't blame you. You had no emotional connection to me or Midland."

"About that," said Jean. "If I did meet my grandparents in 1997, and it wasn't here, then where was it?"

Annie turned toward her and took her hands. "Do you trust me?"

"Yes."

"We'll get there, but not just yet, okay?"

Jean nodded. She wanted to know everything immediately, but she needed to let Annie tell her in Annie's way.

"Okay," Annie said. "The present."

"The present," Jean replied.

Annie squeezed her hands and then walked back toward the couch across from her.

18

"Just to get my bearings, can you tell me what you know about your Uncle Brett?" asked Annie. She was snuggled under her Pendleton blanket once more, and they had both taken a sip of tea and observed the fire roar in the brick hearth.

Jean told her—trucker, divorced, one son, and Jean had last seen him when he had driven through Billings and stopped over at their house when she was around five or six.

"That's not much," said Annie.

"I know that he and my mom are on good terms, but they have drifted apart over the years. No one's fault, it's just hard to keep in touch with anyone who lives in Alaska, especially Mom, who is not a phone or social media person. She's always been an out-of-sight, out-of-mind type."

"I'd be surprised if they weren't on good terms. She mentions him every once in a while when we talk. I seem to be an exception to her phone-call boycott." Annie took a sip of tea. "Know anything about his ex-wife or why they divorced?"

"No."

Annie leaned back once again, the friction between her sweater and the leather cushions making a cracking noise. "Well, you know from our storm prep session earlier that I'm a stickler for details, so I'll give you a proper update."

"I know you will. It's one of the reasons I trust you and have reached out to you tonight."

Annie gave a slight bow, seemingly satisfied with Jean's reply. She cleared her throat and then began. "Brett is not just a trucker, he's an OTR—an 'over the road' trucker, which means he transports materials and goods long distances, almost always across multiple states. This is definitely why he was trucking through Montana when you were young. He's a well-known small business owner now as an independent owner-operator, got his Class A Commercial Driver's License, owns the vehicles he uses to transport loads—he's got two trucks that he alternates between to haul heavy freight and machinery—and, since he runs his own show, he's responsible for all routine maintenance and repairs on his truck. And, my gosh, does he ever stay on top of everything. His company's slogan is, 'Over Thirty Years Without a Missed Load.' He updates it every five years. Let's just say that he is *in demand* right now. And," she said, pausing. "He makes over three hundred thousand dollars a year."

There had been times during her life when Jean had thought about looking up her uncle, but she had never followed through with it. Those instances were more fleeting flashes of interest while she was doing something else, such as running on a treadmill, where the interest would disappear a few paces later or, at most, moments after she got off the treadmill and headed for the shower. The dismissal of her interest was most likely due to the straightforward nature of what she perceived as his work. For Jean—and her parents—life was all about one thing: work. He's a trucker—drives a truck, delivers things, returns home, then the cycle repeats itself. That's it. She had never considered that he was self-employed, and three hundred thousand bucks for onloading, driving, and unloading? She would have never guessed it.

"His shifts are usually three weeks. So, he's spending a lot of continuous time on the road, traveling a great distance each shift. You're probably putting two and two together here and seeing why his marriage didn't work out. But we'll get to that in a minute. He lives in Fairbanks, Alaska, has since he left Michigan when he was nineteen. Yes, his decision to leave coincides with the event in 1992." Annie coughed and took a sip of tea. "Apple didn't fall far from the tree as far as his son Brandon was concerned. He's twenty-six now and drives a truck. Already making eighty-five thousand a year."

Jean thought that she had said this last statement with an air of pride, almost as if it were meant to elicit a reaction from Jean. *She must not know how much I make a year, or I don't think she would have said it like that.* And it made sense that she didn't know, because Jean had not discussed it with her mother, so the chances that Lori had told Annie were slim. Did Lori know how much Jean's condo in Soho cost? Probably. Lori had confided in Jean that she was addicted to Zillow, but Jean's parents were usually only concerned with the value of their property and their substantial accumulated wealth, which had grown over the years as they built their formidable law firm, Mercer & Mercer. Jean had been raised to believe that money was the only marker of success, because it could be measured—salaries, bank accounts, investments, and properties all had exact numbers associated with them at any one moment in life. There was no debate. You make *this amount* each year; you have *this amount* in your checking account; your investments are worth *this amount* today; your home's current value is *this amount*. Any inquiry into your finances led to a number, and that number told the naked truth of how successful you were. Feelings were not to be trusted— they could not be measured because a baseline could never be established, and they could never be compared to a database of other people's feelings because *they* could not be measured. There was no reference point and never would be.

Happiness was unquantifiable and an illusion. Unwise investments aside, currency, death, and taxes were the only certainties.

Then again, maybe Annie *did* know how much Jean made and was making a point about the value of forgotten or taken-for-granted blue collar workers like Jean's cousin—a mission statement that read: *You may be thirty and a millionaire, advising people how to best seduce consumers into purchasing goods and services that may or may not be necessary for life, but there are people out there like the cousin you've never met who are keeping the world running.*

She took a breath and exhaled before picking up her cup of tea. *Stop overanalyzing already.*

Annie continued. "Your Aunt Carrie still lives in Fairbanks. Manages the Red Lantern Steak and Spirits restaurant in the Westmark Fairbanks Hotel and Conference Center. Always liked her, and I have to hand it to her and Brett. They co-parented Brandon peacefully and shared the load as much as they could. Carrie shouldered most of it when Brandon was young, but as he grew up, he spent more and more time with Brett in the truck. Now, I wouldn't say that Carrie and Brett are still friends because I have a theory about that." She leaned forward. "If you break up and are still able to be friends, then you are either still in love with that person or you never were in the first place." She leaned back and stretched. The leather couch cushions made a cracking sound once again. "Well, I shouldn't take credit for that theory as mine—heard it somewhere—but it's a good one." Annie paused. "A bit unsettling to know that Brandon is now a year older than his parents were when they got married."

She was still trying to take in Annie's statement about relationships when the practical part of her brain overrode the philosophical part, and she asked, "How long did the marriage last? I don't remember Uncle Brett, Mom, or Dad saying anything about it when he came to visit us, which doesn't surprise me. I do remember him mentioning Brandon and that he was walking, but that's about it."

"They got married in 1998 when you were four. Your parents attended the wedding but left you with friends of theirs in Billings. I thought they should have brought you, but, well . . . Anyway, Brett and Carrie got divorced two years later. Couldn't handle the separation when Brett was on the road."

"Makes sense." She immediately wanted to add to her crass statement, which she had delivered like she had just been told that there was treasure on the sandy bottom of the ocean where a ship had wrecked that was carrying gold. She had never noticed before how cold she could be in her replies, but she was noticing now. *Your uncle's life got rocked by something that happened between him and your grandparents, and then, eight years later, his world got upended again by divorce. These are people's*—family members'—*lives you are talking about here.* "That's tough," she managed to say. "Especially on Brandon." *Not much better, but I am trying.*

"Divorce is always hard. I got lucky, and so did Shirley Ruth; we never had to go through it, but we each had a child who wasn't as fortunate. My son, Scott's father, has never been the same. What a mess. Put a big hole in our family's heart that won't ever heal. They were together twenty-three years . . . ah," she said, waving her hand like she was backhanding a fly. "If I go there, I'll get all worked up." She closed her eyes, took a deep breath while tapping her fingers on her lap, and then exhaled. Jean wondered if this was a procedure that Annie had devised long ago and followed ever since to reset herself.

With her eyes still shut, she said, "I feel bad every day for Scottie and his younger sister Heather. They suffered." She took another breath, exhaled while tapping, and then opened her eyes. "Three years ago, your grandmother and I were clinging to each other for dear life after we'd just lost our husbands. It also became a period of reflection. There had been divorces, disappointments, detours, and destruction, but also good times, moments of clarity, and accomplishments. We were still standing. Never moved in with each other, but we maintained a daily routine and stuck to it—meals, walks, goddamned pills, reading, board games, card games, crossword puzzles, morning and evening check-ins, and on and on. So many of our friends had already died—it seemed like someone we knew passed away every week. Your grandmother and I relished the fact that we still had each other. Pretty rare to have a best friend for over fifty years."

"I don't have a best friend."

"Not even from high school or college?"

"No. I had friends—people I hung out with—but no one with whom I would say I was close." Her eyes wandered over to the fire. *What am I feeling? Embarrassment . . . like I've missed something essential? Is everyone supposed to have a best friend? Marissa and I were close, but after the holiday concert . . .*

"You still have time to form a friendship like Shirley Ruth's and mine. Beware, though, because it crushes you when they're gone." She glanced over at the rocking chair next to the fire. "That was her favorite seat. I'd poke at her for not wanting to sit on one of the couches, but she liked being able to rock while we chatted or while she stared into the fire. Didn't surprise me. Your grandmother had to be moving constantly."

"She was fidgety?"

"No, she was always in control of her movements—wasn't anxious. She just glided everywhere with the consistency of a pendulum, moving back and forth in the most calm and graceful motion I've ever seen in a human being. And it was so discreet that, after a while, you didn't notice it. Never distracted me." She laughed. "I always thought she would outlive me because I have my sedentary periods. She never did." Annie rubbed her hands together. "And now she's gone. I'm eighty-three, Jean. My best friend and husband have passed away, and my children live thousands of miles from here. All I've got for family is Scottie. Sometimes I think I'm beyond reflection now, but I've never lost my purpose or the undeniable drive to survive. I cherish my daily routine, although having a full house is a gift, especially this time of year—I wish it weren't because of the storm—and I *live* for visits from Scottie."

"You also keep in close contact with your neighbors."

"Yes. Community is key. You said you didn't have a best friend, but do you stay in contact with anyone whom you grew up with? That you went to school with?"

She didn't. Jean had been semi-social throughout the years but never really belonged to anything of an organized nature beyond high school choir—a school club, a thespian group, the Girl Scouts—not even a Facebook group. She preferred the sanctuary of her own space. When casual acquaintances started to confide in her about problems in their lives or ask for advice about a particular matter, she would begin to distance herself from them. And, eventually, they all got the hint without her ever having to say a word, which was what she had intended. No adversarial untethering. No questions. No drama. People flowed in and out of her life freely and without attachment or expectations. The only people she felt somewhat attached to were her coworkers, but those relationships were all about the bottom line and collaborating on exciting projects and managing interesting clients. Professionalism, with defined boundaries and accountability, was a pleasant experience.

It was also superficial—everyone got into character and assumed their work persona. Even drinks after work or holiday parties, like the one she had attended at Pier Sixty, were always, in their most square and concrete spirit, anchored to work topics, and, in their most relaxed manner, anchored to at least some informal shop talk or company gossip. She didn't *know* anyone she worked with, which was fine with her.

She also didn't know anyone *outside* of work, which was . . .

"No, I don't keep in touch with anyone from my past," she said, her eyes returning front and center. "I wouldn't be opposed to it if someone reached out to me, but there would have to be a reason for them to do so, and I'm not sure what that would be. I never delved too deep into anyone's personal life and kept my own guarded. So, I'm not sure what we would talk about beyond catching up on what has transpired since we last saw each other, but those basics can be gleaned from my LinkedIn profile. And that's all I would feel comfortable sharing. I would never initiate contact. I have social media accounts, but don't use them."

"You seem a little less guarded around me," Annie said. "Is that because I have something you want?"

The statement's truth did not surprise Jean. Annie had proven herself to be direct, clear, and perceptive. In terms of advertising, Jean would have recruited her to serve on her "first impression" panel, as initial, unvarnished feedback guided much of the early work in her company's ad research and development phase. *"You can't teach those instincts,"* Urian had once remarked after being impressed by a new team member who, when shown a draft video ad for hot dogs that had a horse that was made out of leaves of kale sitting in the stands at a baseball game, wearing a ballcap and eating hot dog after hot dog, had said, *'I don't get it. Nothing will convince the consumer that hot dogs are natural and will make you strong like a horse . . . especially one that looks like a green 'Pizza the Hut' from* Spaceballs. *And no one goes to a baseball game to eat healthy."*

Urian.

Will I even make it to Greece?

As her eyes began to tiptoe over to the window, she remembered what Annie had said and turned back toward her. "You do have something I want, which, until this point, I have never wanted before. But, there is something else about you, about this house, about the conditions that we're in that makes talking to you easy. I'm much more of a thinker than a feeler—not good with emotions—but your kindness, your straightforwardness, and your genuine manner have lowered my usual defenses and awakened a curiosity that I believe was always there about my family's past."

"I don't have the luxury or time for games anymore, my dear, if I ever had the stomach for them. It's why I get straight to the point. Easier that way. You have your grandmother's honesty." Her voice trailed off, and she was silent for a bit. When she began again, she said, "Well, at least her honesty later in life."

What did that *mean?*

19

Jean watched as Annie returned from the kitchen with two snifters of brandy. "Here we are," she said, handing one to Jean. "We're beyond tea now, Miss Jean. A little extra warmth."

After the statement about Shirley Ruth's honesty, her host had excused herself to use the restroom and then had thrown another two logs on the fire before pouring the brandy. Jean had her first experience with the drink the night her ex-boyfriend had tried to convince her that she would enjoy a cigar more if sips of good brandy accompanied it. He had not been wrong; now, once or twice a year—usually when she closed a large deal—she would go to the Soho Cigar Bar for a brandy and her favorite cigar, a Room 101 Farce Connecticut. And she would think nothing of her ex as she sat at her usual table in the back room. Sights, tastes, and smells—the sensory accelerants of memory and feeling retrieval—never took her out of the present moment, never made her remember a past relationship or event for too long. The cinnamon smell she had experienced earlier had done something to her, prompting her curiosity. However, since she had no previous experience associated with the spicy scent, nothing had flashed across her mind other than a parallel experience with her own Pura diffuser.

"Thank you," she said, lifting the snifter to her mouth and inhaling the sweet scent coming from the brandy in its bowl.

Annie sat down and took a sip—then, she surprised Jean and rose from the couch with her snifter. "A bit of music, I think."

Music? Her eyes followed Annie as she walked away from the couch—the one with the component stereo cabinet behind it—and crossed in front of the fire on her way to . . .

She's going to play the piano, almost certainly Christmas music.

Am I ready for this?

And suddenly, all Jean's thoughts about why Shirley Ruth might not have been an honest person in her younger years were diminished by the overriding need to hear the Steinway & Sons Classic Grand played in this setting. The high wall, symbolizing her primary defense against allowing music that she had once performed back into her life, had crumbled. Her fear and anxiety disappeared. She longed for her once domineering life force, which had supported and sustained her. That particular type of music had never turned its back on her; she had turned her back on it.

I need to hear Annie play . . .

But what about our discussion?

Was Annie avoiding the subject, regretting what she had divulged, or was this her way of easing into a more difficult topic?

No one is going anywhere tomorrow, Jean thought. *I have time.*

As Annie moved out of view behind her, Jean picked up her drink, stood, and turned around in time to witness Annie place her snifter on top of the piano and sit down behind it. For a moment, Annie morphed into Ms. Janie, and Jean's mood soared, feeling reunited with a long-lost friend. Jean had broken her heart, too, and she wanted to reach out and comfort her. Make things better again.

The image disappeared, and Annie was back.

She lifted her fingers and held them above the keys, but instead of playing, looked over at Jean. "Only one request."

"Name it," Jean said.

Annie's eyes motioned toward the rocking chair. "Sit in it for me. It will be like old times, like I'm playing for my friend."

Jean studied the chair—the beautiful craftsmanship, the detail, and the Pendleton blanket, which Annie had folded and hung over the backrest once again. For a moment, she thought she could see her grandmother—an earlier version, perhaps, when she was around Jean's age, which is to say that Jean saw herself in the chair—rocking back and forth, listening to Annie play the Cole Porter songbook. Shirley Ruth/she was smiling.

"Of course," Jean said. "Time to find out what the fuss is all about." She was using humor and wit to conceal the tears building behind her eyes. *Just hold on until the music starts,* she told herself.

"Quite right," Annie replied, and when Jean had taken her seat and started to rock back and forth slowly, the first bars of "The Christmas Song" filled the air.

This was followed by "White Christmas," "A Marshmallow World," and "Silent Night." For the final song in her set, Annie played "Have Yourself a Merry Little Christmas" and sang along as she played. She had a beautiful voice, and Jean felt the pull to join her as the song's lyrics came back to her. However, for the moment, she remained silent. The only time she listened to Christmas music was when she had to be at the company's holiday gathering—before and after that event, she steered clear of anywhere that might be playing holiday music. Every Thanksgiving, she left the city to avoid Macy's parade; she did all of her Christmas shopping online; and she ordered takeout from her favorite places to avoid restaurants that would be decorated for the season and playing holiday favorites over and over again. December was Christmas time, and Christmas time was gathering time, and she had no one to gather with, and all the holiday music did was remind her of that fact.

Still, being here alone downstairs with Annie, as if she were attending a private concert, was a different experience. She was already overwhelmed by the sound of the piano, which Annie played softly not to wake the family upstairs. As Jean listened to Annie sing the lyrics of the last song with an honesty and joy she had not witnessed since Ms. Norman had sung a solo in front of the choir as inspiration during a challenging practice, Jean allowed herself to get swept up in the words and realized that, with no one around whom she knew or spent time with, she could admit that the song's words had a heartfelt message that she had denied herself all of these years.

As the song neared its conclusion, Jean's emotions ran high, and she saw the high school senior version of herself, dressed in her black choir dress, signing the song at the Holiday Traditions concert—her eyes fixed on Ms. Norman. And, suddenly, the pain of her parents not showing up was replaced by a wave of relief, and the release from years of tension, disappointment, and abandonment gave way to an unstoppable urge to . . .

. . . *sing.*

Annie finished the song and drank from her snifter of brandy. As she rose from the piano bench, she said, "There. I always feel better after playing."

Do it, Jean told herself. *Before she gets to the couch!* "Annie?"

Annie stopped just a few feet away from the piano. "Yes, dear?"

Jean swallowed, gathering her courage. "Could you play one more?"

"Of course!"

"And . . . would you mind if I performed the song while you played?"

"Are you serious, child? I would love to hear your voice! What a team we'll make!" She sat back down behind the piano and stretched her fingers. "What shall it be?"

Jean walked over and stood next to the piano. She felt comfortable, energized, and ready to sing the one song she *needed* to sing. The *only* song that captured her lost innocence and, by singing it, would allow her to defy the song's bittersweet lyric and return, momentarily re-crossing the uncrossable border, to childhood. To her dreams.

"Could you play 'Toyland'?"

"Oh dear, it would be an honor."

Remembering that it was the Doris Day version that Ms. Norman had used for their concert, Jean said, "Do you know the Doris Day version?"

Annie snapped her fingers. "By heart. Very much my generation."

Jean took a deep breath. She exhaled and nodded to Annie.

As the first notes of the intro came from the piano, Jean felt transported back in time and remembered why music had meant so much to her in her youth. Most of all, it had brought her a sense of serenity and filled her with wonder, and it was doing so again. Annie continued with the beautiful opening, and Jean grinned at her as she anticipated the upcoming moment to join in . . .

When Annie held the note Jean had been waiting for, she took a breath, closed her eyes, and sang, "Toyland. Toyland. Little girl and boy land. While you dwell within it, you are ever happy then . . ."

A minute later, she arrived at the point where she remembered that the chorus took over for Day, and Jean wondered what to do. She needn't have worried. Annie gave her a wink and sang, "When you've grown up, my dears, and are as old as I, you'll often ponder on the years that roll so swiftly by, my dears, that roll so swiftly by."

She gave Jean a nod, throwing it back to her, and Jean sang the final verse. "Childhood's joy-land. Mystic merry Toyland. Once you pass its borders, you can ne'er return again."

As Annie played the closing, Jean's body became enveloped in a cloud of happiness that held her high above the world of confusion, hurt, and shattered dreams. She had done it. She had sung again.

When she opened her eyes, the song had ended, and Annie was standing next to her. They embraced.

"That was beautiful," Annie said, rubbing her back.

"Thank you. Please don't tell anyone about this." They broke their hug. "It was an important first step for me."

"Won't say a word."

Annie took up her position once again on the couch, and Jean returned to the rocking chair.

"You play very well. I enjoyed that more than I can put into words."

"Thank you, sweetie. Not what I once was, but it still fills me."

There was silence for a few beats, and then Jean thought she heard the distant hum of a motor.

Annie seemed to hear it too as she sat still and leaned toward the front of the log cabin. "Snowmobile," she said.

"Scott?"

"Maybe. Maybe not." She rose. "Let's head to the foyer."

Jean set her almost-empty glass of brandy on the kitchen counter on the way there—Annie had already disappeared down the hallway.

20

They stood in front of the large windows next to the front porch's door and peered out into the dark patch of woods on the far side of the front lawn. The sound of the machine's motor continued to grow.

"Definitely headed this way," Jean said.

"Down the driveway, if I had to guess," Annie replied.

Finally, Jean saw the snowmobile's headlights cut through the patch of woods, and soon the machine cleared the forest and drove down the rest of the winding driveway toward the house.

Before reaching the pad where the vehicles were parked, Jean could see the SnowCoach behind the machine. Annie exhaled. "Thank God. It's Scott." She hugged Jean.

An hour later, the snowmobile was refueled and stowed in the pole barn along with the SnowCoach. Scott had showered and come downstairs in leather slippers, gray sweatpants, and a navy hooded sweatshirt. His work clothes were being washed, and his snowsuit, hat, and gloves were in the dryer.

Annie handed him a snifter of brandy, and he joined Jean on the couch.

"Okay, now that I know that you're safe and sound, I'm heading to bed. I'll be up early tomorrow for breakfast."

"Thanks, Gram," Scott said, taking a healthy pull on his brandy. "Sleep well. I'm going to crash down here on the couch after I finish this."

"Why not up in your room?"

"I'll keep the fire stoked and will also be able to answer the front door if we get any new visitors."

Annie took a drink from the glass of water she held in her hand. "Do you think we'll have any?"

He told her about the abandoned Ford Taurus he had found and his search for the person who had left the vehicle. "The tracks ended at a road across the field that he or she went across. There were recent vehicle tracks in both directions, so I couldn't determine which way the person went. I walked down the road in both directions for a while but didn't see anyone. It's still haunting me. I hope he or she is okay."

"Maybe one of the vehicles picked him or her up," Jean said.

"Definitely a possibility. I radioed in the license plate, so, by now, someone at the police station knows whose car it is and has probably been trying to track the person down." He turned back toward Annie. "So, yes, from what I saw on M-20, it's possible we could get some visitors. Even though everyone has been advised to stay off the roads, there'll be at least someone who tries it and gets stuck."

"But it's after two a.m.!" Annie said.

"Still wouldn't surprise me. It was almost one a.m. when I reached the road where the boot tracks ended and the fresh vehicle tracks were." He took a sip. "At eleven thirty, I was at the junction of M-20 and another road, turning cars back around."

"Anyone get pissy?" asked Annie.

"One guy demanded that he be allowed to take M-20 into Midland so that he could pick up groceries. Said it was his constitutional right to drive his truck wherever the hell he wanted to. Then, he exaggerated and said that he only had peanut butter and a jar of pickles back at the house."

"What did you say to him?" Jean asked.

"I said, 'The grocery stores are closed, sir. It looks like you're eating peanut butter and pickles until at least tomorrow.' He had a few choice words and then, of course, attempted to go around the snowmobile to get on M-20, but he spun out and almost went into the ditch. Thankfully, that changed his mind, and he turned around."

Jean wondered what she would have done. "Could you have stopped him if he had made it onto the road?"

"No. But he would have gotten stuck within a hundred yards, and then I would have had one more person to take to a shelter, which would have ticked him and me off."

He took another pull. "Anyway, if someone got into trouble, they could follow my fresh snowmobile tracks here. Can't blame 'em—it's what I'd do."

When Scott had first arrived home, he had told them how the night had gone. He described the first two hours as a free-for-all with dozens of vehicles stuck on M-20 and everyone needing help as their gas started to run out. Right before he was relieved by another snowmobiler who also had a SnowCoach attached to his machine, every stuck vehicle on the stretch of M-20 between Midland and Mt. Pleasant had been checked, and the passengers transported to shelters. He'd heard that there were major concerns with the number of vehicles stuck on the highways, but the majority of the police force, fire department, and other first responders were deployed there, along with volunteers who lived close to the highways and had snowmobiles. The police captain whom Scott had been reporting to all night had told him that everyone needed to focus on their assigned area; depending on how things looked tomorrow morning, they would reassess where to deploy their resources and divert transports where necessary.

"So, it's possible but *not likely* that we'll get visitors," Annie said.

"That's how I'd put it, since there are other places between the house and the highway, but throw logic out the window."

For a moment, Jean thought about sleeping on the other couch. If there was any trouble, she wanted to be as close to Scott as possible. Yes, she was an independent woman, but she was also aware of her current situation. Plus, besides the fear of the unknown concerning the rest of the night, she wanted to be around Scott. She liked the way his sweatshirt and sweatpants hugged his fit frame, and she had caught a pleasant whiff of some fresh shower gel he had used. She remembered being jealous of Dial for Men Triple Action Wash's marketing slogan, "Maintenance for your man suit." Renault Impact had lost the bid to come up with a slogan for a rival company, and it bothered her, not only because they lost the bid but also because she was struggling to think of a slogan that could rival Dial's.

Her mind started to drift to Scott entering the shower upstairs and applying whatever shower gel he was using, so she picked up her brandy.

Annie said good night and padded off to bed. Before handing Scott his brandy, she had recharged Jean with a finger of the smooth, amber liquid, and Jean now took a sip.

"Everything go okay with our guests upstairs?" Scott said, leaning his head back on the soft leather cushion and closing his eyes.

"Yes. They're a nice family."

He smiled, keeping his eyes closed. "Kids keep you up at all?"

She laughed. "Let's just say some bumps and thuds were coming from their room earlier."

"Those kids are so rambunctious. It's like they have an unlimited supply of energy. Although when I showered twenty minutes ago, I didn't hear a peep. I think they're all finally down."

"Long night for them. Maybe the kids will let them sleep in."

"Fifty-fifty," Scott said. "Hopefully, they get power back at their place soon."

"What time are you getting up tomorrow?"

"I told the Michigan State Police that I'd be out on M-20 by six a.m."

Damn, I thought we'd get to chat a little, but he needs sleep. She took a sip of her brandy and rose. "Well, I'll let you get some sleep. Be careful out there."

He opened his eyes. "Thanks for staying up with me a bit."

"Oh. Of course."

He finished off his drink, set the snifter on the coffee table, and curled up on the couch.

She finished her drink and entered the kitchen, putting her glass in the dishwasher. As she left the space and headed for the hallway, she heard him say, "Good night, Jean."

She stopped and glanced over at the couch. His head was raised off the armrest cushion, and he was staring at her. "Good night," she said and walked out of the room, a warm feeling coursing through her body that was not because of the brandy. As she walked down the hallway toward the foyer, her mind drifted to the future and her potential relationships:

She saw herself with Scott. They were on a foggy London street at night, dressed in overcoats and both wearing hats—he a fedora, she a pillbox. It was a scene out of the 1940s, in black and white with one exception: her red lipstick.

Then, Scott's face morphed into that of Urian's, and he adjusted the front brim of the fedora while moving closer to her . . .

Urian disappeared, and she was alone.

A figure materialized out of the fog—a man wearing the same overcoat and fedora as Scott and Urian, but his facial features were blurry.

Who is this?

She reached the foot of the stairs, and her thoughts about potential suitors were replaced by Annie's last words about Jean's grandmother—*'Well, at least her honesty later in life."*

There was still much to learn about Shirley Ruth and her family's history. *Maybe tomorrow, I'll get a chance to find out more.*

Jean looked over her shoulder at the swirling snow outside, hearing the biting wind rattle the porch window's shutters. She headed upstairs.

PART III

Clearings

21

Jean awoke to the sounds of feet hurrying down the hallway, along with laughing and yelling. Then, she heard a loud bang, as if someone had run into a wall, and heavier-sounding footsteps passed by her room.

She heard Carole's voice, a raised growl of a whisper. "Brittany! Ethan!"

There was more laughing, then running down the stairs.

Jean wiped her eyes and picked up her phone . . .

. . . 11:53 a.m.!

As if she had done something wrong and was about to be caught, she threw the covers off, dressed, got ready quickly in the bathroom, and then headed toward the staircase—all the while thinking: *How did I sleep in that long? I never sleep in!*

As she started down the stairs, she heard a growing commotion on the first floor. She reached the foyer and was surprised to see everyone except Scott there and in good spirits.

"Good morning," said Annie, who was dressed in jeans and a black crewneck sweater, and was helping Carole with the children's jackets and gloves.

"Good morning," Jean replied.

Carole, the kids, and Geoff all said hi, and then, after Geoff had put on his jacket, he said, "The power is back on at our house, so Scott is taking us home."

She looked around for Scott—down the hallway, around the corner, and finally outside—but there was no sign of him. "That's great," she said. "When was it restored?"

"We got the word half an hour ago," Annie replied, pulling a knit hat over Ethan's ears while Carole did the same with Brittany.

Carole met Jean's eyes. "So sorry these critters kept you up last night. We tried to keep them as quiet as possible this morning. Please tell me you got some solid sleep."

"Once my head hit the pillow, I didn't wake up until a few minutes ago."

"Thank God," Carole said.

"I haven't slept this long since—" She yawned, stretching her arms toward the ceiling. "Well, I can't remember when."

Annie finished with Brittany and came over and gave Jean's arm a loving squeeze. "I bet you're starved. I'll get something for you as soon as they leave."

Jean went to protest, being uncomfortable with people waiting on her who had been up hours before she had, but the snowmobile and SnowCoach came into view as it sped down the driveway toward the house.

Ethan started jumping up and down. "It's Ranger Scott! It's Ranger Scott!"

Jean turned toward Annie, and Annie said, "He's been out on M-20 since six a.m., says he'll go until around four this afternoon and then be back. Asked how you were doing when we told him the power was back on at Carole and Geoff's."

"What did you tell him?"

"That you were sound asleep, and that made him happy. He appreciated you staying up with him for a bit before he conked out."

Jean had hoped to be up when Scott left in the morning, but knowing that he had probably gotten up sometime around five to be on M-20, helping at six, made her realize the absurdity of that desire. She was tired—she just had not known *how tired* until waking up at almost noon. She theorized that it was the emotional energy expended yesterday that had worn her out—seeing Shirley Ruth's home, her cancelled flights, learning some of her family's history from someone she didn't know, the texts from Urian and Chantel, meeting Scott and already feeling something for him, even though she wasn't exactly sure what it was yet, and the general discomfort of a major change in her plans, resulting in a loss of control. The last item was on full display with her arrival downstairs after everyone else had already been up for some time. She wondered, *What will today bring?* Her phone was in the back-right pocket of her jeans, and there was an urge to pull it out and see if any flights were going out today, but as she looked outside and watched the blizzard continue to swirl, she thought, *There's no way.*

They all watched as Scott pulled up, his bright Polaris monosuit glowing against the landscape like an orange placed in front of a piece of printer paper.

"Santa's coming tonight!" Brittany yelled.

"He certainly is," said Geoff, picking his daughter up and hugging her.

Scott stopped the machine and SnowCoach right in front of the porch and hopped off. Jean saw him take the green Stanley thermos and a small backpack out of a rear compartment and then walk toward the porch.

He entered and was greeted with a hug from Annie and Carole, as well as a hearty handshake from Geoff. Jean stayed in the wings and gave him a smile when his eyes met hers. He handed the thermos and backpack to Annie.

She said, "I'll be right back," and headed off toward the kitchen.

He excused himself for a minute to use the restroom, and when he came back, Annie had his thermos refilled with coffee and fresh food loaded in his backpack. Scott looked at the family, all bundled up. "Ready to go home?"

The two children yelled, "Yes!" in unison.

"Okay, I'm going to put this stuff in the aft compartment, then drive the Grand Touring and SnowCoach into the pole barn and gas up. When I return, I'll wave you out and we'll get you all situated in the SnowCoach like before. Sound good?"

The kids cheered again, and Geoff and Carole expressed their thanks.

Scott slid over to Annie and Jean. "I should be back around four, and I'll be home for the night. Still looks like the storm will slow down this evening, which means things might start moving again around the state tomorrow." He stared into Jean's eyes. "I don't think there will be any flights, but maybe there will be on the 26th."

Jean wanted to say so many things—*Thank you for what you're doing; I wish I would have been up when you left this morning; I'm embarrassed that I just woke up and haven't checked my phone for any weather or travel updates; I'm . . . glad I won't be leaving for another few days*—but, she knew he was in a hurry. All she could do was say, "See you then. Stay safe."

He nodded, and in ten minutes, after heartfelt goodbyes in the foyer, the house was empty except for Jean and Annie. As they watched the snowmobile and SnowCoach disappear around the side of the house, Annie said, "I've got coffee and homemade blueberry muffins if you're still in a breakfast mood, or I have French onion soup and chicken salad sandwiches."

"You made that all today?"

Annie patted her arm. "My dear, I've been up since Scott left this morning. I've already got the corn casserole, potato casserole, ham, and raspberry pie prepared for tomorrow's feast."

"I'm sorr—"

"Now, don't you apologize one bit. You needed rest. Your schedule got turned upside down, and you're in unfamiliar surroundings with unfamiliar people—two toddlers last night, at that! If those things didn't drain you, then the heavy topics we covered did." She hugged Jean. "We don't have to discuss anything more if you don't want to."

She released her hug, and a part of Jean didn't want her to. She felt cared for in Annie's arms, like genuine kindness—a consideration for her well-being that she had not felt . . . "This is all more than I deserve," said Jean.

"Wrong again," Annie said. "You are my best friend's granddaughter, and, from my side of the hug we just had, that means you are family to me. I consider it my privilege and duty to look after you until this storm has passed. Got it, ma'am?"

Jean blushed and nodded. A tear slid down her cheek. *Why am I crying?* Before she could answer, Annie had embraced her again.

"There, there, child. There, there. Let's get some nourishment in you." She gently pulled away from Jean and made eye contact.

Jean removed her glasses and wiped the tears from her eyes. She said, "I still want to know everything, but I will not argue with you that I need something in my stomach first."

Annie touched her cheek. "Follow me."

Almost an hour later, Jean was full from the soup and sandwich. Annie had given her a lime sparkling water to go with the meal, and now the two of them were seated across from each other on the living room couches, sipping fresh coffee. Carole and Geoff had called and were settled back in, enjoying Christmas music and savoring the children's excitement for the big day tomorrow. Annie had also heard from Tammy and Rob, and they were fine, settling in for a cozy Christmas Eve. Scott had also called and said that every vehicle had been checked and that all people had been transported to shelters. He was stationed back at the intersection he had covered the previous evening to turn any vehicles around and send them back home unless someone inside needed emergency transport to a hospital. A female state police officer named Shelly and a male EMT named Greg had joined him at his station and were on standby to evaluate situations and deploy Scott as needed. He told Annie that he was still on schedule to be relieved at quarter to four and would drive straight home, park the snowmobile and SnowCoach in the pole barn, and then head inside.

Before they had left the kitchen, Jean had helped Annie make a tray of lasagna for dinner. *"Per our shopping list—a touch of Italy tonight,"* Annie had said. *"Lasagna, garlic bread, Caesar salad, and a bottle of Honig Cabernet Sauvignon Napa, 2021. Your grandmother got me interested in Napa years ago—we took a tour there—and I still receive two shipments a year. Scottie got us a few extra Cabs at Meijer if we need them, but we'll start with this one."*

The fire in the hearth blazed away, and the house creaked and moaned as the wind outside picked back up, the storm refusing to go away. They sat for a minute listening to the sounds, sipping on their coffee, both alone with their thoughts. Jean glanced at the piano, remembering the previous evening. *That was special, and something inside of me has changed for the better, but it's back to business now.*

Jean set her mug down on the coffee table and said, "Last night, you mentioned something about my grandmother being honest later in life. Maybe we could start there?"

Annie took one more drink and then set her mug down. "In 1983, Shirley Ruth's parents—your great-grandparents—left Michigan to retire in Great Falls, Montana." She stopped and leaned her head to one side, seeming to study Jean. "I should have known. Your mother never told you any of this, did she?"

"No."

"I suppose I'm not that surprised. Even though she didn't tell you much about your grandparents, I thought she might have mentioned your great-grandparents and how they chose Great Falls as a destination. It's quite remarkable, even silly perhaps."

"I've never heard about it."

"Hmm. Well, it was all because of an author, believe it or not. Richard Ford. Your great-grandparents were well-read people—they put my bookshelf to shame—and they enjoyed what is now termed 'literary fiction.' Highbrow, timeless—whatever snooty descriptor you prefer. And they passed this passion on to their daughter, but Shirley Ruth also enjoyed airplane fiction, as I still do. Her parents even occasionally drifted toward the realm of popular fiction, especially in their later years. It started when Shirley Ruth caught her mother with a copy of *The Hunt for Red October* when she visited them in their new home during Christmas in 1984, but her mother was quick to justify it, saying, *When President Reagan calls the book his kind of yarn or the perfect yarn, then I make an exception.*" Annie chuckled. "They were literary enthusiasts but die-hard Republicans. Go figure. Our nation in a nutshell, contradictions abounding from sea to shining sea. Anyway, in 1983, your great-grandparents read Ford's short story 'Great Falls' and became interested in Montana. At that time, Richard Ford was not the household name he is today. I love his works."

Jean winced. "I've never heard of him."

"Really?" Annie said. "You never saw the 2018 film adaptation of Ford's novel *Wildlife*? It had Jake Gyllenhaal and Carey Mulligan in it."

Jean shook her head. "I haven't." She did not fault Annie for the suggestive nature of her inquiry, which came across as, *Well, you know of those two popular actors, so you must have seen everything they are in, right?'* She knew that Annie intended to establish a connection and interest, based on a lifetime of existing and participating in the communal theatrical experience, where almost everyone saw the same films together and followed the same stars, choosing to see future movies based on whether those stars were in them or not. It was what Annie's generation did, and, applied in a general sense, it explained much of their overall consumer behavior, which Jean had learned through an extensive study prepared for Renault Impact in preparation for a product that was to be pitched to that particular age group a few years ago.

"Huh. Well, you should check it out and then explore Ford's work if you're a reader. Are you one?"

She's doing it again. "Yes, I like to read."

"Then I think you'll enjoy Richard Ford." She rubbed her tongue across her upper lip. "I know Scott loves his stuff."

And again!

Jean nodded. "All right. I'll give Mr. Ford a try. Where should I start?"

Annie laughed. "Now that's a loaded question. Your grandmother and I were always at odds when friends asked us where to start. We weren't Ford fanatics like your great-grandparents, but we always recommended him to people when they asked us what or who they should read next." She tapped her fingertips together. "How about this? I'll tell you where *Shirley Ruth* thought people should start." When Jean nodded again, Annie said, "*The Sportswriter.*"

After a moment of silence, Jean said, "Any particular reason?"

Annie seemed to weigh her words. "Yes . . . and it's not a happy one. She never told people why she chose that book as the Ford jumping-off point, but I knew it, and those who were close to her put it together. It became one of those ah-ha moments where your eyes go wide and you snap your fingers, saying something like, 'I get it, now.'"

Jean was captivated. "What's *The Sportswriter* about?"

She read Annie's frown as one not of disappointment but of sorrow, pain. "It's about a failed novelist turned sportswriter dealing with the aftermath of a failed marriage and other losses—most notably, the death of his son."

22

Jean waited for Annie to continue. She didn't immediately make the connection between the novel's premise and her grandmother's life, but her mind continued to work on the problem of how the two were related, and she eventually formed a working theory. My grandmother's children never died, but she did lose them both at some point and dealt with it for the rest of her life.

Annie asked, "Any ideas as to why she would choose that particular work?"

Jean told her her theory.

Annie took a pull on her coffee and said, "My Lord, girl. You have Shirley Ruth's instincts and her ability to read situations."

"It's been a cloud that has hung over my family's past since I was old enough to ask about it and be told, *'One day, I'll let you know.'* Which, *that day*, as you know, never came."

"That day is today."

"It is."

"Yes," Annie said. "Okay, back to the move. There's also a Michigan connection to Mr. Ford. He attended Michigan State University and even taught junior high school in Flint, Michigan, about an hour away from here.

Even though your grandmother and I were teachers, we never knew him, naturally, but it is interesting. I know your great-grandparents found it *interesting,* and, in their later years, claimed that Ford's time in Michigan, coupled with 'Great Falls' and his other Montana writings, were undeniable signs that they were meant to retire there."

Jean smiled, breaking some of the tension.

"I know," said Annie, smiling back. "People have their reasons, don't they?"

In advertising and in life, Jean thought. It could be argued that the secret behind any successful campaign lies in understanding *why* people are drawn to certain things. "They do," she replied.

"From what your grandmother told me, your great-grandparents had an idyllic retirement out there, fueled by the good Mr. Ford and his writings. In 1987, he released a short story collection titled 'Rock Springs.' Most of the stories are set in Montana, so it only solidified their belief that Richard Ford had brought them there. Then, in 1990, came the whopper: *Wildlife,* which is set *in* Great Falls. It was a novel that Shirley Ruth enjoyed reading with her parents, but it also later broke their hearts—the story was about a fracturing family. We'll get to all that in a minute, but I'll fast forward. When Ford's other "Montana novel," *Canada,* came out in 2012, Shirley Ruth couldn't read it right away. It wasn't until 2018 when the movie version of *Wildlife* came out that I was able to get her to read it." Annie stopped, seemingly lost in another memory, her eyes drifting toward the fire. It took a few seconds until she returned to the present, and she blinked and then swallowed before continuing. "So, they moved there in '83, and kind of shocked Shirley Ruth. She was very close to her parents. But she eventually accepted it, and she, your grandfather, your mom, and your uncle started taking family trips out there to see them a few times a year. Your mom and uncle loved their grandparents."

Jean sighed once again. "She never told me about them."

Annie pursed her lips. "That's too bad. Your great-grandparents were such kind people. I know for a fact that your mother discovered her love for Montana during those visits. Things were nice for all of them, easy and relaxed." She leaned forward. "However, in the spring of 1992, everything changed. Shirley Ruth came over one Saturday afternoon in April and told me that she had just spoken to her mother, who had asked if she and Martin would be willing to move to Great Falls and take care of her and her father. They were still self-sufficient, but it was becoming increasingly difficult to manage certain aspects of their lives without assistance. One thing was for certain: they did not want to move into an assisted living facility. As I listened to Shirley Ruth, I felt that horrible emptiness in my stomach that many people experience when life changes. Even though she told me that she and Martin were thinking the request over, I knew I was going to lose my best friend for a while—maybe forever."

"How did you know?"

"For a few reasons. One, your grandmother was a caretaker—sometimes to a fault due to her pushiness—and she would never fail to honor her duty to her beloved parents. Two, she and Martin were empty nesters; your mom was twenty-three and in her first year at the University of Michigan's Law School, where, as you know, she met your father." She gave a sudden grin, which surprised Jean. "In the early seventies, *Richard Ford* received a three-year appointment in the University of Michigan Society of Fellows. But, I digress. I need to shut down the Richard Ford talk right about now."

Yes! Please do! Jean thought but couldn't keep a laugh of bewilderment from escaping her mouth.

"Ha! Message received, my dear. Although you are much nicer about it than your grandmother would have been. She would have cut me off at his name, looked me in the eye, and said, 'Annie, shut the fuck up about Ford, will you?' And she would have meant it with love, but, my God, could the woman swear with authority."

Jean bit her tongue, wanting to laugh at Annie saying the f-word. Some people sounded so unnatural when they swore, whereas some possessed the gift to say expletives with panache. Annie was in the former category; Jean's boss, Chantel, was in the latter, as was, apparently, Shirley Ruth. She grinned, thinking of her favorite audiobook narrator, who was the most gifted deliverer of profanity that she had ever heard. Jean loved a particular series he narrated where, at least once in every novel, the author would have his main character address that particular book's villain, saying, "Who in the *fuck*, do you think you are?"

Annie took a breath, joined her hands, and exhaled in a reset of sorts, gathering herself for the rest of the story. She continued. "Your Uncle Brett was nineteen and a freshman at Michigan Tech. Did your mother ever tell you that he scored a *thirty-five* on the ACT? No? Well, because of his score, he had received a full academic scholarship to Michigan Tech, which had made your grandmother and grandfather so proud. You have a brilliant family, dear."

She did not know what to do with the compliment. *I don't know about Uncle Brett, Aunt Carrie, or Brandon, but for my family: They might be book smart, but in terms of emotional intelligence, my mother and father are pretty much in kindergarten. Me? From what I gathered from Psychologist-Samuel-forgot-his-last-name before he forgot to put on pants, I was stuck there too before starting my work.* She gave a nod and said, "Wow."

"Extremely smart," Annie said. "So, a few days after she came to visit me, your grandmother invited me over for a glass of wine after school. I had a feeling that she was going to tell me their decision, and I was right. Immediately after we toasted, she said that she and Martin would be moving to Great Falls that summer. I broke down. Believe me, I understood the decision, but it devastated me. I didn't know if they would ever return to Michigan. She teared up, but that was as emotional as Shirley Ruth got."

"She wasn't retired yet, was she?"

"No. She was fifty-two, and I was fifty-one. We were definitely in the late stages of our careers, but we both needed to keep working. When she flew out there a few weeks later to look for a house, she interviewed at Charles M. Russell High School and was hired. Even in 1992, there were not many female high school teachers who held PhDs. She also found them a house a few blocks away from her parents' home, so when she returned to Midland, she let everyone at school know she would be leaving at the end of the school year. Until that point, I had never seen our good friend Bob Sympkins cry, but he wept that day; there would be other occasions that would follow, but they were many years in the future. More coffee?"

"No, thank you."

"I can see the confusion on your face," Annie said. "Minus the difficulty in saying goodbye to your place of work, your friends, and the home where you raised your children, it seems like a pretty straightforward move in life. If your mom and uncle would have still been at home, I could have seen how uprooting them would have been added stress, but they weren't—Lori had her apartment in Ann Arbor, and Brett was planning on staying in the Upper Peninsula over the summer working as a tutor and getting to live in the residence hall rent free, pretty good deal. It seemed like the perfect time for Shirley Ruth and Martin to make the transition. We were empty nesters too—my kids, J.J. and Michelle, were twenty-two and twenty, and both were in college. I think that made the move even more difficult, because both couples were looking forward to spending time with each other without having to care for the kids. We all loved our children, but we were also eager to reclaim some of our lives. For John and me, it was a sigh of relief—We made it! We wanted to reclaim our relationship, rekindle it, remember what it was like before we had kids. And, we looked forward to celebrating adult milestones that our children would reach." She laughed. "You've got to take your victory laps when they come. However, reaching that particular milestone of regaining your independence, unfortunately, sets into motion a countdown clock to reaching a host of other milestones that you wish you never reached—physical deterioration, medical issues that you didn't have to deal with before, the fading of your mental acuity, going from taking care of your kids to having them take care of you, and on and on. None of those things had happened yet, but we knew they were inevitable consequences that would come with reaching the milestone of our children leaving home. Of course, there were compensations that old age could bring, such as financial security and career achievements, but these were still in the distance, if they were attainable at all. I think that's why we were all so excited to get busy with life again when our last child left the house—a spirit of 'Let's get the entire bucket list checked off before those things start to happen.' Even if it was only for a decade or so, we considered ourselves *back*—back in the game. Well, in our haste, we had forgotten about the other side of the equation; yes, the kids had left the nest, but our parents were about to return to it. It ended up that John and I got a lot more freedom back than Shirley Ruth and Martin did, like fourteen years more. Their brief gift of liberty got ripped away."

A log in the hearth surrendered to the heat and fell off the pile, and Annie glanced that way. Without turning back, she said, "Sometimes, I wonder if your great-grandparents held on for a few extra years until Brett was out of the house so that they wouldn't put your grandparents in the situation of having to move with him while he was still in high school. It wouldn't surprise me if they had needed help a few years earlier. The more I have thought about it over the years, the surer I am that that is what happened. When Shirley Ruth and Martin arrived in Great Falls that summer, they had a ton they had to do to take care of Shirley Ruth's parents."

"Well, I haven't read any Richard Ford—"

Annie's eyes left the fire and met Jean's.

"—but I have read enough stories to know that we've reached the point where the unexpected happens, and things go to pot."

"Unfortunately, we have," was all Annie said.

"I just cannot imagine what it was," said Jean.

"And I don't think you ever would. But," she exhaled, "here it is."

23

"The end of the school year came, and there were tributes to Shirley Ruth and goodbye parties thrown for her and Martin. It made saying goodbye more difficult. Felt like the end of an era that had been cut short. Your grandmother and I thought we would retire together."

Jean watched as Annie's hands squeezed the couch cushions and then released.

"They sold the house in late June, and we celebrated the 4th of July at their place. This is, of course, when we both still lived in town and not out here. The 4th was on a Saturday that year, so Lori and Brett had both driven home on Friday, and my kids had come home too, so we could all celebrate one last holiday together at their house, which was like a second home to all of us. Also, Lori and Brett had arranged their schedules so that they could stay for a few days after the weekend to help their parents pack for the movers who were coming at the end of the week. They had to be out of the house by Wednesday the fifteenth because that was when the new owners were moving in; I remember because it was smack dab in the middle of the month. Naturally, my entire family volunteered to help them pack, but Shirley Ruth said that she would only need my help on Monday, the sixth, because that was when she was going to pack up the kitchen. So far, so good, right?"

Jean nodded. *What in the world happened? These people are all so sweet!*

"I come over on Monday and help her out. It took us all damned day. Sorry, I'm swearing again. On Tuesday the seventh, things go well. We talk at night, and they're all exhausted, of course. I go to bed sad, because the more they pack, the closer they get to leaving us. Then, on Wednesday, July 7th—one week before they're supposed to move out—it happens, and everything changes forever." She dabbed the corner of her eyes with the sleeve of her sweater. "Still gets me." Annie sat back, resting her head against the couch cushion as if she had just said, *"Oh, I give up!"*

She hesitated and then continued. "Late Wednesday morning, while Shirley Ruth and Martin were in the garage organizing items into bins, Brett and Lori picked up a file cabinet that was in the bottom of a hallway storage closet. Lori lost her grip, and the cabinet tipped over, spilling its contents onto the hallway floor. As they picked up the files, papers, and other documents your grandparents had filed away, Brett found a heavy, nine-inch-by-twelve-inch manila envelope that had faded in color, sticking out from a file folder. When he opened the folder to stick the envelope back in, he saw his name written in permanent marker near the top of the envelope." She exhaled toward the ceiling, stared at the wooden beams for a beat, and then met eyes with Jean. "He opened it and examined the contents. What he discovered was that he was adopted. Neither he nor Lori had any clue of this beforehand—Shirley Ruth and Martin had kept it from them both."

"Oh, God," said Jean. "Why would they do that?"

"Brett's biological mom died giving birth to him when she was 19. Brett's father was 18 and a senior in high school. They were both from low-income families who lived near Lansing and had decided to give the baby up for adoption when he was born. After Shirley Ruth had nearly died giving birth to

Lori, the doctors had advised her not to become pregnant again, but they always wanted to have another child. So, they started the adoption process, which led them to Brett's parents because they were having a boy, and that is what Shirley Ruth and Martin had decided they wanted. They thought it would make the perfect family. When Brett was born, Lori was three years old, about to turn four, and we all wondered if she would remember her mom not being pregnant. Obviously, she never did, and neither did my oldest, J.J., who was almost three. Back then, things were a lot more private than they are today. No one ever told Brett he was adopted. It also helped that his biological parents resembled Shirley Ruth and Martin." She sat up. "Now, the reason why they didn't tell him. By 1979, when Brett was six, Shirley Ruth had told me that they planned on telling him when he was a little older. But, in 1980, they found out that his biological father, twenty-five years old at the time, had murdered his parents and then committed suicide. After Shirley Ruth and Martin heard that, their attitude changed. I am not saying I agree with their decision to keep everything from him, but I know that they intended to shield him from the horrific deaths that his parents and one set of biological grandparents experienced. They wanted to protect him, thinking it would all be too much for him to handle, even if he was older. I think they also weighed what good it would do to tell him; there was nothing he could do to change the situation, and both of his parents were now dead. Some children would have forgiven their adopted parents, but it was not meant to be for Shirley Ruth and Martin. Brett and Lori exploded on them in the garage, and there was a huge shouting match. I got the feeling that something was going on when I made my nightly call to Shirley Ruth, and no one picked up the phone. That had never happened before, when I knew that they were home. I explained it away at the time, thinking that they were just busy or had maybe gone out for pizza. I thought of calling again later, but decided against it because I planned to bring them breakfast the next morning. So, I went to bed. When I showed up with a thermos of fresh coffee and a dozen donuts, I found a broken Martin and an angry Shirley Ruth. They gave me a quick summary and asked for some space. I left the thermos and donuts and headed home, crying all the way."

"Did Brett ever find out what happened to his birth parents?"

"Lori told me that the information about his mother dying during childbirth was in the documents in the envelope, but that the information about his father's and grandparents' deaths was not. Your mom helped him track down those details that summer. They discovered that Brett's dad had an older brother, and Brett considered reaching out to him but wanted to learn more about him first. They found him in Lansing and followed him for two days. From the moment a dive bar opened, he was in there drinking and then selling drugs in a back alley. Brett decided not to make contact. I guess one of the hardest early moments came a few days after they left Lansing. Brett thought about the first six years of his life and all the things he did while his dad was still alive. Then, he thought about being seven in 1980 and all the things he did around the time that his dad murdered his parents and took his own life. It absolutely crushed him. And that was the one thing that separated him from Shirley Ruth, Martin, and Lori: he showed emotion, and they struggled to deal with it. Mostly, they tried to suppress it, which just made it worse. I think he had a lot of pent-up emotion when he found out that they had never told him the truth, and that is why the split was so volatile . . . and permanent."

Tears slid down Jean's cheeks as she thought about what Brett had gone through. In a way, she was proud of her mom for sticking up for her brother; in another way, she was angry at her for never telling her what had happened.

"I know, dear," Annie said. "Do you want to take a break?"

Jean shook her head no and removed her glasses to wipe the tears. "Please, continue, Annie."

"All right," whispered Annie. She cleared her throat and raised the volume of her voice to her normal speaking tone. "So, Brett dropped out of college and moved to Alaska. Lori told me something interesting early on in the estrangement—I became her confidant, although I never got in between her and Shirley Ruth. Your mom knew that I thought she should meet with Shirley Ruth and try to clear the air. More on that in a bit. In the manila envelope was a copy of Brett's father's and mother's SAT scores. Somehow, Shirley Ruth had acquired them. I never asked her, but Lori and I assumed that Shirley Ruth and Martin wanted to adopt a baby that had intellectual potential. Brett's mother scored 1490 out of 1600—incredible. Brett's father's score was interesting. He scored 800 overall. But the breakdown was an 800 on the math section and a *zero* on the verbal section—he skipped the verbal part of the test. The tragedy is that they both had the smarts to get themselves out of their unfortunate situation. Brett's biological father was a junior in high school, and his mother was a senior when she became pregnant. It stands to reason that they were thinking of a better future by putting the baby up for adoption. Brett's father was even enrolled in Lansing Community College, but he dropped out after Brett's mother died, and Lori and Brett found no record of him ever enrolling in college again.

"Brett's intelligence was another aspect that helped keep the family secret intact. Everyone just thought he was a product of a brainy family. As a side note, he is one of the most intelligent people I have ever met, and he's a lifelong learner. Lori told me that his love of learning and curiosity never stopped—he just went about things more informally after he dropped out of Michigan Tech. From the age of nineteen until now, he has educated himself by listening to books on CD—now digital audiobooks on his phone's apps—while driving his truck all over the country; he must be one of the most well-read individuals on the planet by now. Plus, Alaska was a great fit for him. He loves cold weather. Most of us in Michigan tolerate it, and there are some fun times to be had out in the snow—right now, not being one of those times—but during winter, most of us cannot wait for things to warm up. Not Brett, though. He always hated to see winter go. We all thought he was a little crazy, but he's stayed true to who he was. Plenty of cold up in Alaska!"

Jean welcomed the bit of humor. Her different emotions vacillated like waves that were out of sync—she felt all of them, none of them dominating the others. *It is strange to be laughing while also feeling pain, sorrow, disappointment, confusion, and frustration,* she thought.

"And he liked to travel. Whenever we pulled out of Midland, he was always the most excited out of both families." She put a hand on her heart. "Being someone who is emotional, I always had a special place in my heart for Brett."

Jean finished her coffee and sat back. "I find it ironic that my mother and father moved to Billings in 1994. One, she was pregnant with me, so it must have been a difficult move. Two, the only reason I know the year is that my parents just celebrated thirty years of practicing law in Billings. They had a small office party. I received an invitation, more out of courtesy than the expectation that I would attend. They kept the date of the party separate from my birthday, which was . . . well, whatever. But I do know that my mother practiced law from her hospital bed the day I was born. It's become kind of a family legend, but I think it's ridiculous." She pulled out her phone. "How far is it from—"

Annie cut her off. "It's a three-and-a-half-hour drive from Billings to Great Falls."

Jean put her phone on the table next to her empty mug. "That's not far at all. I don't know exactly when my great-grandparents passed away, never looked it up and never asked, but if my grandparents arrived in the summer of 1992, then unless my great-grandparents died right away, there had to be some overlap."

"There was quite a bit of overlap," said Annie. "Your great-grandparents lived until 2006, when they both passed away within a few months of each other. Your grandparents were in Great Falls from 1992 until 2007."

Suddenly, the filled-in chronology returned her to Annie's statements from before, and they made more sense—*"We all loved our children, but we were also excited to get some of our lives back . . . It ended up that John and I got a lot more freedom back than Shirley Ruth and Martin did, like fourteen years more. Their brief gift of liberty got ripped away."* Just as both couples, Annie and John and Shirley Ruth and Martin, had become empty nesters in 1991, Shirley Ruth and Martin had gotten their independence cut short almost immediately, just a year later in 1992, when they had to move to Great Falls to take care of Shirley Ruth's parents. They ended up taking care of them for fourteen years and then returned to Michigan the following year in 2007.

Mom and Dad had twelve years of overlap with Mom's grandparents and thirteen years of overlap with Mom's parents. "Did Mom and Dad ever visit my great-grandparents or grandparents? I mean, did they ever take *me* to see them?"

Annie's eyes dropped to the floor and then slowly rose. "Yes, there were visits. Your mother made it clear that she did not want contact with her parents for a while, but *did* want contact with her grandparents. It was awkward and hurtful for Shirley Ruth and Martin to know that Lori was a few blocks away visiting Shirley Ruth's parents, but her parents allowed the visits because they loved Lori and thought that if they maintained ties, then one day her heart would open up to her parents again."

"And, there was me, right?"

"Yes, dear. That was probably the strongest argument for them maintaining contact. They ate you up every time Lori would bring you along."

"I have no memory of them," said Jean.

"Shirley Ruth wrote letters to me while she lived in Great Falls and said that her dream was to see her granddaughter one day. After a few years, she didn't understand why Lori hadn't moved on and reestablished contact. At that point, which was around 1996, I briefly entered the fray, telling her that she needed to apologize to Lori and Brett."

"She hadn't even apologized yet?"

"Your grandparents were stubborn. They felt bad about what had happened and how it had happened, but they still believed they had not done anything wrong or hurtful intentionally. They thought Brett and Lori were being too emotional—Brett's reaction didn't surprise them, but Lori's did. They felt that they had been protecting Brett—and, to an extent, Lori—and they refused to offer an apology. There were times when my husband, John, wanted to contact Martin and talk to him, man-to-man, but I told him not to. Our only chance at helping was for me to try to convince my best friend of what she should do."

"What happened when you gave your advice?"

"I called her—thought it was the right way to do it. Being an introvert, she much preferred letters, which is why she later preferred texts over calls. However, I felt she had opened the door for me to walk through when she asked me why things weren't coming back together, and I told her I would answer her, but that I had to do it my way. So, we talked one Saturday afternoon in the summer of 1996. The Olympics were on, which we both loved. Since they were in Atlanta that year, we had even thrown around the idea of taking an anniversary road trip there together to mark our trip there eighteen years prior to—"

She stopped abruptly.

"Are you okay?" Jean asked.

Annie rolled her eyes up at the ceiling. "Sorry, Jean. I almost gave something away about later tonight that has nothing to do with your family's estrangements. Whew! Glad I caught myself."

Jean was utterly baffled. *Why would Shirley Ruth and Annie have traveled to Atlanta in 1978? And what in the hell did it have to do with later tonight?* "I'll just have to trust you on that one," she said.

"Thank you. It will make sense later. Now, where was I . . . Right, the phone call. We both agreed to keep the Olympics on to distract us if things got too tense. It was more for me than her, because I can get worked up when something bothers me. And, believe me, it bothered me that she and your grandfather had not apologized, yet expected things to heal on their own. Ridiculous, right?" She didn't wait for Jean's response. "We talked, and I felt heard—knew this would be my only chance because that is all Shirley Ruth ever gave anyone. She didn't like to revisit topics."

"What did she say?"

"There were some grunts and sighs, but then I got an 'Okay, I'll think about it,' which was more than I thought I would get concerning this topic. On almost anything else, we enjoyed bickering and trying to convince each other of things—'I'm right, and you know it,' or, 'My position is stronger than yours,' that kind of competitive squabbling. But not this time. I talked and she listened. This conversation led to her and Martin calling both kids, but it took over half a year."

"It took *that* long?" asked Jean.

"They never rushed into decisions."

Who does that sound like? thought Jean.

"After a few months, so this would have been late September, Shirley Ruth called me and said they were leaning toward contacting their kids. But they didn't want to call around any of the upcoming holidays—Halloween, Thanksgiving, Christmas, or New Year's. So, they decided that they would probably call Lori first in mid-January. I politely told them that it was late September and that they could call her right now, avoiding all the holidays, but they wouldn't budge. I know they were afraid and didn't want to chance either ruining their kids' holidays, and, if I'm being honest, their own. Mid-January was safe, and they followed through. Lori picked up. I still remember her words when she called me afterwards. 'They both gave a roundabout apology of sorts, which was better than anything they had done so far, and I decided to introduce Jean to them.'"

"She brought me?" Jean asked.

"Yes."

"What about my father?"

"He stayed in Billings."

"Brett?"

"Your grandparents asked Lori for Brett's phone number, and she reached out to Brett. He declined. Later on, they asked for his address. Once again, he declined. When they learned that he was living in Fairbanks, they sent a letter, but he never wrote back. They asked me every few years if I had his phone number, which I didn't. He always called me from pay phones when he was on the road; he never called me from his house. At one point, your grandparents thought about hiring a private detective to track down his number, but they decided against it. They also considered flying out and showing up on his doorstep, but each time they worked up the nerve, they backed away, afraid of being rejected on the spot. I told them they should both just do it. Then, Martin got sick, and, well, the window closed. I'll skip right to the end before I tell you about your visit to them with your mom: Brett never saw or spoke with his parents again."

Jean felt an immense sadness overtake her, her chest muscles contracting, her body feeling like it was going to collapse. Even though she was not a part of what had taken place more than thirty years ago, it involved her family members, specifically Shirley Ruth, with whom she felt a growing connection. *I might have tried to shield my child from pain and heartache, too, but at the expense of the truth?* She was not sure. *I can sit here and say I would have apologized, but when I think I'm in the right, I can be stubborn, too!* She grieved for Brett; she grieved for Lori; she grieved for her great-grandparents who, knowing that Lori had taken her over to see them, had held and kissed her when she was a baby; she grieved for

Shirley Ruth and Martin, whose absence of self-awareness and, therefore, the requisite emotional intelligence to navigate the situation had been the architects of their prison. *How would I have dealt with decades of heartache? A complete loss of control.* Jean's chest heaved, and she put her head in her hands.

The next thing she knew, Annie was by her side, rubbing her back.

"Quickly," Jean said. "Tell me the rest of it."

"I will, but are you sure you don't want to rest a while?"

Jean sat up, her eyes red. "I am sure. Please?"

"Okay," Annie said. "There was one visit, and it didn't go well. After a half-dozen phone calls between January and May 1997, in June, your mom decided to bring you to your grandparents' house. All I ever got from Shirley Ruth about the visit came a few weeks after. She wrote me a letter, mentioning the visit only in the final paragraph, stating that it had not gone well and that she was unsure about the future of the relationship. She added that she loved holding you and meeting you and that an on-again, off-again relationship with you, your mother, and your father would be too tough to handle. Lori eventually called me and said that after twenty minutes of stiff, safe conversation, the chat moved into dealing with the past. And at that point, your grandmother and grandfather said what was in the past was in the past, and they didn't want to talk about it anymore. Naturally, this didn't sit well with Lori, who, even though she was more of a thinker like them and less emotional, wanted to talk things through—especially about what had happened to Brett. She felt that was the only way to reset things and move forward. Shirley Ruth and Martin thought differently, and it cost them. The result of the visit shattered your great-grandparents. They sided with Lori and could not understand why Shirley Ruth and Martin had not just swallowed their pride and heard Lori out. Things could have been repaired that afternoon, and it's a shame."

Jean began to cry, and Annie held her. Finally, she said, "I never saw any of them after that, did I?"

Annie teared up. "No, you didn't."

Not wanting to believe it, Jean said, "My mom didn't even take me over to see my great-grandparents? They lived for nine more years."

"She didn't," Annie said. "Your mom stopped visiting them after the June 1997 visit."

Jean screamed.

24

Jean lay on the couch, facing the hearth, with a pillow behind her head and the Pendleton blanket draped over her. Annie sat on the other couch, sipping tea and watching over her.

She had apologized for her outburst, which Annie had not accepted, saying the apology was unnecessary. Still, she felt that she had embarrassed herself by losing control—especially as a guest in someone's home. Annie would hear none of it, holding her until she calmed down enough to take a drink from the glass of ice water that Annie had brought from the kitchen.

Jean's teeth had been clenched, her eyes burning with rage as she had taken the glass and brought it to her mouth. After a few seconds of holding the glass to her lips, her jaw muscles relaxed, and she had taken her first drink. The primordial scream had shocked her system as she had never become so worked up to release such a sound, and what bothered her most was that it had slipped out uncontrollably. It wasn't until the horrible sound ceased that she even noticed that it had come from her. The other cue of realization came from the fact that Annie had slid away from her in fear. As Jean's senses had struggled to clear, she noticed that her host sat a few feet away and was no longer holding her, looking at her with what Jean thought to be surprise, wonder, and then pity on her face.

Annie had left at that point to fetch the ice water, and after Jean had swallowed the first gulp, she had turned to the old sweet lady and said, "Sorry. I—"

"You have nothing to be sorry about, Jean. I wish the story you wanted me to tell you were different."

She finished the glass of water, the cool liquid feeling good on her throat, which was now sore from the intensity of her yell. Then, Annie had lain her back on the couch and brought her the pillow and blanket.

Now, a stream of imagined memories appeared in her mind that were similar to the ones that had flashed in there yesterday when she had visited her grandmother's house. They moved faster and faster until coalescing into an alternate reality of what might have been for the past thirty years. The images of herself, her mother, and her father were always clear as were their aging and actions along with the various settings she imagined—Billings, New York City, Shirley Ruth's house in Michigan, Annie's log cabin, and her great-grandparents' home in Great Falls, even though she had no frame of reference to base the setting on. What was not clear were the features of her grandparents and great-grandparents—it was as if she were watching a home movie, where everything else was clear, but the blurry figures of her elders were each labeled with a name tag that moved with them in the scene. She could not hear their voices, their dialog appearing as subtitles across the screen of the moving image; she could only hear the voices of people she had heard in real life—her own, her mother's, her father's, Annie's, and . . . Scott's. He had appeared throughout the reels, mainly as a teenager, riding bikes with her down Shirley Ruth's winding driveway during one of her imagined family visits with her grandmother and grandfather. She had mentioned to Annie that the 3,500-square-foot house seemed big for just two people, but Annie had explained that

Shirley Ruth and Martin loved to entertain their friends there, and, Annie thought that they still clung to the shred of hope that the family would be reunited and their children and their children's families would one day stay with them there.

The moving images and sound continued until Shirley Ruth's funeral came into view, and everything slowed down. Jean saw herself sobbing as her grandmother's casket was lowered into the earth, but somehow she could feel what the alternate version of herself in that moment felt. Gathered around her were her parents, Annie, Scott, and her Uncle Brett. She felt comforted, whole—not alone.

What would my life have been like had the 1997 visit gone the other way? Her pragmatic and logical side, which usually dominated her thinking, told her not to concern herself with this line of thinking. The past could not be changed, and she had no control over the situation. However, that did not mean that it was futile to try to make sense of what had happened, and she found herself frustrated. She felt anger toward Shirley Ruth, but also pity; she felt irritated, even bewildered, by her mother's actions, yet also in awe of Lori's ability to stand by her brother. There was a part of Jean that wanted things to be different, but there was also a part of her that did not. She had become who she was because of these events, and she liked the person she had become. But the tension inside her had been building ever since she had first seen her grandmother's house yesterday, and today, it had reached a point where it could no longer be contained and needed to be released. *This* she needed to understand, and she believed it started with the person who had triggered her journey down this path: Shirley Ruth.

She and Annie had remained best friends through the entire ordeal, and Jean's grandmother and grandfather had moved back to Michigan, only increasing the distance between themselves and their family in Montana and Alaska. Why?

She asked Annie.

"I think it was acceptance, maybe a touch of avoidance as well. After her mother and father passed away in 2006, Shirley Ruth realized that the chances of having a relationship with her son and his family were close to zero, and the chances of having a relationship with her daughter and her family weren't that much better. In 2007, when they moved back and had the house that you're selling built, Shirley Ruth was sixty-seven, and Martin was seventy-two. They were retired; we were retired; and we missed each other." She rested her voice for a moment. "They decided that they wanted to be around close friends as they entered their third act in life. Of course, John and I were ecstatic. From 1992 until 2007, we had enjoyed being empty nesters but had also taken on the responsibility of caring for our elderly parents. John's father had passed away when he was in his early thirties, so we looked after his mom, who lived in Saginaw until she passed in 2002. My parents lived in Mt. Pleasant, and my mother died in 2001 and my dad in 2005. The log cabin was finished near the end of 2006, and it has been my residence ever since.

"With our kids out of the house and our parents living so close, it had not been too much to manage over the years, but it was enough so that after one trip out to Great Falls in 1995 to visit with Shirley Ruth and Martin, we didn't make it back out there, and they never traveled back to Michigan. So, when they came home in 2007, we had not seen each other in twelve years."

Jean turned her head, the pillow underneath it making a crackling noise, and looked over at Annie. "Must have been quite the reunion."

"Would you like to hear about it? Might give you something optimistic to think about."

And at that moment, something inside her settled, like a plane that had found a smooth path through the air. She wanted stability, but what she yearned for was positivity—a good memory to latch onto. She answered,

"Yes," and then turned her head so that she could focus on the comforting view of the fire in the brick hearth.

25

The Tridge, Midland, Michigan, August 25, 2007

I, Annie Sharon Brady, stand next to my husband and Bob Sympkins and his wife in the northeast corner of Chippewassee Park, perhaps twenty yards from the entrance to the Tridge, a three-legged wooden footbridge that spans the convergence of the Chippewa and Tittabawassee Rivers. It is one of my favorite places in town—so scenic—consisting of a single 31-foot-tall central pillar that supports three spokes, each 180 feet long and 8 feet wide. I remember when it opened in 1981 at a total cost of $972,000. Rumors are circulating throughout town that it will require a major renovation within the next ten years to extend its lifespan, at a projected cost of well over $2 million. It will be worth every cent.

I have always thought that the structure symbolized a coming together of different people or entities, meeting and communing in the center, observing the smooth-running water of the rivers below—their disagreements melting away like the ice in spring. Moving outward from the center, it symbolized different paths one could take at key junctures in life, leading to different yet beautiful lands beyond each spoke's wooden decking. However, more than the Tridge's picturesque nature or the fact that people from all over the country travel to visit it, it was my favorite place to spend time with Shirley Ruth. I cannot remember how many walks we have taken over these three spokes or how many cups of hot apple cider we have shared, standing in the center at night around Halloween with the Tridge lit with orange and purple lights or how many mugs of hot chocolate we have shared standing in the same place around Christmas time with the structure lit up with red, green, and white lights.

It is for this reason that I have chosen this place today.

We await the guest of honor, my best friend, Shirley Ruth White, and her husband, Martin. There are nearly one hundred people spread out behind me—old colleagues from Midland's H.H. Dow High School, former students of Shirley Ruth's, and our joint friends from a golden age in our lives when all we cared about was being together, teaching, learning—giving back—raising children, and enjoying life. They are as anxious as I am to see her. For me, it's been twelve years; for others behind me, it's been fifteen or more.

It is 11:55 a.m., and I can smell the hamburgers and hot dogs on the grill by the pavilion, behind me and off to my left. It and the surrounding area—we've rented dining tents, tables, and chairs for the celebration—have been decorated in H.H. Dow's school colors, green and gold. There is enough food to feed an army back there, and it will be a glorious afternoon. We couldn't have asked for better weather, either—eighty-one degrees, no clouds, and a slight breeze.

The man who was principal when Shirley Ruth left, Don Wharton, is here. He's retired, and he traveled all the way from Florida to surprise her. When he heard what I was putting together, he suggested we get the school marching band to play the fight song as she stepped onto the Tridge—he's still an old high school football coach at heart, which was what he was for fifteen years before becoming our principal—but I reminded him that although Shirley Ruth had always been respectful of the Chargers' fight song and cheered when she went to games, she secretly disapproved since the song was "Across the Field," which is Ohio State's fight song, and she is a Michigan fan. Don, as he had when Shirley Ruth would present him with a superior argument at a faculty meeting, backed down. They were close, and she always had a special place in her heart for him, which only Bob Sympkins and I ever knew. There have been a few surprised stares directed at him today, but mostly, he's been warmly embraced by everyone. His former players worship him, and a few are here this morning. I know it will mean the world to Shirley Ruth that he is here. His wife died last summer, and this will be good for him. He needs to be around people. He also needs not to be forgotten.

I check my watch.

11:56 a.m.

Shirley Ruth and Martin are due here by noon, and if I know my old friend, then she'll be right on time but not a minute early. My eyes nervously scan the Tridge, looking for any sign of her and her husband. They arrived in Ironwood, Michigan, just after 5 p.m. yesterday and made it as far south on I-75 as Grayling, where they stopped just before midnight. We spoke to each other this morning, and they were up and had eaten breakfast. The drive down to Midland is only about an hour and fifteen minutes, and they were going to stop by their new apartment to pick up their keys and drop off some things before coming over. The apartment is ten minutes from the Tridge, and the apartment manager called me on my cell phone fifteen minutes ago and told me that they had just left. So, they should be here any minute. They think it's just a ceremonial and sentimental picnic gathering between the four of us to welcome them home. Dear Lord, are they in for a shock.

"Why are you doing this? Why are you making their return a big deal?" Those were the questions Bob had for me a month ago when I started planning everything.

Because my friend needs it. Her husband needs it. We're all getting older. We can do less than we used to. Both of their parents are now gone, and their children are estranged from them, maybe for good. They've made mistakes, but they have suffered too. I don't judge either them or their children for what has happened; it's for the family to figure out. But I do know that they are our friends—she, my best—and they need to feel welcomed back. They need to feel they are valued. They need to feel that they belong. They need to feel loved. I don't know what the future holds for any of us, and I pray that she and Martin will be able to see their children and grandchildren again, but it has been ten years since they last saw Lori and Jean, and fifteen years since they last saw Brett. I'm not sure it will ever happen. But today is happening, and they need to know that they can have a life here with us and their other friends. We're not the same people we were fifteen years ago—battered in some ways, better in others—but we're still here. Those long-ago lakeside conversations during our joint-family summer vacations in Curtis about staying busy in retirement— getting involved as senior citizens in election administration and volunteering at the salvation army, going to get senior citizen coffee at McDonald's, trying yoga, and joining a reading group at the library—well, they're no longer hypothetical courses of action. We're there. At first, I thought I was on a mission to ensure that we reclaim something that was lost: our time together. It did not take me long to come to the reality of the impossibility of that dream. We can't have those years back, but what we can have—and I hope today is the start of it—is a reaffirming of our deep friendship.

Even Shirley Ruth's old nemesis at H.H. Dow, Julie Sayers, is here—mainly keeping to herself, but I've seen her touch base with a few old friends. It doesn't surprise me. She burned a lot of bridges with our cohort early on, but in my last few years of teaching, I saw her grow into who I always thought she could be—a leader and maternal figure for new teachers. She is nearing her twilight years as an educator, almost fifty and now an elder stateswoman at

Dow. Still, in the early '80s, she was new to the faculty—a twenty-two-year-old firecracker straight out of Michigan State. Seeing her today makes me remember that young woman, full of the reckless spirit of invincibility we all had when we were her age. She has finally found a positive channel to funnel all of that energy, and she seems much happier now. The battles between her and Shirley Ruth over the direction of public education were legendary, and I used to marvel at their resilience and stamina during those after-school sidewalk showdowns on the way to the parking lot. I was touched when she showed up a half an hour ago and surprised by her hug. Her presence here is proof of Shirley Ruth's magic: she could feel like your enemy, but you could not deny the impact that she had on you.

I feel a tap on my shoulder.

"Gram?"

It is my fourteen-year-old grandson, Scott, who is staying with us until Wednesday, when he returns home and prepares for the start of the school year after Labor Day weekend. I turn my head so that I can see him and still keep an eye on the Tridge. "Yes, Scottie?"

"Any sign of her yet?"

He is sweaty from throwing the football around with some kids his age, probably grandchildren of our former colleagues who are here, or even children of some of our former students. Of course, "Coach" Wharton got in on the action and started throwing passes and pulling some of them aside to provide instruction. I almost teared up, seeing my old friend back in his element. Speaking of sports, John and I are treating Shirley Ruth and Martin to a Great Lakes Loons baseball game tomorrow night. Before she was ever a Michigan fan, Shirley Ruth was a Detroit Tigers *fanatic.* And do I ever have a surprise for her. The catcher from the 1984 World Series Championship team, Lance Parrish, is the manager for the Loons. She'll get to see one of her all-time favorites tomorrow evening and watch some quality Class A baseball. Dow

Diamond is a beautiful stadium that just opened in April. I don't think she knows about it. Hmm . . . lots of players trying to make it into the big leagues, and Lance is the guy to get them there.

"Expect her at any minute," I say to Scott.

He gives me a hug, getting sweat on my summer dress. Do I care? Hell no. "Excited for you!" he says and runs off to play again. That boy has an old soul about him. What teenager would pause playing sports to check on his grandmother?

Scott Joseph Brady.

I grin as he catches a ball and then throws it back.

Off to my left, I see the towering figure of our retired union rep, Robert Oakley, holding court with a dozen current teachers and a few of the old guard. I catch a snippet of his booming voice. "Those are *your* tax dollars at work," he says, pointing his index finger into the chest of a terrified male teacher, who is a head shorter than Robert and still looks like a teenager. The legendary labor warhorse pulls back his finger and gestures with his arms and hands in a dueling cyclone motion, which puts a smile on my face. Then, he sees our mutual emeritus teaching friend, Brian Hubbard, walking toward the pavilion and shouts, "Brian! Brian!" and waves him over to join his growing circle. I chuckle as I watch Brian laugh to himself and start heading that way. Reminds me of the old days.

Then, I turn my full attention toward the Tridge. Still don't see them.

I hope this doesn't overwhelm her and Martin. They have driven from Montana and have to be tired, but I've never known Shirley Ruth to shy away from a crowd. Is she introverted? Absolutely. Can she switch and become an extrovert when she senses energy? I've seen her do it more than once.

Bob Sympkins says, "Eleven fifty-eight. She always cut it close." He laughs. "Or was that you?"

I give him a playful punch on his shoulder and eyeball him. "I was always early."

He smiles. "That's right." Suddenly, he becomes stone-faced, as if he can't believe what he's seeing. Oh my God, his eyes are starting to water.

I snap my eyes over at the Tridge, specifically the leg that starts from the sidewalk that extends out from the parking lot at the end of Ashman Street . . .

I see two people walking together: a man with a ball cap on and a woman a bit shorter than him with . . . Gray hair! It was black when we last saw each other, if this is indeed her.

After a few more paces, I know it is them. She has always had a distinctive, very upright stride.

They're picking up their pace, nearing the center where we used to spend countless hours, sitting and chatting, and where they will turn right and come across the section that leads them to me.

Bob Sympkins has made it known that John and I will receive them first, and I see now that he has turned around and slid behind me, politely saying, "Let's back up a bit, team. Give Annie some room."

I love that man.

I move toward the Tridge. The plan was for them to get all the way here to the park before embracing them, but the hell with that.

Tears are streaming down my face, and as my feet hit the wooden boards of the Tridge, Shirley Ruth and Martin turn onto that section, and we see each other for the first time.

She yells, "Hey!" in joy, and now we are running toward each other. I see now that Martin is using a cane to walk, and he appears to be a little heavier, but he is moving as fast as he can, for he sees me now, and then I hear John's broken voice from a few steps behind me shout, "Martin!" And I completely lose it, because when my husband loses it, I lose it. He shouldn't be running because of his heart, but I know that I couldn't stop him if I tried. We are caught up in one of life's strongest and most precious currents.

She is feet away from me now—slender, powerful, like she could move heaven and earth—and I can see the tears coming from her eyes. Not even she could hold back in a moment like this.

Our bodies collide, and we embrace like we never have before. She kisses the side of my head—another first—and holds me tightly. I never want to let go; I never want her to let go. We've let too much time slip by. Never again.

I feel a slight brush to the side and open my eyes to see John give Martin a big bear hug, and I hear John's sniffles as they squeeze, followed by Martin's strong, "Old friend, I've missed you."

Then, I hear loud cheers and clapping, and Shirley Ruth and I part for a second as she surveys the massive crowd on the park's bright green grass behind me.

Her shaky voice says, "My God . . ." She squints, and then her eyes open wide. "Is that Bob?"

I say, "Yes. This is for you both. We're so glad you are home," and then we clinch together again, and I feel whole for the first time in years.

26

St. Barths – Eden Rock Villa "Rockstar" – Christmas Eve

Naked, Chantel Renault stretched out on the fluffy comforter of the king-sized bed in the villa's upstairs "Lennon" master suite. Her hair was wet from the shower, and she could hear the water still running in the ensuite bathroom's separate shower that was next to the one she had just exited. Her husband, Alec Rio Mar, was passed out in their downstairs "Bowie" master suite after downing five margaritas while lying on one of the sun beds by the villa's pool. She had enjoyed one drink, which was just enough to lower her defenses and arouse her curiosity in the up-and-coming musician who was visiting for the afternoon. He was thirty-one to her fifty-five, but age was just a number . . . until it wasn't. His stamina was ten times that of her loving, fifty-seven-year-old Alec, which he had displayed as they had made ample use of the sofa bench at the foot of the large bed before working their way into the ensuite bathroom and into the stone bathtub where he had displayed his endurance once again. She was satisfied from the afternoon of, well, *fucking*—there was no other way to put it—but the encounters had also drained her energy. She wondered if she would be able to react to him with the same enthusiasm if he came out of the shower ready for one more joining. Her desire was still triggered, and she moved her hand between her legs. As she began to rub, she found the arousing sensation mixed with another, more subtle feeling: a dull ache. She continued, not surprised by the soreness that had started to pulse in waves in conjunction with the mounting pleasure.

He's so much bigger than Alec. I'm going to be feeling him for days.

Listening to the running water and thinking of the wet drops splashing all over the musician's toned body, Chantel rubbed faster until her fingers moved in a frenzy, and she soon climaxed. Breathing fast, she moved her hand away and peered up at the ceiling.

Her parents were out on a sailing charter that would return in time for dinner; her children were away at an all-day scuba diving class; and the rest of her extended family were either at the pool or in the adjoining villa called "Nina." Her lover had dropped by right after Alec had drifted off to a deep, inebriated afternoon sleep, and she had shown the musician the villa's state-of-the-art music recording studio, which had impressed him. Then, she had led him upstairs and impressed him with her energy, which had been primed by a late morning workout in the villa's glamorous gym, followed by a relaxing swim in the pool, ending in a half-hour soak in the hot tub. She had closed and locked the suite's windows and doors and tried to stay quiet during their hour-long tryst, but his skill in the art of making her orgasm had resulted in a few loud exclamations of the world he was taking her to, which she hoped no one had heard. On her way up to the room, she had slid one of her bodyguards, Ariel, a stack of one-hundred-dollar bills to redirect anyone who neared the "Lennon" room. Thank God Chantel's brother and his wife would not be arriving until tomorrow. If they had been here today, the sex would have had to have taken place in the recording studio, which she had only done once ten years ago with a friend of Alec's. It had seemed like salacious behavior at the time, but it was nowhere near her risqué act of performing fellatio on her superior while they were seated next to each other on a ski lift in Aspen. She laughed to herself, remembering the man's skis dancing all around like erratic helicopter blades right before he climaxed. In any event, every time Alec suggested the recording studio setting for a "strategic and picturesque romp"— his vile phrasing, not hers, delivered with his eyebrows raised in a mischievous manner, which annoyed her—she had lured him into their suite instead, preferring to preserve the singular memory of her wild ten minutes in the studio a decade prior. On one occasion, after she had denied him the experience a few times, he had shown her a black wig he had ordered. The cardboard in the flimsy plastic package the wig was in said "'80s Heavy Metal Rockstar" and showed an Alice Cooper lookalike strumming a guitar. Before she could say anything, he had taken it out of the package and put it on, saying, *"Please, Chantel? You know it's every man's fantasy, right?"* She doubted that and had given him a firm, *"No. Now, remove that thing."*

She heard the shower turn off and began to rub both of her hands over her smooth body, feeling restored and wondering if they had time for a final session before he left. It was four.

The kids got back at six, her parents at six-thirty; dinner was planned for seven; and the annual Christmas Eve present exchange would follow dessert. Maybe Alec would be up by then—she'd have the villa cook make him something to fight the inevitable hangover that would hit him.

Anticipating her lover's entrance, she turned on her side and dug her left elbow into the puffy comforter, propping her head up with her left hand. She waited.

When he did not emerge, her mind began to scroll. Then, she realized that he had brought his clothes into the ensuite bathroom when they had run the bathwater in the tub. As soon as the words *he's getting dressed* entered her mind, out walked the music celebrity in his sandals, tan shorts, Vans T-shirt, and straw cowboy hat.

She pouted as he sat down on the edge of the bed. "I know, right?" he said. "Believe me, I want to stay." He ran a hand through the thick, damp hair on the top of her head. "We've got to do this again," he said. "My villa should be pretty quiet on the twenty-seventh or twenty-eighth—the Christmas crowd will be gone, and the New Year's guests won't have arrived yet."

Chantel smiled. "What about your girlfriend?"

He winked. "I'll think of something."

Using his right index finger, he made slow circles around the nipple on her right breast, while looking into her eyes. Then, he leaned over and gave her a sensual kiss on the lips, using his tongue sparingly, which she appreciated. Some men she had been with used their tongues as if they had run out of air and were desperately searching for a pocket of oxygen.

The kiss ended, and he tipped his cowboy hat to her. "Text me . . . *cowgirl*," he said, shaking his head with a grin of slight embarrassment. He rose from the bed, his fresh scent lingering in the air, and left.

Cowgirl. Her grin said "triumph" as she rested her head back on the fluffy pillow, remembering her favorite position with him. She preferred the words "on top" instead of the irreverent term he had used. Regardless, it was her preferred posture when she slept with anyone. She enjoyed power. She was keen on being in control, and the musician had submitted to her direction as she maneuvered into that place of physical supremacy over and over again during their coupling in the bedroom, each change dictating a shift in authority, sending her into periods of maintaining a frenetic pace she didn't think was possible, going longer than the one before until she finally broke him, and he released with a ripple that matched her own deep, molten explosion. The bedroom had been her time, the bathtub, his. There, in the soapy water, she had relinquished control, and, taking advantage of this, he had displayed dexterity beyond what she expected—his flexibility, his athleticism, his movements . . . all of it.

I will *be texting you.*

Chantel dressed and exited the room. After looking down the stairs and seeing her other bodyguard, Marcus, positioned at the bottom, who waved up at her, she re-entered the suite and stepped out through the suite's sliding glass door onto the upper floor's spacious wooden deck. There, she saw Ariel leaning against the glass railing that overlooked the villa's courtyard below. Chantel approached her and asked, "Anyone get curious?"

"Quiet as a mouse."

Chantel rubbed the woman's arm. "Good. I saw Marcus stationed at the bottom of the stairs."

"We had everything covered."

"Yes, you did." She looked around. "Could you discreetly have the room and bathroom cleaned and prepared for my brother and sister-in-law?"

"We'll do it right now."

"Has he—"

"Yes, madam. He's already left the villa."

"Thank you," Chantel said, and she walked toward the sliding glass door.

She entered the "Bowie" master suite and found Alec spread out on the massive bed, snoring. She gave him a look of pity and then changed into her bikini. Grabbing her sunhat and phone, she exited the suite, closing the door behind her.

A staff member casually strolled around the outdoor dining area and bar, waiting to assist her or anyone else at a moment's notice, as she walked past and headed toward the pool. She continued until she exited the villa via the red gate that led directly onto St. Jean Beach. The white sand was warm and firm, feeling marvelous under her feet. The color was so light compared to other beaches she had been on, and she remembered her father telling her when she was a child that it was just a different kind of snow that Santa landed his sleigh on. Even though the innocence of both the moment and explanation had long since passed, she would always think of the sand on St. Jean Beach as snow.

The water was a glorious shade of aquamarine and crystal clear. She saw a Boston Whaler anchored twenty yards offshore, and a kayaker directly in front of her, perhaps another ten yards seaward of the Whaler, made smooth strokes with his paddle as he headed down the coast. And it wasn't just any kayaker. It was a kayaker of the 2-time-Academy-Award-winning-actor variety. Chantel waved, and he stopped his paddling to wave back. Her whole family was invited to his New Year's party and would probably attend. His villa was even more spacious than the musician's, and old friends, dating back to the time of her father, would be in attendance. There would be stories of time gone by and reminiscences of good times had, and, in the spirit of the new year and renewed possibilities, there would be passionate pledges—delivered with hijacked emotions, fueled by expensive alcohol—to see everyone more often . . . *Let's not let another year go by* . . . which would go unhonored without offense or further mention.

Ahead of her, was a row of sun loungers with umbrellas open above them, reserved explicitly for Villa Rockstar. She made her way across the warm sand and sat down on one of the loungers, and, after taking in a minute of the glorious view, called Urian.

"Enjoying the warmth of the sun?" he asked, answering the phone.

"Never gets old," she said. "Your reputation as a night owl is secure." It was after eleven p.m. in Mykonos. "How is *your* island?"

"Refreshing. Quiet. Just the way I like it."

"Getting lonely yet?"

"I'm always lonely at night, probably why I stay up and keep busy. I just finished a run." There was a pause. "Or, do you mean that I'm lonely *for you* or someone else?"

A staff member from the villa placed a red plastic bucket in the sand to the right of her lounger and disappeared. Inside the bucket were two bottles of water packed in ice. She lowered her voice. "Well, you'd better be lonely for *me*."

There was a short laugh on the other end of the phone. "Of course, boss."

"And who might the 'someone else' be?" she asked.

"If that annoying Michigan snowstorm doesn't clear up, then Jean might miss her flight, and . . . well, I don't want to even think about that."

"I texted with her—"

"So did I," said Urian, cutting her off. "She's in a cabin right now with some eighty-year-old. Lame, and beneath her. Haven't we taught her better than that?"

"If I didn't know you, I'd think you were getting attached."

"You know I'm attracted to her—"

"Uh, huh."

"—but I'm not in *any way* attached. At least . . . not yet."

"Well, don't." Chantel massaged her right thigh, then her left. The quadriceps were still tight from her time with the musician. "Remember, the only reason you're getting a chance to bed her is because I approved it."

"If I didn't know any better, I would say that you have your eye on her."

"Ha. Ha." Her face broke into a sly grin. "Maybe I do."

"You are something else, you know that?" There was a pause. "Just make sure you let me know if it ever reaches that point, okay? I don't ever want to walk in on the two of you, especially if I start dating her."

"Yes, you do, and I'd welcome it."

Another laugh. "You're crazy."

She shook out a water bottle from the bucket and took a long drink. Then, she rested her two front teeth on her bottom lip. "If things progress, are you going to tell her about us?"

"I hadn't planned on it, but, hey, if the potential scenario that you just said you would welcome happens, my telling her would be irrelevant, wouldn't it?"

"Yes, it would."

"However, if it does happen, we need to have a line ready when she calls you out about your supposed monogamous and special relationship with Alec. You know, the perfect family image that you project."

"Already prepared. Here it is. 'I don't know what came over me, Jean. I—I've never done anything like that before. Oh, please don't judge me. Alec is the only man for me, and I'm loyal. But, I'm attracted to you, Jean, and, well, things just happened. You're not ashamed of what we just did, are you? Have you ever done anything like this before?' Then, I'll give her a sheepish giggle and say, 'You seemed more experienced with it than I was.' Something like that, and she won't be ashamed after I get through with her. She'll be coming back for more—like that tech CEO I was with. Now, whether you get *invited* to become involved with us is, hmm. I'll have to think about it."

"I should have known. But. If all of that—you and her . . . you, me, and her—*doesn't* happen, I don't think it would be the best idea to tell her about *us* as we occasionally . . . *rekindle* things."

"*You and I* are uncomplicated, which is why I like it."

"Business trips together are the perfect cover, and when we're not traveling, meetings serve the same purpose."

"You're boring me. It just works between us. Leave it at that."

"Agree. It's perfect how it is. The question is, however, will you let me have the same thing with Jean?"

"She wouldn't be coming to visit you if I were against it."

"Well, that's a relief then. And you're okay sharing me with her?"

"Urian, I can have anyone I want."

"Fair enough, fair enough."

Chantel watched as the actor tried to maneuver his kayak around a group of twenty-somethings splashing around in the water. He almost flipped the boat. "I won't have anything to share, though, if she doesn't come visit you."

She heard him exhale. "Yeah, I need to touch base with her today and see how things look. I've checked about every weather app that's been invented, and they all say the same thing: The storm is going to continue through Christmas, which means flights out of Michigan are going to be backed up forever."

Chantel grinned. "You're in a pickle, aren't you? Thinking about flying back to try and rescue her yourself?"

"I wouldn't go that far."

"So what if she doesn't make it to your little island? You've got time, and . . . you've got me."

His voice started to show annoyance. "But I had everything planned. The place is all set up. If she doesn't come, I won't have anyone here to . . . *entertain*."

The actor cleared the swimmers, giving them a wave as he passed by. The group ignored him, not noticing who was underneath the straw hat and behind the sunglasses. *Fools.* She took another drink of water, savoring its coldness. "That's a load of shit. What about your beloved Eidothea? The sea nymph with legs that stretch into the sky—even farther than Jean's?"

"Jesus, you should try saying her name out loud when you're about to climax. I couldn't do it, got tripped up—any name over two syllables always throws me off. I prefer 'Chan—Tel,' which has two syllables, allowing me to sync with my movements. 'Jean'—one syllable—even better."

She giggled, remembering one of their private "meetings" in her office. She, with her blouse and suit jacket still on but wearing nothing below that, was lying back on the top of her desk with her legs spread while he stood pantless, still wearing his shirt and tie, driving his member in and out of her, saying

"Chan—Tel. Chan—Tel." *The pig, he had been in sync!* "Fuck you," she said. "You're so childish sometimes."

There was a laughter of satisfaction on the other end of the phone, and Urian said, "Okay, I deserved that." There was a pause. "I suppose Eidothea will do if Jean can't make it. I should probably check and see if the sea nymph is even here."

"You should."

"Hey, how about some optimism?"

"I'm not familiar with that word."

She imagined him shaking his head, frustrated with her needling.

"Oh, listen to you. You've got a smorgasbord to choose from down there."

She instantly slipped into her Chantel-is-bewildered-by-that-statement tone, which she leveraged to great effect in business negotiations that veered off track, which she knew Urian would recognize. "I don't know what you're talking about, sir. My ship is anchored to Alec, and we've been having a splendid time down here together."

"You should be spanked for that statement."

"I thought we didn't do that anymore." She chuckled. "After you hurt your hand."

"*Dear Lord*, Chantel."

She watched as the actor turned his kayak around and then began to paddle back toward the water, directly off where she sat on St. Jean Beach. The young crowd continued to splash, dunk each other, and laugh as he moved seaward to avoid them this time. "It's so relaxing and warm today. I don't know why you and Jean just don't come here instead. You're not bundling up and walking through snowbanks where you're at, but you're not exactly sunbathing either, are you?"

"Maybe next year. I need to have her all to myself for this first visit, and, plus, every place in St. Barths is booked. You pay me well, but I don't have two hundred thousand to drop on Villa Rockstar for a week."

"Two hundred and fifty thousand," Chantel said.

Urian grunted. "Oh, my mistake."

"We have plenty of room for you both to stay. And, after the twenty-eighth, there will be three empty master suites between the two villas; remember, we have Villa Nina next door rented out, too." The words had slipped out before she had time enough to realize what position she would be putting herself in.

Balancing Alec, the musician, and Urian?

The beginnings of regret soon gave way to exhilaration. *What a challenge! What fun!*

"Why are people leaving?"

"Right before we arrived, my sister-in-law told me that she had pushed my brother to ring in the new year at their new vacation home in Malibu. She wants to reenact the Streisand-Redford fantasy from *The Way We Were*, complete with walks on the beach and so forth. She even had a cream-colored turtleneck sweater handmade that is a perfect replica of the one Redford wore while walking on the beach with Babs. Right now, it is wrapped up and under the Christmas tree in Villa Nina, where they are staying. In a few hours, we're going to do our annual Christmas Eve gift exchange, and that's the present she's giving him tonight."

"That's romantic."

"It's total cheese. He hates that movie, but it's her favorite."

"I like it."

"One of my favorites, too."

"We'll have to watch it sometime."

"No. I only watch that film with Alec—it's one of our traditions every fall when the leaves change and are at their peak." There was silence for a beat, and then she said, "Anyway, they're leaving, their kids are leaving to stay with her parents in Miami, and my other brother's son, Rich, and Rich's fiancée, Jazz, are flying to Maui to link up with a few couples for New Year's." She scoffed. "And here I thought it was sacrosanct that the family all stays together here for the full vacation. I guess the departing members cleared everything with my parents, and I was one of the last to know, which pissed me off." Chantel sighed. "Nothing I can do about it—I guess all traditions come to an end. I just never anticipated *this one* coming to an end." Her voice became stern. "I would have *never* dreamed of asking my mother and father to leave the annual winter vacation early. Then again, I'm the oldest, and the oldest child always ends up getting screwed."

"So, you'll have some extra room. Isn't that less hectic?"

"You don't understand. This is the only time of the year when I *want it* to be hectic. I love my family, and I don't like change."

"And yet, you're inviting me and Jean to come stay? Or, was that another insincere jab at me?"

She sat up, bringing her knees closer to her chest. "No, it was sincere. Since everyone else is allowed to break the long-standing rules, I suppose I am entitled to do the same. No pressure, but you have to admit that it would be fun."

"It would, but—"

"Just think about it. I understand if you want this time with Jean all to yourself, but the invitation stands, all right?"

"All right."

She felt good—more in control. If they showed up, then that was fine. If they didn't, then she would have plenty of playtime with the musician and maybe even the actor. It had been years since their affair, but seeing him in the kayak had reminded her of those dazzling weekends in his palace in Pacific Palisades. Additionally, if Urian and Jean declined her offer, she would find a way to leverage the decision against Urian later on to manipulate him, framing his move as a rejection. "You doing anything else tonight?" she asked.

"Mass at midnight. Then, thank God, a huge meal when we get home. We've all been semi-fasting for forty days. I told you about that, didn't I?

"I think so. Kinda sucks."

"You get used to it. We had a few groups of children come by the house earlier to sing Kalanda."

She cut him off. "Kalanda?"

"Carols. I used to go around with my friends singing them on Christmas Eve too. I'm glad it's still a tradition."

"That's it? The kids come by and sing carols?"

"And we give them treats and money afterwards. It's very festive."

"What about tomorrow?"

"Our cook will prepare a large family meal—pork, lamb, a loaf of Christopsomo, Christmas bread—and then we'll have Melomakarona and Kourabiedes, which are honey-soaked cookies and almond cookies. They're the best. I'd better stop talking about food, or I won't make it to mass. The heavenly smells from the kitchen are filling the house, which is why I had to leave and go on my run."

"You have a tree, right?"

"Yes, we have a beautiful Christmas tree, but our yacht anchored offshore is also decorated."

"Why is your yacht decorated?"

"Tradition—there's that word again. It's called Karavaci. We do it to honor our maritime history and Saint Nicholas. You should see all the boats anchored around the island at night—it's gorgeous, like a ring of different colored lights. I have liked to look out at the boats at night since I was old enough to remember."

"Send me pictures."

"I will."

"Presents tomorrow?"

"Celebrations will continue through New Year's until January 6th, which is Epiphany Day. We'll exchange some gifts tomorrow, but our main exchange will be on New Year's Day and Epiphany."

"Why didn't you tell me any of this before?"

"I'm not sure. You never asked, and we have always treated this break as just that: a break. I always knew you went to St. Barths, but I never knew any of your rituals. This is the first time I have heard about the Christmas Eve gift exchange."

She decided to backtrack a bit. "Well, just because my family traditions seem to be imploding, I don't want to take you away from your traditions, especially since you will be introducing Jean to them."

"Nonsense," he said. "My family is flexible and would be fine with us coming to visit you in . . . *paradise*. Let's keep the communication lines open."

She felt even better, more at peace—like she couldn't be blamed now for taking him away from his family. It also gave her room to maneuver in terms of changing her mind. Perhaps in a few days, she wouldn't want them to visit, and she would drop hints about someone being under the weather—a time-tested and worthy deterrent. Of course, if she did want them to come, she would ratchet up the pressure and start sending him pictures—of the water, of the beach, of the pool, of the villa . . . of her.

"Yes, let's stay in touch," she said. "I want to hear if there's any news regarding Jean's predicament, okay?"

"You got it. Merry Christmas, boss."

She playfully rolled her eyes. "Merry Christmas, *underboss*." As soon as she heard his chuckle, she ended the call.

Staring out at the turquoise water, she was reminded of her children, Odell and Keely, who had been scuba diving all day. *I need to find more things for them to do to keep them away from the villa.* She thought about their nanny, Sonja. *She needs to step up. We've been here two days, and I'm already tired of spending time with them. They demand too much of me, and Sonja knows it. I'll make it through tomorrow—maybe the presents will keep them busy—but she'd better have something planned for the twenty-sixth.*

As she took a drink of water and scrolled through social media on her phone, she thought about what her father had said to her about children: *Kids are a pain in the ass, muffin.*

As usual, he had been right. But Alec had wanted them so badly, and he was a decent father, but he also loved it when they were away on some excursion so that he could concentrate on Chantel or his friends or his drinking. She'd let him have it if he couldn't rise and join the gift opening ceremony later. Her thoughts wandered to Jean Mercer, her prodigy. *Oh, to be young, unattached, and rich!*

Bitch.

Envy turned to sorrow, and her eyes became glassy. *Sometimes, I feel so alone. And older.* She slipped into her script, whispering to herself, "You're fifty-five. You want to re-experience being twenty—the looks, the pain-free body, the lack of expectations, the lack of pressure, the lack of responsibility, the carefree and . . . *happy* Chantel. And yet, you want that, and you want to have all of the things that it has taken you thirty-five years to acquire. It doesn't work that way. You get one or the other. Not both." She exhaled and felt a tear slip down below her sunglasses. Chantel looked around and saw no one on the beach. She squeezed her eyes shut, experiencing a searing pain. *It's happening again.* Her self-whispering ceased, and the words now became imprisoned in the self-talk boundaries of her mind. *I can't help myself—It's because I want to go back. I want to walk into a club, hearing Oasis—because they're* new, *not for nostalgia—and drink and dance all night. I want no responsibilities—no one counting on me. No husband. No goddamned kids. No co-workers. No attachments. I want to be flirted with because it's* me *they want. I want freedom. I don't want to be around people I know—don't want to socialize, don't want to 'get into character,' don't want to pose for pictures. I want to get away.*

. .

Chantel let out a brief and barely audible guttural growl. She had completed the cycle—*I want to go back; I want freedom; I want to get away.* Then, there was silence except for the sound of the waves coming ashore. She opened her eyes, saw that the beach was still empty, and wiped her eyes and cheeks.

Her discharge over, Chantel rose, tossing her water bottle at the bucket. It missed.

Whatever.

She left the bottle and the bucket and started back across the sand.

27

Midland, Michigan – Christmas Eve, 7 p.m.

Jean followed Annie and Scott into the living room and sat down on one of the couches next to Scott. Annie handed them each an identical present, which was the size of a square tissue box. They had finished dinner twenty minutes ago and, after Scott had dashed upstairs and come back, had just exited the kitchen after cleaning everything up.

Holding the wrapped gift in his hands, Scott shook his head in acknowledgement, as if he knew what the contents were. Jean thought about risking a shake of the box but decided against it.

Annie took a seat behind the Steinway. "Okay, open them."

They did, and Jean now held in her hand a heavy, round globe ornament decorated with snowflakes that had her name written on it in puffy, red, cursive letters. There was a small brass ring at the top, and through the ring was a loop of green ribbon tied into a bow, which she could use to hang the ornament on the tree.

She looked over at Scott and saw that he held a similar ornament with his name on it.

Jean went to speak, but Annie said, "Shhh, my dear. Follow Scott."

And with that, she began to play "Christmas Time Is Here" by the Vince Guaraldi Trio, from the soundtrack of *A Charlie Brown Christmas*.

Scott, looking rested and wearing black dress pants with a white collared shirt and a crimson V-neck sweater, rose and extended his hand to Jean, who took it, and he helped her to her feet. Everyone had showered and changed before dinner, but she had not smelled any cologne on him—at least not the luscious scent he had on the other day. But, after he had sprinted up to his room and then come back down, she noticed the glorious scent once more, determining that he had just splashed some on, which made her heart start pounding.

"Tradition," he whispered.

He squeezed her hand and then let go. As he moved past her, she caught another whiff of his cologne, and her eyes stayed glued to his trim figure as she stepped off after him toward the tree. After the emotional talk that morning, she had washed her maroon turtleneck and charcoal-colored dress slacks, which she had changed into the previous day, and Annie had pressed them for her. The Brady family matriarch had on cream-colored tights and a black sweater dress with a bright red scarf, and Jean felt at ease, assimilating perfectly into the evening's dress code with her outfit.

They reached the tree, and the first thing she noticed was that there were more presents underneath it. Then, she saw her name on a few and felt both gratitude and guilt. It was so kind of Annie to think of her, but she had no gifts to give *her*. Scott's movement took her away from that line of thinking, and she watched as he hung his ornament on a branch next to the one that held his grandmother's globe. On the other side of Annie's was a matching globe that had John written in cursive on it. Scott stepped to the side, and Jean moved forward, her eyes scanning the tree until she found Shirley Ruth's and Martin's side by side. The branch next to Shirley Ruth's was empty—*On purpose?* she thought—and she carefully hung her ornament there.

Her eyes met Scott's, and she raised her eyebrows as if to say, *What now?* His eyes moved from her to her ornament and then back to her, and he gave a smile that she thought conveyed approval and understanding. Had he and Annie talked about the conversations that had taken place between her and Annie while he was out? Perhaps. When he arrived home at four, she was taking a nap that had started at three and lasted until five thirty.

They stood there, eyes glued to each other and then to the tree as Annie continued to play. The Christmas music fed her soul, and she knew she would never again avoid the songs of the season. She missed singing. *There has to be a choir I could join back home,* she thought.

As Jean's eyes moved to the presents, she wondered what Annie had put in the packages for her. Whatever the items were, they could not match the gift she had given to Jean yesterday and today: her family's past. She now knew why her mother had wanted her to visit her grandmother's best friend.

Annie's story about Shirley Ruth and Martin's return to Midland had warmed Jean's heart and indeed given her something positive and uplifting to hold onto amidst the heartbreaking history that she had discovered. Moreover, it had reminded her that human beings were complex, *"mixed bags,"* Annie had said, and that it would take time for her to process the information. She felt empowered to meet with her mother at some point and talk about things— especially why her mother had lied to her. Jean would not force the meeting to happen, but knew that her mother would have never had her meet Annie if she didn't want Jean to talk to Lori one day about what she had learned. After speaking with Annie earlier, she had gone upstairs and sent her mother a simple text.

I spoke with Annie about our family. Processing things right now. Thank you for introducing me to her.

Her mother had just "liked" the message, which was all Jean had expected. She was relieved that Lori had not written more, and Jean did not plan on texting again or calling her while she was here. The type of conversation she wanted was in-person.

She wanted to hear her mother's side; she wanted to know what her father thought; she wanted to take a trip to Alaska and meet her Uncle Brett, Aunt Carrie, and her cousin Brandon.

I want to tell her that I started singing again and let her and Dad know that what they did to me when I was in choir was cruel. Not one *performance!*

However, there was one thing she didn't need to process. In addition to already mourning the fact that she never got to meet her grandparents, she was also sad about never being able to visit them in the house she had walked through the day before. What she had felt while inside and outside of the house had been real—a queasy emptiness at what could have been. She was thirteen when they returned to Midland, so she would have been fourteen when they moved into their new house. The Christmases and summers she could have spent there, getting to know them, going to Loons games at Dow Diamond, and maybe even meeting the man who was standing next to her in front of the Christmas tree right now.

Would we have struck up a summer romance? She thought, looking into his eyes.

What about now?

Annie finished the song, and Scott clapped. Jean joined in.

"Please sit," Annie said. "I'll be right back. It's present time."

They took their places back on the couch, and Annie went into the kitchen. When she returned, she had three snifters of brandy. As she set them on the coffee table, she said, "I always break out the Calvados on Christmas Eve—an upgrade from last night's selection." They toasted and drank. Then, Annie set her snifter down and walked toward the tree.

❋ ❋ ❋

Just a quick hello before we carry out our tradition, my love, Annie thought as she approached the tree.

She stopped just in front of John's ornament, her face inches away from it.

"I miss you," she whispered. Her eyes became glassy. "I love you."

She reached up and traced the letters of his name with her right index finger. "It probably won't be long now. There's no one left except for Scottie. I can't wait to see you again."

Annie looked back over her shoulder at Scott and Jean, who were watching her. She smiled at them and then faced the ornament again. "Yes, they'd be perfect for each other," she said, continuing to whisper. "Reminds me of us."

She kissed the ornament, wiped her eyes, and then turned around and stepped off for the couch opposite Scott and Jean.

❋ ❋ ❋

Annie sat down and said, "Scott, will you be our Santa?"

He leaned forward and placed his snifter on the coffee table. "Of course, Gram."

I've never seen anything that sweet, Jean said to herself, thinking about the kiss that Annie had given John's ornament. *What was she whispering?* Jean looked again at the presents underneath the tree. "Can I just say something?" she asked, making eye contact with both Annie and Scott.

Annie motioned Scott to stay put. "Of course, dear."

"I don't have anything for either of you. If I had known—"

Scott put his hand on her shoulder and said, "That's good because I don't have anything for you, either." He pointed at Annie. "This is all her doing."

269

"You bet it is," Annie said. "Wouldn't have it any other way. And don't you worry, Jean. I didn't expect anything in return." She smirked. "I knew what I was doing."

Scott removed his hand and picked up his snifter once more. "I've been looking forward to this since yesterday." He took a drink.

Now, she was intrigued. First, there was the fact that Annie and Shirley Ruth had visited Atlanta years ago and that it had something to do with tonight. Additionally, Scott had some insight into what was going to happen. Her mind searched for answers. *Did he buy the presents yesterday?* He could have, but they would have been from Meijer, which she was unfamiliar with, but knew the store sold groceries.

I give up.

She was a bit surprised that she was yielding so soon . . . *But, hey, maybe I need to do that more often—go with the flow and not overthink everything to death.* "Well, now I'm in," she said, picking up her snifter and toasting them both through the air. She swallowed the warm, spicy, and delicious brandy. "But, before Santa here distributes the gifts—" and now it was she who touched *his* shoulder, "—tell me the story behind what we just did with the ornaments."

Annie slapped her thigh. "I'd be delighted!" She crossed her legs. "It's quite simple. Everyone in our family, including close friends, has an ornament with their name on it that I made by hand. Thank God you slept in this morning!"

They all laughed.

"The tree decorating ceremony would always be the weekend after Thanksgiving, usually on Saturday night. I would play the entire Charlie Brown Christmas album while we strung lights, hung ornaments, and drank eggnog. Sorry, none of the latter tonight, although I do have some in the fridge. I figured we had wine and were going to have Calvados, so I didn't want to mix too much in our bellies. Anyway, when Scottie was little, I would play the CD when his family visited us over the Thanksgiving weekend. When Scott's parents were little, I would play the record album. Over the years, if people could not be here for Thanksgiving but were able to make it for Christmas Eve, then John and I, along with Shirley Ruth and Martin, would follow our usual tradition at Thanksgiving and hang our ornaments then. Still, we would have a second ceremony on Christmas Eve when those who could attend got to hang up their ornaments. If no one was able to make it for Thanksgiving and Christmas, then John and I hung up their ornaments for them when we hung ours." She beamed at Scott. "Scottie, did I explain it right?"

"Gram, you could have skipped half of that and still done better than me. When I was a kid, all I looked forward to were the presents—well, I still do—but now, the thing I look forward to the most every year is hanging my ornament on the tree."

Annie lifted her chin in victory. "Thank you, child."

"When did the tradition start?" asked Jean.

"*A Charlie Brown Christmas* came out in early December 1965 when I was twenty-four—I was working my way through my Master's degree at that point—but the show struck a chord with me. John and I had only been married a few years at that point and had never had any Christmas traditions. I mean, we put up the tree and exchanged gifts, but didn't have any set routines. So, for that particular Christmas, I went out and bought the record album when it came out that December, and we played it when we got our tree a week before Christmas. Back then, we waited until the last minute. Just young and busy, I guess. Anyway, I played it while we decorated the tree and on Christmas Eve— maybe we were a little more punctual that year—we decided to exchange one gift. Then, as we had kids and wanted to set up the tree earlier and earlier so we could enjoy it for longer, our traditions just evolved. I made ornaments and that got put into the mix, and it all coalesced into a routine that we loved." She broke eye contact with them and stared at the window.

Jean followed her gaze. If the weather was supposed to clear sometime in the middle of the night, it sure didn't look like it was going to right now.

Still looking out at the storm, Annie said, "Then, the kids grow up, move away, and everything contracts. I dislike downsizing, especially at this time of year. I want things big, noisy, festive—*busy*." She turned her attention back to them. "What a gift I have been given this Christmas. I pray everyone affected by the storm is safe and can carry on like before once it passes, but I don't think I will. The past two days have been very special. Tomorrow will be, too."

"Sorry about later tonight, Gram," Scott said.

Annie shrugged. "Nothing we can do about it, kiddo."

"What about later tonight?" asked Jean.

"I always go to Midnight Mass on Christmas Eve," Annie said, "but because of the weather, they've cancelled it. Never seen it happen before."

Jean had no memory of church, although she had once seen a picture of herself as a toddler in a pew around Christmas time, or maybe it was Easter. "I'm sorry to hear that," she said.

"I'm still waiting on word to see if they'll give it a go tomorrow. If so, we'll adjust our dinner schedule."

The room was quiet for a minute as they all took sips from their snifters and watched the fire or looked at the tree. Jean felt her emotions peaking again—she felt the urge to hug someone and to be held.

Annie broke the silence. "Okay, Scottie, get the gifts."

Scott rose and walked past Jean, brushing her leg as he passed. It wasn't hugging, but it was contact. She liked it and followed him with her eyes. He bent over by the tree, picked up five packages, and then approached the couch.

Why does he have five *packages? Maybe they exchange two each?*

Scott tucked a large wrapped box underneath his left arm and first handed Annie his gift to her, the shape looking to Jean like a thin, department store collapsible box that would typically hold a men's fitted shirt snugly inside—the red wrapping paper was neatly folded and taped, and the package had a green bow off-center on top. Then, he walked over to Jean and handed her the three remaining packages—all wrapped in the same manner as the one from Annie to Scott: brown paper with a white string, which formed a perfect cross in the center of each gift.

Jean exhaled, once again uncomfortable. "Annie, why do I have *three* packages?"

"All will be explained when you open them, my dear," said Annie. "And since you are the guest, you get to go last. Scottie . . . you first."

Scott stood his package up on his thighs and attempted to pull the string over one of the four corners. Failing, he tried another corner. The box started to bend, and he released the string. He said, "Oh, come on . . ." and then pulled his Swiss Army knife from his pocket and cut the string.

Annie tittered over in her chair, and Jean pulled her hand up to her mouth, hiding her grin.

He tore the paper off the box, lifted the top off, and then pulled out a bulky navy-colored fisherman's sweater. Scott held it up, admiring it.

Jean thought it was beautiful—classic and . . . there was something different about it. *What is it?* Her eyes scanned the sweater, moving from the tightly knitted, ribbed strip on the bottom up to the . . . there, the collar. She saw no tag on the inside.

"Might be the last one I ever make you, boy."

He lowered the sweater. "Gram, don't say that."

"Might be true this time."

"You said it last year and the year before that."

"Well—"

He walked over and wrapped his grandmother in his arms. "Thank you. I'll wear it tomorrow."

She kissed his cheek. "You're welcome, and I approve of your decision. The weather calls for it, don't you think?"

He moved back to the other couch, and Annie turned her attention to Jean. "Do you sew or knit, dear?"

"I don't," said Jean. "And looking at what you made for Scott, I don't think I should ever try. How long did that take?"

"Oh, a while," she answered. "But don't you shy away because of that. My God, you should have seen some of the first sweaters I made for John. The pattern looked like some modernist mishmash you'd see on a painting in the Midland Center for the Arts. It's relaxing, and you should try it sometime." She shrugged. "Not for everyone, but you'd be surprised how quickly you can catch on to something, and you, my young friend, seem to pick up on things fast."

It was pointless at this point to argue with her. The woman had a way of nudging but always leaving the receiver of those nudges a way out. It was an effective means of persuasion—gentle, understated, but encouraging. "All right. Maybe I'll give it a go sometime."

"Bravo," said Annie.

Scott balled up the brown paper and placed it in the fire. Then, he flattened the box and set it on the coffee table. "It's ready for next year. Okay, your turn, Gram."

She opened the package from Scott methodically yet slowly, seeming to savor the buildup. After slipping off the shiny wrapping paper, she took the bow off and neatly folded the paper, placing both it and the bow on the couch beside her. Then, she lifted the top off the flimsy white box. Jean saw Annie part the tissue paper that was inside and heard the woman say, "Oh, Scottie." She placed a hand over her heart and fought back tears. "It's—it's like brand new."

"I took the original and had a friend from college who works in digital photography see what he could do with it." He pointed at the box. "The original is in an envelope in there."

Annie let the top of the box fall to the floor, and she pulled a picture frame from the bottom half of the box and then looked down. "Got it," she said, removing the envelope and placing it on the couch next to the folded wrapping paper and bow. She held the picture frame in front of her face and then kissed it. Lowering it, she said, "Jean, would you like to see your grandmother and me at the height of our powers?"

Immediately, Jean went over, and when Annie handed her the frame, she became transfixed by the image it held.

"New Year's Eve 1969. John took this just as the clock was about to strike midnight, ushering in the 1970s. If only we knew what a crazy decade we were in for!"

If Jean didn't know any better, she would have thought that it was a picture of herself, transported back in time to take a photo with a 30-year-old version of Annie. The two women were sitting on a brown, burlap-cushioned couch with worn wooden armrests at each end. Annie wore black slacks and a purple blouse with her hair done up. She was holding a bottle of beer, wearing the same huge smile Jean had seen many times in the past few days. Shirley Ruth wore bell-bottom jeans and an emerald turtleneck sweater, accompanied by a gold necklace that hung down. Her black hair was long and silky, falling around her shoulders. Her smile was more reserved than Annie's, and her eyes, behind glasses that were similar to Jean's, were fixed on the camera. In her hand was a glass of red wine, and her long fingers curled around the stem. *I look exactly like my grandmother in this picture.*

"That's why I stared at you for an extra moment yesterday," Scott said. "I couldn't believe the resemblance."

Jean looked up from the photograph, remembering how he had looked at her like he knew her when they met the previous day. "I can see why."

Annie chimed in. "See? We were just long-lost friends, my dear."

Jean handed her back the frame and then did something on complete instinct. She leaned over and hugged Annie, whispering, "I can see how much she meant to you."

She heard a sniffle, followed by, "Other than my family, she was my world. Never had another friend like her. Never will."

Jean pulled back, and then, feeling the emotion of the moment, she went over and hugged Scott. "That was a kind thing to do," she said, and then sat back down next to him. Taking a sip of brandy, she realized that her gesture had been more about honoring his kindness to his grandmother and less about her desire to know what it felt like to be in his arms. However, now that the rush of her emotions had subsided, she focused on how it had felt, which was divine—a feeling she wanted to experience again, and soon.

"I'd be happy to have my friend make one for you if you want," he said.

"Yes. I'd like that."

Annie clasped her hands together. "Wonderful idea, Scottie! Now, it's your turn, Jean."

She opened the three gifts and was both grateful and confused by them. A book, *Didion & Babitz* by Lili Anolik, a CD—*The Tony Bennett Bill Evans Album*—and the film *Jaws*. She had never heard of the book, although it looked interesting. She had listened to Tony Bennett before, but never this album, and she did not own any CDs or a CD player. *Jaws*, she had heard of but had never seen—she thought it a pure horror film, and those scared her.

However, an hour later, she had a completely different outlook on the three gifts. Without ever "experiencing" any of them, they meant more to her than any gift she had ever received before. To hear Annie's reasoning behind the purchases, the story of her trip with Shirley Ruth to Atlanta, and the history of their annual gift exchange of exactly three specific items—something to read, something to listen to, and something to watch—touched Jean's soul. Materialism was a realm she operated in constantly—her profession drove it— but until now, she realized that she had never had any emotional attachment to material gifts beyond a polite thanks and then appreciating the utility which each item offered. Suddenly, the things she associated the items with changed.

Didion & Babitz went from "book" to "my grandmother and her best friend."

The Tony Bennett Bill Evans Album went from "CD" to "Annie and Shirley Ruth's enduring, odd-couple friendship and music that entertained and relaxed my grandmother."

Jaws went from "horror DVD" to "two independent women taking a long road trip and their annual summer vacation in Curtis."

They all took their gifts to their respective bedrooms and put on their pajamas, meeting back up on the living room's couches ten minutes later. Annie went over to the Steinway and played Christmas music while Jean and Scott sat and listened. Tonight's playlist featured "Sleigh Ride," "Winter Wonderland," "It's the Most Wonderful Time of the Year," "Hark! The Herald Angels Sing," "Silver Bells," "O Tannenbaum," "The Christmas Waltz," and one more passionate rendering of "Christmas Time is Here."

Neither she nor Scott had their phones, and their eyes had met periodically throughout the half hour of music. Earlier, when she had gone upstairs to put the gifts in her room, she had seen a text from Chantel, but had decided to look at it later before going to bed. When she had seen Chantel's name and the first few words of the text ("Hey there, cabin girl"), she had been a bit snippy in her thoughts. *I get it—you're down there in the sand and sun with your perfect family, enjoying Christmas vacation without a care in the world, and, yes, I'm still here in a cabin.* Now, as they took their empty brandy glasses into the kitchen, she felt sorry that she had reacted negatively to the notification. *I shouldn't judge her for having a wonderful relationship with her husband and kids. I would like to have that someday myself. And she's just being nice, checking up on me.*

Annie took the glasses from them and placed them in the dishwasher. "I haven't forgotten about your special drink, Jean." She winked. "Tomorrow afternoon, I'll make you a Sprite with Maraschino cherries." Before Jean could respond, Annie's phone beeped, and she picked it up off the counter. "Okay! Just got a notification that if the weather gets better and they can get the roads cleared, then they are going to have two Christmas services at the church in the evening tomorrow, one at six and one at eight." She turned to Jean. "Mass on Christmas Day is usually at eight and ten in the morning. Nothing we can do about it this year." She closed her eyes and smiled. "Thank God. I feel off if I get out of my routine, and I must hear the children sing." Her eyes opened. "No pressure, but you are both invited to attend with me."

They both nodded, and Jean was unsure what the nod meant from Scott. For her, it was a polite way of thanking Annie, but she would probably decline—except . . . Annie had said the children were singing.

"The children sing?" said Jean.

"Absolutely," Annie replied, her eyes full of joy. "The children's church choir always performs at Midnight Mass and mass on Christmas Day. It's my favorite part of both services, but—" she laughed, "—don't tell my priest that."

I haven't heard children sing since . . . well, since my last high school concert. It would be wonderful to experience it again.

"Okay, I am heading to bed," Annie said. "Best option for me since they canceled Midnight Mass tonight." She put her phone in her pocket and looked around the kitchen. "Still, even without the morning service, it will be an early day for me tomorrow."

"I'll set my alarm so that I can help," Jean said.

"Oh, no, no. You and Scott sleep in, and I'll have breakfast all ready for you. The majority of the work was done today. Tomorrow's the fun part."

Scott yawned and stretched.

No. Don't go to bed now, Jean thought. *I want to spend some time together; I want to get to know you.*

"Gram," Scott said.

"I don't want to hear it. You were up early today, out in that cold, and didn't take a nap. As your grandmother, I order you not to set your alarm, young man."

He gave a fun-loving frown. "Okay. But if for some unearthly reason I'm not up by nine, then please, kindly kick down my door."

Grinning, Jean asked, "Can I set my alarm for nine?"

"Beautiful, young lady," Annie said. "Approved."

Scott took a glass down from one of the cupboards and walked over to the refrigerator. Jean heard the ice cubes rattle into the cup, followed by the steady stream of water. "Well, I'm bushed," he said.

Damnit!

"Jean?"

Wait a minute! Maybe tonight's not over. "Yes?"

"After breakfast, if the weather has cleared up, would you like to take a walk with me? It's another family tradition."

Okay, tonight is over, but this sounds nice. "I'd love to."

He took a drink of water and then nodded. "Great. Sleep well."

"Goodnight," she said.

He gave Annie a hug and a kiss on the side of her head and left the kitchen.

They were alone for a few seconds before Jean said, "Thank you again for the talks. I texted my mom. I think at some point, we'll probably have a conversation about everything."

"I think that would be good for both of you," Annie said. "I love that woman, but I think she has a lot inside of her that she needs to unload. Before you showed up yesterday, she told me that she wanted me to text her updates on how things were going. I've sent two texts—one last night, and one this afternoon. Sometimes brevity is not my strong suit, but those two times, I just said that things were going well."

"Did she write you back?"

"No, but she did give both messages a thumbs-up emoji."

"That's her."

"That's a start."

"I hope so."

Annie gave her a hug, said goodnight, and they both left the kitchen.

In her bed upstairs, Jean turned off the bedside lamp and opened her text messages. There were now two messages—both from Chantel—one earlier, and one from ten minutes ago. She clicked and read.

Hey there, cabin girl . . . LONG text coming your way. Hope this message finds you not bored to death and not freezing your buns off. App says your weather will be clearing by tomorrow morning. Consider it an early Christmas present from me. Ha! I used a variation of that in my gift exchange speech tonight. I said, "Did you like the weather today? I did my best." The fam loved it. A little humor on the cusp of presents galore. Spoke with Urian. He's so sweet . . . and still a bit high schoolish at times. He's afraid you won't be able to make it. He's got everything set up perfectly for you, and with the weather, he keeps telling himself that it's not going to happen. He needs to chill out, right?! With the weather improving tomorrow, you'll make it there no problem. Uh. Men. I wish he were more like Alec sometimes when it comes to his personal life—more assured.

I told him, "Jean will love your family. You all are going to have a great time. Relax." Maybe you can mature him up a bit while you're out there. You're now in my inner circle, QUEEN . . . been waiting for the right female brains to join me in the upper echelon for a while. Grateful for you. Well, you're on my mind, and I wish you an early Merry Christmas. Got a bit wistful twice today—don't you dare tell anyone, haha—thinking about my kiddos and how fast they're growing up. Need to make every second with them and Alec count. Hugs.

Hey! Just about to turn in, but I remembered one more thing. There's a corporate getaway at the beginning of February. You know, the one that I always take Urian to every year. Well, I'm thinking of it being a girls-only trip this year—you and me. It's in GRAND CAYMAN. When I thought about you traveling to Greece, well, it's not exactly the Caribbean, is it? You deserve some sun, queen. Great networking too—always walk away with new clients. Don't mention it to Urian—I'll let him down easy when we reconvene in Jan. Night, night. You've almost survived the cabin! haha

Before responding, she swiped out and checked the weather. Scott and Chantel were right. The snow would stop and the winds would die down right after midnight. Tomorrow looked clear, as did the 26th. *Looks like I* will *be going to Greece.*

She thought about Urian and the preparations he had made for her. It was sweet, and she wasn't sure that she agreed with Chantel. Urian's worry that Jean wouldn't make it to Greece might not be a sign of immaturity—it could be a sign that he cares. Or, if he was like Jean, then it might be a fear of having wasted time and energy preparing for a visit that now wasn't going to happen. Putting effort into something that yielded no results was one of her triggers. Perhaps it was one of Urian's. She didn't think of the vacation as any 'desired result'—and didn't think that Urian thought of it that way either—but she empathized with the possible predicament he was in.

This, and the change in the weather, reassured Jean of her commitment to him. Did she want to stay and get to know Scott? She did, but he had a chance tonight to see where things could go and decided to head to bed.

No, stop it. Stop being selfish. He was out helping people and was tired. Of course, he needs rest. He asked you to take a walk with him tomorrow.

Still, where is it going? Her eyes moved over to the door, and she envisioned him in his bed down the hall. *What is realistically possible here? I live and work in New York City, and he lives and works in Michigan's Upper Peninsula. We haven't even known each other two days yet. We're in different tax brackets, different social circles . . . Does that even matter?*

Maybe I should just let it go, let him go.

She felt her stomach turn.

I don't know what to do.

She put the phone down, closed her eyes, and did four cycles of box breathing.

When she opened her eyes back up, she thought, *You've got a lot of emotions going through you right now, some you aren't even aware of. Just text Chantel something short and kind, and then go to sleep.*

She did.

If she had stirred a few hours later, perhaps having to use the bathroom, and checked her phone, she would have seen a text from Urian. But she did not stir.

She barely moved and did not wake up until her 9:00 a.m. alarm went off.

Then, she saw the text from Urian.

28

Christmas

J ean read the text and felt her enthusiasm rise. Urian was flying to Detroit Metro Airport and was scheduled to arrive at 8 p.m. on December 26th— tomorrow night. He had arranged for a private charter pilot to fly her out of MBS International Airport in Freeland to Detroit Metro on the 26th at noon, and he had rooms for them at The Westin hotel in Metro's airport that night. She could check in once she got there, rest, and then when he arrived, they'd have a late dinner together.

The final part of the text came as a complete surprise. The next evening, on the 27th, they would be flying from Detroit to St. Barths for a few days with Chantel and her family, and then flying to Greece on the 30th. He'd cleared it with Chantel for them to stay an extra week in Mykonos, and he could not be more excited about the trips.

She was ecstatic at the development. *Maybe things happen for a reason,* she thought. *Annie was in my life this Christmas to serve a purpose for which I can never repay her, and now it's time to move on and continue living life, just as my grandmother would have. Annie will never be out of my life. This is a relationship I intend to maintain.*

And Scott—

The knocking on the door down the hall interrupted her thought, as she heard Annie say, "Scottie? Merry Christmas. Time for breakfast, my boy." Jean did not hear Scott's reply, but she heard Annie add, "Aw, thank you. I'll see you in a few minutes."

She could hear Annie's footsteps approaching her door. When she heard them stop, Jean forced herself to cough loudly. The footsteps continued down the hall and then down the stairs.

Do I tell them the new plan?

No, not right away, and I don't have to share all the details with them. I'll wait until later and then tell them that I've got a flight out of MBS at noon tomorrow. I have to return the rental car, so that will make it easier. I'll leave here around 8:30 a.m. just to be safe. Yes, everything will work out fine. Let's just enjoy today.

She texted Urian back and then Chantel. Within minutes, she heard back from both of them. They appreciated her flexibility and wanted to reward her for it. They said they both felt guilty for putting her in her present situation, as they had been the ones who had adjusted her plans to visit Michigan later than she had initially planned. St. Barths was going to be relaxing and fun, and they were thrilled. Chantel started a group text at the end, attaching a picture of the beach and writing:

It. Is. ON. Get ready to be spoiled.

Jean "loved" the text and then set down her phone. *Time for coffee and breakfast!* She entered the bathroom and began brushing her hair. After a few strokes, she stopped. Staring at her reflection, she put the brush down and then removed her glasses. "Why not?" she said, and got out her contact lenses.

When she arrived in the kitchen, Annie had already laid out the glorious spread on the kitchen table—bacon, eggs, toast, croissants, fresh fruit, and French toast. There was a pitcher of orange juice along with cream and sugar set out for coffee.

"Merry Christmas, dear," Annie said, wiping her hands on a dish towel while standing in front of the sink.

"Merry Christmas."

Three place settings were staged with a crisp white cloth napkin folded and standing up in the center of each plate. Scott had not come down yet, but she thought she heard footsteps in the hallway.

"Sure you don't want to stay the rest of the week?" Annie asked, giving Jean a quick hug.

"If breakfast looks like this, I'm not giving up my room key."

Annie laughed and gave her a poke in the side as she walked away. "Why, Jean, there is a sense of humor in that lean frame."

"It won't be lean for long. Annie, this looks and smells . . . well, *wow*."

"Way I planned it. Now, sit." Then, she gasped. "Dear God! Look at those beautiful eyes!"

Jean had wondered if or when anyone would notice. "Thought I would change things up for today."

Annie put a hand on both of Jean's cheeks and studied her face. "It's like a completely different you. I love you with your glasses, but I love this too." She lowered her hands. "Those baby blues, they're radiant."

"I'm glad you approve."

"Did Santa come?" Scott said, entering the kitchen. Like Jean, he still had his pajamas on from last night—navy sweatpants and a white round-neck t-shirt that was tight around his shoulders and biceps. *He looks refreshed*, Jean thought. *I hope he slept well. Why do I immediately feel nervous at the first sight of him?*

"Not for you if you don't get over here and sit down right now."

"Morning, Jean. Merry Christmas," he said with a cute grin. He did a double-take. "Whoa! Where are your glasses? I mean, they're probably upstairs, but, well . . . well, you surprised me."

"Pure majesty," Annie said.

Jean looked at Scott, who looked like he swallowed a squirrel.

"Yes, uh, yes they are," he said.

She felt bile rise in her throat and swallowed it down. *I'm feeling something else. What is it?*

He hugged Annie. "Merry Christmas, Gram."

She kissed his cheek and then walked over and grabbed the coffee pot.

"Let me get that," said Jean, trying to take her mind off her nervous stomach.

"No, ma'am. You stay put. Maybe later, with the dishes."

"Yes, and you are not stopping me." She swallowed again.

"A sense of humor, *and* she's assertive. My, my, dear, you're on a roll this morning."

Scott looked confused. "What does she mean by that?" he asked Jean.

"Oh, you just sit down," Annie commanded him.

Scott gave a joshing shrug and joined Jean at the table; Annie filled all three of their mugs with fresh coffee and then poured the rest of the pot into a tan pitcher and screwed on the lid, which had a push button and spout so they could easily refill their mugs. "Got it for special occasions like this," Annie said, tapping the side of the pitcher with the empty pot.

Jean watched as she walked across the kitchen, put on a fresh pot, and then removed her apron. She sat down; they held hands; and she said grace. "Okay, eat up." Jerking her thumb behind her, she added, "We haven't even gotten to the good stuff yet."

Jean looked over at the double oven. The appliance's lights were on, and she could see a large dish in each port.

"Did you make all of that this morning?" Scott said.

Annie had scrambled eggs and two slices of bacon on her plate and was using her fork and knife to cut the bacon. "Heavens no. Prepared everything yesterday." She motioned her hand at the counter next to the sink. "Pie's already done, though."

Jean saw a large dish with tin foil spread over it. Still feeling queasy, she poured herself a glass of orange juice and buttered a piece of toast. After a few bites, followed by sips of the OJ, her stomach calmed down, and she added cream and sugar to her coffee.

"We'll open presents after breakfast—that will give your food time to settle—and then you two can bundle up for your walk."

The walk. She hadn't even looked outside yet.

"Beautiful sunny day," said Scott. "I took a peek out my bedroom window before coming down. No clouds, no snow, and no wind. It's like a still picture everywhere you look—not a snowflake moving." His eyes worked their way over to Jean. "On my phone, I saw that MBS and Detroit Metro are back up and running as of this morning." He stabbed a piece of bacon with his fork and took a bite. "I suppose you'll be leaving us."

Annie jumped in. "Oh, but not today, right?"

She had wanted to postpone the conversation, but she was now forced to have it. *Maybe it will be better this way.* Then, like an uninvited guest, her queasiness returned, and she took a drink of orange juice. "No, I have a flight that leaves tomorrow at noon." She grinned. "So, I'll have to mooch off you for one more day."

She had expected Annie to join her in the lighthearted joke, but instead of seeing Annie's lips curl into a smile, she watched as a wave of sadness washed over the sweet old lady's face. Eventually, she nodded and said, "Well, at least we get a little more time with you."

Jean looked to Scott for a more positive reaction, but his expression looked pained as if the Michigan State Police had just told him that they found the person who had abandoned the Ford Taurus two nights ago and that the person was dead, frozen in a snowbank. "I thought . . . well, forget what I thought. We were lucky to have you here as long as we did." He took a sip of coffee. "You got your return flight scheduled pretty fast. Mine to California didn't even have an update. Did the airline contact you this morning?"

"No," she said. *God, I wanted to avoid this part of it!* "My bosses arranged a private flight out of MBS."

"Oh," said Scott.

"Where are you going, dear?" asked Annie.

"I'm meeting up with my immediate supervisor in Detroit, and then we're both flying down to St. Barths to join our boss for a few days." *There. Please, let's leave it at that . . . No, let me add one more thing.* "They did it as a gesture of kindness since I got stuck here."

Scott nodded, and Annie just raised her eyebrows.

Damnit! I just made it worse! "What I meant to say is that they feel a little guilty. I was originally supposed to fly here last week, but they wanted me to attend our company's annual holiday party, where I was to be honored. So, they arranged for my flight to be changed, and then, voila, the snowstorm hit."

"That's nice of them," said Annie. "I wondered what had happened. Your mother had provided me with your flight information, and then the week before you were coming, she texted me with the updated information." She smiled, and Jean knew it was genuine. "Everything always works out like it's supposed to, I guess. If you had come before, then you wouldn't have met Scottie."

"If that's the case, then I'm glad your plans changed," Scott said. "Sounds like you work for a good boss." He took a bite of toast and washed it down with coffee. "What did they honor you with at the holiday party?"

She exhaled, trying to relax. "I got promoted to be a member of the lead team."

"Congratulations," he said.

With every nice sentiment delivered by him, she felt her stomach turn more and more. *What is going on with me?*

"Doesn't surprise me," Annie said. *Gosh, she could trademark that phrase,* Jean thought. "You could be running the company in a few years."

"What company do you work for?" asked Scott.

She told them and explained a little about what she did.

"The state and national parks could use some of your magic," he said, frowning. "We're seeing declining numbers. Fewer and fewer people are spending time outside."

Before she could process what he had said, Annie scoffed. "Enough of that negative energy. I know, I know, you're right, Scottie, but we won't solve it now." She reached out and gave Jean's forearm a few quick rubs back and forth. "If all we get is one last day with you, then let's make the most of it."

Jean detected a current of anger underneath the statements. She did not think Annie was upset with her. Instead, she sensed that Annie had taken her sadness at Jean leaving and funneled it into anger to help her deal with it. *Why can I read her right now and not myself?* She wondered.

Scott took a drink of his coffee, and Jean saw his face brighten. "You're right. Let's make it a great day."

"Do you think you'll still be flying west at some point?" Jean asked him.

He shook his head. "At this point, I don't think I'm going to go. I'd rather stay here for a few more days until I need to head back up."

Annie beamed.

They finished breakfast, and Scott and Jean helped Annie clean up. She did a little more preparation in the kitchen for their big meal later, while Scott and Jean showered and dressed. Then, they all met in the family room, where they opened presents, listened to Christmas music on Annie's stereo, and had more coffee.

While she was upstairs changing before coming down to open presents, Jean had received a text from Sarah.

Merry Christmas, boss lady! What a storm here! Hope you are good wherever you are—probably should have checked in earlier, but we lost power. Got it back last night. Weather has improved. Roads pretty much cleared around here now, plows worked all night. GREAT "magic" news (lol): The water heater and HVAC crews will be able to start work at the house tomorrow. Thought it would be at least the 27th or 28th, but Michiganders bounce back quickly, ma'am. More updates to come!

When they had met in the family room, she had told Annie and Scott about Sarah's message, and they were happy for her. Jean loved the leather journal, leather bookmark, fountain pen, and her stocking stuffers, and she enjoyed watching Scott and Annie exchange the rest of their gifts. Everything was slow, and, more than once, she caught Scott staring at his grandmother, taking in each moment. *She's eighty-three, and I've never seen anyone that age move the way she moves or who possesses her mental acuity,* Jean thought. *But, still, at eighty-three, it can all go away in an instant.* If Jean had to guess, she believed Scott was not doom-scrolling his way through the gift exchange, putting pressure on himself like, 'This is the last Christmas I'll ever have with her,' but he seemed to be in tune with the fact that the next one with her was not guaranteed. This made Jean think about her relationship with Annie. *I don't want this one to be my last with her either.* She was already thinking about a visit back here this spring to catch up and learn more about her family's past. Annie had mentioned that she would be happy to let Jean look through some of her family photo albums. Maybe she would be up for getting them out after their big dinner this afternoon.

Annie had said that she was going to attend the 6 p.m. Christmas Day Mass, and Scott had said he would drive her and attend as well. With nothing to lose and wanting to spend more time with them both and hear the children's choir, she agreed to go. Hence, the plan for the rest of the day had become: a walk with Scott now, light snacks until a pre-dinner drink—Sprite and Maraschino cherries for Jean—by the fire at two-thirty p.m., dinner at three instead of six followed by hot chocolate in Annie's 'Christmas Room,' which Jean was anxious to see, and then they would leave for mass at 5 p.m. to, in Annie's words, *"Make sure we get a seat. It's going to be packed, and I'm not standing or sitting in the cry room."*

They sat in the living room, and Annie took her position behind the Steinway. "Okay, I'll play while you two dress in the foyer. Think of this as your pre-walk song."

As they rose, Jean heard the first bars of "Snow" and felt a pep in her step as she followed Scott to the foyer. Remembering the horrific walk to the chorus room after singing that song to end her final high school concert—she had quit choir two days later—Jean took comfort in the fact that this walk would be different. *If Annie only knew what a favor she is doing for me by playing it now, giving me the power to use it as a beginning instead of the ending I have always associated it with. Bless her.*

Maybe I will tell her about it when we get back. We've got all afternoon.

The song was still playing as they opened the front door and stepped onto the porch.

"Will she stop now?" Jean asked.

"Not a chance. She always finishes the song."

They exchanged a smile and stepped off.

It was a magisterial scene—bright green pine trees, shagged with snow and ice, dotted the landscape. A warm, yellow-orange sun was above, and large trunks of bare trees rose to the sky, lining the property in the distance. A thick blanket of snow seemed to cover everything else. The air was crisp; there was still no wind; and the sun felt warm on Jean's face underneath her knit hat.

They stepped onto the driveway, which Annie's neighbor Rob had plowed for them early that morning. Annie had told them that she had given him a mug of coffee and thanked him for everyone, while Jean and Scott were still asleep. *Would my neighbors be that generous, and on Christmas morning?* she thought. An answer she did not like entered her mind, and she focused on her stride to distract herself. With each step, Jean could hear the snow crunch underneath their boots. It was a comforting sound, like a gentle, aesthetic reinforcement signifying their continued progress down the drive.

Seeing the large banks that rose on both sides of the driveway reminded her of how she had described Scott's pained expression that morning when he learned that she would be leaving tomorrow.

The anonymous traveler in the Ford Taurus.

"Did they ever find the person you tracked? The one who left the Taurus in the ditch?"

"They didn't, but I did get a text this morning that the car was gone."

"Gone?"

"By late last night, when the snowfall started to slow down, they had been able to pull every vehicle from the ditch on M-20. Then, this morning, when the State Police made their rounds, the car was gone."

"I guess that's good news."

"Yeah. I don't know what else to think. Just weird. Like I chased some ghost."

"My life feels like that right now."

"How so?"

"How much has your grandmother told you about my family?"

"Not a lot, but she did mention that you didn't know your grandmother and grandfather, who lived in the house you came here to sell."

"Did you know them? I mean, beyond playing cards with my grandmother?"

"A little. I heard that Gram told you about their return to Michigan. I was there." He made eye contact with her. "It was powerful. My grandparents and your grandparents embraced on the Tridge for a long time before they joined the rest of us." He looked straight ahead again. "How are you holding up?"

"It's a lot to take in. I'm lucky to have your grandma to talk to."

"She makes it easy, doesn't she?"

"Yeah." She listened to her breathing and the sound of their boots for a few more steps. "So do you."

"Oh, thanks. I don't have a lot of in-depth conversations. Don't have many conversations, period—just small talk with my staff and people who come into the park. A little sad."

"What would you say if I told you that I was the same way?"

He chuckled—it was something she loved about him. "I'd say we're both sad then."

She joined him in laughter.

"Truth is, though, I like people. Minus some of the pains in the ass who I have to deal with in the park—you know, the kind of people that will never be happy—I have a skewed perception because almost everyone else who comes to camp or just be outdoors is content, and it makes me feel good."

"I sense a 'but.'"

"There is one. When I get outside of my park, it flips, and almost everyone I come into contact with is miserable." He rubbed his gloves together. "I don't like it."

They reached the tree line, and soon the cabin and pole barn went out of view behind them.

"What about you?" he asked.

"Most people I come into contact with start either even-keeled or unhappy, but after our team helps them boost the sales of their product, I hear from their corporate leadership that they are all now happy. The thing is, I never get to see it. I'm on to the next job when the advertising package for the previous one goes into effect."

"Do you think that happiness is long-lasting?"

"I don't know. Money and happiness have always been strange bedfellows."

"What about you? Are you happy?"

"In my job?"

"Yeah."

"I am. I like to work hard and help our customers achieve their goals. What about you?"

"I can't see myself doing anything else, which is rare for our generation, I guess. We're supposed to be switching jobs or careers every couple of years."

"We are known for that."

"So, what's wrong with us?"

"Guess we didn't get the memo."

"Guess not."

They walked in silence for a while, just taking in the sights, smells, and sounds. When they reached the end of the driveway, she asked, "So, how long is the traditional Christmas-Day walk?"

"I'm not sure there is a predetermined length. I usually hang a left here and walk down to Geoff and Carole's, then turn around. Road looks great. Sarah was right about the plows. How about it?"

"After that breakfast, how can I say no?"

"We did put away some food."

They turned and started down the road.

She found him to be laid-back yet assertive as they walked and talked about their lives. Where they had grown up, who their friends had been, what schools they had attended, and how they had landed the jobs they were currently in. Never for one moment did she think that he wasn't engaged, and yet he wasn't overly engaged, which would have made it seem like he was trying too hard.

She felt comfortable with him and around him. When he talked about a trip his family had taken to Florida during one of his spring breaks while growing up, she thought of sun and sand and was reminded of where she was heading with Urian. And instead of this recollection lifting her spirits and energizing her steps, she felt the emptiness of impending separation. She was sure she would see Annie in a few months, but would she ever see Scott again? There was no guarantee that he would be able to take the time off to come down and see her when she visited Annie, and would it seem awkward if she came up north to see him while he was working? Maybe. She didn't want anyone to visit her while she was at work.

As they reached Geoff and Carole's mailbox and turned around, she concentrated on what she was feeling. Halfway down the road back to Annie's, she had it.

It came to her in the form of a series of questions. *Will I be okay if I never see Scott again? Is there something here worth pursuing? Will I always wonder what could have been?*

As the last question ran across her mind, he asked, "Are you excited to be going someplace warm?"

The honest answer was that, yes, she was. *Be straight with him,* she told herself. "I am. It will be nice. New York City is beautiful this time of year, but it can get dreary some days." However, she knew there was another part of her answer that she would not share with him. *I am excited to go, but there's also a part of me that wants to stay here and see if there's something between us.*

"I can't blame you. Summer seems far away."

"You could still go to California."

"I could. But I won't. I'd take Gram and the cold weather over my family that's out there and warm weather any time."

"That bad, huh?"

He shrugged. "I wouldn't say it's bad. It's just not good, if that makes any sense."

She couldn't have explained what it was like to go home and visit her parents any better.

As they took another few steps, a jumble of thoughts coalesced into a statement Jean's mind wanted her to consider now. *You have to go on this trip because it is the only way you'll discover if you truly* need *to see Scott again.*

She was surprised by the clarity of the declaration, but it gave her a newfound confidence and validated what she had been feeling. Yes, she wanted to stay and get to know Scott better. Yes, she worried about leaving without knowing if something was there. And, yes, she was attracted to Urian and wanted to know if something was there as well, because her current situation could be turned around. And if it was, then she realized that all the questions and fears she had regarding Scott also applied to Urian. Now, was there a little voice on her shoulder telling her that when she was with Scott, her feelings for Urian vanished until she was alone again. She couldn't deny that this was true. Yet again, she could also end up forgetting Scott when she was with Urian over the next few weeks. She made up her mind.

It will be hard to leave tomorrow, but I have to.

She looked at him. *God, his eyes are dreamy, and I feel so safe when I'm with him. Not that I'm a shrinking violet or need a man to always be with me, but I feel like he is someone who would have my back, and I usually don't feel that way about anyone.*

"Yes?" he said.

Shit! I was staring too long. Quick, what was the last thing we were talking about? Ah! Right. He said that visiting his family was neither good nor bad. Perfect. "Sorry," she said. "I was thinking about the last thing you mentioned . . . about it not being good or bad seeing your family. That makes perfect sense."

"Really?" he asked.

"I feel that when I visit my folks."

"It's just awkward, right?"

"Superficial."

"That's a good word for it." After a few more steps, he said, "So, New York City. Do you like living there?"

"I do."

"Only been there once, and there's no place like it."

"In a good way or a bad way?"

"Neither. It's just different. I understand the attraction, though—Broadway, Madison Square Garden, Yankee Stadium, the museums, the libraries, the galas, the parades, the celebrations, the nightlife, Central Park, not having to do yardwork or worry about a car."

"All true," she said.

"Devices with internet connectivity have brought the vices and virtues of a big city into the palm of one's hand, which, for better and for worse, has blurred the lines between living where you do and where I do. With what is accessible online and on television, I think there are more and more people who visit New York City virtually and believe it's just as good, or even better, than visiting in person. And that's a shame, because it's not the same. This shift makes me wonder about sustainability. I remember walking down a street in Manhattan and looking up at all of those skyscrapers, wondering, 'How are all of these architectural marvels going to be maintained in the years to come?' and

'What happens when people abandon going to live theater?'" He met her eyes. "Do you ever wonder about stuff like that?"

"Not often," she said. "I probably should, though."

"No judgment on my part. I tend to get contemplative around the holidays when things slow down. I wonder sometimes about what society—the earth—will be like when we're around my Gram's age."

"That I do think about," she said. "With the way things are moving at light speed right now, it's hard to see, but I'd like to think that the improvements will outweigh the costs."

"Me too." He hesitated, then said, "We'll see."

They reached Annie's driveway, and soon they were climbing the stairs to the porch.

"I think we cleared some space for dinner. How about you?" he asked, patting his stomach.

"Couple of calories burned there."

"Thanks for the walk," he said, and then he gave her a quick hug.

Just as she started to enjoy it, he pulled back and opened the door for her.

They entered, and he said, "We're home."

There was no answer, but they could smell the delicious food.

Suddenly, Scott stopped, and he took a deep breath in with his nose. "Smells like something's . . . burning."

Before Jean could say that she smelled it too, he was already sprinting toward the kitchen.

29

Jean had nearly caught up to Scott when she heard him shout in horror. "Oh, Gram! Oh, no!"

They entered the kitchen, and Jean saw Annie lying on the floor, her head a few feet from the oven. Scott had already dropped down to the ground and was checking to see if his grandmother was breathing and had a pulse. Jean's eyes started to water as she knelt next to Scott. "What can I do?" she cried.

"She's still alive," he said in a panic. "Breathing and has a pulse." He pulled out his phone and dialed 9-1-1. Jean looked around the kitchen and saw that the oven was still on, and whatever was inside was burning. She leaped to her feet and turned off both oven chambers.

Next, she listened as Scott talked to the emergency personnel. He was still shaky but gave Annie's condition and address. Fifteen minutes later, an ambulance arrived, and Annie was loaded into it and taken to Midland Hospital. Jean rode with Scott in his truck, trying to hold back her tears, as they followed the ambulance and then parked in the hospital parking lot.

They raced inside, just in time to see Annie being wheeled into emergency. Before the doors closed, Scott shouted, "I'm right here, Gram. They're going to take good care of you. You'll be all right." The doors closed, and the waiting area fell silent. By now, a nurse had come around the front desk and was approaching them. Scott broke down in tears and collapsed into a chair in the lobby.

Jean heard the doors to emergency open, and a tall, stocky African-American male doctor walked out and approached her and Scott.

She nudged Scott, and he stood up immediately, rubbing his eyes. He had fallen asleep twenty minutes ago, exhausted.

In the deepest baritone voice that Jean had ever heard, the doctor said, "Mr. Brady?"

Scott's head swiveled around, still in a daze and apparently not exactly sure of his surroundings. "Yes, I'm Scott Brady."

Jean stood up next to him. "You dozed off for a little bit. It's okay."

"This is Jean Mercer," Scott said, introducing her. "What time is it?" Scott asked, his forehead beaded with sweat.

"It's just after six-thirty," Jean said. "They've had Annie in there for almost four hours."

The doctor spoke again, calmly and evenly. "Hi, Scott. Hi, Jean. I'm Dr. Arthur Prater, and I operated on your grandmother, Scott—"

"Oh, God. Is she . . ."

"She made it through surgery and is in intensive care. We had to do a triple bypass, but she's a tough lady."

Scott broke down in tears once again and was unable to speak for a minute.

Jean stepped in. "His father is flying into Detroit tonight and driving up here."

"That's what the nurse told me," said Doctor Prater. "I'm glad that you have family coming in and that you have your friend here with you now. The next twenty-four to forty-eight hours are critical in your grandmother's recovery. She's getting the best care possible in our ICU, and they are monitoring everything, looking for potential complications—bleeding, infection, etc.—and helping her manage any pain that comes her way."

"Pain?"

"It's common after a procedure like we just performed. We'll have her on medication to keep her comfortable."

"If everything goes as planned, when could she be out of the ICU?"

"It's usually one to two days. When she stabilizes, we'll move her to a regular room."

"How long in the regular room?"

"Let's get her out of ICU first, okay?"

Scott wiped his eyes, and he could finally speak. "Please, I'd like to know. I think information will comfort me right now."

In the four hours she had been waiting alongside Scott, she had scoured the internet, almost as if she were attempting to become an expert in heart attacks and the associated surgery and recovery. She couldn't help herself. It was all she had known in life—an unlimited supply of information at the push of a button. Scott had looked too, but in his stress, it appeared that the information had vanished from his head or at least become blocked with the doctor's news that his grandmother had survived. Or, he just needed to hear everything again. So far, according to what she had researched, the doctor's answers were spot-on.

The doctor put his hand on Scott's shoulder. "Sure. Other than the blockages we fixed, she's in terrific shape for her age. I could see her leaving for home in a week, maybe a little less after she's transferred into a regular room."

"Thanks, doc," said Scott.

"You're welcome. Now, I'm going to go back and check on her, okay? A nurse will be out shortly to speak with you and gather additional information. She'll also ask you if you need anything." He looked around and lowered his voice. "May I recommend a cup of coffee from the nurse's station. It's the best in the hospital. Tell her I said it was okay."

Jean said, "Thank you," and shook his hand.

Scott hugged him.

She was not used to seeing a man display emotions—not on this level for sure—and it unsettled her, not because she thought it was wrong, but it made her feel like she needed to find a way to fix things and make him stop. *I don't do well around people in pain. But that is who I was,* she thought. *Who am I now? Haven't I been moved to tears in the past two days more than . . . well,* ever? Scott hadn't been emotional the past few days. Yes, he had been warm to her and Annie and wasn't afraid of physical touch, but beyond those moments, he was rather stoic, which is why his unleashing of tears and loss of that stoicism had surprised her, no, *shocked* her. However, as the afternoon hours had passed, Jean reminded herself that she had witnessed Scott with, perhaps, the most important person in his life. She could not take the fact that he had fallen apart in an unpredictable situation where he could have lost his beloved grandmother— could still lose her—and make a sweeping generalization about how emotional a person he was.

"My pleasure," Doctor Prater said. "You two hang in there. I've got a great team in there looking after her."

He left, and they sat back down. While he walked over to a corner on the other side of the room and made calls to his family, Jean texted her mom and dad with an update. She was surprised at how much her mom was texting back, asking what they could do for Annie, Scott, and the family—even checking in on how Jean was holding up.

The other message she received was from the group text between her, Chantel, and Urian. They both wished her a Merry Christmas, and Urian texted a countdown clock that he had set up, the hours, minutes, and seconds winding down until Jean left the next day. She had held off on responding, waiting to see if Annie would pull through. Watching Scott sleep on her shoulder, she had determined that if Annie died, she would cancel her trip and stay with Scott and the family to help out.

Now that Annie had survived, and Scott's father would be here tonight, it opened up the possibility of her continuing with her plan to leave tomorrow. She had discussed none of this with Scott and would not until later out of respect for him and Annie.

The nurse arrived and asked if she could get them anything. When Scott mentioned coffee from the nurse's station, she whispered, "That man! I'll see what I can do."

A few minutes later, she came back with two large cups of coffee.

Scott and Jean thanked her, and after reiterating that she was there for them, the nurse returned to her station at the front desk. A half hour later, she came back and delivered the good news. Annie was looking stronger already.

Finished with her coffee, which *was* very good, Jean took her empty cup and threw it away in the trash can next to a vending machine. When she returned to her seat next to Scott, he was still sipping from his cup.

"My dad texted me. He landed in Detroit and is now on the road."

Earlier, Scott had briefly mentioned that his father was remarried, but had not said whether his stepmother was traveling with his father. "Is your stepmom with him?" she asked.

"No. *Megan* stayed in Santa Barbara." He made eye contact with her. "Typical. I didn't expect her to come."

"Did you reach your mom?"

"I did. She was kind. She always got along well with Gram." He then gave an overview of how his father had cheated on his mother, and that Annie had found it hard to forgive his father for breaking up their family. Then, shrugging his shoulders, the floodgates had opened, and Scott told her of his limited contact with his sister, who had experienced the worst of the divorce, and that his father's sister, Michelle, had little to no contact with Annie because of her jealousy of his father's relationship with Annie, even after the divorce. He ended by saying that Michelle's daughter, his cousin, Victoria, also now had nothing to do with Annie, which broke Annie's heart—a heart that had almost killed her today. "So," he said, concluding the story of his family saga, "it looks like it will be me and my father taking care of things in the short term. My aunt Michelle hasn't returned my text yet, and I'm unsure if she will. I called my sister, Heather, and she was comforting—surprised, maybe more than anyone, at what had happened, because she had just talked to Gram, wishing her a Merry Christmas, after we had stepped off for our walk. Said she talked to her for about twenty minutes while Gram moved around the kitchen working on the big dinner. It must have been *minutes* after they got off the phone that Gram collapsed."

"Do you think she'll travel up here at some point?"

"Maybe. She said her girlfriend is taking off a week from work around New Year's, and they might come up to see Gram." He stared straight ahead. "She asked me if I needed her here right now, which was sweet of her to do . . . I said I'd be okay. And, as long as Gram pulls through, I will be."

For as private and reserved as Scott had been during the past two days, including their walk where she thought he had opened up to her more than at any other time, she had discovered that in the right circumstances, he had no problem talking about his family and how imperfect it was. There was a hint of disdain toward his stepmom, but his other statements came across as matter-of-fact, as if *this is the way it is*, which made her take notice. He had welcomed any conversation about his family, but he had not made it seem like he needed to keep talking about it, where she might have felt dragged into something she did not want to be a part of. Even though the subject matter was heavy, it didn't come across as heavy. At first, she had reasoned that Annie's heart attack had created the "right circumstances" for him to open up to her, but then she thought, *maybe he feels as comfortable around me as I do around him.*

He turned toward her and held her hands in his. "Thank you for being there for me today. I've never dealt with anything like that before." He cleared his throat. "And I mean what I'm about to tell you—"

Say you want me to stay. There was a level of clarity in her thoughts that she trusted. *Say you want me to stay.*

"I am happy that you are heading out tomorrow."

What?

Perhaps, he picked up on her confusion. She didn't think that her body language had given anything away, but she was not one-hundred percent sure. "Well, not happy in the sense that we're parting company, because I have enjoyed our time together. What I mean is that you were thrown into a situation by the storm, and you deserve to have some time off to relax. And I don't mean that as if I have the right to determine what you need or want. It comes from a place of gratitude and respect. The way you treated my grandmother and helped us out was something special. It meant a lot to her, and it meant a lot to me." He squeezed her hands and then released them, just as his grandmother had done. "Maybe we'll stay in contact, but we're both experienced enough to know that, even with the best intentions, it might not happen. I'm not big on melodramatic or hyperbolic statements, but Jean, I'm glad you came into my life for these two days. It has given me some hope for the future." He grinned at the floor. "Okay, end of big speech."

With a lump in her throat and her hands trembling, she pulled his head to hers and kissed his lips.

❄ ❄ ❄

Noon, December 26th

With a glass of white wine in her hand and her feet propped up in the leather recliner she was seated in, being massaged by a flight attendant, Jean looked out the window of the Bombardier 7500 at the snow-covered landscape of Freeland, Michigan, as the luxury jet climbed into the sky.

Her glasses were back on, and she took a sip of her drink and then set the fine crystal glass down on the polished tray table in front of her seat. *I never did get my Sprite with Maraschino cherries.* The thought lingered in her mind for a couple of seconds, but then vanished. She picked up her phone.

When she arrived at the airport, she expected to be flying on a small charter plane to Detroit, which was why she was surprised to see an attractive female flight attendant dressed in a white blouse, short navy skirt, and navy heels approach her when she entered the terminal and asked Jean to follow her. As soon as she was welcomed aboard the private jet by the captain, she messaged Chantel and Urian This is not a small charter plane! in the group text. Chantel had taken the lead and written:

Sit back and relax, QUEEN . . . and text us AS SOON as the wheels leave the ground.

Jean closed her eyes for a moment, feeling wonderful as the flight attendant who had gathered her at the airport continued to knead her feet. Imagining her blood pressure dropping as fast as the aircraft was ascending, she exhaled and opened her eyes. She typed a message into her phone and hit send.

Okay, I am now airborne.

Immediately, there were bubbles from Urian, and a few seconds later, he wrote:

Surprise! You're not landing in Detroit. WE'RE flying to St. Barths . . . Right. Now.

She cocked her head to the right, looking confused. Then, the flight attendant who was massaging her feet started to giggle. Jean typed:

WE'RE?

Then, Chantel texted:

Ah! Look behind you.

She turned her head to see Urian, wearing leather sandals, tan shorts, and a form-fitting turquoise Polo shirt, walking toward her from the plane's aft cabin.

40 Years Later . . .

EPILOGUE

Jean awoke to the haziness and dull headache that reminded her of how much red wine she had consumed the night before. Unfortunately, her friends in Silicon Valley had not yet managed to eliminate the hangover. She blinked, and her eyes slowly adjusted to the darkness of the room. Soon, she became aware of the figure standing at the foot of her massive bed.

"Good morning, madam," said the female voice of her robot maid Ainsley. Decades ago, a female audiobook narrator had sold her voice to a gigantic tech company for a landmark amount of money, and the company had used the woman's soft, soothing voice for its humanoids ever since.

"A glass of whatever I was having last night, four PF super gels, and my B-12 poke, please," Jean said.

Ainsley was the newest model to come off an exclusive line of only one hundred made. She had been a member of their household for two months now, replacing Jean's long-time robot maid Audrey, who had been given a new program and reassigned to work in the estate's extensive garden. Even in her morning fog, Jean still marveled at how human-like Ainsley was: six feet tall with smooth skin the shade of sand, which felt like real skin, fitted over her frame composed of aluminum alloys, steel, polycarbonate, carbon fiber, and Kevlar. Stripped of her clothes, which was how she arrived in a special casket, she had been designed to have an athletic frame, and, from the neck down, at a distance of perhaps ten yards, Jean thought that a beautiful woman model was standing in front of her. Ainsley's hair was the color of gold and styled in a shoulder-length cut. Her face was pretty, with a pleasing smile fixed in place, exposing high cheekbones. However, when she spoke, her face did not move—the only thing that ever moved above her chin was her eyes, which had blue irises. Perhaps the next model, due out in two years, would have facial muscles and lips that moved when it smiled and talked. Her husband had told her that there was an ongoing discussion at the company that produced the robots about whether the machines should ever be programmed to frown on occasion. Jean was not sure that it was a good idea.

Ainsley turned and then pushed a cart around the side of the bed until it reached Jean's nightstand. For the maid's clothing, Jean had chosen black heels, charcoal-colored dress slacks, and a crisp white blouse. The machine wore no jewelry, but her fingernails and toenails were painted crimson. Other than the skin and the constantly improving interface program, guided by state-of-the-art artificial intelligence, which determined Ainsley's responses to humans who addressed her, the humanoid's physical movement was the most noticeable upgrade from Audrey: Ainsley moved—walked, ran, jumped, massaged body parts, lifted things—like a human female who was around thirty years old, the age of a woman's peak physical strength (according to the company that had designed her).

"I know I've mentioned this before," Ainsley said, gesturing to the glass of wine, syringe, and two round blue pills on the silver tray resting on top of the cart, "but this mixture is not good for your overall life expectancy. Naturally, I had it ready for you per your instructions last night, but your daily wine intake has gone from seven hundred and fifty milliliters per day up to one and a half liters a day in the past month."

I know. It's because of him!

"I'm sensing the onset of depression, madam. Shall I load my counselor program? We could have a nice chat over some green tea, which I can make in five minutes, and that accounts for the three minutes of steeping."

Jean ignored her and picked up the glass of wine and four pills. She placed the capsules in her mouth and washed them down with the entire glass of wine. "One more glass before breakfast, please," she commanded Ainsley.

"Of course," the robot said. "But, with your big night tonight, I recommend against any more until after the celebration. You know what happened the last time your two daughters saw you in that state." Ainsley paused. "They should be here by four in the afternoon. It will be an honor to get all three of you ready for the party."

My daughters. Why are they coming? For money, probably, or to manipulate me by threatening to cut me off from my grandsons.

She hadn't seen them in almost a year.

"I knew you would remind me. Those engineers did an impressive job transferring Audrey's database over to yours."

"Audrey? Our lead harvester?"

"Never mind. You're right about my not having any more wine until later. Maybe one tiny snort, though?" The mention of her daughters had triggered her, and she demanded immediate release from the horror filling her mind. *I have no patience. Who am I?* "It's been a while."

"Four days, five hours, thirty-seven minutes, eighteen seconds. I've been instructed to deny you that luxury until after you are honored this evening. Your husband told me that he wants tonight to be *perfect* for you. Almost fifty years with the company! The last thirty-five as CEO! And, it's Christmas Eve!"

Jean didn't even recognize the advertising world anymore, let alone the company she had helmed for the past three-plus decades. With almost everyone in the United States on universal basic income, only the most powerful companies had survived, typically two or three per market, and they only used small, targeted campaigns for the pockets of wealthy enclaves that remained scattered across the country, whose residents could afford their products. "You spoke to him?"

"Yes—last night. Now, time for your shot."

Jean rolled onto her stomach and pulled down a corner of her pajamas, exposing the upper outer quadrant of her left buttock—just below where she had a tattoo removed.

Immediately, she heard Ainsley say, "Remain still," and seconds later, she felt the slight pinch of the needle entering her skin, followed by an immediate boost of energy. The robot gently pulled Jean's pajama bottoms back over Jean's rear and said in an encouraging tone, "All done. As good as new."

Jean turned over and placed two pillows behind her head, propping herself up. "Ainsley, have you seen my husband this morning?"

"I have not."

"Do you know where he is?"

"In the north-wing master suite."

Thank God we don't live in the city anymore—Soylent Green. Jean gritted her teeth. *But, in our thirty-two-thousand-square-foot house, he couldn't stay any closer than two wings away?* "Is anyone in there with him?" She already knew the answer, but wanted to make sure that he had not fiddled with Ainsley's main programming. Adjusting her settings to deny Jean the purest form of cocaine that Jean had ever had before the evening's events was one thing. Adjusting her to lie about Jean's husband's serial philandering was another. Then again, Jean wondered if he knew about the younger men who had stayed with her in this room over the years. *Probably,* she thought. Audrey had been designed to report everything. Jean wanted Ainsley to maintain this level of surveillance regarding her husband's movements and relationships, but hoped the maid would be more discreet when it came to her paramours.

She started to tear up. *Why did I stay with him? Why did I even* begin *with him?*

The answer to the first question was complicated; the answer to the second question was not.

However, both answers included one person: Chantel Nadine Renault.

Chantel had steered Jean to Urian, and, when Jean had heard about *their* relationship, she had stolen Urian *from* Chantel and destroyed her boss, which had paved the way for Jean to become the youngest CEO in Renault Impact's history. Five years later, Chantel was dead from an overdose, and her husband, Alec, had committed suicide.

I need to be careful with the white powder, or I might join her, Jean thought.

"Yes," Ainsley reported. "Krystal entered the north-wing master suite at nine p.m. last night and has not left. Same as the previous two nights. And the night before that, it was—"

"Marlene."

"Well . . . yes, madam. Of course, Balara and Orah were—"

"I already know about his sex androids!" Jean picked up the empty wine glass and threw it across the room; it shattered against the brick hearth, sending shards of glass onto the cobalt blue carpeted floor. In addition to Renault Impact's forty-seven-year-old Chief Financial Officer, Marlene Dunne, the company's twenty-eight-year-old virtual reality advertising lead, Krystal Pfarr, was also now involved with her husband, Urian Phineas Nikolaidhts. "You would have thought they all could have waited until *after* my retirement ceremony!" she screamed. "And I thought you could re-program Balara and Orah!"

"I apologize, madam. Their models have formidable firewalls. I was blocked. Also, the two are very strong. I was unable to access their manual panels physically. They told me to stay away."

Jean yelled, "What good are you?"

There was a moment of silence, and then "Toyland" by Doris Day started playing from Ainsley's front speaker, as if Ainsley was singing it.

"Turn that horrible sound off!"

The music stopped, and Ainsley said, "I'm sorry, madam, it's just part of my holiday soothing program."

Jean started to cry. "Don't ever play music for me again!"

"There, there," Ainsley said, extending her right arm toward Jean. "Let's not think about any of this. I'll clean everything up. A sedative, perhaps? Counteract the booster? I can administer another one later. Maybe a little more sleep . . ."

Jean's heart was racing—the pain from her headache was gone, replaced with fiery spasms in her legs and arms. Her neuropathy was acting up again, and she was sweating—a clammy, breath-skipping variety that had her chin vibrating.

"Oh, my," said Ainsley, reaching for Jean's wet left cheek. "My sweet madam. Oh, this will not do for you. This will not *do*."

Her hand was inches from touching Jean's skin. *You will not touch me!*

There, there . . . there, there . . .

. . .

"Gram?"

Jean bolted upright in bed, her head turning side-to-side. The room was pitch black.

"Gram?" a little voice whispered again. "Are you okay? You yelled something."

Jean's eyes adjusted to the dark, and she felt a tiny hand on her right arm. She looked down to find her three-year-old granddaughter, Connie, at the side of her bed. "Oh, sweetie, I'm sorry. Gram was having a bad dream." Jean lifted her into bed, and Connie got under the covers. Their heads lay back on Jean's pillow, and they started snuggling. "Are *you* okay?" Jean asked.

"I got ascared," her tiny voice whispered back. "Where's grandpa?"

Jean lifted her head and, turning it, saw that the other side of the bed was empty; the covers were pulled back. *What time is it?* she thought.

She glanced at her watch.

6:03 a.m.

She lay her head back on the pillow. "He's up already. Must be downstairs. You know grandpa, right?"

Connie giggled. "He's always up."

Jean smiled and kissed the top of her granddaughter's head. *She's already forgotten why she was scared.* "Yes, he is. But, hey, *we* don't have to get up yet."

Connie whispered, "Okay. Let's get more sleep, Gram. Then we'll have a *big* breakfast. Santa's coming tomorrow night."

"Yes, he is," said Jean. "I almost forgot."

"Grrrraammm, how you could almost forget?"

"Hush, sweet child. I remembered. Let's close our eyes."

"Uh-huh," Connie said and then rolled over, adjusting until she was still.

Jean gave her back a rub and then shut her eyes.

Soon, they were asleep.

Perhaps it was the smell of fresh coffee that woke her up. Perhaps the scent of the cinnamon candle that he always lit in the kitchen at the start of every day had finally made its way into the bedroom. Or, perhaps, she was finally rested and her morning rhythms had taken over, even with the nightmare that had woken her up and her granddaughter hopping into bed.

Jean yawned and reached for the child—all her hand found was the covers. She turned her head.

She was alone in bed.

Didn't even feel or hear the munchkin leave.

After rubbing her eyes, she stretched her arms and then stared at the wooden beams high above that crisscrossed below the pitched ceiling. After today, she would be retired.

How do I feel about that?

She shivered at the thought of her dream. Her imagination—one that had led her to great heights in the advertising world—still never failed when it came to creative interpretations. She laughed to herself. *Ainsley . . . where had that name come from?* Even she was surprised by what her mind had conjured up regarding what a life with Urian might have been like. The vision of him grasping her right wrist and trying to pull her hand underneath his swimsuit on the second night in St. Barths and the follow-on vision of her resisting made her quiver again.

From what she had seen last year online, perhaps his fourth wife *was* living that nightmare—reports of infidelity, abuse, and financial woes. Chantel had been wife number two, after she had divorced Alec, and when her marriage to Urian disintegrated because Urian got both his personal secretary and one of the company's lower-tier financial analysts pregnant, the company almost imploded. He left to join a promising startup, and Chantel stayed on as CEO for another ten years until cancer forced her into retirement. A year later, she was dead, and the startup had gone bankrupt. Meanwhile, Alec had found love and safety in the arms of a widow of one of Silicon Valley's largest companies. There had been an article written about him fathering an estimated two hundred children because the widow had convinced him to be a sperm donor due to his gentle manner and welcoming personality. *"We need a* world *of Alec Rio Mars, not these soulless robots,"* she had been quoted as saying in the piece. Predictably, this had led to the sensationalism that had followed ten years later: The video of a dying Alec in his hospital bed being wheeled into the hospital's commons area, where he became surrounded by almost all of the children he had fathered via the sperm bank. However, what had made the image stand out was that a video engineer for the broadcasting company had digitally inserted dollar signs in place of all of Alec's children's eyes as the camera panned across the massive field of his issue, with members ranging from over twenty years old to a few months old. The widow had sued the company and won the case. It was later discovered that the widow owned over *fifty* androids, one of which was modeled after Alec—and she had married it.

Aside from the personal texture of the dream, other aspects—such as the increasing number of humanoids present in homes and workplaces and the growing portion of humans who had been relegated to accept universal basic income—inspired terror in her.

Perhaps the dream was her subconscious preying on her fear of retirement. Was her family financially set? Yes. Did she deserve to have some downtime in her golden years to relax? Yes. Did she have her health? Yes. Was she happy in her life? Absolutely. Was her advertising company, Outdoor Charms, that she had built from the ground up, after leaving Renault Impact almost forty years ago, in a good place? Without a doubt. Tonight, she would officially turn over the reins to her son, Teddy, who would carry the company's banner: a singular mission of attracting people to national and state parks—to get them outside and *moving* and spending quality time with each other and with nature, living with the land and each other.

All of her effort and the company's innovation had paid off. Attendance in national and state parks had hit an all-time high this year.

And yet, when I leave my professional work behind, will I lose my purpose?

She knew that she wouldn't, for many years ago, Jean had found equilibrium and peace between her entrepreneurial life—the work-is-life instincts that drove her—and the most amazing adventure she had ever been on in her personal life with Scott Brady. Their first kiss had been at the hospital, but the kiss that had sealed her feelings for him had occurred months later on the living room couch in front of a blazing fire in the hearth of his small house in Munising. She remembered the warmth of his touch, the strength in his arms that held her tightly, and the gentle way he kissed her slowly, then deeply—she had never let him go.

He had softened her, rounded her out, balanced her. He was the reason— the torch in the darkness that would not go out—that she had opened herself to feelings, which had led to her eventual belief that she could unconditionally trust some people, count on them, believe *in them*, and that being vulnerable with them was not a weakness but rather a strength. Together, they had strived not for wealth but for understanding during the decades of their marriage— there was passion and energy, compassion and patience with mistakes, humility and grace. She had strengthened his belief that work, *meaningful* work, brought true satisfaction to one's life and gave it substance, which many people chased but never found. When she met him, he was enjoying being a park ranger, but she had shown him *why* the job was essential and then proved it by leaving her company to start a business that doubled down on that importance. On the flip side, he had taught her that she didn't need to do it all alone.

That's why right now, he's downstairs taking care of anything that needs to be taken care of, like he always has, and loving me and the life we've made, and our family. The gift of being able to count on something like that! She teared up. *He's probably reading a book to Connie by the hearth and Christmas tree, getting her excited for Christmas Eve.*

She wiped her eyes.

Where did it all start?

She knew.

That weekend, long, long ago, with Annie—sweet Annie, who had lived three more years after her heart attack, which was long enough to see them married and the birth of their first child. Gracious Annie, whose cabin had been the model for their home. Heaven-sent Annie, who had roused Jean's locked-away love for music. *"You have brought back something in me that I thought was lost forever,"* she had told Annie when she returned to Michigan two months after that first Christmas. Determined Annie, who had summoned the strength on her deathbed to stare into Jean's eyes with an intensity she hadn't displayed for months, saying, *"You are strong. You can adapt to the changes in life that are coming, the horrible ones and the unexpected joyful turns. You have your grandmother's indomitable spirit—don't ever forget that. I am in awe of your power; I am in awe of your grace. You feel and aren't ashamed. You are the perfect wife for my grandson. And you are a wonderful mother. Never doubt yourself, Jean."* Then, she had shared private words with Scott, and, satisfied that her final mission was complete, she had slipped away.

Jean looked at the Pendleton blanket draped across the rocking chair, resting in the corner of their bedroom. They had been the final items in Annie's will.

She felt Shirley Ruth's presence today—that unconquerable lifeforce that had carried on amidst the mistakes and disappointments in life. Jean felt the presence of her late mother and father, as well as their spirit of survival, which had been instilled in her by a generation that could be distant and mercenary. They had worked—built careers—and been self-sufficient, which, beyond all of their shortcomings, had garnered Jean's respect.

Hanging in Jean's closet was her trademark black suit and white blouse, which she would wear one last time tonight as she passed the company torch. Afterwards, she would don her traditional red scarf and affix a golden angel to her right lapel. Both items had been gifts from Annie during the present exchange on Annie's last Christmas Eve. Jean and her family would attend Midnight Mass, where she would direct the children's choir as the sweet young ones sang a handful of beloved Christmas songs. It would be her final time leading the choir as she would retire after serving for thirty-five years as director. Remaining eternally efficient with her schedule, she had synced both retirements.

A member of her very first choir group, Maddie Drummond, who was now forty-one and had been helping Jean for the past few years, would take over as director after tonight.

"No one stays with anything this long anymore. There is no replacing you, but I will carry on what you have built," Maddie had said at the start of their final rehearsal yesterday.

Jean had replied, *"Nonsense. Make it your own. You have the gift, the love of music and the compassion for children. I'll be watching from the pews with pride."* And at that moment, Jean remembered Ms. Norman and Ms. Janie flying from Montana to Michigan to support Jean during her choir's first performance with her as the director. *I will be here for you like they were here for me,* she thought. *"Now, let's run through the program one more time,"* Jean said.

After they finished the final song, "Silent Night," she shared some heartfelt words with Maddie and the children before dismissing them. To Jean's astonishment, not a soul moved. Then, the youngest choir member, six-year-old Lucy Timmons, stepped down and disappeared behind the risers. Seconds later, she emerged with a red poinsettia and presented it to Jean. Jean's eyes watered as they sang "Have Yourself a Merry Little Christmas" to her.

After the song had concluded and hugs had been shared, Maddie pulled her old director aside and said, *"I decided to do this now instead of at the service tomorrow night, because I know you would never want anything to take the spotlight off the choir's performance. You've never once made it about you."*

Jean gazed at the bedroom's ceiling for a few seconds more and then shut her eyes.

I am ready to let go . . .

. . .

She opened her eyes, hearing the creak of the bedroom door.

A silver-haired Scott Brady, holding Connie with one arm and a steaming mug of coffee in the other, entered the room.

"Gram! I knew you were awake!"

Jean watched as Scott let her down, and the tiny girl ran toward her and jumped up on the bed. After a barrage of hugs and kisses, Jean looked up at Scott, who was next to the bed, and accepted the mug of coffee he held out for her.

Scott laughed. "Couldn't hold her off any longer."

She still loved his laugh.

Jean took a sip, savoring the taste of a cup brewed to perfection, and then swallowed, letting the coffee warm her insides.

Scott gave her other hand a loving squeeze.

Jean squeezed it back and then said, "Okay, are we all ready for Gram to attack the day?"

They both answered in the affirmative, and as the three of them left the room and entered the long hallway, Jean saw the picture of Annie and Shirley Ruth from New Year's Eve—enlarged, framed, and hanging on the wall—and she heard the unmistakable, beautiful, and uplifting beginning notes of "Snow."

AUTHOR'S NOTE

Thank you for reading or listening to *Snow*. As an author, my success greatly depends on reviews and referrals. If you enjoyed the book, it would be greatly appreciated if you could leave a quick review and then pass on the recommendation. For more information on upcoming books and exclusive discounts, please sign up for my email list on my website (landonbeachbooks.com) or follow Landon Beach Books on Facebook, Twitter, or Instagram.

*** *Snow* ***

Novel #10.

The ending is the one I always envisioned. My goal was to get Jean to a point where the stakes were high and she had to make a decision. Then, I thought it would be a fun and fresh approach to fast-forward forty years and let you know how things turned out. I am always trying to give you something new to experience, while still providing you with something in line with what you want and expect. It isn't easy to accomplish.

I hope you enjoyed the novel. My readers mean everything to me.

Snow, of course, is purely fiction. However, I come from a broken home, and my heart goes out to those—especially the kids, like I was when my parents divorced—who have had to endure a family disintegrating before their eyes and survived.

Many thanks to MB, EL, JG, JB, RR, and DB, who provided helpful comments on early drafts of the manuscript. I also thank my wife and two daughters, who saw me through novel #10 with love, patience, and unwavering support.

On to novel #11.

Merry Christmas, Happy Holidays, Happy New Year, and Happy Beach Reading!

L.B.

If you enjoyed *Snow,* expand your adventure with *Huron Breeze,* the first book in Sunrise-Side Mystery Series. Here is an excerpt to start the journey.

HURON BREEZE

Landon Beach

PART I

The Beach House

Landon Beach

1

South of Hampstead, Michigan, June 2022

The bonfire on the beach was almost dead—a circular carpet of red embers left on the white sand after tongues of flame had murdered the logs and kindling. Christine Harper ran a hand along the smooth, brown skin of her left forearm and then picked up her plastic cup of wine. She was ready to call it a night and should have felt relaxed, but there was something elusive, perhaps just beyond the realm of her reasoned awareness, that had her feeling uneasy. What it was, she couldn't say. Her intuition only whispered that forces as strong as the fire, which had consumed itself, were at play.

The last few drips of Chardonnay hit her tongue, and she swallowed, savoring the taste. She glanced at her watch. 10:45. It had been nice to sit and enjoy her drink and the fire without any company, well, at least the company that would be arriving in another week: her family.

The company she was supposed to have with her by the fire tonight had been caught in bed with their dental hygienist a month ago, which had ended her 3-year relationship with Danny Lee. The virtues of living together without the legal binds of marriage had been liberating, relaxed, with a come-and-go-as-you-please philosophy. It was uncomplicated with no restrictions. No pressure to settle down and have kids from parents because *"the relationship could end at any moment,"* according to her mother. If anything, the pressure was leveraged in the opposite direction: *"Don't have any kids until you're officially together."* The money situation had also been simple and straightforward. He had his checking account, and she had hers. He was a financial planner, and she ran her own book reviewing and promotion company, Harper's Highlights. They split the rent, went out to eat most nights during the week, and had no pets or other items to tie them down. The future? Well, when you were twenty-nine and twenty-seven, the future was a long way off. The only condition that they had discussed and agreed upon was monogamy. And so, in a life of freedom and choice, the only restriction had been the first one tested; Danny's eye had wandered from the comfort and security of Christine to their 23-year-old hygienist, Alyssa, and her glowing smile of perfect teeth, short golden hair, and cute laugh.

Looking back, the relationship had become stale over the past year, from the lack of quality time to the virtual elimination of their morning workouts together to the uninspired sex. She had lived in denial, knowing that the magic had fizzled but not knowing how to end the relationship. They had only had one major argument during the stretch, which had ended with him saying, *"Hey, I'm sorry. Let's just forget it and get counseling when we're like forty or something, okay?"* She had laughed, and the disagreement had been pushed away, but his words lingered, never quite exiting her thoughts. Now, on the cusp of turning thirty in a month, she felt free again. He had kept their apartment, and, as soon as she was out, the hygienist had moved in. Best of luck, sweetheart.

Her new place was a second-floor apartment in a complex on the other side of town. But, because her job was one-hundred percent online, she considered the move temporary. Escape wasn't the right word, but she had grown bored with living in Detroit. Yes, she would miss the summer evenings at Comerica Park and the nightclub scene with her network of friends that she and Danny had established; the term *young professionals* had been coined by someone, and it fit. However, what she wanted now was solitude—time to think, time to re-center, and time to consider what thirty to forty might have in store for her. And, minus her family, who would be showing up next week, there was no better place to contemplate her next move than the Harper family beach house that was here, fifteen miles south of Hampstead, on the shore of Lake Huron, where the summer breezes seemed to rejuvenate, inspire, excite, and calm all at once.

Speaking of the Huron breezes, the wind had picked up since she had started the fire. It had been from the west but had shifted and was coming out of the southwest now. She turned her attention to the large waves hitting the beach; the blaze of her fire had now been replaced with the roar of whitecaps breaking on the shore. Her flat-ironed, black hair blew away from her face, and she closed her eyes, feeling the cool wind on her face and neck. She heard a fresh set of waves reach the beach and visualized the sheen of water sliding across the wet sand toward the cool, dry sand above, like an athlete stretching her arms up toward the ceiling, trying to touch it with her fingertips, and then lowering her arms back to her side. She would unlatch and raise her bedroom window tonight and fall asleep to nature's finest lullaby.

After another full breath, she opened her eyes and gazed out over the water. Ten miles directly offshore was Beacon Island, a paradise that was privately owned by the Knight family. The closest she had ever been to the island was on summer sails in her father's 28-foot O'Day before he sold it. She swiveled her head and looked south. The white strip of beach extended for half a mile and then bent inward. Half a mile after the bend was the Knight's beach estate—a place she *had* visited.

She faced the water again and pondered going down to dip her feet in. Then, she saw the familiar glow of Beacon Light in the distance and watched as the light shined brightly for three seconds and then went dark. She counted off ten seconds in her head, and, right on cue, the light lit up for another three seconds straight and then went dark again. The lighthouse was located on the northern tip of Beacon Island and had served as an eternal night light for her as a child as she would leave her second-story window open and look out from her bed at the light as she drifted off to sleep. She planned to do the same thing tonight.

One more look.

The light came on, and she counted to herself, "One, tw—"

The light went out.

She set her plastic cup in the sand and then rubbed her eyes. *I've had three drinks, but I can still count.* She blinked twice and then looked back at the far end of the island. *Okay, 3 seconds. Let's go.* She narrowed her eyes and waited, but then a dark shadow of movement caught her attention.

Something had emerged from the water.

She stood up and observed the dark silhouette of a person against the clear, moonlit sky. The shadow started toward her. At this distance, perhaps twenty yards, she couldn't tell whether it was a man or a woman. Whoever it was moved irregularly—a mix of stumbling and limping. A drunk? She leaned over and grabbed her heavy-duty Maglite with her right hand. Her left hand had closed and become a fist.

Before she could turn the flashlight on, she heard the first moans from the unknown person.

She stepped to the side of her chair, giving herself a clear path to sprint back to the house. She turned the flashlight on and aimed it at the silhouette that was now fifteen yards away. "Who are you?" she said.

The flashlight's white beam illuminated a man wearing shorts and a collared shirt that were drenched. The man's hair was also wet and matted against his forehead. His eyes did not flinch from the sudden spotlight but rather opened wide as he pleaded, "Heeellllppp, muhh." He staggered to one side, held up only by his left leg. "Mmeeee." His eyes rolled back, and he fell forward, his chest and head hitting the sand with a thud.

Her altruistic instincts kicked in, and she rushed toward the man to help. A few yards away, though, her survival instincts hit right back, and she stopped. The man did not move as she started to circle his body, aiming her light at his bare feet and working her way up to—

She stopped.

Sticking straight out from in between the man's shoulder blades was the stainless-steel handle and curved butt of a knife.

Christine screamed, but there was no one to hear her cries.

2

Over two hours later, Christine Harper stood next to Hampstead Police Chief Corey Ritter as they watched the forensics and K-9 units finish up and then walk past them, heading toward their vehicles in Christine's driveway. The German shepherd, named Mario, stopped right before the sand ended and took a big dump.

As the handler started to guide Mario away, Ritter yelled, "Hey, pick that up!"

"Sorry," came the reply as the handler reversed course and scooped up the pile of feces with a pea-green colored bag.

Ritter looked down at where his feet should have been but only saw his bulging belly covered by the tan-colored summer uniform shirt of the Hampstead Police Department. He'd lost fifty pounds by Halloween on some kamikaze diet plan of celery, pills, sparkling water, and black coffee. Before that victory, he'd tried every diet plan known to the human species—Weight Watchers (the hell with counting points), Atkins (the fifth day of two steaks for dinner had led to an accompanying bottle of red wine, which had led to a second bottle, which had led to…), South Beach (when he hit phase two, his justification for adding back things he had deprived himself in phase one was 'I can handle it.' He couldn't handle it).

Anyway, after his latest diet had succeeded, his moment of triumph had come when he had paused thrusting and told his on-again, off-again girlfriend that he could finally see his cock again while having sex—'He's back!—which had immediately stopped their tryst. Then, like all perfect autumns up north with the leaves in full bloom and the smell of hot apple cider around every corner, Corey Ritter's return to glory had ended. The winter had snuck up on him like a strung-out burglar, and the good old Michigan time swap of spending one-third of your day inside and two-thirds outside from April to October to two-thirds inside and one-third outside from November to March sabotaged his food and drink intake.

The return to fast food, raspberry mochas, Sweetwater's donuts—of course—and a six-pack of longnecks before he drifted off to sleep in his burgundy recliner had been gradual at first. Six pounds in two weeks. Then, he played the mind game of, "You're fine. You just gotta work out to eat." The fallacy of riding a stationary bike for an hour each morning to work off the previous day's calories became apparent after an additional ten-pound gain after three more weeks. The morning biking came to a halt with the declaration, "I'm gonna return this piece of shit and get my money back!" He stopped weighing himself until a week ago; he was now right back where he had been last summer. The monster truck tire was around his waist again, but he had vowed to his lady that this summer he meant business—even called his nightly walk around the neighborhood his "constitution." The revival was on, and he was on day eight of *clean* eating, whatever the hell that meant. The internet nutritionist had introduced him to the term, and he'd been telling everyone about it when he announced that Corey Ritter was back on the weight-loss wagon, riding shotgun, and headed back into the wild west of hunger pains, hot sweats, and night terror about chocolate cake. He'd even upped the stakes and taken a break from the cancer sticks, which was like lopping off a limb—coffee and cigarettes in the morning, brandy and a cigar on his back deck at night. Then, tonight, he'd received the call about the body on the beach, and his car had swerved into

Walmart on the way over, where he picked up a dozen donuts from the bakery. This was followed by a stop at the Shell station for gas, coffee, and a pack of Marlboros. It was a twenty-minute drive out to Christine Harper's, and there were nine donuts left in the box when he had arrived.

Ritter said, "Asshole," and kicked a shoe full of sand in the direction of the K-9 and his handler, but they were twenty yards away now, and the only thing the theatrics of the kick did was make the overweight police chief almost lose his balance and have to grab Christine's arm to save himself. "Sorry," he said, taking in a few deep breaths.

Christine looked away and rolled her eyes. He had been overdramatic since arriving. When the body bag carrying the corpse of 35-year-old Kaj Reynard had been carried away by his deputies, Ritter had said, "Let's go," about a hundred times and had kept snapping his fingers and adjusting his pants. The body was now with the medical examiner, and Ritter had explained to her that his deputies were back at the station filling out paperwork. *They're pretty much useless, but they'll get it filed before morning,* "he had said.

When conducting his official questioning of her, every question had been asked with his head cocked to one side, and his eyes narrowed as if to say *Corey Ritter was now in charge, and thoroughness flowed as easily through his veins as the blood that flowed out of Kaj Reynard's back.* He was pushy, impatient, and she judged that if a person was robbing the Hampstead bank and Corey Ritter was the only police officer to give chase on foot, then the robber would never get caught.

She'd told him everything, which wasn't much.

Two cars started in her driveway, and she could see the lemon beams illuminate the woods to the right of her house. Then, the beams swung in an arc and faded down the driveway. She and Ritter were alone now on the beach, and Ritter turned toward her. "So, you were sitting here enjoying a fire, your family," he said, pausing to open his pocket notebook, "mother, Roberta Judith Harper, father, Stanton Daniel Harper, brother, Keagan Michael Harper, who all live in Florida, and uh—" he flipped a page "—your aunt, let's see here, yeah, your mom's sister, Gail Leigh Kimball, and uncle, Alan Robert Kimball, who live in Seattle, are all arriving a week from now and haven't been here since last summer."

Jesus, the middle names. He was a slow writer, and it had taken him forever to scribble down the names earlier—making sure he had every single one spelled correctly. When she had asked him why the full names were so important, he had eyeballed her and said, *"Gives me perspective—and gets me inside their heads."*

What? Talk about amateur hour.

He walked closer to the fire, but the light from the pulsating embers was fading. He switched on his flashlight. "Your folks moved away from Hampstead eleven years ago when you graduated high school. Your older brother went to college in Florida and decided to stay down there. And your aunt and uncle moved out to Seattle before you were born." He flipped to another page. "But, they all—your mom, dad, aunt, and uncle—graduated from Hampstead High School. Dad and uncle, 1982. Mom, '83, and aunt '85—same as me. I remember all of 'em. Wanted to date your aunt, but..."

Are you serious?

"You didn't see anything in the water. No boat, no canoe, no kayak, no one else swimming, nothing." Ritter pointed at the ebony-colored water and started gesturing with his arm as if re-enacting the scene. "You saw Mr. Reynard, who you claim you've only seen a few times before but don't really know—" he raised an eyebrow "—emerge from the water, scaring the shit out of ya; he hobbled a few yards on the beach toward the fire, and then did a faceplant on the sand. You see the knife handle coming out of his back; you scream; you don't remember anyone else noticing your scream—no neighbors who turn on their lights or ask you what's wrong; you sprint to the house, go inside, and call us." He closed the notebook, put it back in his pocket, and locked eyes with her. After staying silent for a few seconds, he raised his right eyebrow. "You stay inside until we arrive twenty minutes later."

For the third time tonight, yes!

Christine gave a devious smile. "Not much to go on."

Ritter rubbed his goatee. "No, it isn't. His tracks come straight from the water and end where he fell by your fire; forensics went up and down the beach and didn't find a thing. And, it looks like the murder weapon won't help us either. A stainless-steel Cuisinart 8-inch chef's knife with an ergo—" He flipped open his notebook again. "Ergonomically designed handle. No prints, and that knife is common enough to make it impossible to track down."

"Not even a partial print?" She'd seen the forensics team member approach Ritter before heading out.

"Nope. Whoever stabbed him was probably wearing gloves. Evidently, Kaj Reynard got away from his assailant, which, I think, rules out the murderer asking him to pause for a minute while he or she wiped off the handle." He exhaled. "So, if it's gloves," he said, miming putting on a pair, "we're talking about, then this was most likely a premeditated murder." Ritter tapped the top of his notebook, apparently happy with his conclusion.

Christine nodded and remembered her mother's fifteen-piece Cuisinart knife set on the kitchen counter inside the beach house. Now that she thought of it, a few of the knives were missing, along with the scissors that had come with the set. She knew about the scissors because she had been in the kitchen when the plastic handle had snapped off when her mother was trying to cut a zip tie. *Was one of the missing knives a chef's knife?* "For sure," she said.

Ritter looked away from her and scanned the dark water offshore. "Going to be a tough one to solve."

Even if it was an easy case, you couldn't solve it. She closed her eyes and rubbed the bridge of her nose with her right thumb and index finger.

Don't be a bitch. You're still in shock, and he's just doing his job.

"Anything else, Chief?" she said.

Ritter pulled up his pants again, smoothing the shirt wrinkles above his belt with his thumbs. "Not right now."

They left the beach, and he offered to send a deputy back to stay outside her house for the rest of the night. She declined, even though her entire body felt as tight as a drum. It was unlikely that she'd get back to sleep, and part of her didn't want to. She'd stay up the rest of the night, and when the safety of a Lake Huron sunrise arrived, drift off then. She had already spoken to her mother and would call her back after the police chief left. During the last call, words of comfort had been given and offers had been made for the family to change their travel plans and arrive early, but she had said she'd be all right.

Will I?

Ritter swung his enormous gut into the patrol car, and she swore the vehicle almost touched the ground when he sat down. After starting the car, he rolled down the window. "Sure you'll be okay?"

Absolutely not. She lied by nodding yes.

"I'll be back out this way tomorrow just to take another look. By then, I'll know if forensics or the medical examiner have been able to come up with anything else. Instincts tell me no." He turned on the radio. Eighties greatest hits. *Ugh.* "My guys have already interviewed your next-door neighbors. And they—"

"Didn't hear or see anything," she said, cutting him off.

Ritter frowned. "Sorry. I know we've been over it a lot." He lit a cigarette, inhaled, and blew the smoke out of the open window. It smelled delicious. Maybe she'd buy a pack tomorrow. "We'll probably interview them again. Get some rest."

She thought about her friend, Rachel Roberts, who lived a few houses south of her. They'd probably talk to her sometime tomorrow.

He pulled out of the driveway, and as the golden bloom of his headlights disappeared down the road, she felt a tingle of fear slide up her spine. The woods on both sides of the house were a mixture of swaying black tree trunks, reaching for the sky, with a maze of gray tunnels between them. She shivered.

Get inside and get it together.

She listened to the little voice inside her head and jogged to the front porch.

The sound of a box fan at the top of the stairs greeted her as she stepped into the foyer. After locking the door, she turned on every light in the downstairs, grabbed a beer from the fridge, and turned on the TV, finding a *Lost* re-run marathon.

An hour later, she was snoring away on the couch—unaware of the vehicle that had stopped at the end of her driveway for a few seconds and then continued off into the night.

ABOUT THE AUTHOR

Landon Beach was born and raised in Michigan but now lives in the Sunshine State with his wife, two children, and their golden retriever. He previously served as a Naval Officer and was an educator for fifteen years before becoming a full-time writer. Find out more at landonbeachbooks.com.